THE BISHOP'S RESONANT VOICE
HAD RISEN TO FEVER PITCH

"As we consecrate the union of this young Amish couple, I must insist that the single and widowed men and women among us find mates *immediately*," he exhorted. "Before the snow flies, I expect to see you— Matilda Schwartz, Christine Hershberger, Rosetta Bender, Amos Troyer, and Marlin Kurtz—standing before me to take your wedding vows! It's unnatural for God's children to live alone, or for women to engage in any business other than making a home for their families. Moreover," he continued, gesticulating dramatically, "our colony cannot condone the inter-marriages of Old Order members with those of more liberal Plain faiths. When we take on the ways of a lesser faith, we weaken the very foundation of our colony—and we risk losing our salvation in our Lord."

Amos gripped the edge of the preacher's bench until his hands hurt. This was not the proper time to challenge folks by name, telling them to find mates. He couldn't miss the way Truman Wickey, their Mennonite neighbor, had also tensed.

To Amos's right, Preacher Eli Peterscheim shifted on the wooden bench as the bishop continued preaching. "That's just wrong," he muttered under his breath. "You can't tell me God instructed Floyd to name names and set a deadline for marrying!"

Christmas At PROMISE LODGE

Charlotte Hubbard

ZEBRA BOOKS
KENSINGTON PUBLISHING CORP.
http://www.kensingtonbooks.com

ZEBRA BOOKS are published by

Kensington Publishing Corp.
119 West 40th Street
New York, NY 10018

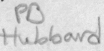

All Kensington titles, imprints, and distributed lines are available
at special quantity discounts for bulk purchases for sales promotion,
premiums, fund-raising, educational, or institutional use.

Special book excerpts or customized printings can also be created
to fit specific needs. For details, write or phone the office of the
Kensington Sales Manager: Attn.: Sales Department. Kensington
Publishing Corp., 119 West 40th Street, New York, NY 10018.
Phone: 1-800-221-2647.

First Printing: October 2016
ISBN-13: 978-1-4201-3943-3
ISBN-10: 1-4201-3943-6

eISBN-13: 978-1-4201-3944-0
eISBN-10: 1-4201-3944-4

10 9 8 7 6 5 4 3 2 1

JUN 29 2017

Printed in the United States of America

For my Aunt Sandra,
who celebrates a Christmas birthday!

ACKNOWLEDGMENTS

Thank You, Lord, for Your guidance as I continue this series!

Thank you, Neal, for all the wonderful Christmases we've shared.

Continued gratitude to my editor, Alicia Condon, and to Evan Marshall, my agent. I'm thrilled to be working with both of you as we continue this Amish story journey together.

Special thanks to Vicki Harding, innkeeper of Poosey's Edge B & B in Jamesport, Missouri. Your assistance and friendship have been invaluable! Thanks and blessings, as well, to Joe Burkholder and his family, proprietors of Oak Ridge Furniture and Sherwood Christian Books in Jamesport.

Luke 2:4–14 (KJV)

4 And Joseph also went up from Galilee, out of the city of Nazareth, into Judaea, unto the city of David, which is called Bethlehem; (because he was of the house and lineage of David:)

5 To be taxed with Mary his espoused wife, being great with child.

6 And so it was, that, while they were there, the days were accomplished that she should be delivered.

7 And she brought forth her firstborn son, and wrapped him in swaddling clothes, and laid him in a manger; because there was no room for them in the inn.

8 And there were in the same country shepherds abiding in the field, keeping watch over their flock by night.

9 And, lo, the angel of the Lord came upon them, and the glory of the Lord shone round about them: and they were sore afraid.

10 And the angel said unto them, Fear not: for, behold, I bring you good tidings of great joy, which shall be to all people.

11 For unto you is born this day in the city of David a Saviour, which is Christ the Lord.

12 And this shall be a sign unto you; Ye shall find the babe wrapped in swaddling clothes, lying in a manger.

13 And suddenly there was with the angel a multitude of the heavenly host praising God, and saying,

14 Glory to God in the highest, and on earth peace, good will toward men.

Chapter One

Mattie Schwartz slipped into her new navy blue dress earlier than she needed to because today—November fifth—was no ordinary Thursday. In about four hours, her younger son, Noah, would be marrying Deborah Peterscheim. It was the first wedding to take place in the Promise Lodge colony she and her sisters had founded last spring, and she'd been awake since three o'clock this morning, too excited to sleep. She left her two-room apartment and went downstairs to join the Kuhn sisters, who were overseeing the preparation of the wedding meal in the lodge's kitchen.

Mattie inhaled deeply. The entire building smelled of roasting chickens, vegetables, and perking coffee. The huge kitchen, which had provided meals for kids when Promise Lodge had been a church camp, bustled with the ladies who lived here now. As soon as Mattie stepped through the door, however, seventy-year-old Beulah Kuhn pointed at her with a vegetable peeler.

"This is the day the Lord has made for your Noah

to marry Deborah," she paraphrased from the stool where she sat peeling potatoes.

"'We will rejoice and be glad in it!'" Beulah's sister, Ruby, added with a wide smile. "The mother of the groom gets time off from cooking and cleaning up. It's your day to party, Mattie!"

"We've already sent Alma Peterscheim out of here," Mattie's sister Christine remarked from the stove, where she stood stirring gravy. "Didn't want Deborah's mother sitting through church with food on her new dress, after all."

"You were here all yesterday afternoon baking pies with us, Mattie," Frances Lehman, the bishop's wife, pointed out. "So it's your day to visit with the family and friends who'll come to celebrate with you. We'll allow you a cup of coffee and one of the biscuit sandwiches from the counter, and then you're to forget all about the kitchen."

Mattie chuckled. As one of the three original owners of the property, she'd considered herself more outspoken and independent than most Plain women, but the other ladies who'd made their homes here were proving to be every bit as stubborn and insistent as she and Christine and Rosetta.

"All right, just this once I'll do as I'm told," Mattie teased as she picked up a warm breakfast sandwich. "But we're not making it a habit, understand."

The kitchen filled with laughter, a sound that lifted Mattie's spirits. When she'd been widowed in Coldstream, and Christine had lost her husband, and Rosetta had been left alone after their parents had passed, they'd each known the lonely silence of roaming around in their separate farmhouses. Living in the lodge together, along with Plain ladies who rented apartments from Rosetta, made for a far more cheerful life. Mattie closed her eyes as she bit into a big, soft biscuit filled with ham, a fried egg, and cheese that dribbled down the sides. Eating food someone else had cooked was a treat that made her son's wedding day even more special.

"We've told Rosetta and my girls to stay in the dining hall, setting tables," Christine remarked, pouring more flour and milk mixture into her gravy. "Phoebe and Laura are so excited to be serving as Deborah's side-sitters, I didn't want them getting their dresses dirty, either."

"*Jah*, what with Noah being sweet on Deborah all through school, your girls have waited a long while to sit up front with her," Mattie said before taking another gratifying bite of her breakfast.

"And what a blessing that Noah and Deborah can hold the wedding in their new home," Frances put in with a big smile. "It's truly amazing, how many houses have gone up since Floyd and I moved here with the girls this past summer."

"*Jah*, what with Preacher Amos's being a carpenter and Floyd and his brother Lester running a siding and window business, we've got one of the nicest-looking Plain communities I've ever seen." Beulah rose from her stool to carry a big pot of peeled potatoes to the stove. "Ruby and I never dreamed we'd have our cheese factory up and running so fast, either, but the fellows here can build anything. And we couldn't ask for richer milk than we're getting from Christine's cows."

"My bees love the orchard, too," Ruby said happily.

"Every morning when I get up and look out the window, I see their white hives amongst the apple trees and tell myself we've found the Garden of Eden."

"The produce stand's open later in the season than I'd figured on, too," Mattie said with a nod. "Local folks are snapping up the last of our pumpkins and squash now, and I suspect they'd continue coming all winter if Deborah kept selling her baked goodies there."

"Maybe she could sell them from the cheese factory," Beulah mused aloud. She turned on the gas burner and put the potatoes on to boil. "Truth be told, Ruby and I could use her help running the counter out front while we stir up batches of cheese. But she might change her mind about working now that she's getting married."

"Last I heard, Deborah was excited about having a new kitchen to bake in, especially while Noah's out on his welding jobs," Mattie said. "At least until she's got wee ones to watch after."

"I'd be happy to have Deborah's goodies in my gift shop, too," Rosetta called from the large dining room. "I figure to open it one of these days to sell my home-made soaps, and anything else the rest of you ladies might want to offer for sale."

"Deborah was amazed at how well her breads and bars sold over the summer," Christine said. She smiled at Mattie. "I suspect she sees the three of us Bender sisters running businesses and understands what an advantage it is for a woman to have some income. For us unattached gals it's our living, but for a wife it means a little more leverage when things around the house wear out or need fixing."

Frances was listening to this thread of conversation as though Mattie, Christine, and the Kuhn sisters were speaking a dialect she didn't understand. "Where I come from, the menfolk have always brought home the bacon and the women have cooked it up," she said softly. "Married women are homemakers without any businesses, and widows and *maidels* depend upon the men in their families to support them."

"That's how it was for Beulah and me before we ran away from home," Ruby said. "Once we *maidel* school-teachers retired, our brother Delbert took us in—"

"But we felt he and his wife, Carol, should be raising their five kids without having to support us, as well," Beulah continued. "Delbert was against us living here—"

"*Jah*, he came in his truck and hauled us back home," Ruby recounted.

"—but when his mother-in-law had to move in after Carol's *dat* died, we decided that was just too many folks in a one-bathroom house. So here we are," Beulah said, raising her arms victoriously. "We're making our own way with our cheese and our bees, living in Rosetta's lodge. Life is fun again!"

"We're too young to get old anytime soon," Ruby chimed in matter-of-factly. "God is *gut*, and so's the life He's led us to here."

Frances smiled despite her misgivings. "It's invigorating to come to this new colony where everyone's starting fresh—and I'm grateful to everyone for being so accepting of my Mary Kate," she said in a voice that quivered a bit. "With Floyd's being the bishop in our previous settlement, and Mary Kate's being in the family way after that English fellow took advantage of her, we prayed that Promise Lodge would be a safe haven for her and the baby."

"I think she's very brave, wanting to raise the baby rather than give it up for adoption," Mattie remarked. She placed three biscuit sandwiches on a paper plate and covered them with a napkin. "If I don't take these to Preacher Amos and my two boys, they might not eat anything before church and the wedding. *Denki* to you ladies for cooking on our special day, and for seeing to our breakfast, too."

As Mattie passed through the large dining room, she smiled at the way white tablecloths had transformed the old, careworn wooden tables into the perfect setting for their celebration. Her younger sister, Rosetta, was setting a glass to the right of each plate. Christine's girls, Laura and Phoebe, were going down the sides of the tables with forks and knives while Mary Kate Lehman followed them with the spoons.

"Looks like you've got a *gut* system going, girls," Mattie said brightly. "How many folks can we seat at once? Today will be the first time we've filled this room."

"A hundred and fifty—which includes the wedding party up on the *eck*," Rosetta replied, gesturing toward the raised table in the far corner. "We figure most of the guests will fill up the first sitting, and then we worker bees can eat during the second sitting."

"It'll be *gut* to see our friends from Coldstream, along with our cousins, aunts, and uncles who're scattered around Missouri," Phoebe said. She turned toward Mary Kate with a smile. "We used to live about three hours from here, but the bishop's son Isaac was causing so much trouble—"

"Setting barns afire and drinking with his English friends," Laura put in with a shake of her head.

"—that our *mamm* and aunts decided to move away," Phoebe continued. "And as if that weren't enough, Isaac came here with one of his buddies, thinking to get back at Deborah for calling the sheriff on him."

"But we sent him packing!" Rosetta recalled with a chuckle. "I doubt the Chupps will come today, not after all three of our households plus Preacher Amos and the Peterscheims moved here to get away from them."

Mary Kate stopped placing spoons on the tables. Her hand slid over the swell of her belly as her eyes widened. "You—you're sure Isaac won't be coming?" she murmured fearfully. "After that English fellow pulled off the road and—and tackled me in the ditch, I don't ever want a man getting that close to me again, or even *looking* at me."

Mattie hurried over to the bishop's daughter. "Mary Kate, don't you worry about a thing," she murmured as she slung her arm around the girl's slender shoulders. "If my boys or Preacher Amos spot Isaac Chupp, they'll be swarming around him like Ruby's bees. Here at Promise Lodge we don't tolerate men who bully women."

Mary Kate was breathing rapidly, sucking in air to settle her nerves. "Maybe when we're finished setting up here, I should go home instead of attending the wedding. Dat says that in my condition, I shouldn't be showing myself in public anyway."

Mattie chose her words carefully, not wanting to contradict the bishop—yet hoping Mary Kate would feel comfortable enough to enjoy today's wedding festivities. At eight months along she was obviously pregnant, but her guilt and shame bothered Mattie more than Mary Kate's appearance. It wasn't as if this shy eighteen-year-old girl had gone looking for trouble the day she'd been raped while walking home from a neighbor's.

"I don't see the harm of sitting with your *mamm* during church and the wedding," Mattie said gently. "What with Laura, Phoebe, and Deborah—and your *dat*—all sitting up front, you and your mother could keep one another company. There'll be a lot of folks here that neither one of you knows."

Mary Kate looked down at her clasped hands. "*Jah*, there's that, but—"

"And it might be a long while before we have another big event—unless Rosetta and Truman Wickey decide to get hitched," Phoebe said with a teasing glance at her aunt.

Rosetta waved them off, but she was smiling. "Don't hold your breath for *that* wedding, seeing's how Truman's Mennonite and I'm Old Order Amish."

Laura let out a frustrated sigh. "I don't see why that's such a big deal," she protested. "Everybody knows you and Truman are sweet on each other. In some Plain settlements, folks are fine with interfaith marriages."

"Well, that's an issue to take up on another day," Mattie remarked in a purposeful tone. Her nieces meant well, but their romantic notions about Truman and Rosetta would get Bishop Floyd going on another one of his lectures. As bishops went, he was very conservative and insisted on following traditional Old Order ways. "Our concern now is for Mary Kate, and we want her to enjoy our special day instead of feeling she has to hide herself away. Think about it, all right?" she asked softly.

Mary Kate nodded. "You and your sisters keep telling me I should have some fun before the baby gets here. I'll give it my best shot—unless I chicken out, come time for church."

Squeezing the girl's shoulder, Mattie left her sister and the girls and strode through the lobby to the front door. When she stepped out onto the lodge's big front porch, she stopped for a moment to take in the plowed plots where they'd grown vegetables all summer for their roadside produce stand . . . the small white structure alongside Christine's red dairy barn, where the Kuhn sisters made several varieties of cheese . . . the new road that wound between homes and barns belonging to Noah and Deborah, Preacher Amos, the Peterscheim family, and the Lehmans—as well as the two partly completed homes, one for their newest residents, Preacher Marlin Kurtz and his kids, and the other for her older son, Roman. Every morning she stood here gazing toward the orchard, Rainbow Lake, and the tree-covered hills that provided such a rustic, lovely setting, amazed at how their colony had progressed since spring.

Denki, *Lord, for Your providential care*, Mattie prayed. *We ask Your blessings on Noah and Deborah today as they become husband and wife. If You'd bless Mary Kate with health and healing and more confidence, that would be a gift, as well.*

When she saw Amos Troyer stepping out onto his porch, Mattie waved and started walking toward him. His new home was modest and small compared to the others, because as a widower he wasn't going to raise another family—although it was no secret that he hoped Mattie would marry him someday soon. Truth be told, she savored her independence after enduring a husband who'd mistreated her, but she enjoyed Preacher Amos's company.

"I've got a surprise for your breakfast," she called out as she approached his tidy white house. "The Kuhn sisters were kind enough to make us some biscuit sandwiches—"

"Did somebody say biscuits?" Roman hollered as he came out of Noah's house, which was next door to Amos's. Queenie, Noah's black-and-white Border collie, rushed out into the yard, barking excitedly.

Behind Roman, Noah was stepping outside, buttoning his black vest over his white shirt. "Hope you've got more than one of those sandwiches, Mamm," he said with a laugh. "The pizza Deborah made for us last night is long gone—and she's not showing her face until church starts."

"You poor, starving things," Mattie teased as she started up the walk toward her sons. "Deborah deserves a wedding day away from the stove."

"Or you could get by on bacon, eggs, and toast like I do," Preacher Amos teased as he strode across his small, leaf-covered yard. He stopped a few feet away from Mattie to take in her new dress—and the plate in her hand—with an appreciative smile. He lowered his voice before Roman and Noah reached them. "Of course, if you married me, Mattie, I wouldn't be threatened by starvation or depression or any of those other maladies a man alone endures."

"*Jah*, so you've told me," Mattie teased as she removed the napkin that covered her plate. "Maybe someday I'll feel sorry enough for you to give up my cozy apartment in the lodge."

The moment her sons joined them, the three sandwiches were snatched up. With a welling-up of love, Mattie watched Noah eat. Although he was twenty-one, it seemed like only yesterday when he'd been born. He and Deborah had known each other all their lives, had become sweethearts in school, had gotten engaged—until Deborah broke off their relationship, claiming Noah didn't communicate with her or have a concrete plan for their future. The nasty incident involving Isaac Chupp had brought Noah out of his shell, awakening his protective feelings for Deborah, and all of them at Promise Lodge had breathed a sigh of relief when the young couple reconciled this past summer.

"I'm proud of you, Noah," Mattie murmured as she stroked his unruly brown waves. "I wish you all the happiness that marriage and your faith in God can offer."

Blushing, Noah eased away from her touch. "*Denki*, Mamm. I think Deborah and I have figured out how to stay together now," he said as he offered his dog the last bite of his biscuit.

Mattie shared a smile with Preacher Amos. "When you're my age, son, you'll look back to this day and realize how young and innocent you were," she murmured.

"And clueless." Amos laughed. "We fellows like to believe we've got everything figured out and under control—until life starts tossing monkey wrenches into our well-laid plans. I'm a different kind of man than I imagined I'd be when I was your age."

"Did folks hitch their rigs to dinosaurs back then?"

Roman teased. He, too, fed the last bite of his sandwich to Queenie and then rubbed between her black ears.

"Puh! I didn't have much money when I married," the preacher reminisced, "but I drove fine-looking retired racehorses. Not that my bride always appreciated my priorities," he admitted. "I hope you'll give a thought to Deborah's needs before you devote the household budget to your own whims, Noah. I had a spendy streak—"

"But all the girls liked what they saw and thought you'd be a fine catch back in the day, Amos," Mattie cut in with a chuckle.

"Back in the day?" he challenged. The way he held her gaze made Mattie's cheeks prickle. "Might be a little snow on the roof, but there's still a fire down below."

"And with that, I'm going to finish getting dressed," Roman announced, pointing toward the rigs coming through the camp entrance. "We've got guests arriving. I hope you two won't be gawking at each other all during the service, embarrassing us all."

Mattie smiled, watching her two sons and the dog enter Noah's white frame house. "I'm so glad we came to Promise Lodge," she murmured to Amos. "So glad we risked buying this property so we're no longer living in Obadiah Chupp's shadow. If I'd still been shackled to that farmhouse in Coldstream, I couldn't have given my boys plots of land where they could lead lives of their own."

"You're an innovator, for sure and for certain," Amos agreed. "The best thing I ever did was sell my place and come to the tiny town of Promise with you and your sisters. I feel like my life and my efforts *matter* now, as we build houses for our new neighbors. The land is like a paradise and the air smells cleaner—"

"That's because I showered this morning," Mattie teased.

She faced Amos, loving the way his laughter eased the lines time had carved into a masculine face weathered by the elements and life experiences. Her life would've been entirely different had her *dat* allowed her to marry Amos Troyer when she was young instead of insisting she take up with Marvin Schwartz, who'd come into a farm with a house on it. Amos had been a fledgling carpenter without two nickels to rub together.

At fifty, Amos was five years older than she, but his strong, sturdy body showed no signs of softening with age or health issues. He was a man in his prime, and he'd made no bones about wanting to marry her now that both of their spouses had passed. Sometimes Mattie was on the verge of blurting out a *yes* when Amos talked of getting hitched—and then memories of Marvin's abuse would come rushing back to her.

No, she wasn't in a hurry to take on another husband, another household. But if she ever did, it would be with Amos.

"I hope you'll allow me the honor of sitting with you at dinner as we celebrate your son's big day," he murmured, squeezing her hand.

Mattie smiled up at him, gripping his fingers before releasing them. His silver-shot hair and beard shimmered in the morning light, and he cut a fine figure in his black suit and white shirt. "I'll be happy to, Amos. God be with you as you find the words for your sermon this morning."

Amos flashed her a boyish grin. "It'll be God I'm listening to as I speak," he said, "but it'll be you I'm looking to for inspiration, Mattie. I hope today's celebration turns out to be every bit as wonderful as you are."

Mattie flushed with pleasure, watching him walk to Noah's new house to prepare for the service—the home Amos had designed and then built with the help of the other local fellows, with interior walls that could be removed to accommodate large crowds for church services. Amos's hands were calloused from years of carpentry, but there was no softer, more loving heart on God's green earth.

A few hours later, Amos sat on the preacher's bench trying not to scowl. After a full-length church service they had progressed into the wedding, and he had preached the first sermon on the thirteenth chapter of First Corinthians—about how love was patient and kind, an example of the humility Plain folks were to strive for. Bishop Floyd Lehman was now delivering the second, longer sermon before he would lead Noah and Deborah in their marriage vows, and his tone was becoming more strident as he discussed the duties of husband and wife to each other and to God. It was an appropriate topic, but some of the folks in the congregation appeared to be shrinking into themselves like turtles retreating into their shells, probably because the bishop's resonant voice had risen to fever pitch.

"As we consecrate the union of this young Amish couple, I must insist that the single and widowed men and women among us find mates *immediately*," he exhorted. "Before the snow flies, I expect to see you—Matilda Schwartz, Christine Hershberger, Rosetta Bender, Amos Troyer, and Marlin Kurtz—standing before me to take your wedding vows! It's unnatural for God's children to live alone, or for women to engage in any business other than making a home for their families. Moreover," he continued, gesticulating dramatically, "our colony cannot condone the inter-marriages of Old Order members with those of more liberal Plain faiths. When we take on the ways of a lesser faith, we weaken the very foundation of our colony—and we risk losing our salvation in our Lord."

Amos gripped the edge of the preacher's bench until his hands hurt. This was not the proper time to challenge folks by name, telling them to find mates. He couldn't miss the way Truman Wickey, their Mennonite neighbor, had also tensed. Truman sat on the front pew bench of the men's side, serving as one of Noah's *newehockers* along with Roman, so his reaction was easy to see. Amos suspected that on the women's side, Rosetta, Mattie, and Christine appeared equally perturbed.

To Amos's right, Preacher Eli Peterscheim shifted on the wooden bench as the bishop continued preaching. "That's just wrong," he muttered under his breath. "You can't tell me God instructed Floyd to name names and set a deadline for marrying."

Amos agreed with Eli's assessment. Why on earth had Bishop Floyd used this wedding sermon to single out the three women who'd founded their colony—and then named him and Marlin, as well? Why was Floyd so set on following the very strictest formula of the Old Order faith, when other communities allowed intermarriage and home-based businesses run by married women?

On Amos's other side, Marlin Kurtz, the colony's new preacher, leaned closer. "That's outrageous— I've only lived here a couple months," he whispered. "I've had no time to court anyone while building a house and getting my kids settled in. Is Floyd always this intense?"

Amos stifled a cough. "If the bishop thinks the un-attached folks here are going to bang his door down, asking him to officiate at their weddings in the next few weeks, he's in for a rude awakening."

And I probably am, too. Mattie will most likely dig in her heels and refuse to marry me now, just to spite the bishop.

Sure enough, when Amos peered toward the side of the expanded front room where the women sat, he saw that Mattie's lips were pressed into a tight line as though she might explode from suppressing her irri-tation with Bishop Floyd. Rosetta's face was as red as an apple from the orchard, and Christine's scowl could've curdled milk. Amos suspected the three sisters would express their opinions openly once they were out of church, and he prayed the bishop wouldn't spoil this festive occasion by lashing out or ordering them to pay some sort of penance for chal-lenging his decree. Amos predicted that Mattie's frus-tration would get her into hot water one of these days, and unfortunately, Floyd Lehman would always have the upper hand and the last word.

Help us serve You, Jesus, even when our passions and loyalty blind us, Amos prayed. *And help me walk in Your way if push comes to shove between Bishop Floyd and the Bender sisters.*

Chapter Two

Mary Kate Lehman sat on the front porch swing of the new house, wrapped in a cozy old quilt. She gazed toward the white frame home where Noah and Deborah were being married—barely able to see it between the large old maple trees that shimmered in shades of gold, orange, and crimson as the late-morning sunshine struck them. She'd been ready to enter Noah's house with the other ladies before the church service began, until her *dat*'s disapproving glare had sent her trundling awkwardly up the road, clutching her belly as she blinked back tears. Why did life have to be so hard, so harsh, after that English stranger had taken advantage of her?

As an obedient bishop's daughter, however, Mary Kate knew better than to voice such a question aloud. All her life her parents had insisted that she was to listen and obey rather than to question the path God had chosen for her. Sighing, she rocked back and forth in the swing. The sound of more than a hundred voices singing a hymn drifted down the road, telling her that the wedding ceremony was almost over. She'd planned to join everyone in the lodge for the wedding meal—she ate there on Sundays with her new friends at Promise Lodge—but the thought of so many guests and strangers staring at her gave her pause.

In Amish society, there was simply no place, no explanation, for an unmarried girl who was eight months pregnant. She was grateful to Mattie Schwartz, Rosetta Bender, and Christine Hershberger for welcoming her so warmly to this new colony. At times they seemed more sympathetic to her situation than her parents or her older sister, Gloria.

Mary Kate leaned forward, straining to see the guests as they came out of Noah's house in a steady stream. Lots of people had arrived from Coldstream, where the Schwartzes and Preacher Amos had lived before, not to mention kinfolk of the Peterscheims who'd come from other towns . . . folks she didn't know and would likely not see again. They would figure she'd crossed the line with an errant boyfriend, and they would judge her. She rose from the swing, resigning herself to a cheese sandwich and a glass of milk.

She was slicing a ball of creamy, pale mozzarella cheese the Kuhn sisters had made when rapid footsteps clattered across the porch out front.

"Mary Kate? Mary Kate, you won't believe it!" her sister called out as she entered the house. Gloria burst into the kitchen, her dark eyes alight with excitement. "Guess who kept looking at me all during the church service?"

Mary Kate shrugged, arranging the cheese on a

slice of bread she'd spread with mayonnaise. "Could have been anybody, seeing's how so many folks from out of town are—"

"Roman Schwartz!" Gloria blurted. "It was easy to see him, of course, because he was in the front row with his brother and that Mennonite guy Rosetta likes."

"Truman Wickey."

"*Jah*, but the *best* part," Gloria continued in a breathless voice, "was how Roman was sneaking peeks at me. I'm going back to the lodge now, because if I help refill water glasses or hand out the sliced pie, I can keep an eye on him—and convince him to ask me out! You'd think he'd take the hint after I've been talking to him all summer, but I feel like today's going to be my lucky day!"

Mary Kate gazed at her sister, unsure of what to say. Not so long ago she and Gloria had held similar conversations about the boys they saw around town or at weddings, but now that she was pregnant with an unknown man's child, the prospect of attracting a boyfriend was a dream that would never come true—not that her sister noticed. Gloria was twirling a *kapp* string around her finger, smiling and batting her long lashes as she anticipated what she'd say and do when Roman finally noticed her. At twenty-two, Gloria had left a few boyfriends behind when they'd moved here from Sugarcreek, Ohio—and Mary Kate had no illusions about her sister's ability to attract additional young men here in Missouri. Gloria had always been prettier than she, and more outgoing, and better at flirting and making small talk, and—

Well, everyone knows she'll be getting hitched before long,

Mary Kate mused with a sigh. *The Bible tells us of the haves and the have-nots, and Gloria's got her share of blessings and mine, too.*

Gloria blinked. "Oh—Mamm wants me to ask if she can bring you some food from the wedding meal. We can fix you a plate—"

Mary Kate's lips twitched. It would be like Mamm to think of feeding her, while Gloria had mostly hurried home to share her plan for enticing Roman. "No need for that," she assured her sister. "Maybe if there's food left after all the guests have eaten a plate, it would be nice, but I've got some of Beulah's cheese and—"

"All right then, I'll get back to the lodge," Gloria replied as she hurried out of the kitchen.

The screen door banged behind her, sounding very much like the lid of a coffin falling shut. Mary Kate blinked rapidly, determined to enjoy her fresh cheese sandwich instead of crying. It was a beautiful, warm autumn day to eat outside on the porch, and she would not fall prey yet again to the emotions that surged like a rollercoaster, from highs to lows, without any warning. She had to believe that her life would go on, that her outlook would improve once she held her newborn baby.

"Kitty kitty?" Mary Kate glanced toward the mudroom where the two cats had their bed. As she pressed a second slice of fresh bread onto her cheese to form a thick sandwich, her white cat and its ginger companion peered out at her, blinking as though she'd wakened them from a nap. She took a few cat treats from a container in the pantry, capturing their attention.

"I've got something yummy here. If you come out

to the porch with me, we can have a picnic," Mary Kate murmured as she placed the treats on her plate. "If we're lucky, maybe later Mamm'll bring a go-box of something with gravy. I could really go for a big dollop of mashed potatoes smothered in chicken gravy. Or just a go-box full of gravy."

Sugar and Spice followed her out the front door, meowing softly. When Mary Kate settled on the swing, the cats leapt nimbly up on either side of her, watching closely as she lifted the sandwich to her lips. As she chewed a huge bite of the soft cheese and fresh bread, she placed treats on the swing's padded seat for her pets. When she looked down the road again, the last guests were leaving Noah and Deborah's new home, ambling toward the dining room in the lodge to enjoy the wonderful meal she'd helped prepare yesterday.

Mary Kate had a sudden yearning to sink her teeth into Rosetta's moist, savory baked chicken and to cram her mouth full of the dressing the Kuhn sisters had made. Mamm had told her that cravings were common during pregnancy, yet deep down she wanted the fun and fellowship of the wedding dinner even more than the delicious food. Would it be this way for the rest of her life—sitting alone with the cats and the baby while the rest of the world passed her by? She sighed as she set her boring white sandwich on her plate and gave Sugar and Spice another treat.

She was almost ready to go inside, to search the cabinets and the fridge for something more tempting, when a movement at the back door of the lodge caught her eye. A tall, lithe figure jogged across the road toward Rainbow Lake and then disappeared into the orchard. The black pants, white shirt, and lean body build meant it was one of the young men attending the wedding, but why had he left the dinner that was just being served? And what was in the container he was carrying?

"There's a story there," Mary Kate murmured. At the cats' nudging, she dropped another treat on either side of her. Absently, she took a bite of her sandwich as she tried to recall the guy's hair color. She was cramming the last of the sandwich into her mouth when a voice startled her.

"Here you are! I've been looking for you all morning, Mary Kate."

Mary Kate's eyes widened as Roman Schwartz came around the side of the house and stepped up onto the porch. The cats, always wary of strangers, scurried to the far corner. With her mouth so full, all Mary Kate could do was hold up a finger in a plea to wait until she'd chewed and swallowed her unladylike mouthful of food. Why would Roman be here instead of on the *eck*, eating with the rest of the wedding party? Did she dare hope his lidded glass pan held food from the lodge kitchen?

And where's my sister? she wondered as she finally managed a smile. "I—I wasn't expecting you," she blurted. Feeling suddenly fat, she tried to cover her belly with her plate, knowing that trick wouldn't work.

Roman's lopsided smile made him look like a kid, although Mary Kate knew he was twenty-three or twenty-four. "I saw you going into Noah's house before church, but when I looked for you during the service, I only saw your sister. Are you all right?"

Mary Kate's cheeks prickled with heat. "Um, Dat sort of told me to go home," she murmured. "He has a thing about women being seen in public when they're . . . carrying."

"Ah. I thought it might be something like that. Not always easy, being the bishop's kid, I bet." He glanced down as though he'd just remembered he was holding something. "I brought you some dinner."

Had anyone ever done such a thoughtful thing for her? Shyly, Mary Kate held out her hands, and when Roman gave her the warm container, she caught a whiff of chicken that nearly made her swoon. Remembering her manners, she scooted to one end of the swing. "Sit down if you want," she murmured. "But then, I guess you'll be heading back to eat with the bride and groom—"

Roman shrugged and sat on the other end of the swing. "Plenty of time for that, seeing's how the party will last all day. Can I get you a fork or something?"

Once again Mary Kate marveled at the kindness her visitor was showing. She chuckled as she lifted the container's lid and took a deep breath. "How did you know I'd been sitting here wishing for chicken and gravy?" she murmured ecstatically. "Oh, Roman, *denki* so much!"

He cleared his throat a little nervously. "I thought I'd visit awhile—unless you don't want me watching you eat."

"We could share. You loaded enough into this pan for three people—which will work out just right, considering I'm eating for two," Mary Kate teased. Then she nearly choked. Had she really made a joke about her condition to a *guy*? The fellow her sister was crazy for?

Roman laughed. "I'll get two forks. We'll see how much you leave for me."

"*Jah*, it'll taste better now than it will later."

By the time he'd reached the door, Mary Kate was ready to grab one of the seasoned chicken legs and stuff it unceremoniously into her mouth. Roman had mounded mashed potatoes at one end of the glass pan, along with a generous portion of dressing, and he'd poured creamy chicken gravy over it all. Alongside four pieces of baked chicken, he'd spooned some creamed celery and several slices of apples simmered in butter, brown sugar, and cinnamon. She inhaled deeply, closing her eyes.

"Did I pick stuff you like?" Roman asked as he returned with their forks. "I was trying to get out of the kitchen and across the road before your sister realized what I was doing. She's been, well . . . gawking at me a lot today."

Mary Kate's heart skipped a beat. Who would ever have imagined Roman Schwartz—the guy who milked huge black-and-white dairy cows every day—trying to escape her sister's schemes? "Gloria wants to go out with you. But you didn't hear that from me."

Roman handed her a fork and sat down in the swing again, close enough that they could eat from the glass pan he held between them. He seemed to be considering his response.

Mary Kate, however, wasted no time dipping up a big blob of potatoes and gravy. It was a mouthful of heaven. She closed her eyes over the combination of creaminess and warmth and smooth, well-seasoned chicken gravy. "Ohhh," she murmured. "You have no idea how I was craving potatoes and gravy."

Roman's smile made his brown eyes sparkle. His dark blond waves shifted in the breeze as he took a forkful of the dressing. "I could eat this kind of food every single day and not get tired of it," he remarked. "But I don't know how to make potatoes and gravy and dressing—much less how to cook chicken the way my aunt does."

I would make you mashed potatoes and gravy and dressing every day, Mary Kate suddenly thought. But where had such an idea come from? Roman was at least six years older than she was, and he wouldn't be hanging around once the baby came. He'd felt sorry for her, being here by herself instead of attending the wedding, and she didn't want his pity. It occurred to Mary Kate that just this morning she'd told the gals at the lodge she wanted nothing to do with men, ever . . . yet Roman was making her forget her aversion. Could he be as genuinely nice as he seemed?

"You have *gut* taste, Roman," she said as she reached for a chicken leg. "And *denki* again for thinking of me."

"You're welcome." He took hold of the pan so Mary Kate could use both hands to eat her chicken. He was polite enough not to comment when she made very short work of the leg and then set the bone against the side of the pan.

They spent the next several moments eating in companionable silence, careful to avoid each other's forks as they dipped into the container. When they were down to scraping the sides of the pan, they both sighed contentedly—and then laughed at themselves.

"I feel so much better," Mary Kate said. "It was awfully nice of you to come."

Roman smiled at her. "I'm glad I did. For guys my age, weddings feel like the first day of deer hunting season, when all the single gals behave as though the guys are walking targets. I suppose I should get back, though."

"*Jah*, your brother and the bride probably are wondering what's happened to you." *Not to mention Gloria,* Mary Kate thought with a smile.

"I guarantee you that Noah and Deborah aren't thinking about me," Roman teased. "You did miss a pretty provocative wedding sermon, though. Your *dat* told my *mamm* and aunts, along with Amos and Preacher Marlin—by name—that they were to be married before the snow flies and that he'd allow no marrying of Amish to Mennonites. He also preached that the women's only business should be keeping house for their families."

Her jaw dropped. "He really said those things? In front of so many people?" she whispered. "*That's* not going to go over with Rosetta or your *mamm* or—"

"Preacher Amos was gripping the bench so hard, I thought he might crack it in half. Preacher Marlin looked ready to stand up and leave—and Truman Wickey was as mad as I've ever seen him." Roman shook his head as he rose from the swing. "I'm sure we've not heard the last of this. After all, who's to run the produce stand or manage the lodge apartments if my mother and aunt aren't allowed? I can't see them handing over those businesses to men—even their husbands—after they've poured themselves into making a go of it here."

Mary Kate sighed loudly. "My *dat* believes women should know their place and stay there, without making any fuss," she murmured. "I don't see why he's so old-fashioned about stuff like that, when other Amish settlements allow women to work from their homes—which is what your *mamm* and Rosetta are doing. And anyone can see that Truman and Rosetta are meant for each other."

"It'll all work out, somehow." Roman gazed at her. Although he stood nearly six feet tall and had a sturdy, muscled body, he didn't give the impression of looking down at her, or of intending to keep her in his shadow or under his thumb. The slow smile that overtook his face appeared open and sincere—not a sign of derision or pity. "You take care, Mary Kate. It was nice visiting with you."

As Roman strolled down the road leading back to the lodge, Mary Kate wanted to clap her hands and whoop and dance. Never in her wildest dreams had she anticipated a visit from a good-looking guy after she'd resigned herself to spending the day with her cats. Her smile grew even wider when she realized how upset Gloria would be when she found out why Roman had left the wedding dinner.

It wasn't that she wished her sister ill. For the first time, Mary Kate had enjoyed the attention of a very eligible, upstanding young man who'd escaped pretty, vivacious, accomplished Gloria to spend time with *her*. That would never have happened back in Sugarcreek, where her sister went out quite often while Mary Kate hadn't been out on a single date. Ever. To the young men there she'd apparently been invisible, yet when Roman Schwartz had looked her over moments ago, she'd felt a connection.

She'd felt pretty. *Happy*.

If God had led her father here to become the bishop of Promise Lodge, maybe He had some plans for her, as well. Maybe this new settlement in rural Missouri held more promise than she'd thought.

Chapter Three

"Mattie, we've excused you from kitchen duty today," Beulah Kuhn insisted as she playfully swished her apron to usher Mattie toward the dining room.

"*Jah*, I figured you and Preacher Amos would be enjoying the meal—and maybe the whole afternoon—together," Frances Lehman joined in. "We've got plenty of help here, so—"

When Frances's smile fell, Mattie realized how fierce her facial expression must be. She inhaled deeply, reminding herself that Frances and the Kuhn sisters had graciously agreed to oversee the final preparations of the meal rather than attend the wedding, so they weren't yet aware of Bishop Floyd's decrees.

"You'd better put me to work washing dishes or filling plates or *something*," Mattie murmured as a movement at the doorway caught her attention. Rosetta and Christine were entering the kitchen with the same idea, it appeared—wearing expressions that suggested they'd tasted lemon pie made without any sugar. "Busy hands might be happy hands," Mattie continued, "but—"

"*My* hands feel like wringing somebody's neck," Rosetta muttered. She grabbed a flour-sack towel and began drying the big metal pots Ruby had scrubbed.

"And just who am I supposed to hitch up with in the next few weeks?" Christine demanded in a low voice. "If that wasn't the most preposterous, inappropriate—"

Mattie slung her arm around her sister before her rant went any further. "Keep in mind that our friends here have been cooking, so they don't know about Bishop Floyd's sermon. Frances shouldn't bear the brunt of our hissy fit, because she's not responsible for what comes out of her husband's mouth."

Frances's expression tightened, while the Kuhn sisters came over to huddle with Mattie, Christine, and the bishop's wife. Mattie understood perfectly why Rosetta remained beside the sink, wiping a big metal stockpot as though she intended to remove the burnt-on grime that dated back to when the lodge was a church camp.

"Oh dear," Frances murmured. "Something tells me Floyd went beyond his usual spiel about women knowing their place."

Christine exhaled, crossing her arms over her apron. "Can you imagine how we sisters felt when the bishop called us by name—along with Preacher Amos and Preacher Marlin—"

"And informed us we were all to be married before the first snowfall?" Mattie continued in a hoarse whisper.

"Just who does he think I'm to marry?" Christine's voice cracked and she looked ready to cry. "Marlin Kurtz hasn't been here but a couple of months—not that he seems any more inclined toward hitching up with me than I am with him."

"And where does it leave me if Bishop Floyd's forbidding me to marry Truman because he's a Mennonite?" Rosetta blurted. She set her pot on a metal table with a *clank* that echoed in the kitchen. "I've known all along that he feels that way, and I've had many a conversation with God about the consequences of leaving my Amish faith to become Truman's wife, but—it's just the *nerve* of that man! Calling us out in front of a roomful of wedding guests!"

Frances covered her face with her hand. "Oh my. I had no idea he'd go so far as to humiliate you that way."

"What'd he say about Ruby and me?" Beulah muttered. "If he thinks we two *maidels* intend to get married at this late date—"

"Not to worry, Sister," Ruby said as she patted Beulah's arm. "This new colony welcomes all manner of Plain folks, but we who are Mennonite rather than Amish don't answer to Floyd, remember."

"I'm afraid my husband's as hardheaded as he is hard of hearing," Frances murmured. "I suppose he also preached that women shouldn't be running businesses—even though that has little to do with Noah and Deborah getting married."

"*Jah*, we heard that sermon again," Mattie replied. She suddenly felt very tired, unwilling to carry this conversation any further. "Now that I've let off some steam, I want to find Amos. I could tell by the look on his face that he was no happier about Floyd's ultimatum than we women were."

Mattie smoothed her apron, hoping her bad mood would dissipate as she stepped into the doorway of the dining room. What a sight it was! The long tables covered in white cloths gave the large hall a simple elegance. Every seat was filled with friends and family members who visited happily as they ate their meal. The aromas of baked chicken, stuffing, and warm bread soothed her as she gazed from table to table, trying to locate Amos. She hoped he hadn't given up on her. He'd be disappointed if she didn't join him for dinner.

Her gaze lingered on the raised *eck* table, where her younger son sat with his new bride. The sight of them sitting so close, lost in each other's gazes, made Mattie's heart overflow with a special love. *It's their happiness that matters*, she reminded herself. *They're the future of Promise Lodge no matter how things work out— or don't—with Floyd Lehman.*

Mattie wondered why Roman was returning to his place at the wedding party's table with a secretive smile, appearing slightly out of breath. He waved off Noah's teasing question, squeezing his younger brother's shoulder as he sat down beside Laura Hershberger—his cousin and Deborah's closest friend. What a blessing that her boys were so close, and that they remained so connected to Christine's girls, as well. Once again, as she gazed at their earnest faces, she wondered how those four kids— and Deborah—had reached young adulthood already.

If your sons are twenty-four and twenty-one, there's no denying how old that makes you, Mattie realized wistfully. *Maybe Amos has it right. Maybe you should accept his proposal, for who knows how long he'll keep asking a middle-aged widow to make her home with him? Roman's building a house now, so he'll have a home to offer the right young*

*woman when she comes along. Do you want to grow old
alone?*

Another quick look around the crowded room convinced Mattie that Amos wasn't seated yet—and that
was just as well. As soon as these guests finished eating,
the serving crew would clear the dirty dishes and set
up for a second, smaller shift for the kitchen helpers
and the remaining guests and family members who'd
waited patiently to enjoy their dinner.

Mattie felt calmer as she made her way to the *eck*
table. The bride and groom sat in the center, and
behind them rose a white cake decorated in pale blue,
displayed on the glass cake plate Mattie had used
when she'd married Marvin Schwartz—an idea Beulah
and Ruby had suggested after they'd baked and decorated the cake together.

"It's *gut* to see all you kids enjoying this wonderful
day," Mattie murmured as she reached for Noah and
Deborah's hands. "And I wish you two a lifetime of
God's blessings as you begin your life together."

Deborah grabbed Mattie's hand between both of
hers and squeezed it. "We can't thank you and Amos
enough for our plot of land, and for building us a
beautiful home," she replied earnestly. She leaned
farther over the table, lowering her voice. "And I
hope you and your sisters and Amos can work out a
solution—a sensible peace—about running your
businesses and marrying in God's *gut* time rather than
in Bishop Floyd's."

A sensible peace . . . in God's gut *time rather than Bishop
Floyd's.* Was that too much to hope for? Too much to
ask of God, the father of them all?

"*Denki*, Deborah. That's a lovely idea," Mattie murmured. She felt blessed indeed, witnessing the mature,

sincere faith reflected in all the young faces at this table. "Our mission as God's Plain people is always to attain the peace He desires for us—in our relationship with Him, and amongst ourselves, as well."

"We'll put in a *gut* word for Truman when we pray about this situation," Phoebe said as she patted the empty spot beside her at the end of the table. "He apologized for not sitting up here with us, and for getting riled up about the wedding sermon. I hope he'll spend some time with Rosetta today—"

"*Jah*, I was honored that he served as my side-sitter," Noah chimed in. "He's a bit older, as *newehockers* go—and he has a lot to think about now that our bishop's spoken out against intermarriage again."

"I hope Truman won't think we no longer value his friendship—or that we don't appreciate all the ways he's helped with digging foundations, pouring concrete for our roads, and helping us restore the orchard," Roman said as he picked up his fork. The food on the plate the servers had brought him a while ago had gone cold, but he didn't seem to mind. "Fact is, we'd still be struggling to build Noah's house, not to mention the others that have gone up so fast, had Truman not brought his crew and equipment over to help us."

"He's the best sort of neighbor and a fine friend," Mattie agreed. "I'll pass along your words of thanks when I see him. He needs to know that Floyd doesn't speak for the rest of us."

And that's a sad thing—a dangerous thing—to say about the bishop of our new colony, Mattie realized as she made her way toward the door. Her spirits lifted as she passed the tables where friends from Coldstream voiced their congratulations about the wedding and

the way Promise Lodge had come together so quickly
and beautifully. A few of those folks appeared ready to
quiz her about Bishop Floyd's marriage ultimatum, so
Mattie kept moving between the tables, determined
to find Amos. If her former neighbors asked about
their bishop, who claimed God had led him from
Ohio to their new Missouri colony to be their leader,
what could she say? Only the Lord knew Floyd
Lehman's true motives. It wasn't her place to question
the bishop's sincerity—or God's plan.

When Mattie stepped out of the dining room's back
door, leaving the laughter and loud chatter behind
her, she savored the serenity of the sun-dappled
shade. The huge old maple trees were dropping their
leaves, so the grassy yard resembled a green quilt with
a freestyle design in brilliant shades of red, gold, and
orange. The breeze held a hint of winter, reminding
Mattie that she'd soon be wearing her coat every time
she stepped outside.

The row of brown cabins, which had served as tem-
porary homes for incoming residents, would be
closed up in a few weeks because they didn't have any
heat. Amos, Noah, and Deborah had devoted a lot of
time to refurbishing those cottages over the summer.
Preacher Marlin Kurtz and his kids, Fannie and
Lowell, fourteen and twelve, were now living in the
largest cabin while Marlin's son and daughter-in-law,
Harley and Minerva, were staying in another one—all
of them awaiting the completion of a roomy new
home on the double lot atop the nearest hill.

Mattie was pleased that the Kurtz family had joined
them, because Preacher Marlin, a widower in his
fifties, delivered salt-of-the-earth, thought-provoking

sermons as only a man acquainted with the highs and lows of life could do. Marlin had asked the construction crew to finish his shop first—he built all sorts of wooden rain barrels, barrel furniture, and buckets that he sold through regional stores and a mail-order catalog. His daughter-in-law, Minerva, was a midwife—a welcome addition to any Plain settlement—and Harley's herd of sheep already grazed the grassy hills he'd fenced off last month.

When Mattie glanced toward the pastures, she saw Queenie lying at the top of a hill, keeping watch over the flock as though the sheep were her special responsibility. Mattie was about to head across the lawn to see if Amos had gone home when male voices made her stop to listen.

". . . you've pretty much guaranteed that Mattie won't marry me now, provoking her with your sermon ultimatum."

"I spoke the words God gave me. *Family* is everything in our faith—as you well know, Amos," came Bishop Floyd's reply. "It's time for you to provide Mattie a home and a more fitting full-time occupation."

Mattie frowned, her irritation rising again as the conversation drifted from the screen door of the cabin Marlin Kurtz was staying in.

"Floyd, I must ask you to remember that Christine kept her husband's dairy herd because she needs an income—just as Mattie began her produce stand and Rosetta opened apartments for single women because they have no men in their family to support them," Amos continued. His voice was calm but insistent. "It would be a shame to shut down the produce stand now that local folks are so eagerly supporting it—and it provides jobs for some of our other residents, too. I doubt you'd be agreeable if someone suddenly ordered you to quit running your siding business—"

"But that won't happen," Floyd interrupted testily. "If you can speak so eloquently in support of Mattie's business, why can't you persuade her to marry you?"

Mattie's jaw dropped. The bishop's impertinence bordered on disrespect, especially because Amos had maintained a low-key response to the ultimatums they'd heard during Floyd's wedding sermon.

"While marriage is the traditional vision for Old Order adults," another fellow joined in after a few moments of silence, "I can't believe you're suggesting that Christine and Marlin should get hitched—since there's nobody else for them to choose from. They hardly know each other."

"That's how I see it," a fourth fellow chimed in emphatically. "I'm sure Christine's a fine, upstanding woman who'll make some fellow a *gut* wife, but I have a business to get re-established and a house to finish before winter. And frankly, I'm still in mourning for my Essie. I doubt my heart will welcome another wife anytime soon."

Mattie's eyebrows rose. She recognized the voices of Preacher Eli Peterscheim and Preacher Marlin, which meant that either the bishop had called the three ministers together or they had cornered him to challenge his sermon. It was improper to eavesdrop on their meeting . . . but anyone coming out of the lodge could've heard them talking.

"And the way *I* see it," a fifth man added testily, "Rosetta and I could probably be husband and wife before the snow flies—but you've forbidden a Mennonite to marry her! And you insinuated that I'd be putting her on the path to perdition if I did. I resent that, Floyd. I'm every bit as sincere in my love for Christ—the Savior of us all—as you are. God sent his Son to save the world, not to condemn it."

Truman Wickey, you said that just right, Mattie thought as she walked a little closer to the cabin where the men were meeting. Although she'd been instructed all her life that the Old Order Amish faith was the one true church—the sole path to God's salvation—she was having a harder time believing that as she got older. She'd met plenty of Christians of other persuasions who believed God's grace and mercy were intended for them—and for all of His children. Why would He create so many followers, so many souls who called Him their God, only to condemn them to hell if they weren't Amish?

"And we know of other colonies hereabouts that permit Amish and Mennonites—or German River Brethren—to marry each other without any shunning or separation from the Amish congregation," Eli pointed out. "Here in Missouri—"

"Well, I come from an Ohio district that has remained true to the Ordnung and the old ways," Bishop Floyd interrupted loudly. "I believe that if Amish congregations start allowing small changes in the faith—like permitting intermarriage, or allowing women to own businesses—before you know it our people will be driving cars and using cell phones. Just like English."

Amos cleared his throat. "There are cell phones without Internet connections made especially for Plain people," he pointed out. "You see them advertised in *The Budget* all the time."

"Seeing something in print doesn't make it appropriate!" Floyd countered.

Mattie stopped at the corner of the cottage where the men were talking, noting the rise in the pitch and volume of their voices. She stood where the curtain panel would hide her, and when she glanced through the window she could see the five fellows in the main room. The three preachers and Truman were seated in chairs or on the edge of the bed while Bishop Floyd remained standing . . . as though using his stature to place himself above the others and refute everything they said. It made for a very uneven conversation, from her viewpoint—

Not that Bishop Floyd cares about your viewpoint.

Mattie blinked. The thought had come to her unbidden, yet unerring. It was wrong for her to judge the bishop, but her sudden flash of insight resonated with an uncomfortable truth. No matter what any of the other men said, Floyd Lehman would remain rooted in his own convictions, his mind closed to their ideas. And if he paid no attention to what the three preachers suggested, he certainly wouldn't listen to the women's opinions.

When she focused on Amos, who sat facing the window, Mattie admired him for speaking his mind—and for standing up for her and her produce stand. He looked robust and handsome dressed in his wedding best, with his hair and beard neatly clipped to follow the shape of his weathered face. Apparently the men in Floyd's previous district preferred the U-shaped style of beard that was allowed to grow as it would, untrimmed—messy, in Mattie's opinion. It shouldn't matter how their bishop looked, yet Floyd's unkempt, unruly appearance made it harder for her to accept his criticism.

But Mattie forgot all about beards and grooming when she realized Amos had spotted her. His face remained placid as Floyd pontificated further on the merits of the one true Old Order faith, but Amos stood up, waiting for a break in the conversation.

"No offense, Bishop, but I sense you'll remain unconvinced of anything we're going to say," Amos remarked quietly. "Rather than wasting any more of this special day, I'm going to eat some of the fine meal the ladies have prepared and visit with friends who've traveled here to celebrate with us."

As Amos headed for the front door, Mattie's heart sped up. Would Floyd see her through the window and realize she'd been spying? Perhaps she should slip back to the lodge and wait for Amos there, so Floyd wouldn't—

What do you have to hide? Any of our guests might've walked over this way to look at our cabins, and they would've overheard the men's conversation.

Smiling resolutely, Mattie held out her hands to Amos when he stepped outside. "I was beginning to think my dinner date had ducked out on me," she teased. She turned to smile at the men who were following him out. "Truman, Eli—the first-shift folks are coming out of the lodge, which means the tables are being reset for the rest of us. I know a couple of ladies who've been cooking and serving all day, who'd be grateful to sit down and eat with you. Marlin, we'd be pleased if you'd join us," she added as their newest preacher stepped outside.

Amos tucked her hand under his elbow and started

toward the lodge with her. "*Gut* timing, Mattie," he murmured near her ear. "Had you not given me a reason to leave, we might've been stuck in there with Floyd all afternoon. And we wouldn't have accomplished a thing, unfortunately."

"*Jah*, I'm ready for some pleasant company," Truman remarked softly as he fell into step with them. "We might as well have been talking to the wall—and I'm sorry to say that about your bishop, understand."

"Oh, we understand," Mattie replied with a sigh. "We started our Promise Lodge colony hoping to allow for a more progressive, positive lifestyle that would still embrace our bedrock faith. The bishop God brought us has different ideas, however."

As they met up with folks coming out of the lodge, Mattie and Amos stopped to talk with them, which allowed the serving ladies time to reset the tables for the second dinner shift. She felt a little odd not helping them, but she also felt good standing beside Amos, who'd kept her hand tucked in his elbow for all the world to see.

When did Marvin ever touch you in public? Or stand up for things that mattered to you?

Mattie blinked. Most Amish men didn't display affection in public, even when they dearly loved their wives, so it pleased her that Amos wasn't afraid to show his feelings—and that he wasn't keeping her hand in the crook of his elbow to establish his control over her. And he certainly wasn't cozying up to her to win Floyd's favor.

Amos enjoys being with you. He respects you and your opinions. He's an even-tempered fellow who lives his faith every day and doesn't consider men's matters more important than women's.

When they'd finished talking to some of the Peterscheims' cousins, Amos smiled down at her with his warm brown eyes. "Let's head on in to eat, shall we?" he murmured. "I hope it's all right that I let Marlin and Truman go in ahead of us, hoping to have you to myself for a little while."

Mattie's heart fluttered. She couldn't seem to stop gazing up at him. "That sounds lovely, Amos," she murmured. "*Denki* for thinking to do that."

Amos's smile brought his dimples out to play. "It's a rare day when you're not bustling around cooking and serving. I'm glad you've taken some time off, and that you're spending it with me."

Amos has been crazy about you since you were kids—how much more of your life will pass by before you allow him to make you happy? Why spend any longer living in the lodge with the other unattached women when Amos wants you to share his home, his life?

Mattie's thoughts were spinning rapidly. Her resistance to Amos's proposal suddenly seemed silly and irrelevant. "What if I want to spend more than just today with you?" she blurted. Her heart was pounding so hard she wasn't sure she'd get any more words out. "I—I want to accept your offer. I want to be your wife."

The sudden joy on Amos's face stunned her. He glanced around, slipped his arm around her waist, and quickly walked her behind the lodge. "Really?" he whispered as he pulled her close. "You're not saying this because of what Floyd preached—"

"Puh! He'll probably take credit for it," Mattie said

with a short laugh, "but no bishop is going to tell me—or you—who or when to marry, Amos."

"*Jah*, you've got that right. Oh, Mattie!" Ever so gently, Amos took her face between his large, sturdy hands and kissed her. It was a feathery brushing of lips, mere seconds of contact, yet it awakened feelings she'd not known since she'd been an innocent young woman.

"I was seventeen the first time you kissed me, and so crazy head-over-heels for you," she recalled in a dreamlike voice.

"I remember that day like it was yesterday," Amos murmured. "We were kids taking the long way home after a Singing when I finally worked up the nerve to kiss you. But we knew our hearts. We would've made it work."

"I believe that, too," Mattie whispered.

"I've always loved you, Mattie. I buried those feelings when your *dat* wanted you to marry Marvin and I hitched up with Anna," Amos recalled softly, "but that doesn't mean my heart forgot you. And now, at long last, you're making my dreams come true."

Mattie felt tears trickling down her cheeks as she buried her face against his sturdy chest. She felt the rumble of his chuckle as he wrapped his arms around her. For several moments she savored Amos's warm strength as they stood in blissful silence. The beating of his heart calmed her, set her life into rhythm again like the steady, dependable ticking of the clock he'd given her as an engagement gift . . . the clock she'd stored away during her marriage and had taken out again after Marvin's passing.

"I love you, too, Amos. *Denki* for your patience, your understanding—"

His kiss was more fervent this time, sweet and tender. Then he eased away to look at her. "I suppose we'd better behave ourselves, considering how many folks could catch us spooning out here. But I'll take up where we left off, next time we're alone together." He gently thumbed away the wet streaks on her cheeks. "Take a minute to pull yourself together, dear."

Mattie chuckled, dabbing at her eyes with the hem of her apron. "I'm out of practice at feeling so happy—but I think I can get used to it."

"I'll be sure you do," he murmured. "I intend to make up for a lot of lost time and make you glad you married me. Every single day. Ready to go in?"

Mattie nodded, straightening her *kapp* and smoothing her apron. "Ready—for whatever comes along."

Chapter Four

As Roman polished off his slice of peach pie, he eyed the untouched slice of coconut cream pie beside his cousin Phoebe's plate. Phoebe was chatting with Gloria Lehman, but the bishop's daughter wasn't fooling him: she was standing in front of the *eck* table to be sure he saw her. Gloria's behavior was about as subtle as a wag-tailed puppy's, so he looked for a way to stall getting up from the table. She was sure to follow him wherever he went.

"You going to eat this, Cuz?" he asked, tapping the pie plate with his finger.

Phoebe shook her head. Her knowing smile suggested that she knew what Gloria was up to and that Roman intended to avoid spending time with her. "Go for it. I'm saving room for some wedding cake later."

"Happy to help," Roman said as he set her plate on top of the one he'd just emptied.

"So you like coconut cream pie?" Gloria asked coyly. "I'll have to bake one for you sometime. I use cream instead of milk—and lots of brown sugar."

Roman shoved a large bite of the pie into his

mouth so he wouldn't have to answer. He knew a lot more about eating than about cooking, but it seemed odd to him that anyone would make a creamy-white coconut pie with brown sugar.

"That looks like the pie Ruby made, using milk from the cows Roman milks. She puts toasted coconut on top of hers," Phoebe remarked matter-of-factly. "The Kuhn sisters say Christine's Holsteins give such rich milk, their cheese tastes better than any they've made before."

"Mmm," Roman said, nodding in agreement. The pie was fabulous, thick and creamy and sweet. The second bite he took was smaller so he could stretch out the time it would take to eat the rest of the slice.

"You must make a lot of money for your aunt, selling her herd's milk, if she can pay you enough to build a new house," Gloria said. She gazed sweetly at Roman, batting her long eyelashes.

Roman stopped chewing. It wasn't particularly a secret that his mother had given him and Noah their choice of lots or that Amos had insisted on building him a home before winter set in. Roman had bunked in the barn loft over the summer so the lodge could be properly maintained as apartments for ladies. Noah and Deborah had offered him a room at their new place, but Preacher Amos had sensed that Roman and the newlyweds would both be more comfortable having separate homes.

Not that he cared to discuss any of this with Gloria. She was fishing for information concerning his livelihood—how well he could support a wife—and he wasn't biting.

"Along with helping your *dat* with his window and siding business, Roman milks twice every day and helps maintain all the common buildings on our property," Phoebe reminded Gloria as she flashed Roman another secretive smile. "Not everyone would rise before the sun, winter and summer, to tromp around in that barn and handle all those cows—and to muck out their manure."

When Gloria wrinkled her nose, Roman wondered if she practiced that expression in front of a mirror. "I sure hope your new house has a mud room—and a hose outside the back door so you won't track in anything stinky."

Roman shrugged. "When you work with cows, you're going to step in it," he remarked, hoping to dissuade her. "Some of my clothes and boots have spent so much time in the barn, no amount of scrubbing gets the odor out."

Gloria pressed a fist to her hip as she twirled one of her *kapp* strings. "I bet *I* could wash up your clothes so they smelled clean!"

"If that's an offer, I'd be silly to turn it down," Roman remarked as he cut another bite of pie. His mother had shown him how to operate a wringer washing machine so he'd be more self-sufficient when he moved into his house, yet he suddenly wanted to see how far Gloria would go in her efforts to impress him. "What say I give you a shot at washing my barn clothes after I tend this afternoon's milking and mucking?"

Gloria's dark brown eyes widened as she considered the pros and cons of making good on her boast. "You're on!" she said brightly. "What time shall I come by the barn for your clothes?"

Roman nearly choked on his bite of pie. Gloria made it sound as if he'd be peeling off his clothes and handing them to her. "Might be better if I brought them to your house," he suggested. "That would give me a chance to clean up and put the clothes into a bag for you. Once I turn the cows back outside—"

"I could come and help you!" Gloria blurted. "I've always wanted to see a dairy cow up close and—"

"Absolutely not." Roman set down his fork and focused on her. "I have to maintain health department sanitation regulations, so I can't have other folks coming in and out of the milking barn on a whim, Gloria," he explained in a low but firm voice. "Your presence—any stranger's arrival—would make the cows nervous, too. If one of them stepped on your foot, I'd have a serious issue to deal with right in the middle of the milking. Stay home. Please."

Gloria's eyes widened as though she might burst into tears. "You don't have to be so mean about it," she whimpered.

From a few seats down, Noah joined the conversation. "Roman's just following regulations, Gloria," he reiterated kindly. "He has set procedures, as far as getting the milk into a refrigerator tank and doing things just right to prevent any chance of contamination goes. Running a dairy's a lot different from a family keeping a milk cow or two."

"And I might work longer than you realize after the milking's done," Roman continued, trying to be patient. "The truck comes to fetch our milk early tomorrow morning, so everything's got to be ready. And then I have to feed and water the herd, muck out the barn, and sanitize the milking equipment."

He smiled, hoping to avoid a scene. His two aunts, Gloria's *mamm*, and the other ladies had probably been following this conversation as they reset the long tables for the second shift of folks that were coming in to eat. "I'll understand if you don't want to wash my clothes, Gloria," he repeated in a low voice. "I doubt you'll want to mix my grungy stuff in with your family's other laundry, and I certainly don't expect you to do my pieces by themselves. Nor would it be nice of me to bring over the whole week's worth of my barn clothes so you'd have a full load."

Gloria's expression told him she hadn't considered these details in her eagerness to please him, to win some time alone with him. "Maybe you're right, Roman," she murmured. "I—I just wanted to help."

"And I appreciate it." He had the distinct impression that Gloria wanted him to make her a better offer—to suggest something fun they could do together—but he kept quiet. After the enjoyable time he'd spent with Mary Kate on the Lehmans' porch, he knew better than to mix it up with two sisters. Gloria was completely different in temperament and intention, and no matter how nice he was to both of them, one sister was bound to get her feelings hurt—or he'd get caught in the middle and they'd both turn on him.

"Well, I guess I'll get back to the kitchen and help with the cleaning up," Gloria said with a long-suffering sigh. "Seems to me that Mary Kate could've stuck around here to help us, considering how Dat told her not to show herself at the wedding. I bet she's had a fine, restful day playing with the cats . . ."

Her sentence drifted off as she turned to leave. Roman glanced at the last bite of his coconut pie and left it. Why did girls have to be so complicated? He hadn't given Gloria any encouragement that he knew of.

Noah, Deborah, and Laura rose from their places

to stretch and walk around as the new shift of folks took their seats. "Careful there," his brother murmured when he passed behind Roman's chair. "Something tells me that the four-legged Lehman cats have nothing on Gloria, when it comes to claws."

"I suspect you're right," Roman replied. He glanced at Phoebe. "*Denki* for helping me out. Gloria's been trying to get my attention ever since the Lehmans moved here—"

"Because you're the only guy her age at Promise Lodge—and because you're building a new house and you have a steady income," Phoebe pointed out. "With Noah married, you're the obvious choice for any single girls who come here. Lucky you, Roman."

"*Jah*, right." He watched his mother come into the dining hall with her hand in Preacher Amos's and a glow on her face. When Mamm beckoned to him and then to Noah and Deborah, Roman stood up. "Well, now. *This* looks interesting."

As he approached them, he couldn't miss the way his mother beamed. Amos's wide smile formed little curves on either side of his mouth. "Noah and Roman," his mother said as she reached happily for their hands, "I've just agreed to marry Amos! We wanted you boys to be the first to know—and you, too, Rosetta and Christine."

Roman's two aunts and Deborah immediately laughed and began hugging Mamm and Amos, congratulating them loudly enough that everyone in the room wanted to be a part of the celebration.

"High time," Noah teased as he pumped Amos's hand. "Maybe Deborah and I were your inspiration, eh?"

Amos laughed. Years had fallen away from his leathery, tanned face and he exchanged yet another smile with Mamm. "Patience and persistence are a man's best friends," he replied. "I've loved your mother since I was a lot younger than you boys. I promise to take *gut* care of her. She's a woman to be prized and cherished."

Roman shook hands with Amos, as well. "Happy for both of you," he murmured as he returned his mother's hug.

He stood back to allow the Kuhn sisters and Frances Lehman to express their congratulations, knowing his mother would be a lot happier with Amos than she'd been alone. His thoughts took him back to his childhood and youth . . . the times he'd realized that Dat was mistreating his mother both verbally and physically, and he hadn't known what to do about it. Their bishop in Coldstream had considered it a man's right to discipline his wife, even after his father had broken Mamm's nose—

But that's behind us now, Roman reminded himself. Amos Troyer was a different sort of man altogether, compassionate and caring even when he had to reprimand church members for behavior that didn't honor their Ordnung or God. Now Mamm had someone to see to her needs and keep her company—

A new household and a new man to be the head of it.

Roman blinked. After assuming responsibility for his *mamm*'s care—considering himself the man of the family after Dat's passing—it seemed strange that his mother would soon be going by a different name. She wouldn't be cooking regular meals for him anymore or confiding in him as much, although he knew he'd always be welcome at her and Amos's table. She wouldn't need him in the same ways—although Mattie Schwartz had never allowed widowhood to hold her back or make her dependent upon anyone. Her successful produce stand was proof of that.

Noah came over to stand beside Roman as they watched other well-wishers crowd around Preacher Amos and their mother. "This should get the bishop off their backs," he murmured.

"*Jah*, and we'll see what happens to the roadside stand and the garden plots," Roman replied. "So, is it just me or does this make you feel kind of funny— thinking of Amos as our step-*dat*? Or is he just Mamm's second husband, because he didn't raise us and won't be supporting us financially?"

"Haven't thought much about such things," Noah replied with a shrug. "But I'm grateful to Amos for seeing to Mamm's needs so we no longer have to, in ways we're not able to. He makes her happy—and their marriage will free up our time and energy so we can focus on our own families. Our futures."

Easy for you to say.

Roman wondered where this unspoken retort had come from, because he wished Noah and Deborah every blessing as they began their life together. He was feeling like the odd man out, however, the last single man remaining—except for Truman Wickey, who had also come into the dining room with Marlin Kurtz and his kids to congratulate the engaged couple.

Preacher Amos flashed Roman a thumbs-up from the center of the crowd that had gathered around him and Mamm. It seemed to Roman that romantic matters must come easier for folks the second time around, because they'd gotten past the bumpy roads of adolescence and dating, finding mates, and setting up households. Older folks had their priorities and preferences figured out and they were established in their occupations. They knew their places in life, and the paths God intended for them to follow—didn't they?

Preacher Amos made love look as easy as casting a line and catching a big fish from Rainbow Lake. Roman couldn't imagine himself looking so happy if he were standing beside Gloria Lehman—not that he'd ever ask her out, much less ask her to marry him.

When he glanced toward the doorway, he saw Mary Kate's unmistakably pregnant profile as she paused to look into the kitchen. Her hand moved slowly over her belly, as though comforting her baby was already second nature to her.

Can she feel it shifting, kicking? Does it respond to her touch? Roman wondered. Curiosity made his fingers tingle—although he would never ask Mary Kate if he could place his hand on her roundness to get the answers to his questions.

As though she sensed his presence, Mary Kate surveyed the dining hall until her gaze met his. Her smile lit her face slowly, much as a sunrise painted the morning sky with strokes of peach and pink and shimmering light. When she entered the kitchen, Roman felt compelled to follow her.

Not while Gloria's there.

He sighed. The gray-haired Kuhn sisters were rolling a cart loaded with heaping plates of chicken, potatoes and gravy, and dressing toward the table nearest his mother and Preacher Amos. "You folks sit down and enjoy your meal together," Beulah urged them as Ruby began setting plates in front of the chairs. "Oh, but this has been a big day! A happy day for one and all!"

Amos pulled out a chair for Mamm, and then he let

his hand linger on her shoulder after he seated her. Mamm beamed up at him so confidently, so joyfully, that Roman almost couldn't stand to watch. Once again he wondered if love came a lot easier to men who'd been around the block before.

Wouldn't it be nice to see Mary Kate smiling at you that way?

Chapter Five

Sunday at last! And no church today.

Amos rolled out of bed with a burst of energy, even though the sun wasn't due up for another hour. Ever since Noah and Deborah's wedding, his head had been in the clouds and his heart had been on his sleeve. Mattie was all he could think about while he'd been working on houses the past couple of days, as well as when he'd gone to the lodge for dinner in the evenings. This morning he was picking her up in the rig and they were going for a long drive and having a picnic to enjoy the end-of-fall weather, and to discuss important details about their marriage without other interested parties listening in.

As Amos chose clean pants and suspenders along with one of his better shirts, he smiled. Someday soon he wouldn't have to do his own laundry, or rely upon lunchmeat and easy-to-heat dinners from the grocery store, or clean the bathrooms—*not* that he saw Mattie merely as a cook and housekeeper. His Anna had been very capable when it came to tending the household and raising their three kids, but she might have been a more joyful, adventurous wife had he encouraged her to think outside the traditional Amish box. And maybe if he'd made Anna happier, their twin girls and Allen wouldn't have moved back east.

He wouldn't—couldn't—follow that pattern with Mattie. She'd lived independently for long enough to know that she didn't really need a man, especially one who expected her to obey his every whim or else suffer the discipline he dished out. Amos's goal this time around was to have *fun* with his wife, to enjoy their time together in his new home—which he was going to allow her to decorate as she wished. The careworn furniture from his first marriage had served its time. New easy chairs and a sofa—and a new bedroom set—would be symbols of their fresh start together.

With Mattie, he wasn't going to be so frugal or stern. Amos considered her his equal. It was an uncommon mindset for a Plain preacher, but it was the only way their union would thrive.

Amos showered, shaved above his silver-spangled beard, and dressed quickly. After a fast cup of coffee and a fried egg sandwich, he went out to tend his two horses. On his way to the barn, he glanced toward the lodge and saw light in Mattie's upstairs apartment window. It was his fondest dream, his firm intention, to make light shine in her life for as long as they lived. He was fifty and she was forty-five, both of them fit and healthy, so they could look forward to a lot of happy years together.

When he drove his open rig down the hill toward the lodge, Mattie was waiting for him on the big porch. "*Gut* morning, Amos!" she called out as she hurried toward him with a picnic hamper.

He hopped down to relieve her of the basket. As his hand closed over hers, Amos brushed her cheek with a quick kiss. "It *is* a *gut* morning, dear Mattie," he murmured. "I've been looking forward to this day with you ever since you suggested it at the wedding. You make me feel like a kid again, you know it?"

Mattie's laugh tickled his ears as he stuck the hamper behind the seat. He lifted her up into the buggy, enjoying the feel of her slender, sturdy body beneath the light coat she wore.

"I'll never be twenty again, but I'm fine with that," she replied. "Now that all my kids are grown up—"

"Are you sure about that?" Amos settled himself on the seat. He raised his eyebrows, partly teasing but gazing straight into Mattie's wide eyes. "We know folks who've had kids at our age."

"But it's been twenty-one years!" she protested. "My baby got married this week. And besides, you built a small house because your kids are married and gone."

Amos clucked at his horse, not surprised at the alarm in Mattie's answer. He considered his response, treading carefully. It was too early to upset her on a day he wanted to go perfectly. "I could certainly expand the house, if need be. Children are gifts from God. We're to welcome them as blessings," he reminded her gently. "And I do enjoy, um, what causes them."

Mattie's cheeks flared. She gazed steadily up and down the road they'd reached, checking for traffic instead of looking at him. "*Jah*, I suppose you would."

Amos wasn't surprised that this subject wasn't her favorite, considering that Marvin Schwartz had once broken her nose. "We'll figure it out, sweetheart," he assured her as he reached for her hand. "But I might as well confess that when you're out working in the garden plots, leaning over to pick beans or pumpkins or whatever, I stop what I'm doing to look at your nice backside."

Mattie's quick intake of breath made him chuckle. He hoped she wasn't ashamed of her body, as so many Plain women seemed to be.

"Puh! I'll be sure to figure out where you're working, then, and point it in the other direction," she said. But a hint of laughter had crept into her voice. "Maybe you should concentrate on your carpentry, Amos Troyer. You've been working a couple stories high, and that's a long way to fall if you get distracted by the view."

"True enough," he replied. "On Friday, we put the roof on the Kurtz place and then shingled it, so now the house is enclosed. Lester Lehman's going to install the siding as soon as he's finished bidding some jobs in Forest Grove. Seems the post office and mercantile want new windows."

"*Jah*, the Lehman brothers are more in demand than Floyd figured on when he was first checking us out," she remarked. "And it's a *gut* opportunity for Lester to complete his house before he moves his family here from Ohio, too—although his wife surely must miss him." Mattie's smile had returned now that he'd changed the subject, and she squeezed Amos's hand. "It was a fine thing to see the walls of Roman's house going up yesterday. Of course, while you were on the ladder I was mostly noticing how you have such broad, strong shoulders and hardly any backside at all."

Amos burst out laughing so loudly it startled his

mare. "Easy there, Mabel," he said, tightening the lines until the horse settled down. Then he smiled at Mattie. "What's *gut* for the goose is *gut* for the gander, I guess."

"No guessing about it, Amos. You have the flattest pants I've ever seen—but your other endearing qualities make up for it."

"Glad you see it that way. Glad you look," he added softly. It relieved him that Mattie's sense of humor had returned, and that she'd left the conversational door open a crack on the matter of revisiting the way husbands and wives behaved behind closed doors. He would never, ever force her . . . might have to entice her past whatever fear or displeasure she'd experienced with Marvin.

But for now, Amos wanted to concentrate on topics they both took pleasure in. "I enjoyed working with your boys yesterday," he said. "Noah's fast with a hammer—has such a deadly aim, I almost felt sorry for the nails."

Mattie chuckled. "Comes from his hours of welding— drawing a bead of solder so accurately—"

"Not to mention his being a crack shot with his rifle. I doubt Rosetta would have any chickens left by now, had Noah not kept the coyotes in check." Amos steered the horse onto the county highway and then over to the shoulder of the road, to stay clear of any cars. "I know he and Deborah were looking forward to their first weekend of collecting wedding gifts. It's an exciting time for them."

Mattie nodded, a wistful expression on her dear face. "They're a well-suited pair. I hope we'll soon settle this matter of wives working at home, because

Noah installed an extra-large double oven so Deborah could continue her baking business this winter."

Amos nodded, hoping to avoid the topic of Bishop Floyd's ultimatums—which would put both of them in an unsuitable mood for such a fine autumn Sunday. The breeze was crisp enough that Mattie pulled her coat a little tighter, but she was gazing at the maples and oaks along the roadside, reveling in their crimson, gold, and orange foliage.

"Seems she's not the only one baking lately," he remarked. "While we were working on Roman's place yesterday, Gloria brought over a pan of bars, still warm enough that the chocolate chips were runny. It was a shame that when she took the first ones out of the pan, they either stuck to it or broke all to pieces."

"That happens when you don't let them cool long enough." Mattie chuckled. "I can just see Gloria getting frustrated and whiny while Roman made out as though he didn't care one way or the other about her goodies."

"He didn't encourage her, that's for sure. Seemed put out that Gloria expected us to stop what we were doing and climb down from our ladders."

"Had it been Mary Kate bringing treats, Roman would've fallen all over himself and gobbled half the bars," Mattie said with a soft chuckle. "But don't tell him I said so. He thinks I don't notice the way he gazes at her."

"Oh, to be the man all the young ladies adore," Amos teased.

"That was you once upon a time, Amos. All of us girls were so envious of Anna when she caught you."

His eyebrows rose. "Even you, although you'd married Marvin with his fine farmhouse?"

"Especially me," she murmured in a faraway voice. "You have no idea. From the first day, my marriage felt like a cage, and I felt like Marvin had thrown away the key. It . . . it wasn't the life I'd hoped for when I was growing up."

Mattie's haunting words made Amos's throat tighten. Although it was pointless to relive their regrets from all those years ago, he still felt deeply sorry that he'd not been able to amass enough money to impress Mattie's ambitious *dat*. Back in that day, so many young men had taken up carpentry that he'd been hard pressed to land enough jobs to keep body and soul together, much less support a wife. He and Anna had lived with her parents for nearly two years before he could afford a one-bedroom rental home down the road a ways from Coldstream.

"I couldn't have provided the life you deserved, Mattie," he murmured. "No matter how much we loved each other then, it wasn't meant to be. But now that we've done right by our first spouses, and endured our time of mourning, God's brought us together again under much better circumstances. So, see?" Amos said in a brighter voice. "It all works out to the *gut* for them who love the Lord and keep His commandments."

"And what about Bishop Floyd's commandments? What do *you* think I should do about my produce business, Amos?" Mattie asked as he steered the rig down a pathway into the woods. "As a preacher, you're supposed to toe a higher mark than other folks. And as your wife, I'll be expected to go along with whatever the bishop sees as God's will for Promise Lodge—no matter how I envisioned our new colony when you and I and my sisters bought the property."

Amos considered his answer carefully as he parked the rig in an open area surrounded by cedar trees and crimson sumac bushes. He went around to help Mattie down, pleased that she'd waited for him when she was perfectly capable of stepping to the ground by herself. He stood before her for a moment, his hands remaining lightly at her waist as he gazed down at her. She smelled fresh and looked particularly pretty in a deep green dress that made her complexion glow— truly a temptation to a fellow who'd lived alone for too long.

"I love you, Mattie," Amos murmured. "I'm going to indulge in a single kiss and then I'll behave myself while we talk this morning. So for now, clear your mind of all those things the bishop said at the wedding, all right?"

Delight lit Mattie's eyes as she reached for him. For a few blissful moments, Amos pressed his lips to hers and held her close, savoring her warmth . . . her eager response to his kiss. Too soon he released her, while his resolve remained strong.

Mattie's sigh told him that she, too, wanted more of such close contact, but she stepped away from him. "What a pretty spot. Sort of secluded," she remarked as she looked around. "I've not explored this area much, so I have no idea where any of these trails in the woods might lead."

"It's a guy thing, to look for potential spots where you can spend time alone with a special woman. And if you follow this trail a little farther, you'll see a surprise." Amos took Mattie's hand, eager to show her what he'd discovered the other day when he'd followed a hunch. Two rabbits sprang from the underbrush at the side of the path, and a woodpecker hammered a nearby tree, far above them. Amos held up a low branch so Mattie could walk beneath it. About twenty feet farther along the trail the view opened up.

"Be careful—the ground drops away on the other side of that outcropping," he warned as he squeezed her hand. "But tell me what you see."

Mattie took notice of the rocks he'd mentioned and leaned forward to gaze out beyond the woods. She sucked in her breath. "Why, there's the lodge! And the cabins, all in a row," she said with awe in her voice. "And there's Rainbow Lake and the orchard, and the new road winding around between the plots we've sold to our new neighbors. Hah! And Queenie's herding Harley's sheep toward his new barn—just for the fun of it, I suppose."

Amos chuckled. "Harley had no idea he'd be getting a four-legged flock manager as part of the deal when he came here, but Queenie's an instinctive sheepdog, it seems."

"It looks like a little toy town from this distance, ain't so?" she whispered.

"Our own little slice of paradise," Amos said. "You probably didn't realize that our property extends this far, to where we're standing. When Truman and I staked out plots and drew our map to show potential residents, we didn't include this rocky hillside or these woods because we figured no one would buy it. Gives us a nice buffer from the traffic and the adjoining property."

He studied Mattie's face. She had a few gray strands in her dark brown hair, and some fine lines around her eyes—and a smile filled with wonderment—and to Amos, she'd never looked prettier. "Don't you wonder what God thinks when He looks down at all of us?" she said softly. "It amazes me that we surely must appear so tiny and insignificant, yet He hears our prayers . . . and answers them."

"And that, dear Mattie, is why you and I are together now," Amos whispered. "He answered my prayers—even if parts of His reply aren't what I wanted to hear."

Mattie nipped her lip, glancing up at him. "Like the part where Floyd is telling us women to get rid of our businesses?" she said ruefully. "Has the bishop said anything more to you about what's to happen to the produce stand? Or to Christine's dairy herd and Rosetta's apartments in the lodge?"

"It would be the natural order of things for your husbands to assume ownership of your land and your businesses—at least in the more conservative Amish communities," Amos replied quietly. "But I have no time or desire to take on the produce business you've established. The gardening season is the best time for me to be building homes for the folks who come to Promise Lodge."

"And what of Christine's cows? When she meets a man to marry, will Roman lose his job when her husband takes over the dairy?" Mattie mused aloud. "And I can't see any fellow managing apartments for single women—just as I can't imagine Rosetta marrying anyone other than Truman."

"If Floyd has his way, Ruby and Beulah will have to move out rather than continue to live in a setting he considers unnatural." Amos exhaled slowly, his eyes upon the cream-colored sheep that were now skittering across the pasture ahead of Noah's dog. "In some ways, the bishop reminds me of Queenie—driving us this way and that at his whim, simply because he enjoys it . . . and because he can. But don't ever tell him I said that," he added quickly.

"Of course I won't. I don't like being herded away from our original plans for Promise Lodge any better than you or my sisters do." She let out a sigh. "I suppose it's wrong to pray for God to intervene with some sort of lightning bolt or unmistakable warning to make Floyd change his mind."

Amos smiled. "Be careful what you pray for," he quipped. "We take our chances when we ask God to do things our way—especially if it involves bringing someone hardship or disaster. And that's what it would take to make Bishop Floyd change his tune. A major disaster."

"No, I don't want that," Mattie quickly clarified. "But a little slap upside the head to let Floyd know he's going about things all wrong would be all right."

"And who are we to say he's wrong? He's following the more conservative ways of the Old Order, after all—and God did choose him for our community."

Mattie gazed up at Amos. "That's what it always comes down to, ain't so? The belief that our male leaders carry out God's purpose."

Amos badly wanted to kiss away the resignation on Mattie's face. She was a steadfast, God-fearing woman who would never knowingly defy His will, and he wanted her to be happy—to be fruitful and multiply, whether that be by raising his children or by producing vegetables that made good use of the fertile soil she'd been blessed with.

"How about if we take a look at what's inside your picnic basket?" he asked softly. "All this serious talk's making me hungry."

Mattie smiled as they turned around and headed back toward the buggy. "Are you saying that whenever I want to redirect opinions I don't like, I can just feed you?" she teased. "That seems easy enough."

"The way to a man's heart is through his stomach," Amos pointed out. "But then, you won my heart a long time ago, dear. You could probably put dirt clods and earthworms on my plate, and I'd be too caught up in my love for you to notice."

Mattie's smile warmed him like the sunshine that filtered through the trees. "Today we've got fried chicken, dinner rolls, slaw, apple salad, and pumpkin pie. But I'll keep your idea about dirt clods and worms in mind, should I ever need to get your attention," she teased.

Amos took the picnic basket from the buggy and handed her an old quilt to spread on the ground. "Oh, you've always got my attention," he said with a chuckle. "And to keep *your* mind from wandering, how soon would you like to get married? If you want me to court you for a while, I'll be happy to—"

"November twenty-first," Mattie replied without missing a beat.

Amos's heart turned a cartwheel. Her immediate answer suggested that she was even more eager to become his wife than he'd anticipated. "That's your birthday, as I recall," he said while they sat down on the quilt. "It's not quite two weeks away. Will that give you ladies enough time to prepare for another wedding meal? I don't want you to feel I'm rushing you into this."

Mattie chuckled as she took the lids from the bowls of slaw and apple salad. "You saw how well everyone worked together at Noah's and Deborah's party. And you and I have known each other for most of our lives, after all," she pointed out. "Once I realized I was wrong to compare you to Marvin, or to assume marriage to you would be anything like the years I spent with him, everything fell into place and my heart fluttered open. I'm ready, Amos. I love you."

"Oh, Mattie," he whispered as he grabbed her hands. "We'll make a wonderful life together. You'll see!"

"We will," Mattie murmured with a decisive nod. She squeezed his fingers as she returned his gaze, a gesture that suggested she wanted to hold on to him forever.

Sunlight shimmered on her dark hair and the breeze played with her long *kapp* strings. Mattie looked younger and happier than she had in years—even more beautiful than when he'd adored her as a young girl—and Amos knew he'd remember this special moment forever.

Chapter Six

Sunday afternoon, Rosetta lingered in the kitchen after the noon meal's dishes were done, hoping the phone would ring. Bishop Floyd had allowed her and her sisters and renters to keep the phone in the lodge kitchen because so many people shared it. Even so, it was silly to think Truman might return the message she'd left him only ten minutes earlier, because he often took his mother to afternoon activities at their Mennonite fellowship hall on Sundays. But the idea Rosetta wanted to discuss with him made her feel as bubbly as a bottle of soda somebody had shaken.

Mattie was getting married!

Rosetta still felt giddy after hearing the news. Mattie had come home from her picnic and announced that she and Amos planned to marry on the twenty-first—not even two weeks from today! Mattie's face had been aglow as she'd entered the lodge, and Amos had worn a smile that suggested the two of them had talked about many important issues, and perhaps had done a little smooching, as well. Rosetta thought it was wonderful that the two of them had rekindled the love they'd shared years ago. If anyone deserved a happy life with a steadfast, affectionate man, it was Mattie.

Rosetta reached for the folder of recipes she'd torn from *The Budget* and had jotted on odd scraps of paper. If she looked for something new to bake, at least she'd have a feasible reason to be in the kitchen—besides waiting for Truman to call. The Kuhn sisters were napping. Mattie had gone upstairs to share her news with Christine, Laura, and Phoebe. Preacher Marlin and his family were taking a walk around the Promise Lodge property to enjoy the fine fall weather, and all the Lehmans were spending the day at the bishop's new house. As winter approached and the ground got covered with snow, Rosetta suspected the lodge building wouldn't be as busy, because most folks would be eating meals and spending their evenings in their homes.

With Mattie moving to Amos's place, Rosetta was glad she'd have Ruby and Beulah for company this winter. She was a bit disappointed that more unattached Plain ladies hadn't written to say they'd move to—

The ring of the phone made Rosetta jump. She laughed as her recipes fluttered to the floor with the swish of her skirt. "*Jah*, hello?" she said as she grabbed the phone. "Promise Lodge Apartments. This is Rosetta speaking."

A chuckle tickled her ear. "*Jah*, dearie, I'm old and alone and I'd like to rent a room at your place," the caller said. Her voice had an odd timbre to it, as though this lady might've suffered some damage to her vocal chords.

"You're in luck," Rosetta said. Maybe her prayer for

more tenants was about to be answered! "We still have several rooms with nice views. We can convert them into apartments or—"

"I'll be right over to check them out," Truman said in his normal voice. "But I suppose I'd have to wear a dress to live there, wouldn't I?"

Rosetta laughed at herself for not checking the caller ID number on the phone's screen—and then laughed at her mental image of the muscular landscaping designer in a cape dress and *kapp*. "*That* would give the bishop something to talk about!"

"But I doubt he'd come any closer to allowing us to court. You sounded excited when you left your message, Rosetta," Truman continued in a low, intimate voice. "What's on your mind? I was glad to hear from you."

"Well, we've learned that Amos and Mattie plan to marry on the twenty-first, so I thought—"

"Of November? Wow, they're moving things right along."

"*Jah*," Rosetta said, "but if you consider that Mattie got caught passing Amos notes when they were kids in school, that's at least forty years they've known each other. Once Mattie decided to put her previous marriage behind her, she became a different woman. She's happier than I've seen her in a *gut* long while."

"That's all that matters. They're both wonderful people."

"Which is why I'd like to throw them a party before the wedding," Rosetta continued excitedly. "Mattie and Amos both cleaned out a lot of their old household stuff when we moved from Coldstream, so it's a perfect time to shower them with new towels and sheets, don't you think?"

"Or even furniture and rugs," Truman suggested. "When I helped Amos carry his stuff from the shed, I was struck by how little he owned. Even though his new house is relatively small, the rooms seemed bare."

"Mattie knew she'd be moving into an apartment when we came here, so she donated a lot of her household stuff to charity. So there you have it! We should plan for some happiness," Rosetta insisted. "We haven't had a picnic since our fish fry this summer."

"We can do that again, if you want. I'll bring my deep fryer, and we could even have a bonfire—burn off that pile of dead wood Roman and I cleared from the orchard."

"And we'll make s'mores and roast hot dogs! And we can get out our mountain-pie irons," Rosetta continued, loving the way this party was taking shape. "The Peterscheim boys and the Kurtz kids will love that! They've been fishing so much, we've frozen a *bunch* of fish fillets since the end of the summer. What better way to enjoy these final autumn days?"

"You're the hostess with the mostest," Truman quipped, "and I welcome any opportunity to spend time with you, Rosetta. Pick a date and count me in."

Pick a date and count me in. Truman's words—and Mattie's afternoon announcement—made Rosetta wish she could pick her own wedding date . . . and then stand beside Truman as they exchanged their vows. For the near future, however, she would content herself with spending time with Truman in public situations, as friends.

"Are you still there, sweetheart?"

Rosetta blinked. It did funny, wonderful things to her heart when Truman used such endearments. "Oh, *jah*," she murmured. "I'm not going anywhere, you know. Promise Lodge is my home, and I love it here."

"Happy to hear that."

She glanced out the kitchen window, wondering how to keep Truman on the line a little longer. "Now that the leaves have turned, it's as though Mother Nature has put away her summer clothes so she can wear Thanksgiving colors. Fall's my favorite season. What's yours?"

"Hmm. I like them all—for different reasons," Truman replied softly. "Autumn's a beautiful time of year here, yet I love the sparkle of the sunshine on snow, as well. And just when I've grown tired of plowing the roads and keeping my clients' driveways cleared, along come the bright green shoots and leaves that signal springtime."

Rosetta nodded. "I'm always glad to put away my coats and do the spring cleaning," she said. "After spending a quiet winter inside, it feels *gut* to be outdoors again, barefoot in the freshly turned garden."

"And now summertime will have a special feel to it because I met *you* then," Truman continued softly. "It's my busiest season for landscaping, and my crews work long hours—but this year my jobs seemed to go faster, more smoothly, because I had your smile to look forward to whenever I stopped by."

"Oh, Truman." Rosetta drew a deep breath, closing her eyes. "No one's ever spoken to me this way."

"No one's ever inspired me the way you have," he said without missing a beat. "I believe God brought you here as a special gift, just for me, Rosetta. He hasn't shown me how to open this present yet—how to make you mine forever—but I trust that He will. The Lord I worship would never be so cruel as to open a beautiful new door without eventually leading me through it, into the next phase He has in mind for me."

Rosetta thumbed a tear from her cheek. "*Denki* for sharing that thought, Truman," she whispered. "You've given me fresh hope for our future. I can be more patient now."

His chuckle caressed her ear. "I wish *I* could. But we're in this together, *jah?* For the long haul, I hope?"

"There's no one else for me."

"Same here. I—I love you, Rosetta," he murmured. "I intended to say that to your face the first time, but there it is. The truth will set us free."

"Ohhh," Rosetta murmured. Her body came alive with goose bumps and joy and crazy little sensations for which she had no words. She gripped the receiver with both hands, as though to hold on to this moment forever.

"I love you, too, Truman. I—I was engaged when I was twenty, to a fellow named Tim," she continued. "But he fell from a tree and broke his neck—and took my hopes to the grave with him. Like a lot of Amish men, Tim wasn't one to express his feelings, so your words make me feel very special."

"Well, you *are.*" Truman's soft laughter delighted her soul. "I've dated a few gals I thought I could make a life with, but the romance went south when they tried to take over my life and reset my priorities. You're wiser than that."

"Puh! I'm older than you are, too," Rosetta teased. "Maybe you should consider that before we take this any further. Maybe there's a reason I've been on the shelf for seventeen years."

"You're thirty-seven to my thirty-three, as I recall?"

he asked. "That's not even a blink of God's eye. It's not as though love has an expiration date, like groceries, you know."

Rosetta chuckled. "I'm glad. I would've shriveled up long ago."

Once again Truman's chuckle lifted her spirits. "I'm glad you called me," he said. "Had no clue we'd share a life-changing conversation, but we've said what's in our hearts."

"We have."

"Let me know when we're having the party for Mattie and Amos. They've got nothing on us!"

"Let's do it Thursday evening. Sooner rather than later," Rosetta suggested. "That gives us gals a week beyond that to plan for the wedding dinner."

"See you then, if not before. Let me know what else I can do or bring."

As she hung up the phone, Rosetta felt as giddy as a girl going on her first date. When she thought back to the Sunday evening Tim had asked to take her home from a Singing—his first display of romantic interest in her—she recalled her nervousness and Tim's shyness, which had resulted in an almost painful silence during their ride home. Most of their early dates had been group activities with the other youth in their church district, and even when Tim had found the nerve to take her out for rides in the countryside, he had remained reserved. He'd asked to court her, and then to marry her, by writing her two short but touching letters.

Rosetta still had Tim's letters tucked away in a special memento box Dat had carved for her. She didn't have to reread them to know that her relationship with Tim had been rather immature. Had he not died, however, she would've married him and been a steadfast wife.

But then you devoted yourself to caring for Mamm and Dat in their final years. And now a whole new life stretches before you, and Truman Wickey—for better or for worse—has become a vital part of it. Wrap yourself in a shawl of patience and be warmed by the deep friendship you share. Someday, when your circumstances are right . . . maybe God will find a way for you and Truman to be together.

Rosetta returned to the table and picked up the pieces of paper that lay scattered on the floor. With an outdoor party planned for Thursday evening, she chose recipes for pumpkin bread, butterscotch cashew bars, and other desserts that her friends would enjoy with their fried fish and hot dogs. She jotted down a list of ingredients they would need for mountain pies—toasted sandwiches made with bread, meat, and cheese, heated over a bonfire in a cast-iron pan similar to a long-handled waffle iron. Already she was anticipating the games they might play, the gifts she might give to Mattie and Amos . . . the time she would spend chatting with Truman, basking in his warm, gentle smile.

"You're here in the kitchen all by your lonesome, missy?"

"Gee, if we'd known you were having a recipe frolic, we would've shortened our naps."

Rosetta turned to smile at Beulah and Ruby. "I'm anything but lonesome. I just got off the phone with Truman—"

"Aha! That explains the light in your eyes," said Ruby.

"I liked that young fellow the first moment I saw him," Beulah chimed in with a nod.

"—and we're planning a party by the lake for Mattie and Amos! A combination fish fry, bonfire, and wedding shower," Rosetta continued in a lower voice. "And it wouldn't be the same without you ladies, of course. Let's keep the shower part a surprise, though."

"Oh, but that sounds like fun!" Beulah said, clapping her hands.

"And an excuse to make all sorts of goodies," Ruby remarked. "We can put together a basket of our cheeses and some jars of honey for the happy couple's gift—"

"With a handwritten certificate that's *gut* for all the cheese and honey they can eat for a year!"

Rosetta smiled. It was a treat to spend time with these *maidel* sisters because their enthusiasm was contagious. "The party is Thursday evening, and the wedding is set for the twenty-first—which is also Mattie's birthday," she added. "We've got a lot of planning and celebrating to do!"

Chapter Seven

As Mattie checked the tables one last time late Thursday afternoon, Rainbow Lake shimmered with sun diamonds and the reflection of trees ablaze in crimson and gold foliage. For the adults who preferred not to sit on the ground, they'd set up a long table with chairs. A short distance from Truman's fish fryer, they'd placed a serving table to hold the plates and the food—and everything was shaping up for a wonderful evening.

The three Peterscheim boys and Lowell Kurtz raced out the lodge's back door with whoops of joy, set free from school a little early by their sympathetic teacher, Minerva Kurtz. Their sisters, Lily Peterscheim and Fannie Kurtz, already close friends, walked quickly toward the picnic site to help with the preparations.

"What can we do?" Fannie called out. At fourteen, she stood a head taller than blond Lily, and her expressive dark brows and hair set off a peaches-and-cream complexion.

Lily went straight to an oblong container near one end of the serving table and lifted its lid. "No doubt you need a cookie tester, and I'm just the one for that job!"

"Cookies! *Jah!*" the boys hollered. They swarmed the table, reaching around the girls to snatch treats.

Mattie laughed, slinging her arms around Christine and Rosetta. "You were right to make a lot of those cookies and to save back another bin of them. What with the kids grabbing them by the handfuls, they're going fast."

"And we'll have a cake, too," Christine said. "Beulah did a dandy job decorating it."

Mattie heard a hint of mystery in her sister's voice but decided not to push for an explanation. It wasn't unusual for the Kuhns to bake cakes, but adding decorations suggested a special occasion . . . perhaps an early birthday celebration. "It was nice of Truman to mow the grass shorter so Preacher Marlin could set up the wickets for croquet—"

"We've decided the old guys should challenge the young bucks to a volleyball game," Amos called over to them. He and Preacher Eli were stretching the net between the two posts while Bishop Floyd and his brother Lester carried buckets of water from the lake to set beside the woodpile that would become their bonfire.

"Hey! Who're you calling *old?*" the bishop teased. "I'm way too young to play on your side of the net, Troyer."

Mattie and her sisters laughed, pleased that the tensions between the men had eased since Noah's wedding. A big pickup truck rumbled as it turned off the county road and approached them.

"There's Truman with his *mamm*," Rosetta said,

waving at the vehicle. "And here come Frances and the girls with the fish and hot dogs."

A series of loud *woofs* announced Queenie's arrival as she escorted Harley Kurtz, along with Roman, Noah, and Deborah.

"What a wonderful party," Mattie said happily. "All of our family and friends, here to play games and eat *gut* food together."

"And we brought you a few little surprises, too," Rosetta said with a secretive smile. "We've stashed them in the shed for you to open after dinner."

Mattie's jaw dropped. "It's not my birthday yet. Why're you giving me presents when I already have everything I—"

"Surprise! They're shower gifts!" Christine blurted. "We thought you and Amos should have some new things as you set up housekeeping together."

"I sure wish somebody would throw a shower for me," Frances teased as she pulled a high-sided wagon to the serving table. "After more than twenty-five years of marriage to Floyd, our towels and sheets are wearing thin."

Mattie blinked back sudden tears and once again hugged her sisters. Frances and Gloria were lifting her favorite glass cake stand from the wagon, and the tall square cake on it said CONGRATULATIONS, AMOS AND MATTIE in chocolate script across the top. Orange and yellow flowers bloomed in the corners and trailed down the sides of the cake.

"What a fine surprise," Mattie murmured. "I didn't expect you to—"

"All the more reason to throw you a party, Sister," Rosetta said. "We wish you and Amos all the best."

"We're calling this a practice run for your wedding cake," Ruby remarked as she and her sister approached the picnic area with bins of bread, hot dog buns, and condiments. "Let us know what colors you want for the decorations—"

"And what you'd like us to cook for your dinner, too," Beulah put in. "We can cook the traditional chicken, dressing, and creamed celery in our sleep, practically, but if you'd rather have something different, we'd love to fix it for you."

"I'll give it some thought and tell you tomorrow," Mattie said. "Let's help Irene to the table so she won't stumble over the volleyball or the croquet wickets."

Rosetta was already heading toward the passenger side of Truman's truck, and when the door opened, his mother waved cheerfully. Irene Wickey didn't often join them for outdoor events because she had trouble keeping her balance on uneven surfaces, but everyone hated for her to be home alone while they were having fun. With Truman standing on one side of his mother and Rosetta on the other, Irene cautiously walked the grassy distance to the table.

Mattie pulled out a chair at the table for her. "Irene, we're so glad you could come," she said, squeezing the older woman's slender shoulders. "It seems these folks have pulled a fast one and turned this into a wedding shower for Amos and me."

"Puh! I've known about that since Sunday, Mattie," Truman's *mamm* teased. "I wore my new flowery dress for the occasion. What do you think?"

Mattie fingered Irene's collar, which lay neatly over the brown fleece jacket she was wearing. "I like the feel of this twill."

"And those deep red and orange mums are perfect for this time of year," Christine remarked. "You and Beulah and Ruby, with your bright floral prints, make me feel like I'm standing in a beautiful garden."

"A garden you didn't have to hoe," Minerva Kurtz pointed out happily. She'd just come from the lodge with several long metal sticks for roasting hot dogs and a big bag of marshmallows. "I think this is the last of the food and utensils from the kitchen. Let's start the party!"

Amos and the other men came over to greet Truman and his mother. "We're thinking we'd best play our all-man volleyball game now, before we load up on food," Amos suggested. "It's the older guys against the kids, Wickey. We'll leave it up to you as to which side of the net you choose."

Truman laughed. "If all the athletic talent is on one team, how do the three Peterscheims and Lavern figure to score any points?" he challenged the boys.

"Oh, *that*'s a funny one!" Lavern cried. "We get Noah and Roman on our team! We'll lob the ball over the net nice and easy until we catch you old guys napping, and then we'll spike it right down on your heads."

"*Jah*, you won't know what hit you—or how your team all of a sudden lost the game!" Johnny said in a swaggering voice. "Let's do it, guys!"

"Won't take but three minutes to win!" Menno chimed in. "Let's let the men serve first or they won't score any points."

The younger boys grabbed Noah and Roman by their jacket sleeves and jogged to one side of the net. The men sauntered over to the other side, chatting among themselves about who should take which position in the rotation. Mattie and the other women set the chairs along one side of the table and took their seats. Minerva and Deborah stood off to one side of the net to watch while Gloria hurried to the opposite side.

"Show them how it's done, Roman!" she called out.

"Somebody grab Queenie," Noah said, "or she'll want to be right in the middle of the action."

Rosetta whistled for the dog. With a glance over her shoulder at the volleyball players, Queenie trotted over to lie down between Rosetta and Christine's feet.

"I know!" Lily said to Fannie. "We could get Queenie's Frisbee and throw it for her. But let's go down by the barn, away from the volleyball game and the croquet wickets. Come on, Queenie! We'll play with you."

Mattie smiled at the young girls, envious of their energy as they began to hurl Queenie's red Frisbee to each other while the dog raced back and forth between them—and then leaped into the air to intercept it. When Mattie saw the wistful expression on Mary Kate's face, she followed the girl's gaze to where Roman was squatting and stretching in front of the volleyball net—and Gloria was murmuring encouragement to him. Mattie patted the chair beside her. "Probably a *gut* idea for you to sit here," she encouraged the bishop's younger daughter.

"*Jah*, away from all that spiking and lobbing the boys are planning," Mary Kate agreed. She settled into the chair and placed her hands on her rounded belly. "The way this wee one's moving around, I wonder if he's playing his own little game of volleyball."

"That's a *gut* sign your baby's healthy." Mattie leaned forward to focus on the formations the volleyball players had decided upon. "Looks like Eli, Amos, and Truman are blocking at the net while Lester,

Floyd, and Marlin are ready to move up and keep the ball from hitting the ground."

"Except for Noah and Roman, the boys' team looks to be a little on the short side," Christine murmured.

"But what they lack in height, they can make up for with speed," Frances pointed out. "Just the fact that their legs are springier gives them an advantage—ah, and Harley's stepping in to play on the boys' side while Lowell acts as referee. That evens out the odds."

"Oh my," Beulah put in. "I hate to think about how sore I'd be for a week after playing one game of volleyball. Our men'll be feeling muscles they've forgotten they had."

"All right, here we go," Lester announced from the back corner. He was several years younger than his brother Floyd, and he gracefully lobbed the ball over the net with an underhand serve. On the boys' side, Harley moved forward to set the ball up for Noah, who passed it over the net—and Amos slapped it back with both his hands. Johnny Peterscheim rushed forward, but the ball went between his hands and bounced on the ground.

"First point," Lowell announced, gesturing toward the older fellows.

Lester served again, and as the ball got volleyed back and forth Mattie enjoyed watching the setups and teamwork on both sides of the net. Some good-natured banter traveled with the ball, and it was fun to watch the boys rush around and dive to the ground to make dramatic saves while the men played more conservatively. Mattie's gaze lingered on Amos as he jumped up to block the ball, or pivoted to watch the men behind him playing their positions as the ball bounced on their hands before he or Eli or Truman spiked it over the net to score.

Within minutes the men had scored five unanswered points. Lester served again. Harley Kurtz rushed toward the ball and hammered it back over the net with the backs of his fists.

"*Ach!* Help us," Fannie cried out from across the lawn.

The men immediately looked over toward the girls, distracted by the plaintive sound of Fannie's voice. When the volleyball hit the ground, the boys cheered. "Score one for us!" Menno hollered. "And it's our turn to serve."

Amos gazed across the lawn. "You girls all right?" he called out.

"*Jah,*" Lily replied, pointing toward the old storage shed. "The Frisbee went wild and landed on the roof. Can somebody please get it down for us?"

As the men murmured among themselves, Amos loped toward the shed, which was where they stored the fishing gear and other equipment. "Won't take me but a minute to get the ladder and fetch that Frisbee," he called back toward the volleyball players. "Then we older guys will show the young bucks what *gut* defense looks like!"

"Cookie break!" Johnny declared.

Mattie and Rosetta stood up to remove the covers from the cookie bins while the other folks chatted among themselves. When she glanced toward the shed, Amos was coming out with a tall wooden ladder, chatting with Fannie and Lily as he positioned it at the corner of the weathered old building. He adjusted the ladder so it was extended as far as it would go, resting against the very edge of the roof.

Mattie was relieved when Truman, Roman, and Bishop Floyd all started toward the shed. "Wait up, Amos," Truman called over. "We'll hold that ladder steady for you."

Amos was already climbing, however, nimble as a monkey. Mattie marveled at how quickly he clambered up the last few rungs, spotted the red Frisbee, and then stretched himself full-length across the old shingled roof to retrieve Queenie's toy with his fingertips. Was it her imagination, or was the corner of the building starting to droop? In a flash of dread, Mattie leapt from her chair. "Amos, watch out!" she cried.

"Hang on, Amos! The roof's giving way!" Truman cried as he, Roman, and the bishop sprinted the last few yards toward the ladder.

For a split second Amos looked toward their voices—and then he lost his foothold when the entire corner of the old roof broke off. As the ladder pitched sideways, Amos floundered and then fell through the air. Mattie felt as though the whole scene was taking place in slow motion. Even though she was running toward the shed, hollering at the top of her lungs, she knew deep down that no one would be able to stop what would happen next. There were no bushes to break Amos's fall, no way to catch—

Suddenly Bishop Floyd rushed forward with his arms extended. "Sweet Jesus, send Your mighty angels," he cried out. "You've got to catch—"

Amos struck Floyd's upper body and knocked the bishop to the ground with him. The men landed hard, both of them crying out. Floyd grabbed his head and rolled away to writhe in pain, but when Truman and Roman reached the two men, Amos wasn't moving.

Mattie stopped, her heart in her throat. Her Amos lay flat on his back with his limbs splayed in various directions. He remained ominously still.

For a few seconds everyone stared in silent shock. Minerva and Frances rushed over from the volleyball net with Eli, Marlin, and the others close behind them. Mattie stood stunned, staring at Amos's inert form as snippets of muffled conversation flew around her.

"He's out cold," one of the younger boys murmured.

"Maybe we'd better call a doctor—"

"No! Amos is strong and fit. He'll come around," Preacher Eli insisted.

"We don't know any doctors hereabouts," Frances pointed out as she and Minerva pressed their hands down on Floyd's shoulders to keep him from standing up.

Truman and Roman were kneeling on either side of Amos, gently smacking his face to bring him around. He wasn't responding.

"Rosetta! Somebody!" Truman called out above everyone's comments. "Call 911. Amos and Floyd should both be checked for broken bones and head injuries."

Rosetta ran toward the lodge, but Menno and Lavern raced past her, their faces tight with worry. Minerva stood up, shooing everyone back. "I'm no doctor, but I've got enough midwifing experience to know that we shouldn't move Amos—and Floyd, you should sit tight," she insisted. "Mattie and Frances, you might want to pack your men a bag before the ambulance comes. I suspect they'll check both of them into the hospital for observation."

"You're not taking either one of us to the hospital!"

Bishop Floyd protested with a grimace. "If you'll give us a minute to catch our breath, we'll be fine."

Ignoring Floyd's outburst, Mattie lingered for a hopeful moment, in case Amos blinked or spoke or grimaced.

Nothing. He was breathing, but otherwise he was lying far too still.

Not daring to think about what sort of damage might've been done when Amos fell from the roof— even with Floyd breaking his fall—Mattie hurried toward Amos's house. She heard voices behind her and saw that Frances, Gloria, and Mary Kate were headed up the road toward their home.

"What on earth possessed your *dat* to catch Amos?" Frances asked in a flustered voice. "He's going to pitch a fit about going to the hospital, but we've got to get him checked over. If he broke some blood vessels, or knocked his neck out of kilter—well, Minerva told me there could be all manner of injuries we won't know about without getting him checked over."

Lord, this is so scary, Mattie prayed as she hurried up the steps to Amos's place. *Help me find what Amos will need. Help me not to panic so I can make the right decisions.*

Because Mattie had helped unpack a lot of boxes when Amos had moved his belongings from the storage shed into his new home, she had an idea where his clothes and toiletries were. She moved as quickly as she could, yet she had the sensation of slogging through suspended time and deep mud, feeling woefully slow. By the time she tucked some pajamas and a change of clothing into a duffle, she heard the distant wail of a siren.

Mattie felt frightened half out of her mind. What if Amos didn't regain consciousness—or if he did, what if he'd suffered the sort of head and neck injuries Frances had mentioned? How could it be that her Amos, so fit and agile, was lying unresponsive on the ground? She hadn't seen a flicker of his eyelids or the slightest motion in his arms and legs.

What if he's paralyzed? Mattie fretted as she hurried out the door with Amos's duffle. *What if he'll never be able to work again—and all because of a freak accident while fetching a Frisbee?*

Stop it! another voice in her head warned. *Thinking the worst will make you crazy. Truman was right to call the ambulance so both men will get the best care.*

A police car sped under the arched entry sign to Promise Lodge, followed by a fire truck and an ambulance, which made Queenie bark frantically as she ran around the yard. Mattie stopped in her tracks, her pulse pounding. So many blaring sirens and flashing lights—so many emergency vehicles—surely must mean the responders had figured on the worst-case scenario. Her hand fluttered to her hammering heart as she watched uniformed officers, firefighters, and paramedics rushing toward the cluster of men who stood near the shed. Mattie was grateful that the sirens had stopped wailing—and that Noah had silenced his dog—so she could think again.

"My word, it's like the lodge and all our houses were burning to the ground," Frances murmured, clutching a small suitcase as she came to stand beside Mattie. Gloria and Mary Kate seemed so intently focused on the throbbing, flashing lights that they couldn't speak.

Mattie gripped the handle of the duffle in both hands, trying to hold on to rational thought. "I'm so grateful that Truman's talking to the emergency crew and knows what to do," she said, shaking her head. "As fast as they're bringing out those stretchers, we should get over there with these clothes."

Mustering her courage, Mattie walked quickly toward the scene of the accident. How could those men who were strapping Amos and Floyd to stretchers work so calmly and efficiently? Didn't they realize that the leadership of this church district—the lives of two vitally important men—were at stake?

When Truman noticed Mattie and Frances, he loped over to meet them. "You ladies need to talk to the ambulance guys. They've got some questions I can't answer."

Mattie shared a startled gaze with Frances. She hurried toward the team of medical workers who surrounded Amos while Frances went to tend her husband. "What do you need to know?" she asked in a tremulous voice. "Amos's kids are married and living out of state—"

"Is he allergic to any medications?" the taller fellow asked in an efficient tone.

"Does he have any health problems, like diabetes or a heart condition?" his partner asked. "And do you know what medications he's taking?"

Mattie's head spun. "Amos is as healthy as a horse— or at least he was until he and Floyd hit the ground," she replied. "Far as pills, he's not even inclined to take an aspirin when he's got a headache, so—"

"Does he have a DNR? Or a living will?"

Mattie went blank. She stared at Truman for help, but he appeared as mystified as she was. "I—I don't know what that means."

"DNR stands for 'do not resuscitate,'" the first man explained. "A living will is a written document that states a person's wishes about life support, if his heart stops beating or he stops breathing."

Oh, dear Lord, please don't let Amos die! Mattie prayed frantically. How could these ambulance fellows ask so casually about such life-and-death situations?

Truman shook his head. "Amos is Amish. We Plain folks don't believe in keeping folks alive on machines, if that's what you mean."

The paramedics nodded and raised Amos's stretcher so it looked like a padded table with metal legs and wheels. "The ambulance is going to be full, what with both men riding in it," the taller fellow said, "but it would be helpful if you folks could follow us to the hospital in Forest Grove." With a renewed sense of urgency, they rolled Amos across the yard and into the waiting ambulance.

Mattie's hand fluttered to her mouth and she looked the other way. This was all so foreign to her, and so frightening.

As the other emergency workers wheeled Floyd into the ambulance, Frances rushed over to Mattie and Truman. "What are we supposed to do?" she wailed, suddenly overcome with tears. "Floyd will fight them every step of the way if they try to check him into the hospital."

"Why did so many rescue workers come?" Gloria whimpered. "You'd think the earth had opened up and tried to swallow us—"

Truman quickly slung his arms around Mattie and Frances, lowering his voice as he addressed the women and Frances's two wide-eyed daughters. "From what I heard when somebody called 911 on one of my landscaping jobs, it's standard procedure to send the police and a fire truck along with the ambulance," he explained gently. "How about if I give you ladies a ride to the hospital? The emergency room folks will appreciate your help when they admit Amos and Floyd."

Mattie nodded numbly. "*Jah*, somebody should be there because—because Amos can't speak for himself," she replied in a halting voice.

"It might be best if you girls stayed here until we know for sure what's going on," Truman continued, fishing his keys from his pocket. "I'll be with your *mamm* the whole time we're there, all right?"

Mary Kate and Gloria glanced doubtfully at their mother, but when Frances started toward Truman's pickup, they nodded. Gloria looked almost relieved that she didn't have to go—a sentiment Mattie certainly understood.

"*Denki* so much for your help, Truman," Mattie murmured as he took her elbow and started toward his truck. "I couldn't handle this without you."

Chapter Eight

As everyone watched the ambulance pull away with a surge of its siren and its lights pulsing, Roman felt a deep, desperate silence settle over the folks gathered near Rainbow Lake. For a few moments after the police car and the fire engine left, they all listened to the wail of the siren as it gradually faded away down the county highway.

Without warning, Gloria threw herself at Roman and wrapped her arms around his waist. "What'll we do without Dat?" she wailed. "What if he's hurt so bad he can't come home? How am I supposed to stay in that house with both of my parents gone, not knowing what's happening to them?"

Roman gingerly put his arms around Gloria. "He'll get the best of care," he insisted, hoping his statement would prove to be true. "With Truman and your *mamm*—and my *mamm*—there, the hospital staff will have the information they need—"

"But what about me? And—and Mary Kate, of course," Gloria added after a moment. "I won't be able to sleep a wink without a man in the house, so maybe—"

"You girls are welcome to bunk in one of the lodge rooms," Rosetta said as she came up beside Roman. "We're all in this together, Gloria. You'll never be alone."

Roman glanced gratefully at his aunt and loosened his arms, hoping Gloria would take the hint. As he caught Mary Kate's gaze from a few yards away, he felt embarrassed that her sister had made such a scene—and in front of all the neighbors, too. Did Mary Kate realize that he hadn't given Gloria any encouragement? It was totally improper, the way Gloria had implied that she wanted Roman to come to the Lehman place, where the two sisters would be home alone.

Rosetta squeezed Gloria's shoulder, easing her away from Roman to steer her toward her sister. "Are you all right, Mary Kate?" Rosetta asked. "It was a shock to us all, what happened to your *dat* and Preacher Amos in the blink of an eye. If you need to sit down, or you want me to take you over to a room at the lodge—"

"I'm okay," Mary Kate replied. Her voice wasn't as chipper as usual, but she appeared to be in control of her emotions. "I don't want to leave Sugar and Spice alone all night, and they'll be *gut* company. *Denki* for asking."

"I believe we should all take a moment to pray for Amos and Floyd," Preacher Marlin said above the crowd's murmurs. "And then I think we should go ahead and eat our meal—"

"*Jah*, we've got all these fish fillets that can't go back in the freezer," Christine put in. "And we'll find comfort in eating together, holding up our prayers for our injured men, and for Mattie, Truman, and Frances as they watch over them."

"Exactly right," Preacher Eli joined in. "Shall we bow our heads?"

Roman closed his eyes in prayer, glad for the chance to avoid Gloria's gaze. He prayed for Amos and his mother, and for Bishop Floyd, and for the rest of the Lehman family, feeling the sense of oneness and purpose these group prayers inspired. In his mind, he saw Mary Kate's gentle smile.

Give her Your strength and wisdom, Lord, as she wonders about her dat . . . *and about her unborn child.*

When one of the men cleared his throat, the folks around Roman began to move. The women headed toward the table and the coolers, while Preacher Eli and Preacher Marlin set fire to the woodpile.

Harley walked over to where Irene Wickey was pouring oil into Truman's big fish fryer. "If you'll show me how to work the controls, I can be the fry cook," he offered.

"That would be dandy," Irene replied as she reached for a large bottle of oil. "And Rosetta, that bin under the table is full of the coating mix. If somebody stirs up the egg and milk mixture, we can set up an assembly line."

Roman felt a sense of calm returning as folks took up the various meal preparation tasks. He smiled at the three Peterscheim boys and Lowell Kurtz. "Who wants to be in charge of hot dogs?" he asked. "And who wants to make mountain pies? I'm thinking we five guys can handle that cooking once the fire gets going, don't you?"

The boys nodded eagerly. "All that commotion with the fire truck and ambulance made me really hungry,"

Menno piped up. "Maybe we should check out the fried pies my *mamm* brought before we start."

"*Jah*, we don't want anybody keeling over into the fire for lack of fortification," his brother Lavern said. "I get dibs on a rhubarb pie!"

"I get apple!" Johnny cried, and away the boys went, rushing toward the bin of goodies.

"Bring me one, too! And fetch the hot dog sticks," Roman called after them. The flames were beginning to lick at the dry branches, so he needed to stay close to the woodpile to keep the fire under control. They had cut a lot of dead wood from the trees in the orchard earlier in the season, so the smoke drifting away from the blaze soon had a slightly sweet, fruity aroma.

When Roman glanced up, he saw Mary Kate approaching him with a plastic cup and something wrapped in a napkin. She appeared calm yet a little subdued.

"Thought you could use some cool water and a lemon bar," she said softly. "It's hot work, tending the fire."

"*Denki*, Mary Kate." Roman gulped the water gratefully and wiped the cup across his forehead. "Won't be long before the fire's ready. Let's stand away from the heat so the sparks won't jump out at you."

She smiled ruefully. "Seems to me you already got burned when my sister launched herself at you. That was so . . . *obvious*."

Roman glanced around the crowd. Aunt Rosetta had convinced Gloria to join Laura and Phoebe, who were dipping and dredging the fish—not that she appeared any too happy about handling the slippery fillets. "I suppose Gloria's scared about what happened to your *dat*."

Mary Kate rolled her eyes and handed him the napkin with a large lemon bar on it. "At least there were other folks around as witnesses. They've got her pegged now, I suppose. Gloria can be such a drama queen."

Roman smiled, closing his eyes over a bite of sweet, tart lemon bar. "This lemon bar sort of makes up for it," he murmured with his mouth full. "Did you make these?"

Mary Kate's cheeks turned a pretty shade of pink. "Baking our bread and goodies is my way of helping *mamm*, since she doesn't let me shift furniture or do the cleaning anymore. I'm glad you like it, Roman."

He nodded, polishing off the final bite of the bar. "You sure you'll be all right at home tonight? My aunts—and my cousins—would be happy to have you stay upstairs in one of the lodge's guest rooms."

"If I'm at home, I'll hear the phone—in case Mamm calls. Dat put the phone out front in a shanty, but he rigged up a ringer in the kitchen," she explained.

Roman nodded. "I can understand that. I figure your *mamm*—and mine—will be calling later this evening when they know for sure what's going on with your *dat* and Amos."

"What exactly happened?" Mary Kate murmured. Her eyes clouded over and she glanced away. "Last thing I knew, Amos was stretched out on the roof— and then Dat tried to catch him, and they were both rolling on the ground. Amos looked . . . well, really gray. Way too still."

Roman thought back to what he'd seen as he'd been jogging toward the shed. "The best I could tell, Amos was just about to grab the Frisbee when the edge of the roof broke off—"

"Oh my," Mary Kate murmured.

"—and the ladder fell away from him," Roman continued, shaking his head. "Then he landed on your *dat*, and I suspect they both whacked their heads when they hit the ground. It's not like either one of them will spring back as fast as, say, Menno or Johnny would," he continued. "And speaking of those boys, here they come. Want to help us roast the hot dogs and make the mountain pies?"

Mary Kate glanced at the four boys, finding a smile. "How about if I put the meat and cheese between the bread slices and you guys can hold the irons in the fire?" she offered.

"And how about if you bring her a chair?" Roman added as Menno and Johnny set down the cooler they'd been carrying.

A few minutes later they had a nice system going. Mary Kate slid the hot dogs onto the metal sticks and filled the sandwiches for the mountain pie irons, and then the boys did the cooking. Roman watched the fire, and he also took the cooked wieners off the sticks and laid them in a metal pan with a lid to keep them warm. The mountain pies, gooey with cheese and ham, smelled so good he almost jammed one into his mouth—except the boys would've followed his example rather than waiting for everyone else.

The smell of frying fish drifted out over their picnic area. As the last of the wieners were roasted, the women called everyone to fill their plates. The sun was drifting low in the western sky and the temperature was sinking enough that the ladies slipped into their shawls and jackets. The serving table was covered with bowls of potato salad, deviled eggs, baked beans, and other picnic foods along with a number of tempting desserts.

Ahead of Roman in line, Mary Kate glanced up at him. "I'll be sitting at the table with Irene and the older gals, because my getting up from the ground makes for quite a spectacle," she murmured.

Roman imagined the scene she described and thought of himself helping her up—realizing she'd feel awkward if he did. "How about if I come to the house later to be sure you and Gloria and the cats are doing all right?" he asked softly. "I won't come inside, of course—"

"That would be nice," she murmured. "Maybe by then we'll know if our mothers and Truman are coming back this evening. I'd hate to have Mamm come home to an empty house after her ordeal at the emergency room."

Roman nodded. Mary Kate's thoughtful remark touched him. "*Jah*, even with Truman there, she and Mamm will go through an ordeal I couldn't even imagine. I've never been to a hospital."

"Me neither. I'll see you later then."

Her smile made butterflies dance in Roman's stomach. As he filled his plate with a couple of crispy fish fillets, a mountain pie, and all the side dishes he could pile on, he thought ahead to his visit to the Lehman house. He'd have to handle it carefully, so no one would misconstrue his intentions. Lester's house was a short distance down the road; if the moonlight was at the right angle, the bishop's brother might spot Roman and figure he was up to no good. The last thing he wanted was to compound Mary Kate's problems as an unmarried mother by appearing to make an improper visit.

But the first thing Roman wanted was another chance to spend time with Mary Kate on the porch ... hopefully without her sister horning in. The thought of seeing Mary Kate again, sitting on the porch swing on a moonlit evening, filled Roman with a sense of peaceful anticipation. It gave him something pleasant to think about as he ate supper on the quilt beside Noah, Deborah, Harley, and Minerva—young married couples who radiated a happiness he hoped to find for himself someday.

And isn't that *an interesting thought?*

Roman smiled. Change was certainly in the air at Promise Lodge.

Chapter Nine

Mattie shivered despite the overheated hospital waiting room. She couldn't ever recall being more scared, more uncertain about what was going on in this strange place where voices came from hidden speakers to summon doctors, using code words she didn't understand. The hard plastic chair was uncomfortable, so she stood up to walk around the waiting area—not that pacing settled her nerves.

Frances had been called to wherever the emergency room staff had taken Floyd, and Truman was at the nurses' station to see if anyone had information about how Amos was doing. It wasn't yet eight o'clock in the evening, but Mattie felt as though they'd spent an entire day at the hospital. Who knew how much longer they might be here?

Mattie sensed Amos wouldn't be going home anytime soon, unless he'd regained consciousness after they'd wheeled him down the corridor into a curtained room. And if he had come around, he surely must feel disoriented and frightened because of all the tubes and monitors he was hooked up to. She and

Truman had shared what little they knew about Amos's medical history with the doctor, yet Mattie wondered if their sketchy information had been helpful—or if these unfamiliar doctors and nurses had even paid much attention to it.

Mattie saw Truman signaling for her from the nurses' station. Bless him, he appeared ragged around the edges with frustration after acting as their spokesman.

"Mattie, they've checked Amos into the hospital for observation," he said in a low voice.

She frowned. "And what exactly does that mean?"

The nurse, a young blonde who wore loose burgundy pants and a matching shirt, gazed at her over the top of the high counter. Her badge said MELODY. "Mr. Troyer is still unconscious," she replied. "Dr. Townsend has ordered a series of tests to determine if he has brain or other internal injuries."

Mattie sucked in her breath. The thought of Amos waking up to learn he'd been seriously hurt—or not waking up at all—sent her mind spinning in frantic circles. "Can't one of us be there with him?" she asked. "If it were me, I wouldn't want to wake up amongst strangers, with so many wires and tubes coming out of me and—"

"HIPAA regulations stipulate that the doctors are only allowed to discuss Mr. Troyer's condition with a designated family member or representative," Melody interrupted. She wasn't snippy, but she wasn't much help, either.

"Hippo?" Mattie asked. "What on earth does a hippo have to do with finding out what's wrong with Amos?"

The nurse cleared her throat as though Mattie were testing her patience. "The government has established HIPAA regulations to insure the privacy of patients. As I was explaining to Mr. Wickey, patients are to name a person from their family—or another advocate they choose—in writing, to confer about their diagnoses."

"But Amos isn't in any condition to choose anybody," Truman pointed out—not for the first time, Mattie suspected.

"He's widowed, and his kids live in Indiana and Ohio," Mattie added, growing even more concerned. "Amos and I are engaged. Does that count?"

Melody appeared doubtful, as well as determined to dot all the I's and cross all the T's of the government regulations. "Do you—or does anyone in his family—have power of attorney?"

"I—I'm not sure what that means, either," Mattie murmured. "We Plain folks don't cotton to all these legalistic things."

"The EMS team—those are the men from the ambulance," the nurse explained tersely, "have told us that Mr. Troyer has no health care directive or living will that will specify what—if any—forms of life support our doctors may use. If he stops breathing or his heart stops—"

"If Amos's heart stops, it means God has called him home," Mattie whispered weakly. "Why would a doctor interfere with God's own will?"

"As a preacher in the Old Order Amish Church, Amos would *refuse* any such means of keeping him alive," Truman insisted earnestly. "He just doesn't have any paperwork to prove it."

Melody scribbled a few lines on a sticky note and attached it to the papers that were in front of her. "I'll confer with the chief of staff about this tomorrow morning," she stated. "Meanwhile, we'll do everything possible to keep Mr. Troyer comfortable and to determine the extent of his injuries so we can get him on the road to recovery. If I were you, I'd go home and get some rest. By midmorning tomorrow we'll know a lot more about his condition."

When Melody headed down the hall with her handful of papers, Mattie's whole body drooped. "What a nightmare," she said softly. "Not only do I not understand the regulations—why they can't let one of us speak for Amos or hear about his diagnosis?—I'm really worried about what they might be doing to him."

Truman wrapped his arm around her shoulders. "Let's sit down until we see what Frances has learned," he suggested kindly. "I feel like praying about this situation—and then I think we'd all feel better if we went to the cafeteria for a bite to eat. It's been a long time since lunch."

"*Jah*, you're right," Mattie replied. "But let's find some better chairs. We don't know how long we might have to sit in them. Or do you think we should go home, like the nurse said?" she continued wearily. "I know you have to work tomorrow morning—"

"I'll call my foreman, Edgar, and tell him what's going on. They can head to the job site without me tomorrow," Truman said as he pulled his cell phone from his pocket. "Who can I call for you, Mattie? Do you want to leave a message on the lodge phone?"

"What would I say? We don't know any more about Amos than we did when we came here." She rubbed her forehead, trying to pull her thoughts together. "I should call his kids after we get home. He hardly ever talks about them, so I suspect they had a falling out after his wife, Anna, passed away."

As they reached a row of upholstered chairs, Mattie sank into the first one with a loud sigh. She felt so helpless. So useless. After Truman completed his call to Edgar, he sat down in the chair beside hers and bowed his head. Mattie did the same.

Forgive me for losing faith, for feeling so alone when You've provided a friend like Truman to look after me, Mattie prayed as she squeezed her eyes shut. *Look in on Amos and guide his doctors, Lord, because only You have the power to heal him and to determine what happens—no matter what government regulations say.*

When Mattie heard a familiar-sounding sigh, she opened her eyes. Frances stood before them, wringing her hands. She had an odd expression on her face.

"What'd you find out?" Mattie asked. "At least you're Floyd's next of kin, so you can have a say in what they'll do to him."

"Puh!" Frances said, shaking her head. "Floyd was raising such a ruckus about the legal paperwork they said he was supposed to have, that they slipped something into his IV to settle him down before he made his injuries any worse."

Mattie's eyes widened. "They knocked him out?"

"Said they had to keep his pulse and blood pressure under control—and they'll be running tests where he has to stay absolutely still," Frances explained with a suppressed smile. "The doctor took me outside the room and asked my permission to proceed. If Floyd finds out I agreed to sedating him, I'll never hear the end of it."

Mattie chuckled, partly because it was funny and

partly because she was feeling so frayed around the edges. "I won't say a word. At least he's got you to help him. They—they won't allow me or Truman in to discuss Amos's condition or treatment with the doctors."

Frances frowned. "Why not? You know more about Amos than anybody else."

"Government red tape," Truman explained. "They're calling it an invasion of his privacy if Amos hasn't named one of us—in writing—to be involved with his care."

"Who could've known Amos would fall off a roof?" Frances protested with a shake of her head. "And how were we Plain folks to know about all those forms we were supposed to have a lawyer fill out? Floyd told them we didn't believe in signing away God's control over us to doctors we've never met—and that it sounded like another way lawyers and doctors were setting themselves up to make more money."

"I'm sure the doctor appreciated that part," Mattie murmured, "even if I believe Floyd was right."

Frances let out a shuddery breath, looking very weary. "They told me to go home and get some rest— puh!—and to come back tomorrow when they had some test results."

"*Jah*, same here. And bless him, Truman has offered to take off work tomorrow so he can bring us back."

Truman nodded. "Do we want to get a bite to eat in the cafeteria, or just head on home?" he asked. "Maybe they have sandwiches already made up that we could eat in the truck."

"Let's see about that," Mattie suggested. "I don't feel like I could eat a bite, but I'm sure you're starving."

About fifteen minutes later the three of them were

walking out to the parking lot with wrapped chicken salad sandwiches. Mattie wondered how it could be such a pleasant evening, frosty but calm outside, after they'd endured such an ordeal in the waiting room. The stars, scattered across the night sky, sparkled peacefully, as though God were still in perfect control of everything that was going on.

When they reached Truman's truck, Mattie turned to gaze at the hospital building. It was impossible to know which one of the many windows belonged to the room Amos was in—or to know if he was awake, or aware of his condition, or in pain . . .

Watch over him, Lord. Help us figure out a way to get him the care he needs. We can't do this without You.

Mattie wiped a stray tear from her cheek before she climbed into the big pickup. She hated leaving Amos in the hospital alone, but it was the best she could do for now.

Weeping may endure for a night, but joy cometh in the morning.

Mattie hoped with all her heart that this verse from the Psalms would prove to be true.

Chapter Ten

Despite the chill in the evening air, Mary Kate sat out on the porch swing swaddled in an afghan. Sugar and Spice were curled up on either side of her, demanding that her hands be on them, but her mind wandered free . . . toward the barn behind the house, where Roman and his brother were doing the livestock chores. It felt good to know they were nearby while she wasn't sure what was going on with her father and mother—even if Gloria was banging around in the kitchen, making a big deal of fixing the Schwartz boys a snack.

At the sound of her sister singing "You Are My Sunshine," Mary Kate shook her head. Bless her heart, Gloria couldn't carry a tune with a bucket in each hand, but she was determined to get Roman's attention by belting out—in a wavering vibrato—her hope that he wouldn't take her sunshine away

A movement beside the porch caught Mary Kate's eye. Roman, Noah, and Queenie came quietly to the porch steps and sat down—and Roman pressed his index finger to his lips and pointed toward the kitchen, signaling for Mary Kate's silence. As more of the familiar old song drifted out through the screen door, the Border collie's ears perked up. When the dog tilted her head back and began to howl along with Gloria's singing, Mary Kate got the giggles.

"Queenie, stop," Noah murmured as he wrapped his arm around the dog's neck.

Roman turned to peer through the door. "Uh-oh. Here she comes," he whispered as he, too, tried to silence the singing collie.

The screen door banged as Gloria stepped out onto the porch. "So what's the deal with your dog? The Peterscheims and Uncle Lester and everyone else will realize you guys have come over here."

Roman shrugged. "It's not like we're trying to hide," he pointed out. "We fed and watered your horses—"

"Queenie picked up on that tune pretty fast, don't you think?" Noah interrupted, trying not to laugh.

Even in the dusk, Mary Kate couldn't miss her sister's irritated expression. "For your information, 'You Are My Sunshine' is one of the most enduring songs of all time," she said archly. "My grand-*dat* used to sing it—to *me*, because he loved me so much."

Mary Kate struggled to keep a straight face. "The neighbors could hear you every bit as clearly as they heard Queenie," she remarked. "They're probably wondering why you're singing so loudly with the windows wide open, chilly as it's getting."

"What do they know?" Gloria muttered. Then, in the blink of an eye, her attitude changed. "Since you fellows were nice enough to tend the horses, I fixed you a little bite to eat," she said in a sugary voice. "Roman, if you'd come in and help me carry it—"

Mary Kate was relieved to hear the rumble of a pickup truck as headlights illuminated the road leading to their house. Poor Roman. Was he as tired of Gloria's overblown flirtation as she was? "There's Truman's truck!" Mary Kate said, easing the cats out of her lap. "Let's go see if Mamm's with him."

"But—but the grilled cheese sandwiches will get cold!" Gloria protested as the two fellows stood up and started toward the road.

Mary Kate didn't miss the chance to join Roman and Noah. If her sister chose to stay behind, whining, that was her choice—Mary Kate was just glad to see her mother getting out of the truck. When Mamm saw her, she rushed toward Mary Kate with her arms open wide.

"Oh, but it's *gut* to be home," her mother said. "If I never set foot in a hospital again, it'll be too soon. Except we're going back tomorrow, hoping your *dat* will be able to come home with us."

Mary Kate hugged her mother tight, then eased away. Even in the darkness, Mamm's face appeared haggard from the ordeal she'd endured. "So he's all right then? Just a bad bump on the head?"

Truman got out of the driver's side, greeting Mary Kate and the Schwartz boys. "We'll know more about your *dat* and Amos tomorrow after the doctors run some tests," he replied. "I hope you'll all get some rest so we'll be ready for whatever they tell us. If there's anything you'd like me to do before I head home, just say the word."

Mary Kate smiled at their neighbor, truly grateful for his compassion. "Roman and Noah have done the chores, so I think we're ready to turn in for the night," she said. "It's a blessing to have such kindhearted friends here looking after us. *Denki* for your help, Truman."

"I wouldn't feel right leaving your *mamms* to face the hospital by themselves. It's a strange world inside those walls," he remarked with a shake of his head. "We don't know a lot more about your *dat* or Amos than we did when the ambulance pulled away, but at least we've done the best we could for them."

"Roman—and Noah—have taken such *gut* care of us," Gloria put in sweetly. "If you'd come inside, we could have those grilled cheese sandwiches I made."

"*Denki*, but I'm heading home," Truman said with a nod to Mamm. "I'll stop by about eight o'clock for you, Frances, if that's all right."

Mamm sighed wearily. "*Jah*, and meanwhile we'll pray that God's holding Floyd and Amos in His hands through the night while they're in the care of strangers."

Gloria reached out to grab Roman's hand. "But you—and Noah—can come on in," she wheedled. "We could visit and have a warm bedtime snack—"

"I'd better check on Mamm and get home to Deborah," Noah said with a knowing smile. "*Gut* night, all."

As Roman watched his brother stride down the road with Queenie trotting beside him, Mary Kate sensed he was desperate to leave, as well. But when Roman met Mary Kate's gaze, he reconsidered. "Well, maybe I could stay for a moment," he murmured. "But you ladies all need to get your rest. It's been a difficult evening."

Smiling triumphantly, Gloria headed toward the house with Roman in tow. Mary Kate hung back, slipping her arm through her mother's. "So will Dat be all right?" she murmured. "I thought it was a *gut* sign that he was calling out orders to the ambulance guys while they wheeled him inside it."

"And he didn't get quiet until the doctor gave him a sedative so they could run their tests," Mamm said with a shake of her head. "When he wakes up, maybe he can talk some sense into those folks about how we Amish don't believe in the medical intervention they were talking about—such as life support machines, if Amos's heart or breathing stops while he's still unconscious."

Mary Kate sucked in her breath. "My word, I've never heard of such a thing," she murmured, massaging the side of her belly. "I—I sure hope Minerva can deliver my baby so I don't have to go to the hospital—"

"Oh no! Fire! *Fire!*"

Mary Kate released her mother to rush awkwardly up the steps at the sound of Gloria's desperate cries. Even from the porch she could smell burning food, but when she entered the house she saw no flames, although Roman was pouring flour into the skillet. Gloria was standing by the open window, fanning at the black smoke that filled the kitchen.

The odor of the burned food made Mary Kate feel nauseous, so she stopped in the front room. "Don't tell me you left the burner on under those grilled cheese sandwiches while you came outside—"

"So they'd be hot when we came in to eat them!" Gloria protested. "I—I just wanted to have a nice snack ready for—"

"There! The food's stopped smoldering now," Roman said as he ran water into the skillet. A sizzling noise filled the kitchen and steam rose from the sink. "Nice of you to think of us, Gloria, but I'll head on back to Noah's now."

Once again Mary Kate felt acutely embarrassed about the ruckus her sister had caused, but what could she do? If she accompanied Roman outside, Gloria would rush out to join them.

She smiled at Roman as he paused in front of her. "Sorry about all the fuss," she murmured. "And *denki* for doing our barn chores."

"You're welcome," he whispered. "Maybe next time we'll be able to visit a bit. *Gut* night, Mary Kate."

As Mary Kate watched Roman leave, she hoped he wouldn't be so put off by her sister's carelessness— and Gloria's singing—that he wouldn't come back.

Mamm went over to the sink and shook her head. "Well, my favorite skillet's so scorched I'm not sure we'll ever get the burnt butter and cheese scrubbed out of it," she murmured ruefully. "But we'll deal with that tomorrow. I've had all of this day I can handle."

"*Gut* night, Mamm," Mary Kate murmured. "I'll keep you and Dat in my prayers."

Her mother nodded sadly and made her way through the unlit front room toward the stairs. With an exasperated sigh, Gloria followed her.

Mary Kate let the cats inside and shut the front door. Breathing shallowly, she closed the kitchen windows against the cold November air, regretting that it would take several hours for the acrid smell of smoke to dissipate. She listened for footsteps crossing the upstairs rooms . . . the sound of water running in the bathroom . . . the silence that told her Mamm and Gloria had gone to bed.

Mary Kate doused the kitchen lamp. She was becoming accustomed to the placement of their furniture and the shadows it cast in their new home, and as she climbed the stairs she felt thankful that their family had moved to Promise Lodge—and that Roman Schwartz seemed to think she was worthy of his time.

As she entered her room, moonlight was casting a soft glow on her hardwood floors. When she looked out her window, she could see Noah's new white house basking in the moon's ethereal glow. A lamp flickered in one of the upstairs rooms.

"*Gut* night, Roman," Mary Kate whispered wistfully. "Sleep tight."

Chapter Eleven

Amos groaned. His head felt like someone was hitting it with a mallet, a pain so deep and intense that he didn't want to open his eyes for fear the pounding would get worse. He tried to lie absolutely still, to recall why he would be feeling so wretched . . . to analyze the odd scent in the air and the foreign feeling of the mattress. What was that whirring noise beside his head? Why did his legs and arms feel bare? He slept in his long johns at this time of the year.

When Amos dared to touch what was attached to the top of his hand, a voice startled him.

"No no, Mr. Troyer—you're not to remove your IV again," a man said. "You gave us quite a scare a few hours ago when you yanked it out."

Amos frowned, which only made his head hurt worse. "Uh?"

A large, warm hand closed gently over his arm. "It's all right. You're bound to be confused, after that hit you took to your head," the man said. "Try to relax. Your friends will be here shortly, after they've spoken to the doctor."

Friends? Doctor? Amos willed his heavy eyelids to open and then wished he hadn't. A blurry male figure—no, two of them—stood beside him. The ceiling was starting to make a lazy circle, and if it didn't stop, he might just throw up. Moments later he was grateful that the stranger had moved fast enough to catch the vomit before it spewed beyond the bed into whatever sort of strange room he was in.

"I'm Gary, by the way. Your nurse for this shift."

Nurse? A guy who's a nurse? The thought jarred Amos enough that he woke up a little more.

Amos sighed, blinking to clear his vision. On either side of him, machines clicked and displayed lit-up numbers. Where on God's earth was he? And how had he gotten here? And why did his head feel like a melon that had hit the floor and split open?

When Amos heard voices at the door, he turned his head toward them and was again sorry that he'd moved even that slight amount.

". . . apologize for the misunderstanding at the nurses' station," another unfamiliar male was saying. "Melody just started working here last week, and she wasn't aware of our policies that honor the religious beliefs of the Plain residents in this area. Mr. Troyer has been resting comfortably with only an IV to keep him hydrated and free of pain."

Amos wanted to refute that part about the pain but he didn't have the energy. He blinked a few more times, trying to discern the facial features of the folks who'd just entered the room. Two men and a woman, from what he could make out.

Gary moved away from the bed, exchanging greetings with the newcomers. Next thing Amos knew, a woman who smelled clean—like the soap he used at home—was grasping his hand and leaning over him.

"Oh, Amos, it's *gut* to see your eyes open," she said. "We've been so worried, ever since they sent us home last night even though I didn't want to leave you here amongst all these strangers and machines and—well, I'm babbling," she admitted with a nervous laugh.

A sense of sweet relief came over Amos, even though the pain in his head threatened to overwhelm his emotions. "Mattie," he whispered hoarsely.

"*Jah*, it's me. Truman's here, too," she replied.

"Hey there, neighbor. Too bad you had to leave your party before we served the food," Truman teased, grasping Amos's shoulder. "*Gut* to see you awake, Amos."

He tried very hard, but for the life of him Amos couldn't figure out what they were talking about. "Party?" he rasped.

"*Jah*, we guys were playing volleyball before the fish fry. You went to get a Frisbee off the roof of the shed, and when the corner gave way, you fell into Floyd when he tried to catch you," Truman explained. "You both hit the ground, and then you took a ride in an ambulance. But you might not remember any of that."

"Nope." Amos closed his eyes again, exhausted. It felt good to have Mattie's hand in his, so he concentrated on her presence . . . willed himself to become more cognizant so he could hold up his end of the conversation.

"Mr. Troyer, I'm Dr. Townsend," the other fellow said as he came to the opposite side of the bed. "The scans we ran last night show that you have a concussion, which means you have some bleeding on your brain. Even though Mr. Lehman broke your fall, you hit the ground at an angle that jarred your head and your body. Nothing's broken, but you're going to be very sore for a while—and limited as to what you can do until your internal bruises heal."

Bleeding on your brain . . . limited as to what you can do. Amos exhaled, trying to rid himself of the fear the doctor's words had inspired. Surely if he rested for a few days he'd be back to work, wouldn't he? The last time he'd slipped off a roof, he'd gotten up and walked away—but then, that had been twenty years ago. When Amos squeezed Mattie's hand, she squeezed back.

"The doctor says we'll have to keep you in a dark room with the curtains shut," she told him. "The part about not watching any screens doesn't mean a whole lot to us Plain folks, but you're to rest in total darkness while you get your strength back."

"So don't get yourself all geared up to finish the Kurtz house, or Roman's place," Truman continued gently. "It might be a while before you swing a hammer or climb a ladder again, Amos. And I know that'll be a real tough adjustment for you."

Images of the large home he and the neighbor men had recently roofed, as well as the rising walls of the home he was building for Mattie's older son made Amos suck in his breath. "But—but we need to get Roman's house enclosed before it snows," he protested. His throat was so dry he could barely speak, but this was an urgent topic, so he kept on talking. "And even if I can't climb a ladder or run the nail gun, I can surely tack on baseboard or—"

As the doctor leaned closer, Amos watched him grow a second head—and then the heads went back together into one again. "That's what Mattie told me you'd say," he remarked kindly. "But if you don't rest in a dark room for the next several weeks, Mr. Troyer, your concussion won't heal. I'm going to set up some physical therapy sessions, to be sure your muscles get back into sync. It could easily be Christmas before you feel up to moving around much, and you might have some lingering symptoms as late as next spring."

Christmas? Spring? What month is it now, for Pete's sake?

Amos tried to recall which page his kitchen calendar showed. He didn't want to ask what day it was, for fear they'd keep him here longer if they realized he was so disoriented. When Amos glanced away from Mattie's earnest face, he noticed the date on the bulletin board: Friday, November thirteenth. Beside the calendar was a page that said HOW IS YOUR PAIN TODAY? A row of circles showed various facial expressions that were numbered zero through ten, with the last one appearing nearly as miserable as Amos felt.

"Twelve," he muttered before the circles went out of focus.

Mattie's brow puckered. "Twelve what, Amos? Twelve months in the year? Jesus's twelve disciples?"

Amos sighed, wishing this conversation were over so he could take a nap. Maybe after that he'd wake up and this nightmare would be over—or he could chase it away with hard physical labor, as he usually did. "Headache," he muttered. "It's at a twelve."

The doctor nodded. "I've written you prescriptions for a pain reliever and an antidepressant. Even so, you really must rest and remain in a dark room," he repeated earnestly. "I suspect daylight will make your head hurt so badly that you'll want to stay in the dark anyway, but the inactivity is going to be difficult for a man who's used to being on the go. Your friends have assured me they'll keep an eye on you so you won't overdo it."

Amos watched both of Mattie's heads nod solemnly.

Well, I know how to talk around her—how to send her off to do me a favor, so I can slip out to one of those houses and get some work done. That's my job, building houses, and in a few days I'll be back at it.

"I'll let Gary remove your IV now, Mr. Troyer," the doctor went on in a more chipper voice. "You can go home as soon as you feel like getting dressed." He signed a couple of forms and handed them to Mattie before he left.

Mattie released Amos's hand to make room for the nurse on that side of the bed. "We'll be right here when you're ready to get up, Amos," she assured him. "Somebody's supposed to stay with you for a while, to help you when you want to walk a bit or go to the bathroom. We can't have you falling and making your head injury worse."

Help him to the bathroom? Was Mattie out of her mind, thinking he'd allow her to hang around while he was on the toilet?

Amos winced when the nurse removed the tape that held the IV contraption to his hand. Looking at the purple bruise that had spread up past his wrist made him feel woozy, so he gulped air and looked away. *I will not throw up . . . I will not throw up. Can't have Mattie thinking I'm an invalid.*

But then, what would Mattie and the rest of them at Promise Lodge think about him holing up at home like a mole? Maybe he'd humor her for a day or two, but then it was back to business as usual. He had houses to build . . . leaves to rake . . .

Mattie reached for his hand. "Shall I call your kids and let them know—"

"No!" Amos blurted. "They're so far away, and they have their own lives and families to look after." Truth was, he didn't want his daughters and his son to see him in this condition—not that they'd be inclined to travel all the way to Missouri now that their mother was gone.

When Mattie left the room so he could get dressed, Amos got another jolt: his legs weren't moving the way they were supposed to. Was this part of the problem the doctor had mentioned, with his muscles being out of kilter? He kept quiet, allowing Truman and Gary to help him into his clothes as he sat on the bed, but worry prodded him to speak up when a lady on the hospital staff showed up with a wheelchair.

"My legs feel like pieces of baked chicken with the bones taken out," he murmured as Truman slipped an arm around his shoulders to help him stand up. "What if my muscles don't get their strength back? What if my head doesn't stop hurting and—"

"Amos! *Gut* to see you dressed so we can get out of here," Bishop Floyd exclaimed as he entered the room. "After the way these people knocked me unconscious—and then who knows what they did to me?—I'm not spending another minute in this place. And neither are you!" he insisted. "God's our doctor and we're going home to heal."

Floyd didn't look very steady on his feet. Amos saw Frances in the hallway, a flustered expression on her face as she talked to Mattie. His head began throbbing so hard he couldn't see straight, so he had no energy to protest. When the aide brought the wheelchair over, Truman helped Amos back up to it. He landed in the seat with a grimace and a groan.

"*Jah*, let's go," Amos said in a shaky voice. He hated it that Mattie saw him looking so weak and out of control, just as he sensed that frustration and pain might be his companions for a long time to come.

Chapter Twelve

Mattie was all ears that evening at supper, when Preacher Eli called a meeting of all the Promise Lodge residents. Rosetta and Christine had simmered a big pot of chicken noodle soup, Deborah had baked bread, and Mary Kate had made orange date bars for their dessert. Everyone was present except for Minerva Kurtz, who was staying with Bishop Floyd so Frances and the girls could attend the meeting. Truman had come over to visit with Amos, so Mattie felt comfortable leaving him.

Once everyone around the tables had prayed, Eli spoke up. "What with both Amos and Floyd laid up for a while, I'm proposing a day when the rest of us fellows finish enclosing Roman's house," he said. "Once we get the roof on, Lester can lead a crew to install the siding while the rest of us get the drywall up. Tomorrow's Saturday. Can we do it then?"

"That's a fine idea," Marlin Kurtz replied as he took two slices of bread and passed the basket along. "If Roman's place sits unfinished, Amos will be stewing about it instead of resting."

"And then we can set aside another day—maybe a week from tomorrow—to do the inside finishing on your place, Marlin," Lester suggested. "Depending on how well Floyd's recovering, I plan to return home to Sugarcreek by Thanksgiving, and I'd like to see those two houses finished before I go. After looking in on my brother when he got home this morning, I can tell you that he's every bit as antsy as Amos about the work he's not supposed to be doing."

"Oh my, but *that's* the truth." Frances shook her head and gazed at Mattie, who sat beside her. "If you thought Floyd was agitated during the ride home from the hospital, he's gotten more cantankerous since he's been home. I hope Minerva's able to keep him quiet—and indoors—while we're here. I wouldn't be a bit surprised if he burst through the lodge door at any moment, even though the doctor told him to sit still so his concussion can heal."

Mattie nodded. "I thought Floyd was going to roll down the window and jump out of the truck, considering how he fussed at Truman for not driving us home fast enough. Did the doctor give you a prescription for something that might calm him down?"

"Oh, I've got pills for settling him," Frances replied with a sigh. "The trick is getting him to take them. Floyd claims he doesn't need any sort of medication because God's his doctor. If we've heard that once today, we've heard it a dozen times."

"Hmm," Rosetta remarked as she stirred her steaming soup. "Minerva might know a trick or two for getting those pills down him. Or you could call the nurse who tended him at the hospital and ask her advice."

"Maybe I should call from here," Frances mused aloud. "Floyd will pitch a fit if he finds out I've contradicted his wishes by sneaking medicine into his food."

"Amos slept like a rock this afternoon when he was napping," Roman said. As he buttered his warm bread, his eyebrows rose. "Once he gets rested up, though, and he's supposed to sit still all day, I suspect he'll not sleep as well at night."

"*Jah*, Minerva's warned us about that—and about something called sundowning, where your body loses track of whether it's day or night," Mattie said with a sigh. She smiled at Roman, proud of him for moving in with Amos to watch over him. "We might need to have other folks spell you at night, son, or you'll be nodding off in the barn while you're milking."

Everyone chuckled, but they murmured their agreement.

"We've all got a part to play here," Ruby put in. "We can take turns sitting with Floyd and Amos—"

"And I'll be in charge of the meals tomorrow and whatever days you fellows will be working on the houses," Beulah volunteered. "It'll save you time if you all eat here instead of going to your separate homes."

"I'll bake some bars and cinnamon rolls," Mary Kate chimed in. "Gloria and I can bring them to the work site midmorning and in the afternoon, along with cider and hot coffee to keep you going."

"Hey, if there'll be goodies, I'm going to work on the house, too!" Menno Peterscheim piped up.

"*Jah*, can we boys all help, Dat?" his little brother Johnny asked excitedly. "We won't fool around or get in the way—I promise! And since you're working on Saturday, it's not like we'll be missing school."

Preacher Eli chuckled. "There's work for every hand, boys—as long as those hands aren't holding cookies," he teased.

Across the table from Mattie, Deborah chimed in. "What's left to do inside the Kurtz place? If the walls are finished, Laura and Phoebe and I could do the painting. We're old hands at that."

"And now that we've finished the rooms here in the lodge," Laura said, "we have a few gallons of ivory and pale yellow paint left—enough to get us started, anyway. But if you want different colors, we could drive into Forest Grove and pick them up at the mercantile."

Preacher Marlin looked genuinely pleased about this idea. "Painting has never been my favorite activity, so I'd be tickled if you girls did that."

"What if we girls left for the mercantile really early, so we arrive when it opens?" his daughter Fannie asked. "We could get the rest of the paint and any brushes and stuff we might need, and then have our painting frolic."

"Count me in!" Lily Peterscheim exclaimed.

"You just want to go shopping," her twin brother, Lavern, remarked.

All the folks around the table laughed, and Mattie got a good feeling about the whole community pitching in to finish the two homes they'd been discussing. In just a few months, these neighbors had bonded even more tightly than she and her sisters had anticipated when they'd first come to Promise Lodge with Amos . . . who would be feeling left out when he got word about their work frolics. She sensed Amos would need a lot of company to keep him from either getting down in the dumps or pushing himself too hard too soon.

"Matter of fact, having you girls go to town is a *gut* idea," Beulah said. She rose from the table with the big tureen to fill it with more soup from the stove. "I'll make out a grocery list to send along—"

"We could use some roofing nails, caulk, and quarter round—and the stain for it, too," Preacher Eli said. He looked down the side of the table where all the younger girls were sitting with hopeful smiles on their faces. "But I'm not sure you ladies would be able to carry all that stuff—"

"Let alone get the *right* stuff," Lowell Kurtz put in. "You don't know heads from tails in a hardware store, Fannie."

"Puh!" his sister shot back. "If the lists are made out right, we'll do as *gut* a job as you would—but I suspect you'll be over helping with Roman's house so you can sample those goodies Mary Kate's making."

"Hold on." Noah held up his hand for silence. "Amos is always saying we should be part of the solution rather than part of the problem, so I volunteer to drive the girls into town. I can oversee the hardware shopping and load all the stuff into the wagon," he suggested. "And I can make sure we get back home in time to do some work, instead of just shopping."

"That's the ticket!" Eli said. "We should write our lists this evening so you young people can get an early start tomorrow."

"The mercantile opens at eight, so we should leave here by seven twenty," Noah said to the girls. "We might as well get the paint for Roman's place, too.

Something like pink or lime green would be his choice, I'm guessing."

Roman rolled his eyes. "You think I'm going to give you *gut* money for such colors?" he teased. "Think again!"

Mattie enjoyed watching Lily, Fannie, Laura, and Phoebe all laughing together, anticipating their adventure in the Forest Grove mercantile. She had a satisfying feeling that these girls and the Lehman sisters would become fast friends over the coming years as they matured into wives and mothers. "I'll get the post office box key from Amos, too," she said. "You can stop in Promise for the mail on your way back. Maybe we'll have more letters from families wanting to move here, and Amos will enjoy reading them."

As Mattie looked at Christine's daughters, another idea occurred to her. "You girls don't happen to know addresses or phone numbers for Amos's kids, do you? He's insisted that we not contact them, but I think they should know about his accident."

Phoebe and Laura glanced at each other, shrugging. "Last I heard, Barbara and Bernice married twin brothers in Ohio," Phoebe replied.

"And Allen's somewhere in Indiana, doing who knows what?" Laura put in. "Allen couldn't wait to leave Coldstream after his *mamm* passed on. Wouldn't surprise me if Allen has jumped the fence, considering how he and Amos used to go head to head over church issues."

Mattie nodded sadly. It was a shame that the Troyer kids had scattered so far away from their *dat*, and that Amos wouldn't be able to do so many things that he'd come to enjoy since moving to Promise Lodge.

She saw it as her mission to make Amos smile and keep him occupied during the weeks he was supposed to rest in dark rooms. Mother Nature seemed to be cooperating, because the days were growing noticeably shorter. From the table she could see the rays of the setting sun shimmering on the frost-coated orange and yellow leaves of the large old maple trees outside the lodge.

After everyone had finished eating, Mattie filled a container with soup, wrapped up some of the bread and orange date bars, and walked over to see how Amos was doing. Her sisters had insisted that she and Frances tend to their men rather than stay to clean up the kitchen, so Mattie walked with the bishop's wife until they reached the bend in the road that veered toward the two Lehman places.

"I sure hope Floyd hasn't given Minerva any trouble—and I hope you'll all get some rest tonight," Mattie said as they paused in front of Amos's house.

"*Jah*, I keep thinking he'll wear himself out soon," Frances replied with a sigh. "We live in hope—and we live in the Lord's keeping."

Mattie nodded and hurried along the lane toward the modest home she and Amos would soon be sharing. Surely he would be recovered enough by the time November twenty-first rolled around—and perhaps they could hold the wedding at Amos's house instead of in the big meeting room at the lodge, to make it easier for him. It wasn't as though he'd be preaching at his own wedding, so he could remain seated if he needed to. Truman had rented a basic wheelchair so Amos could roll from room to room—not that he showed much inclination to move around, with his head hurting so badly.

"Amos? You ready for some soup and fresh bread?" she called out as she entered the house.

"Bring it on!" came his reply from the bedroom in the back. "But bring it in here, will you please?"

Mattie smiled. He sounded stronger this evening, as though resting and spending time with Truman had lifted his spirits. "How about you, Truman?" she asked. "I've got plenty of soup, so you could eat with him."

Truman joined her in the kitchen, where he took his felt hat from the peg on the back wall. "I'll get on home," he replied. "How about if I feed and water his horses before I head out?"

Mattie gazed gratefully at him. "That would be a big help, Truman. We're so blessed to have you for a neighbor." She lowered her voice, glancing over her shoulder to be sure Amos hadn't followed him to the kitchen. "How do you think he's doing?"

Truman shrugged into his barn coat. "He talked some, and he napped some. I noticed that he couldn't quite think of the right words from time to time—but the doctor said that would probably be the case for a while."

Mattie nodded. "I'm going to suggest an early bedtime after he eats. I'm hoping Amos won't feel his pain while he's asleep."

"I'll keep you both in my prayers," Truman said before starting toward the door. "He's taken as much of his pain medication as he's allowed to, but I suspect it's not helping much. Amos is one to put on a happy face and act like he's feeling all right, but I could tell his headache was wearing on him. *Gut* night, Mattie."

"You, too, Truman."

After Mattie put a bowl of soup on a tray along with some buttered bread, she carefully carried it to the bedroom at the back of the house. Amos had joked that this room would become his *dawdi haus* when he got too old and unsteady to climb the stairs. Mattie was glad he'd had the foresight to arrange his floor plan so he could live on the main level now.

She paused in the doorway of Amos's room to let her eyes adjust to the darkness. It took a moment for her to distinguish the armchair positioned beside Amos's bed—and the wheelchair that sat near the head of the bed.

She felt acutely aware that she was entering Amos's bedroom without Roman or anyone else in the house . . . and that beneath the covers, Amos was dressed only in his long johns. Although nothing intimate would take place, some folks—Preacher Eli, for instance—would probably feel she was entering into a sinful situation, considering that she and Amos weren't yet married.

"Are—are you comfortable with me coming in, Amos?" she asked hesitantly. "Roman will be here anytime—"

"Nobody I'd rather have as my nurse, Mattie," he assured her. "And if the neighbors—or the bishop— suspect I'm getting too frisky, well, I guess I'll make my confession at church this Sunday. Even if it's only wishful thinking."

Mattie entered the room and sat down in the armchair, carefully balancing the tray with the bowl of soup on it. It was reassuring that Amos knew they were having church on Sunday, but she didn't want to get his hopes up. "Sunday will probably be too soon for you to get out," she murmured as she handed him the tray. "From the way Frances talks, Bishop Floyd's not doing as well as he thinks he is. Sounds like Eli and Marlin will be preaching—"

"We'll see." Amos grasped the tray and held it for a few moments longer than he needed to, allowing his fingers to close around hers. "God and I have been talking about this today. I feel a lot better this evening, and I predict I'll be right as rain in a few days—sitting through church on Sunday, and helping with Roman's house by next week."

In the back of her mind, Mattie heard Dr. Townsend's warnings that Amos needed to rest for several weeks—at least until Christmas. "Let's take it one day at a time," she suggested gently. "And you shouldn't compare your recovery time to Floyd's, either. Something tells me he'll push himself too hard because he believes he must lead us instead of resting."

In the dimness, Mattie saw Amos concentrating. He set the tray carefully on his lap before he spoke. "Do I recall correctly that as I was falling off the shed, Floyd hollered out for Jesus to send His angels to catch me?"

Mattie nipped her lip, wondering where Amos's question might lead. "*Jah*, he did," she replied softly. "I wasn't sure what to think about that."

"Well, as I've pondered Floyd's plea, I keep remembering how—when Jesus was in the desert fasting for forty days," Amos said in a pensive tone, "Satan tempted Him by telling Him to turn stones to bread. Then the devil told Him to jump from the pinnacle of the Temple to prove God's angels would bear Him up."

"*Jah*, that's how the story goes in the Bible," Mattie murmured. "But Jesus refused, saying it's wrong to tempt God."

"Exactly. The way I see it, I should've known better

than to prop the ladder so close to the corner of that roof that we've all agreed needs replacing," Amos said. "It's my own fault I was so eager to help the girls—and to return to that volleyball game with the fellows—that I didn't pay close enough attention. And although Floyd was making a brave effort to catch me, that wasn't such a smart move, either."

Mattie took Amos's hand, relieved that his thought process seemed as sound and down-to-earth as it always did. "It was nice he broke your fall—but then, he was expecting angels to bear you up."

"None of this was God's fault," Amos insisted, squeezing her hand. "Two men who should've known better made some bad choices. If that subject comes up in church, or if Floyd tries to twist this tale any other direction, I hope you'll set folks straight about how I see it if I'm not there. God did not forsake Floyd by refusing to answer his call for angels. God was being God."

Mattie felt blessed by Amos's words and by the presence of mind it required to share his faith, his opinion. "I'll do that, Preacher Amos. I wish neither one of you had gotten hurt, but I feel a lot better after hearing you say that. I still believe in angels, though."

"So do I. After all, here you are when I need you most." Amos spooned up some soup, inhaled its aroma, and let out a gratified sigh as he swallowed it. "You and this soup are potent medicine, Mattie," he murmured. "With you and God watching over me—and Roman and Truman, bless them—I'll be just fine in a week or so. Deep down in my soul I believe that, Mattie. Do you?"

Mattie nipped her lip. She *wanted* to believe Amos . . . but she didn't think Dr. Townsend would've warned them about a recovery time of several weeks if the test results hadn't indicated fairly serious injuries. "I believe God knows how this will all work out, and when," she hedged. "And I hope we'll all listen to His counsel."

Amos took another bite of soup. "You're a wise woman, Mattie. That's one of the reasons I love you."

Mattie felt a pleasant heat stealing into her cheeks. "I love you, too, Amos," she murmured. "That's why I'll do my best to help you—and tell you exactly what I think, if you're not following the doctor's orders. God guides Dr. Townsend, too, you know. No matter what Floyd says."

Amos burst out laughing, and then he grimaced and his hand went quickly to the side of his head. "*Jah*, well, I feel my instincts come from God, too, so I'll have a lot of praying and listening to do. But we *will* come through this, Mattie. You and me, together."

"Now *that* I believe, Amos," she said, gently gripping his wrist. "You and me, together."

Chapter Thirteen

Rosetta finished arranging the bars of goat-milk soap and then stepped back to see if she liked her new display. Instead of dedicating a room to the gift shop she'd been planning, she had placed a large antique dresser in the lobby of the lodge, off to the side, where folks would see it but it wouldn't be in the way.

"That's better, don't you think?" she asked Ruby, who stood across the lobby. "I like it with your jars of honey in the center and the soap on either side of it—and on days we have Deborah's cookies or other things to sell, we can move our items to make room for them."

"Or—if Deborah bakes the way I think she will," Ruby said with a chuckle, "we might want to have a table just for goodies, to the left of the dresser. What with the holidays coming on, and the way local folks have been snapping up our cheese lately, we might do a brisker business than you think. Even after the weather turns cold."

"We'll hold that positive thought—and plan for

happiness!" Rosetta added resolutely. "And if Bishop Floyd sweeps off our merchandise with his arm like Jesus clearing the money changers' tables in the Temple, then we'll rethink our plan."

"Puh. If Floyd says you're not to have a little shop in the lodge, we'll put your soaps in the front room of our cheese factory," Ruby declared. "He can't mess with us Mennonites."

"I think Floyd's got more important matters than your gift shop to be concerned with," Beulah put in as she came out of the kitchen. "Saw him hobbling around outside his house yesterday, raking leaves. But before he'd been at it for even a minute, he had to sit down on the porch steps."

"Frances is beside herself. She can't make him stay inside, in a dark room, like he's supposed to." With a final glance at the display, Rosetta slipped into her coat and tied on her black bonnet. "Let's hope he's not doing more damage, prolonging the healing of his concussion. But there's no telling Floyd how he should do things."

"Time will tell. I'm glad Amos isn't behaving so foolishly," Beulah said with an emphatic nod. "Better get back to fixing dinner. Those fellows are working away on the rest of Roman's house, and they'll be here to eat in another hour, I'm guessing."

"And I'll be back to help you as soon as I put our new sign out by the road." Rosetta stepped out onto the front porch and picked up the sign Noah had painted for her, along with a rubber mallet to hammer its posts into the ground. When she reached the bottom of the steps, she shivered and looked up at the sky. Gray clouds hung low across the horizon, and a gust of damp, cold wind held a hint of impending winter. Were those tiny snowflakes she felt on her face?

On her way to the road, Rosetta took a moment to watch the crew of men attaching plywood to the triangular roof trusses of Roman's new house. The rapid-fire sound of nails piercing lumber rang out above the hum of the generator that powered their air-driven nail guns. Although all the carpenters looked alike in their dark stocking caps, scarves, and heavy coats, she could distinguish the bulkier frame of Preacher Eli between Noah and Roman's slimmer bodies. Preacher Marlin and his son Harley were up there, as well, while Lester Lehman was beginning to install off-white siding on the front of the house. The three Peterscheim boys and Lowell were on the ground unwrapping large packages of shingles.

Rosetta smiled and hurried toward the road. Even without Amos and Floyd, she was guessing this crew would have Roman's roof shingled and completed by day's end. It was such a blessing that their men worked together as well as the women did. Promise Lodge was indeed the peaceful, productive colony she and her sisters had envisioned when they'd bought this rural property.

They had hoped more families would live here by now, but some of the folks who'd sent letters expressing their interest in the Promise Lodge colony had decided to stay put until spring. Maybe it was time to place another ad in *The Budget*—but she would leave that to Amos. Writing the ad and sending it in would surely be something he could do while he was laid up and not able to build houses.

With several hard whacks of the mallet, Rosetta got

her sign firmly situated beside the sign that advertised the produce stand and the Promise Lodge Apartments.

PROMISE LODGE GIFT SHOP
R & B CHEESE SHOP
NOW OPEN
~
CREAMERY CHEESES
GOAT MILK SOAPS
LOCAL HONEY & BAKED GOODS
COME VISIT US!

Rosetta smiled at Noah's precise black lettering on the white background—and the top of the sign that was shaped like an arrow, pointing toward the buildings. Now that the produce stand was enclosed with the removable white panels Amos had designed, Rosetta and the Kuhn sisters were hoping their regular produce customers—and many new ones—would venture to the lodge to buy their wares.

Time will tell. As Beulah's voice rang in her mind, Rosetta walked beneath the arched metal Promise Lodge sign and back down the lane. She smiled at the sight of her goats lining the wire fence—and Christine's Holsteins clustered around the hay feeders near the barn—all of them watching the construction crew on Roman's roof. Another gust of wind whipped at her bonnet and sent dry leaves spinning in circles across the plowed garden plots. The tall old trees near the lodge stood with their bare branches stretched toward the heavens, looking stark against the gray sky. Once again Rosetta felt the sting of tiny snowflakes hitting her cheeks.

From Roman's house, Queenie came bounding over with a large stick in her mouth. Rosetta laughed, grasping one end of the branch, but the Border collie had a firm grip with her teeth. Growling playfully, Queenie tugged backwards until Rosetta nearly lost her balance. "I suppose the boys are working instead of paying attention to you today," she teased. "*Gut* thing Deborah's allowing you to stay in the house, what with the weather growing colder."

The dog grunted, still holding the stick firmly in her mouth. When Rosetta released it, Queenie ran back to keep track of the carpentry crew. Hurrying up the lodge stairs, Rosetta entered the warm lobby with a grateful sigh. As she removed her wraps, she inhaled the homey aromas of the dinner Beulah was preparing. "What smells so heavenly?" she asked as she entered the kitchen. "It's getting nippy outside. I'll put on a fresh pot of coffee and some water for cocoa."

Beulah closed the oven door. "I've made one of my favorite recipes, called Marriage Meat Loaf," she replied. "As the story goes, some poor Plain fellow married a gal who wasn't such a *gut* cook, but once she served him this meat loaf it saved their marriage. Believe that, or not!"

Rosetta laughed as she filled the percolator and teakettle with water. "No doubt in my mind we'd have bachelors banging the door down with offers of marriage if we invited them for dinner today! What else are you fixing?"

Ruby chuckled. "We've whipped up a cheesy rice casserole, green beans with lots of onions and bacon, and I've just put a big skillet of apples on to simmer."

"And if you ask me, I'm just as content not to have

a bunch of unhitched men begging me to marry them," Beulah remarked. "At this stage of the game, I'm not inclined to change my ways to suit a man—but of course, we'd make an exception for your Truman."

Rosetta's cheeks prickled with heat. "Bless his heart, Truman's catching up on some landscaping work that went by the wayside when he took Mattie and Frances back to the hospital yesterday. So I don't figure he'll be showing up today."

"Not that he needs a meal to convince him to hitch up with you, dearie." Ruby stifled a smile. "This won't sound very Christian of me, but maybe when Floyd hit his head the other night it knocked some sense into him, and he'll change his opinion about you marrying a nice Mennonite fellow."

"Ruby Kuhn, I'll pray extra hard for your soul, for saying that," Beulah chided, but she was chuckling. "If anybody can find a way to bring Rosetta and Truman together, God can. We'll just have to trust that He's got a plan for that—and hope we're expressing an opinion He agrees with."

"So what's for dessert?" Rosetta asked, mostly to change the subject. She appreciated the support of the Kuhn sisters, but sometimes she wished they had someone else to play matchmaker for. "I sure am sorry to see the wonderful-*gut* cake you made for our party still on the cake stand," she remarked as she stepped into the pantry.

"I'll put it in the deep freeze," Beulah said. "We can hope the wedding is still on for next Saturday, and—"

"Do you think Amos and Mattie will call off the wedding?" Ruby blurted. Her forehead creased with concern. "Amos needs a *gut* woman like Mattie more than ever while he recuperates."

"Mattie says Amos can't stand up for any length of time. And his headache's still so intense, he's got no desire to leave his dark room." Beulah raised her eyebrows at Rosetta, as though to ask if she knew whether Amos's condition had improved.

Rosetta shook her head as she lit the gas burner to percolate their coffee. "Unless Amos comes around faster than Mattie thinks he will, I can't see him enduring a three-hour church service and then the wedding ceremony—not to mention all that company and the meal. I predict they'll postpone it for a while, but I hope I'm wrong."

"*Jah*, we always have to allow for a miracle," Ruby murmured. "I've been doing my part, praying for Amos every time I think of him."

Rosetta nodded. She, too, had held Amos—and her sister Mattie—up in prayer many times since the accident. When she opened the bread box, she got an idea she knew all those hungry men would enjoy. "I'm going to whip these day-old cinnamon rolls and leftover muffins into a quick bread pudding. We've got plenty of milk and eggs—and if I make it now, it will still be warm when we're ready to eat it."

"Perfect!" Beulah clapped her hands. "We knew you'd come up with something for dessert, Rosetta, sweet as you are."

What a blessing it was that the Kuhn sisters could always make her chuckle. Rosetta chatted with them as she quickly crumbled the muffins and cinnamon rolls into a large bowl and poured scalded milk over them. When she'd mixed together the sugar, butter, eggs, and other ingredients, she poured the sweet-smelling concoction into a glass casserole and slipped it into the oven with Beulah's meat loaf. Cooking for family and friends was such a soul-satisfying way to spend her morning, and Rosetta was grateful that the dining room would be filled with warmth and delicious aromas when the men came in for dinner.

Within the hour, the carpentry crew and the girls who'd been painting Preacher Marlin's new home were seated around the table. Christine, wearing an old paint-splotched dress and a faded kerchief over her hair, smiled as she gazed at the meal on the table. "You ladies have been busy this morning while I was painting! Let's wait another moment or two, shall we?" she asked as she glanced at the two preachers. "I saw Mattie leaving Amos's place as I was coming into the lodge."

"She'd better get here pretty quick," Johnny Peterscheim said, "or I might just eat half of that meat loaf before we pray. A man works up a big hunger working out in that cold weather."

As the other boys agreed with him, the closing of the back door announced Mattie's arrival. When she saw everyone watching her, she hurried to the table and sat down. After a moment of prayer, the men wasted no time grabbing the bowls and platters within their reach.

"How's Amos today?" Rosetta asked. Mattie was seated next to her, appearing a bit subdued after spending the morning with him.

Mattie spooned some green beans onto her plate. "I'm not sure," she replied after a moment's hesitation. "He says his headache isn't as intense, but he was dozing off a lot. I figured he'd probably sleep for a while, so I came over to eat."

"His painkillers are probably making him drowsy," Ruby remarked.

"His body's telling him it needs rest to rebuild itself," Beulah said. "I'm glad to hear he's taking care of himself."

"Does he still have to use the wheelchair?" Preacher Marlin asked. "I think I'd go crazy if I couldn't be up and around."

Mattie nipped her lip. "I've seen newborn foals with more strength in their legs than Amos has," she said in a low voice. "He's getting pretty depressed about it. I—I'd appreciate it, Roman and Noah, if you'd stop over before you go back to your carpentry work, to help Amos to the bathroom. He says I shouldn't have to do that for him."

"He's embarrassed to have you see him in this condition, Mattie," Christine said with a shake of her head. She looked down the table toward the men, who were now digging into their dinner. "I hate to sound negative, but do you suppose we should be making plans for the possibility that Amos won't walk again? His house isn't set up for a fellow in a wheelchair—"

"And he certainly won't be able to handle the steps going up to his front porch," Roman pointed out. "I've been wondering about that, too. I just haven't wanted to think about him being . . . disabled."

A poignant silence settled over the dining room. Rosetta grabbed Mattie's hand under the table. She could tell her sister was having a hard time accepting Amos's condition.

But then Mattie put on a determined smile. "I think we should allow a little more time before we write Amos off," she said in a voice that quivered a bit. "He's a hardheaded sort, and he wouldn't want us giving up on him—or giving up on God healing his body in ways we can't yet see. But it might not hurt to have some lumber on hand to build a ramp up to his porch."

Roman nodded as he stabbed another slice of meat loaf from the platter. "Amos's arms seem to be just fine," he said. "He'll be a lot happier if he can get around in a wheelchair than if he has to depend on some of us fellows to carry him in and out of his house. Let's keep praying for his full recovery, though. If anybody has the faith to pull himself through, it's Amos."

"Amen to that," Rosetta chimed in. "And has anybody seen or heard how Floyd's doing? I'm awfully glad he's not been trying to help you fellows with Roman's house today."

"I stopped by his place this morning," Lester said. He took a second helping of the rice casserole and passed it to Eli. "Just between us, I suspect Frances slipped some pills into my brother's breakfast, because he was napping in the recliner. She says Floyd's determined to be at church tomorrow, however—and he intends to preach."

Rosetta's eyes widened and a few other folks seemed surprised, as well. "I guess we'll see what happens," she murmured.

Beside her, Mattie shook her head. "*Jah*, I guess we will."

Chapter Fourteen

"Mattie, I'll be fine while you go to church," Amos insisted. He held her gaze to convince her of his sincerity. "I promise you I'll not be running outside the minute you leave, or getting into any other mischief. I really can behave myself while you attend the service and eat dinner with the others."

Mattie's pained expression—the way she looked away from him—made Amos kick himself for his poor choice of words. It didn't take a genius to realize he wouldn't be getting out of his wheelchair anytime soon, and bless her, she'd been avoiding that subject out of the goodness of her heart . . . a heart he feared he'd taken advantage of.

"All right then," Mattie murmured. "I'll be back with your meal. Take care, Amos. We'll be praying for you."

Take care. The words seemed more appropriate coming from other friends than from the woman who'd agreed to marry him. As Amos heard the front door close, he wondered if Mattie was having a change of heart—not that he could blame her. She hadn't figured on his becoming an invalid, after all.

Amos sighed loudly. It was a relief not to have Mattie trying to entertain him with chatter and smiles that were starting to falter. A morning alone would give him a chance to think things through, to pray . . . to plan. He'd fallen from the roof three days ago— had come home from the hospital two days ago, fully expecting that his headaches and inability to walk would have improved by now.

"'My God, my God, why hast thou forsaken me?'" he muttered, knowing he had no right to cry out as Jesus had from the cross—knowing full well he was feeling sorry for himself. But plenty of men in the Bible had railed at the Lord when they'd felt forlorn and defeated—

"Troyer, are you still in that dark room? In that wheelchair?" a loud, familiar voice demanded.

Amos winced. He was in no mood for a visit from the bishop.

"So this is to be the way of it? Are you so pathetic you've also lost your ability to speak?" Floyd leaned on the doorjamb, scowling. "Take up your bed and walk, Amos. A man with any sort of faith—a preacher who believes in the healing power of Jesus—wouldn't be wallowing in self-pity, sitting alone in his room. If you believe in the miracles Jesus performed, come to church with me."

Amos remained silent. Was it his imagination, or did Floyd sound out of breath—and maybe out of his head? Did the bishop's relaxed posture suggest he had recovered from the fall he'd taken, or was he leaning on the door frame because he didn't have the strength to enter the room?

Before Lehman could rail at him again, Amos raised his hand. "I heard you loud and clear," he muttered. "If I were able, I'd be preparing to preach this morning, but my body is telling me to rest instead. The Psalmist tells us to rest in the Lord and to wait patiently on Him—"

"So if I'm the one who took the worst hit—the one who fell to the ground beneath your weight," Floyd countered, "how is it that I'm up and around while you say you're not able to walk? That makes no sense to me."

"I don't like it, either!" Amos retorted. "I don't know the answer to your question, but I'll tell you that my headache was barely noticeable this morning until *you* showed up. Spare me your sarcasm, Floyd. Something tells me you'll need all the strength you can muster to make it through the service."

"Oh ye of little faith," the bishop taunted.

"In Deuteronomy and in the story of Jesus's temptation, we're told not to put God to the test," Amos replied impatiently. "Be careful, Floyd. 'Pride goeth before destruction, and an haughty spirit before a fall.'"

"I can trade verses with you all morning or I can go preach the Word to folks who'll listen. As for me and my house, we'll worship the Lord." Floyd gazed at Amos and then sneered. "As for you, Preacher, this must mean it's God's will for you to be a cripple for the rest of your life."

Amos gripped the arms of his wheelchair to keep from shouting at the insolent man in his doorway.

When Floyd left, the sound of the door slamming echoed accusingly throughout the house.

Amos exhaled. Was he wrong—and was Floyd right? Was he so caught up in the self-pity the bishop had spoken of that he'd lost his will to recover? If he'd prayed harder, or more correctly, would God already have healed him? Or were his injuries linked to his sins? Jesus had often healed people and then added, "Go and sin no more"—

Answer me, Lord! Your servant Amos believes in Your miracles, in Your ability to heal. If it's Your will, help me stand up. Get me out of this chair and out of this misery.

Amos sucked in a deep breath, gripping the arms of the wheelchair. He placed his feet on the floor and pushed himself up, willing his legs to support him. Once he was standing upright, with his arms out for balance, Amos dared to believe that his prayer had been answered—

But a wave of dizziness overcame him. When his knees buckled, it was all he could do to fall back into the chair rather than forward, onto his face. Sweat ran down his temples. He swallowed repeatedly, refusing to vomit. He could not have Mattie find him splattered with his half-digested breakfast.

When Amos's pulse returned to normal, he heaved a sigh. *Well, I didn't like Your answer, Lord, but I see it as a sign I'm to remain in this wheelchair for now. Make Your presence known to those in church this morning, and especially to Bishop Floyd. Forgive my impatience with him. Create in me a clean heart . . .*

As Roman sat on the men's side of the congregation gathered in the lodge's large meeting room, he felt a thrum of tension. Seated with Lester, Noah, and Harley Kurtz, with the younger boys behind them, Roman sang the final verse of the hymn. Preacher Marlin stood up to read from their big King James Bible. Because Marlin had arrived at Promise Lodge after Eli Peterscheim and Amos were already serving as ministers, he had taken on the duties of the district's deacon.

"Our Scripture passage today is from the Book of Luke, the fourth chapter and eighteenth verse," Marlin began, his clear voice ringing in the low-ceilinged room. "'The Spirit of the Lord is upon me because he hath anointed me to preach the gospel to the poor; he hath sent me to heal the brokenhearted, to preach deliverance to the captives, and recovering of sight to the blind, to set at liberty them that are bruised.'"

When Marlin sat down, all eyes were on Bishop Floyd as he rose from the preachers' bench. The bishop looked at the men on his left and then at the women to his right, as though awaiting the Lord's guidance for the sermon he was about to preach. Roman wondered if Floyd was standing with his legs so far apart to keep himself from falling. The bishop didn't look very steady, and one of his arms hung limp at his side.

"The spirit of the Lord is upon me," Floyd began in a booming voice. "As you all know, it was God's idea for me to come to Promise Lodge to preach the gospel, to heal the brokenhearted—or whomever among you needs my counsel—and to—to—"

A couple of the women gasped when Floyd's face went slack and his eyes rolled back. Marlin and Eli quickly stood up and grabbed Floyd from either side so he wouldn't fall. They guided him backwards toward the bench and lowered him so he'd be propped up by the wall, but the bishop showed no sign of opening his eyes.

"Floyd! Wake up!" Lester said as he hurried over to kneel in front of his brother.

Preacher Eli gently slapped the bishop's cheek. "Bishop, you'd better come around, or we'll have to carry you home to bed."

Floyd's eyelids fluttered. He opened his mouth to speak, but no sound came out. When the bishop tried to slap at the hands that were holding him upright, he appeared to be waving sideways, missing his aim completely.

Frances hurried forward and stood in front of her husband, shaking her head. "I was afraid of this," she muttered. In a louder voice, she said, "Floyd, can you answer me? Can you walk home with help, or do we need to make a stretcher and carry you?"

Roman and the fellows around him got very quiet, watching for the bishop's response. Floyd's expression appeared belligerent, as though he intended to rebuke his wife for suggesting he go home, but he couldn't seem to put his thoughts into words. His face looked out of balance, which made his scruffy U-shaped beard lower on one side than on the other.

Frances planted her hands on her hips. "The spirit of the Lord is indeed upon you, Floyd—and He's giving you an undeniable sign that you've got to stop this foolishness and get back to the hospital."

Minerva Kurtz had slipped up from her seat to look at the bishop, as well. Her expression appeared grave as she studied him. "Floyd, listen closely to me. This is a test. Give me a big smile."

The bishop looked ready to do anything but smile, yet he focused on Minerva. His eyes widened and his lips curved—but only on one side.

"Raise both of your arms for me," Minerva insisted.

Floyd appeared puzzled as his right arm rose partway but his left hand remained on his lap. He was trying to talk, but couldn't.

"Someone needs to call 911, right this minute!" Minerva said, looking at Rosetta and her sisters. "Floyd appears to be having a stroke, and every second counts if he's to recover from it."

Rosetta rushed toward the lodge kitchen to make the call, with Frances close behind her. "I'll pack him a bag—again," she said as she left the meeting room. Gloria gazed fearfully at her father and then hurried to catch up with her mother. Alma Peterscheim was talking in a low, concerned voice with Mattie and Christine, while the younger girls whispered among themselves.

When Roman saw Mary Kate rise from her seat, her arms wrapped around her belly, he feared this frightening episode had made her go into labor. He started toward her, but then he realized that while Mary Kate's brown eyes were wide with concern, she seemed calm and in control of her emotions. She walked toward the preachers' bench and sat down beside her father.

"Hang on, Dat," she murmured as she took his hand between hers. "You did your very best to convince yourself you're okay, but your head and body have other ideas now. Do you understand what I'm saying?"

Floyd looked at his younger daughter with eyes that widened like a startled horse's. Then he took a deep breath and seemed to settle himself.

"The ambulance is coming for you," Mary Kate explained patiently. "You're going to the hospital again. *Please* let the doctors help you this time, Dat. We all need you to be healthy."

Roman's heart went out to Mary Kate and his admiration for her soared. She was speaking calmly, showing concern, yet insisting that her father focus on what she was saying.

"When you hit the ground with Preacher Amos last Thursday, you might have caused more than just a concussion." Minerva took up where Mary Kate had left off. "Truly, Floyd, I think the Lord's trying to get your attention. If you don't listen to Him and the doctors this time, you may be incapacitated for the rest of your life."

In the distance, Roman heard the wail of sirens. He went through the lobby and out to the porch of the lodge, waving his arms above his head to attract the attention of the emergency workers. When Queenie raced toward the approaching vehicles, barking as though the drivers needed her directions, Roman called her over and commanded her to sit beside him. He was relieved to see that one of the paramedics hopping out of the ambulance had been here Thursday evening.

"One of the fellows you took to the hospital is having a stroke, we think," Roman said. "He's inside, first room on your left past the lobby."

The men nodded and hurried inside with a stretcher. When the police officer and the firemen established that there were no other emergencies, they went on their way, and by that time the paramedics were wheeling Bishop Floyd through the lobby. Roman held the door for them, and when he saw Frances Lehman rushing around the side of the lodge he called out to the paramedics.

"Could Mrs. Lehman possibly ride to the hospital with you?" Roman asked the men. "The fellow who drove her the other night is attending his own church service—but I bet Truman would join you later today, Frances," he added. "Do you want me to go with you?"

The bishop's wife gave him a grateful smile. "I know more about what to expect this time, and which doctor to request," she replied. "I'm not leaving until I'm sure Floyd is staying put, undergoing treatment. But *jah*, if you could have Truman check on us later, that would be helpful."

Roman nodded and helped her into the ambulance after the paramedics got Floyd's stretcher situated. The array of blinking, beeping medical machinery and the quick efficiency of the paramedics amazed him—and frightened him. The determined expression on Frances's face as she sat on a small bench inside the vehicle suggested she was rising above her fears better than he probably would.

Their neighbors had gathered on the porch to watch the ambulance race down the lane. When its pulsing lights and wailing siren were headed down the county road, everyone began talking at once.

"Frances will have her hands full if Floyd gets contrary again."

"*Jah*, but what if he doesn't come out of it?"

"What are we to do if he can no longer carry out his duties as our bishop?"

"My word, first Amos is laid low and now Floyd. Is

God trying to tell us our leaders aren't behaving the way He wants them to?"

"Let's head back to our worship service," Preacher Marlin said above the chatter. "If ever we needed a time for prayer and contemplation, this is it."

When everyone had resumed their seats, they focused on Marlin as he stood in the space between the men's side and the women's. Roman saw how Gloria clutched Mary Kate's hand, her brown eyes wide with fear.

Lord, we could use Your comfort and consolation, Roman prayed as he briefly bowed his head. *Help me to be a source of strength and reason during this confusing time.*

"The spirit of the Lord is indeed upon us," Preacher Marlin said as he gazed around their small congregation. "We should never forget that even in emergency situations, He is with us—just as He's with Floyd, Frances, and Amos—and He'll show us the path we're to take if we listen for His still, small voice. 'Be still, and know that I am God,' He insists in the Scriptures. Let's unite in silence, praying on our bishop's behalf and listening for God's message to us this morning."

For several minutes the meeting room resonated with the sounds of deep, even breathing, punctuated by an occasional sigh and the soft ticking of the wall clock. Roman felt a unity of spirit among these new neighbors and friends, much stronger than he'd ever sensed during their church services in Coldstream. Or was he simply more attuned to this atmosphere of reverent purpose because he'd taken on more responsibilities as an adult?

"Amen."

When Preacher Eli rose, the folks in the room opened their eyes and sat up straight to hear what he had to say. His solemn expression was accentuated by the deep lines carved around his eyes and bearded chin.

"It's understandable for us to wonder what the future holds, as far as the leadership of our community," Eli began. He clasped his hands and thought for a moment. "While we should indeed consider the need for another bishop, if Floyd doesn't recover as we've prayed he will, I believe we should wait a bit and see what God has in mind for him—and for Amos—before we rush into choosing new leadership. Marlin and I are both experienced in our role as ministers, and unless somebody says differently, I believe he and I are prepared to maintain the Promise Lodge community until it becomes apparent we should hold a drawing of the lot for a new bishop."

A few folks whispered to one another, nodding.

"I'm fine with that, Eli," Lester spoke up. "We've been blessed with three strong preachers—and I believe Amos and Floyd are too tough to let infirmity get them down. I'm confident you and Marlin can lead us in the meantime."

"That's the way I see it, too," Rosetta said, and the women around her nodded in agreement.

"Rather than preaching today, or proceeding with our regular worship service," Eli went on, "I feel God is calling us to a time of silent reflection. There's great power in communion with our Lord, whether individually or as a body united by a common purpose. I would like us to pray again, and then continue in our

observance of the Sabbath by remaining silent as
the ladies set out our meal and as we partake of it
together—and then as we depart toward our homes."

Preacher Eli paused, gazing at each member in
turn. "We have a lot to think about," he continued
pensively. "We might have some amazing insights to
share as we begin our work week tomorrow, after
spending this morning listening for the voice of God
rather than talking amongst ourselves."

The folks around Roman seemed as surprised as he
was by Eli's idea, but everyone bowed their heads
again. After a while, the women and girls got up and
set their simple meal on the table in the dining room.
Everyone passed the food and ate in a contemplative
silence. The mood felt hopeful and helpful—not at all
depressing. No one seemed deprived of the visiting
that ordinarily filled the afternoon of their church
Sundays. In short order, Roman and the other folks
ate the sliced ham, fresh bread, gelatin fruit salad,
slaw, and pies, all of which the women had prepared
on Saturday.

Before he left, Roman filled a plate for Amos and
covered it with foil. His mother nodded at him,
squeezing his arm gratefully. Roman figured she
might clean up the kitchen with the other women and
then rest this afternoon rather than rushing over to
spend the remainder of the day with Amos. He suspected his *mamm* felt bewildered by her fiancé's
condition, and was wondering when Amos would
show some improvement.

When Roman stepped outside to take Amos's meal
to him, fat, white snowflakes were swirling lazily in
the air. He stopped for a moment, looking toward the

sky to enjoy the fluttery, feathery prickles when the cold flakes landed on his face. Although winter sometimes brought on weather-related problems with the cows and other livestock, Roman enjoyed the colder weather . . . the hushed beauty of snow-covered hillsides. He recalled the old sleigh Amos had brought from Coldstream, now stashed in the shed, and an idea made him smile.

Did Mary Kate enjoy riding in a horse-drawn sleigh as much as he did? It was a question worth asking her sometime—at least when enough snow covered the ground.

Roman took Amos's porch steps two at a time and knocked loudly before entering the preacher's house. "How're you doing, Amos?" he called out as he wiped his feet on the rug.

"Still here," came the reply from the back room. "What was all that commotion with the sirens a while ago?"

Roman entered Amos's room and allowed his eyes a moment to adjust to the dimness before he sat in the chair beside the bed. The preacher was propped upright against the headboard with a pillow behind his back, which meant he'd maneuvered himself out of the wheelchair and into bed—a positive sign.

"Floyd was launching into his sermon about how the spirit of the Lord had anointed him to preach, when he nearly fell over," Roman replied. "Minerva believes he was having a stroke—said he might be incapacitated for the rest of his life if he didn't get medical attention right away, so Rosetta called 911."

Amos's eyes widened. "A stroke? They say that's like having a heart attack except it's happening to your brain," he murmured. "Do you suppose this has been building up inside him for a while? Might account for the crazy things Floyd's said and done lately, like running underneath me to catch me when I fell. And this morning he told me it's God's will that I'll always be a cripple, because I couldn't get out of my wheelchair and walk."

"The bishop said that? Well, I don't believe it for a minute." Roman unwrapped the meal and handed it to Amos, observing the way he firmly gripped the plate. Roman was pleased to hear Amos reasoning and speaking clearly. "You might have something, though, about his stroke being in the works for a while. Minerva thought Floyd's fall might've set him up for it."

Amos shifted on the bed. His quick grimace suggested he might not be feeling as chipper as he was trying to appear. "How'd the rest of church go, after the excitement died down?"

"Eli suggested that he and Marlin—and you—would be fine leading the colony until we see whether Floyd recovers," Roman replied. "He had us spend the rest of the morning in prayer and silence, even while we ate—listening for God's counsel rather than finishing the regular service or chatting with each other."

"Really? Peterscheim did that?" Amos bit into a slice of bread, thinking. "That sounds more like what I'd expect Marlin to say. I always considered Eli pretty heavy on the traditional, conservative side—but every preacher's got a few surprises up his sleeve."

Roman wondered if Amos would elaborate on that statement, or reveal his thoughts about his upcoming wedding. He had heard some of the ladies discussing this topic before church—and he suspected Mamm was *very* curious about Amos's plans, what with the ceremony only six days away.

Roman's eyebrows rose as another thought occurred to him. "If Bishop Floyd's laid up, who's going to conduct the wedding service for you and Mamm next Saturday?"

Amos blinked. "That's a very good question, son. And right now, only God knows the answer."

Chapter Fifteen

"That snow we got Sunday afternoon did us a real favor," Mattie remarked as she and her sisters yanked the shriveled squash and pumpkin vines from the garden plot nearest the lodge. "It made these last plants easier to clear away—"

"And it stopped before we had to do any shoveling or plowing!" Rosetta chimed in. "Missouri weather isn't a bit different here than it was in Coldstream. If you don't like it now, wait fifteen minutes and it'll change."

Christine dropped her armload of vines onto the tarp and stood up to stretch her back. "I'm so glad the men got the roof on Roman's house before winter hit us. Now they can take their time with the interior finishing work."

"Marlin's told me again and again how much he appreciated you and the girls doing his painting," Mattie remarked as she, too, stood up. "Now that he and Harley have moved their furniture into the house, Minerva's been sewing the curtains and making everything look real homey. She's really happy to be out of the cabin. Said it was getting chilly at night, without any heat."

"Those little cabins have served us well. We'll hope more folks want to join us here at Promise Lodge come spring," Rosetta said in a wistful voice. "I thought we'd have more residents by now—"

"But what we lack in quantity we make up for with quality," Christine insisted. "We couldn't ask for any nicer renters than the Kuhns. And who would've thought we'd have a cheese factory here, not to mention Marlin's barrel business and the Lehmans' window and siding company?"

Mattie shielded her eyes with her hand, gazing at two cars driving slowly down their lane. The first car parked in front of the cheese factory, and the second one continued until it was a few yards in front of them. "Wonder who this is?"

The lady driving rolled down her window. "Where might I find the gift shop?" she called over. "I want to see that goat-milk soap mentioned on the sign out front."

Rosetta's face lit up like the morning sun. "You're almost there! Follow me to the lodge just ahead of you."

Mattie chuckled and resumed pulling squash vines alongside Christine. The sun was bright, but she was glad to be wearing her flannel-lined barn jacket, which blocked the brisk wind. "Hard to believe we're just a week away from Thanksgiving," she said. "I saved back some of the nice acorn squash we grew to have for our—oh! There's Truman's truck!"

Mattie waved eagerly as the pickup rumbled under the arched metal entry sign. Truman had taken Amos for his follow-up visit at the medical center in Forest

Grove. She'd been on pins and needles all morning, wondering if the doctor had revealed anything new— or promising—about Amos's concussion and his inability to walk. Amos had hurt her feelings a bit when he'd insisted that she not go to his appointment with him, but Mattie had chalked it up to Amos having a tough morning. His headache was back, and he'd complained long and loudly about being cooped up in a dark bedroom for a week. Amos had appeared very downhearted about Truman and Roman making a chair with their arms beneath his bottom and behind his back to carry him to the truck.

"How'd the appointment go?" Mattie asked when Truman stopped alongside them.

"Didn't learn a lot new," Truman murmured. "Amos wants to get to bed now. Maybe he'll feel more like telling you about it later."

Peering into the truck, Mattie gazed at Amos on the passenger side. His head was bowed as though his wide-brimmed black hat was weighing it down.

"I'm sorry to hear that," Christine murmured. "We'll check on him after a bit."

"*Denki* for taking him, Truman—and for all the ways you're helping him." Mattie gazed purposefully at their neighbor, hoping he'd stop on his way out to tell her more about Amos's situation. "He's got clean sheets and towels, and I gathered up his dirty clothes to wash with our laundry tomorrow."

Truman nodded. *I'll be back*, he mouthed as he rolled up his window.

Mattie's heart thudded as she watched the big white pickup roll on down the road toward Amos's house. What could be so wrong that Amos hadn't even looked at her? She'd sensed he wasn't doing well yesterday when she'd taken him the noon meal—he seemed fidgety and depressed—but she didn't know what to do about it. Until Dr. Townsend told them Amos was allowed to open the curtains and spend time out in the sunshine, she intended to be sure he followed the original instructions. Too much was at stake—for her, for Amos, and for everyone at Promise Lodge—if Amos's health deteriorated.

Christine sighed. "I wish Truman had had better news for us. Or even just a hopeful expression on his face."

Mattie nodded, swallowing a lump in her throat. "I'll go in and make coffee and cut one of the pumpkin pies we baked this morning. The least we can do is feed Truman while he talks with us."

"I'll finish up here and send him inside when he comes by," her sister said as she slipped her arm around Mattie's shoulders. "Maybe Truman just didn't want to go into any details while Amos was feeling so poorly."

As she headed for the lodge, Mattie reminded herself that Dr. Townsend had predicted a recovery time of several weeks or maybe months—and who would be in a good mood, having to endure Amos's pain and lack of activity? She was doing everything she could think of—or at least everything Amos would allow—to make him comfortable and cheer him up, but they had a long haul ahead of them. Mattie trudged up the steps and into the lodge, sighing.

"Rosetta, I'm so delighted I've met you. I can't wait to try these soaps!"

Mattie closed the lodge door behind her and

smiled at the English woman standing in front of Rosetta's display. Her plastic sack bulged with several bars of soap, some jars of honey, and she held a covered pan of Deborah's orange bars.

"We're glad you stopped by to check us out, Pam," Rosetta replied, handing her a business card. "Let me know which kinds of soap you like best and I'll keep them on hand for you. With the holidays coming, our Deborah's hoping to take orders for cookie trays or other goodies you might like, too. And the Kuhns are making cheese today, so you might want to stop by their factory before you leave. You can watch them through their showroom window."

"I'll do that—and I'll bring my sisters with me next time!" Pam said with an emphatic nod. She breezed out the door with another smile for Mattie, who couldn't help noticing how depleted the soap and honey display was.

"*Gut* for you, making a new customer so happy," Mattie said. "Truman's just come back with Amos. He's going to stop by on his way out—and I have a feeling his news isn't going to be nearly as cheerful as your visit with Pam."

Rosetta stopped taking fresh soaps from the top drawer of the dresser. "Oh dear. Sounds like we'd better sweeten things up with some of that pumpkin pie—"

"I was thinking the same thing." Mattie turned when she saw motion through the lobby window. "Here comes Truman now."

Mattie added fresh water to the coffee that remained in the percolator and lit the burner beneath it, thinking it would take forever to make a fresh batch. She was grateful for Truman's patience with

Amos, and glad that preparing a snack kept her from wringing her hands. Worrying about Amos wasn't a productive way to spend her time—or a good excuse for losing sleep—but Mattie had been feeling the strain of caring for him the past few days when she'd seen no visible signs of improvement.

"Always smells so wonderful-*gut* in here." Truman closed the door against the chilly breeze and paused in the lobby. "My word, look at your soaps, wrapped in pretty ribbons—and Deborah's been giving her new oven a workout, by the looks of these goodies."

"I bet your *mamm*'s ready for a fresh bar of soap— and here," Rosetta added, "I want you to have a bar of the orange cornmeal soap for scrubbing up, Truman."

"I'll pay you for these when I have—"

"No, you won't," Rosetta insisted as she pressed the two bars of soap into Truman's large hands. "Now join us for pie while you tell us about Amos."

"I want to hear about him, too," Christine said as she came in from outdoors. "Maybe you can tell us what else we can do for him. He looked so despondent when you brought him back."

When the four of them were seated around the worktable in the kitchen with coffee and pie, Truman let out a sigh. "There's *gut* news, and not-so-*gut*," he began. "Dr. Townsend says Amos's healing seems to be on target, far as his concussion goes. But he has no idea why Amos's legs are so weak."

Mattie frowned. "But he's a *doctor*. And he ran so many tests, you'd think—"

"*Jah*, Townsend said the same thing," Truman murmured. "Amos didn't like it one bit that his doctor didn't have an answer—except to recommend some physical therapy sessions. But Townsend wants to give the concussion another couple of weeks to heal before Amos starts any sort of moving around. Needless to say, Amos wasn't happy to hear he's got to stay cooped up in that gloomy room, dependent on folks to help him."

"Can't say I blame him." Christine reached for Mattie's hand. "But if his concussion has improved, then we should keep following the doctor's recommendations, don't you think?"

Mattie nodded emphatically. "*Jah*, we've seen what happened to Floyd when he didn't do as he was told."

"The bishop's in a bad way, but at least he's getting treatment now," Truman said. "Amos and I peeked into Floyd's room at the hospital. He was out getting physical therapy so we chatted with Frances. Dr. Townsend has told them Floyd will be paralyzed—useless—on his left side unless he works with the therapists. I sure don't want that to happen to Amos."

"Nobody does," Rosetta agreed. "I'm just glad Frances convinced the bishop to stay in the hospital."

"This time they didn't give Floyd any say about it," Truman said as he cut into his pie. "He's hooked up to monitors so they can watch his blood pressure, and they've put him on a medication to dissolve blood clots, and meanwhile he's getting speech therapy and seeing other specialists, too," he added. "Might be another day or two before he's released, and Frances says home care therapists will be coming after that."

Mattie set down her fork, no longer enjoying her pumpkin pie. She was pleased to hear about Floyd's treatments, but some of his earlier remarks hadn't set well with her. "Right before Floyd had his stroke, he told Amos it was God's will that he'd always be crippled because he refused to believe he could walk," she murmured. "What's your opinion of that, Truman? You Mennonites sometimes see things in a different light."

Truman grasped her hand and gazed earnestly at her. "I've thought about this a lot lately, Mattie. Amos chose to climb up on that weak roof—just as Floyd, of his own free will, dashed beneath Amos to catch him," he said softly. "I don't believe God wanted that accident to happen, or that He has condemned either man to be an invalid. I do believe the Lord provided emergency services and a *gut*, concerned doctor to help their healing."

Truman's expression grew more pensive. "Now, Amos and Floyd have the choice about accepting medical help. God watches over us all, but He gave us free will—and our bad choices bring on most of our problems, rather than God causing them."

Mattie sighed, nodding along with her sisters. "Religion gets tricky sometimes," she murmured. "I hope we can all have the faith to love and help Amos—and Bishop Floyd—the way God wants us to care for them."

"Amen to that," Rosetta whispered.

Chapter Sixteen

That afternoon Amos sat in his wheelchair in his gloomy room, praying for God's guidance one moment and cursing his condition the next. Why had Dr. Townsend not provided an answer—or at least a timetable for his healing—so he could make plans? Set some priorities? If his concussion was improving, why did his head still feel as if someone was banging on it with a hammer?

"Why can't I walk?" he muttered. "What's happened to my legs? Is this to be the way of it for the rest of my life, God? I am so *tired* of this darkness in my home—and in my soul."

Was that the front door opening? Amos stopped his ranting to listen, hoping his visitor hadn't overheard him complaining to God.

"Who's there?" he called out. Amos hated it that his well-meaning friends came and went whenever they saw fit. Whenever they pitied him.

When he saw Mattie stop in his bedroom doorway, Amos swallowed a loud sigh. He'd figured she would come by, and he wasn't ready to address the issues that loomed between them. How could he say what he needed to without crushing her gentle, loving spirit?

"Amos." Mattie hesitated before coming in, as though she might be afraid of him. When she sat in the armchair, facing him, she put on a smile that looked out of kilter. "It's *gut* to see you sitting up. I hope you feel better—"

"I *wish* I felt better," Amos snapped. "And I wish I knew why I don't."

Mattie nipped her lip. "We've all been praying for you."

"I suppose Truman told you all the bleak details about Townsend not knowing why I can't walk," he blurted.

"He did. I—I'm so sorry this has happened to you, dear Amos."

Dear Amos. He felt like a monster, laying out all his woes like slick mud over ice, knowing that no matter what Mattie said or offered him, she would slip and fall and get hurt in her efforts to care for him.

Mattie reached for his hand. "Let's postpone the wedding, shall we?" she murmured. "We need for you to be feeling better—and it's not like we've got a bishop who can perform the ceremony on Saturday. I doubt you'd want Bishop Obadiah to come from Coldstream to do the ceremony—and I certainly don't."

It had clearly taken all of Mattie's strength to say that, but she'd also opened the door for him to state the obvious. Amos squeezed Mattie's hand, so small yet so strong, already regretting what he was about to say.

"Mattie, I can't allow you to endure another marriage of caring for a sick husband," he began in the strongest voice he could muster. "I can't bear to have you spend the rest of your days playing nurse rather than being the wife we'd both figured on when you agreed to marry me."

Mattie's face fell. In the darkness, Amos saw tears trickling down her cheeks. "Wh—what are you saying?" she whispered. "I believe we're to be together in sickness and in health, or I wouldn't have agreed to marry you. You can't just—"

"You're a strong, desirable woman, Mattie," Amos interrupted. He had all the best intentions, even though he knew he was shredding her heart into tiny pieces. "You have a lot of love to share, so I want you to focus on managing our new colony and your produce business. Take up with another fellow—if one comes along who'll take *gut* care of you," he insisted, forcing the words from his mouth for the benefit of both of them. "I love you but I can't marry you now, Mattie. Don't waste your efforts on a man who'll never be strong again. And don't grow old alone."

Mattie stood up and turned away, covering her face with her hands. "You're having a bad day," she reasoned. "You surely don't mean—"

"A few days ago I was sure I could lick this situation and get on with my life," Amos said bitterly. "But that's changed—*I've* changed. I'm not the man you deserve anymore, Mattie. Please don't make this any more difficult. For your own sake, I can't marry you."

With a sob, Mattie fled his room.

Amos slumped in his chair. He'd said what needed saying, but now his headache was pounding even harder and his heart was broken, too. With a groan he pushed himself up out of the wheelchair and fell toward his bed. It seemed the perfect time to bury his face in the pillow and remain here in the darkness, alone. The way he saw it, he might as well get used to living out his life in this sorry, useless state.

Mattie sat on the side of her bed, staring through her tears at nothing in particular. Why had Amos given up—on himself, and on the love they'd shared for most of their lives? He'd triumphed over many adversities when he'd been younger, remaining strong in his faith. Even when he'd been too poor for her father to consider him a good match—even after his wife, Anna, had died—Amos Troyer had forged ahead, doing the best he could, confident that God would see him through.

Where was God now?

Don't fall into the same trap Amos did, moaning and groaning so loud that you don't hear what God might be trying to tell you, the voice in Mattie's mind warned. But she had a right to feel miserable. The man she loved had just shut her out of his life. Try as she might, she couldn't recall any of the Bible verses that had been written for desperate moments such as these. Her mind felt as empty as her soul.

Mattie sighed and looked out the window of her apartment. The wind whistled, driving thick, fat snowflakes, and the sky looked as dark and dreary as her heart felt. How senseless it seemed, that Amos would now remain alone in his new home and she would continue living in these rooms at the lodge—neither of them happy. What a waste of two lives.

The steady ticking of the clock on her dresser

brought on a fresh round of tears. Amos had given her the clock as an engagement present when they'd been young people madly in love. He'd probably done without groceries for a while after he'd bought it, yet he'd never let on that it was a hardship. Then, when her *dat* had steered her toward Marvin Schwartz as a more up-and-coming husband, Mattie had carefully wrapped the clock and stored it beneath the linens in her cedar chest. She hadn't been able to part with the clock—and secretly, she hadn't given up hope that God's will and circumstances might bring her and Amos together again someday.

And their lives had worked out that way, just as she'd hoped. But this morning it hadn't been a well-meaning father coming between them. It was Amos himself.

Mattie opened the case of the wooden clock and stopped its pendulum. She couldn't bear to hear it ticking away the moments of her life, like a heart that had lost its reason for living yet went on beating.

She decided to allow herself this evening to mourn her loss— *"to everything there is a season . . . a time to weep and a time to laugh."*

Mattie took her flannel nightgown from the drawer. It wasn't even time for supper, yet she was done with this day. No doubt her sisters and the Kuhns would be looking for her when they realized she wasn't in the kitchen helping them cook, but she didn't have the least inclination toward eating—or toward going into detail about why she needed to be alone for a while. They were women. They would understand.

She had just let the nightgown drop down over

her arms and body when she sensed someone else's presence. Mattie turned, reminding herself not to lash out at her visitor the way Amos had done to her. "Ah. Rosetta. I was so caught up in my thoughts I didn't hear you at the door."

Rosetta cocked her head, assessing Mattie for a moment. "What's this? You're not feeling well? Coming down with a cold in this change of the weather?"

Mattie sighed. No sense in gilding the lily. "Amos called off the wedding. Forever."

"He—oh, Mattie, that's his depression talking, not Amos!"

"I tried to tell him that," she explained as she picked up her dress and underthings, "but he insisted I'm not to be his caretaker—not to marry a man who'll never be strong again."

Rosetta's hand fluttered to her mouth and her face clouded over. "I'm so sorry," she whispered. "When Truman said Amos was in a bad way, I never dreamed he'd sunk so low emotionally."

"Me neither. So I've not got any appetite for dinner or company right now." Mattie shrugged, blinking back tears. "I'll start again tomorrow and figure out where to go from there. *Gut* night, Rosetta."

Bless her heart, her youngest sister understood Mattie's need to sort things out alone. Mattie watched Rosetta leave and then turned to look out the window again. The snow was still blowing with a vengeance and the ground below was turning white. It was just as well that the days were short and the nights longer at this time of the year. The thought of sleeping in suited her mood perfectly.

Mattie let down her hair and brushed it, trying not

to imagine how Amos might've reacted to this simple ritual after they'd married, for he'd never seen her with her hair down. Mattie doused the lamp and sat in her rocking chair with an afghan wrapped around her, knowing sleep wouldn't come anytime soon. Back and forth she rocked, slowly, wondering if this would be the way she spent the rest of her years . . . alone in her room . . .

After a little while Mattie heard whispering in the hallway. Behind her, the door creaked and someone entered her room, but she didn't bother to turn around. The soft glow of a lamp made the furniture cast shadows on the wall.

"Nobody felt like cooking supper, Mattie," Christine said.

"And since it's just us girls in the lodge tonight," Ruby chimed in, "we thought a hen party might be fun. How about joining us?"

Mattie smelled something tantalizing. She turned in her chair, ready to insist that she was in no mood for a party. "Oh!" she blurted. "You're all ready for bed, and it's not even six o'clock."

"*Jah*, it's the sort of night to just get comfy and cozy," Beulah said. She was holding a small plate with a ball of goat cheese on it, smiling at Mattie. Her silvery hair cascaded over one shoulder and pooled in her lap as she sat on the edge of the bed in her flannel nightgown.

"And what better time to eat goodies instead of healthy stuff like veggies?" Rosetta asked with a giggle. She set a warm crockery bowl in Mattie's lap. "I can't recall the last time I made chocolate gravy, so I thought I'd refresh our memories about how delicious it is!"

"And we can spoon that chocolate gravy over these pumpkin muffins," Laura suggested as she sat cross-legged on the rug. "I made them for tomorrow's breakfast, but why wait until then when they're warm now?"

"Or we could dip stuff in that chocolate gravy," Phoebe said as she passed a plate of apple slices and cheese chunks under Mattie's nose.

"And we've got a plate of Deborah's cookies, too," Christine said as she pulled an armchair beside Mattie's rocker. "But mainly, we have each other, Sister. We couldn't just leave you all by your lonesome after Rosetta told us what Amos said. We're all in this together, Mattie."

Mattie blinked rapidly. "I'm not very *gut* company tonight, so—"

"Phooey on that! We all love you no matter what, Aunt Mattie," Laura insisted. "And besides, this is a lot more fun than dirtying up dishes and pans and having to clean up the kitchen after we eat. We brought paper plates—"

"And Happy Birthday napkins," Rosetta said as she took a plate and a napkin and passed the stacks around. "Because no matter what Amos did, you'll be having a birthday on Saturday. We all want to celebrate the day you were born, because if you hadn't been—why, we wouldn't be at Promise Lodge!"

"I can't imagine my life without you, Mattie," Christine added. "You've always been the starter-upper, the sister with the best ideas."

"When Beulah and I first arrived and saw how much garden you'd already planted and heard your plans for this place, we knew this was where we belonged, too,"

Ruby insisted with a nod. "So don't go thinking your ideas and your efforts don't matter, Mattie, just because Amos is feeling down on himself."

"We also figured we could set up a schedule so the rest of us gals can take turns looking in on Amos—or not, if he gets cranky with us," Beulah suggested. "If he wants to stew in his own juice, maybe that's the best way to handle him. I suspect Amos has gotten so accustomed to all you've done for him, Mattie, that he has no idea how fast his house and clothes will get smelly without somebody looking after him."

Mattie didn't know what to think. Her sisters, her nieces, and the two Kuhns were all clad in their flannelette nighties with their hair down, passing around the food they'd brought—for a pajama party like she'd had with her sisters and the neighbor girls when they were young. She still didn't think she was hungry, but she split a warm pumpkin muffin on her paper plate and spooned a generous amount of chocolate gravy over it. "It would be very thoughtful of you to look in on Amos," she murmured. "He's quite capable of doing laundry and keeping his house picked up—but that was before he was in a wheelchair. I don't know what's come over him. He seems to have lost all faith in ever recuperating."

"He's depressed and disappointed," Rosetta said as she took a gingerbread cookie from the plate. "He was expecting the doctor to know what's wrong with his legs—like any of us would. Truman told me he and Eli offered to build a ramp up to Amos's porch so he could come and go on his own once he's allowed outside, but Amos wanted no part of that, either."

"Amos is used to being up and around, busy at

building things," Christine put in. She took a few slices of apple and cheese and passed the plate to Mattie. "He doesn't like to feel useless, and if he peeked out from behind his curtains, I imagine it really bothered him to watch the other fellows putting the roof on Roman's house without his help."

Mattie nodded. "You're all right," she murmured. Then she paused to savor the rich sweetness of the muffin drenched in warm chocolate gravy. "Dr. Townsend authorized some physical therapy sessions—but not until Amos's concussion improves. I think that's part of his problem, too. Amos isn't used to sitting. Or *waiting.*"

"I've always considered Amos a very patient man," Beulah mused aloud, "but then, his life was going just fine until he fell off the roof."

For a few moments, the women stopped talking as they enjoyed their food. Mattie watched them close their eyes and sigh with contentment, realizing how grateful she was to be surrounded by so much compassion, so much love. It wasn't the same happiness she'd feel if she were getting married on Saturday, but it was a gratifying peacefulness that came from knowing these women would do everything in their power to make her feel loved and appreciated.

"I hear Frances might be in need of some cheering up—and assistance—as well," Christine said. She plucked a couple of apple slices from Laura's plate and dragged them through the chocolate gravy on her plate. "It sounds as if Floyd is still in much worse shape than Amos, even though he's getting therapy at home. Gloria has told me he stumbles a lot, even with a cane, because his left leg is so unpredictable," she said with a shake of her head. "He can't always keep his food in his mouth while he's chewing, and they have to be careful that he doesn't choke because the stroke affected his ability to swallow."

"We have to wonder if Floyd would be farther along the road to recovery had he stayed in a dark room like he was supposed to," Mattie murmured.

"Or if he'd have stayed in the hospital that first time instead of being in such a hurry to get home. He hasn't been himself since Amos fell on him." Rosetta took a bite and moaned softly. "Now *this* is heavenly— goat cheese spread on a pumpkin muffin with chocolate gravy spread on it!"

"Oh, I'm going to try that!" Phoebe said. She smiled at everyone around their cozy circle. "You know, we really should do this pajama party thing more often. What with winter nearly here, who will care that we're not dressed in the evenings? It gets dark by five o'clock."

"What if we started a crochet club to pass these longer evenings?" Ruby suggested. "Our Mennonite fellowship is big on making blankets and stocking caps and such for homeless folks."

"We could call it the PPCC—the Pajama Party Crochet Club!" Laura said with a chuckle. "I like it! I have a big bag of yarn stashed in my closet, too."

"We left our yarn for our nieces in Versailles," Beulah said, "but I noticed the mercantile in Forest Grove has quite a nice display of yarn and fabrics and such. Maybe we need to make a trip into town when the roads are clear."

"I want to make an afghan for Preacher Amos,"

Laura declared. "Maybe if he wrapped himself up in a snugly blanket, he'd be in a better mood."

"And I want to make one for Bishop Floyd," Phoebe said without missing a beat. "And what about Mary Kate? And her baby? They'll be needing little blankets and booties and caps—"

"Now you're talking!" Rosetta said. "We can plan some happiness for all of these folks. And it'll make the long winter evenings a lot more fun."

Mattie found herself smiling, feeling purposeful again. "You ladies are *gut* medicine," she said as she gazed at each of them. "You've helped me remember that so many folks have a lot more reasons to feel blue than I do—and you've given me something to look forward to. A crochet club wouldn't have interested me if I were getting married on Saturday."

Christine chuckled. "It's just my guess, but I predict you and Amos will get together again. Once he gets past this rough spot in the road—once we find a way to get him motivated, doing something he can handle while he's in his wheelchair—I suspect he'll realize he made a big mistake, calling off the wedding. He's loved you nearly all his life, Mattie. And he hasn't really stopped loving you. He's just gotten sidetracked."

"*Jah*, I think our patience and prayers—and an afghan and some warm food now and again—will go a long way toward helping Amos recover," Ruby said. "Once the doctor says he can come out of the dark, I'm thinking the Amos we know and love will figure out a way to get up and get moving again—or he'll figure out what to do with himself if he can't build houses anymore."

Mattie smiled, feeling much better as she and her

sisters and friends chatted while they ate. *"For where two or three are gathered together in my name, there am I in the midst of them."*

Jesus's words rang true. These women of faith had put together a party to lift her spirits, and Mattie felt the Lord was very much among them as they talked of ways to help Amos and the bishop and Mary Kate. She could move forward now, secure in her life no matter what Amos had decided about marrying her. After all, she'd gotten the idea to move to Promise Lodge when she'd been a woman alone.

Chapter Seventeen

After he finished the milking early on Sunday morning, Roman headed down the snow-packed road, back to Amos's place. The rising sun made tiny diamonds sparkle on the five inches of snow that had fallen in the night, adding a layer of crisp freshness to the lawns and hillsides of Promise Lodge. As Roman passed his new house, he sighed. Lester had installed his windows and siding, the other men had put in his kitchen appliances, and the girls had painted all of his rooms, so the place was finished enough to live in. Roman really wanted to settle into his house, but he also understood that Amos needed help—assistance he was either too proud or too depressed to ask for— so he planned to stay in the preacher's spare bedroom until Amos's health improved.

"*Gut* morning, Amos! You up yet?" Roman called out as he entered the front room. In the kitchen, he filled the percolator with water and coffee and put it on the stove. When Roman paused in the doorway of the dark bedroom, he saw that the preacher had maneuvered himself out of bed and into his wheel-chair, but he was still in his long johns.

"No church today," Roman pointed out, "so what're you going to wear? It's a *gut* day for a heavy shirt, or maybe a sweater, chilly as it is."

"It'll take a lot more than a shirt and sweater to make me feel warm again," Amos groused. "What's clean? That'll make the decision easy for me, won't it?"

Roman bit back a remark about the preacher's irritable mood, because pointing it out would only make Amos grouchier. "Do you want me to do your laundry tomorrow?" he asked as he went to the nearly empty closet. "I've heard Beulah, Christine, and Mamm have offered to wash your clothes, but you've not allowed them to."

"Hate to be a bother."

Roman shrugged, choosing a flannel shirt of deep green. "So run the washer from your wheelchair. Could you do that?"

Amos let out a humorless laugh. "I'm not supposed to leave this cave, remember? The doctor has turned me into a mole, and I'll soon be as white as an albino from lack of sunlight."

"So I'll close the curtains in the rest of your house," Roman challenged. "The doctor didn't limit you to staying in one room. You're only to avoid bright light."

Amos glared at him. "What *gut* would that do? It's not like I can reach the stove—"

"Fine. Put this on." Roman took the shirt from its hanger, deciding it was time for a change of topic. "I've got a favor to ask, Amos. Would it be all right if I cleaned up your sleigh and took it out for a spin? We've got enough snow on the ground for some nice riding now."

"We do?" Amos murmured ruefully. "I—I really feel out of touch. What day is it?"

"Sunday, the twenty-second of November."

"Oh." Amos put the shirt on over the long johns he'd slept in, shaking his head. "I missed your *mamm*'s birthday yesterday . . . not to mention the wedding. How's she doing with that?"

Roman considered his answer. Should he tell Amos about the hen party the ladies had held the night he jilted Mamm? Or make the preacher feel guilty about breaking her heart? "She and the other gals went into Forest Grove yesterday to shop for yarn and fabric," he hedged. "Phoebe and Laura are all excited about the crochet club they've started. They're going to make blankets and booties for Mary Kate's baby, and afghans for folks who need them. It's a mission project to occupy the cold winter evenings."

Amos grunted. "They might as well crochet. It's not like they've got husbands to look after."

As Roman opened the dresser drawer, looking for clean pants, he frowned. It seemed that no matter what he said this morning, Amos was taking exception to it. "At least they're busy and happy, doing something useful," Roman pointed out. "Maybe I should wheel you over there so you could learn to crochet. It would be an improvement over how you've been spending your time alone, ain't so?"

As soon as the words left his mouth, Roman knew he'd been impolite. But maybe he'd made a point. Maybe Amos would take the hint.

With a heavy sigh, the preacher bowed his head. "They wouldn't let me join them—and I can't say as I'd blame them, either. I apologize for my cranky attitude, son. And I'd be delighted if you'd take that sleigh out and enjoy it," Amos went on in a lighter voice. "Hitch Mabel up to it, would you? She loves the snow and she probably wonders why I've not been getting her out for some exercise."

"I'll do that, *jah. Denki*, Amos." Roman flashed him a smile. "If you don't think you'll be needing anything after breakfast, I'll go over to the Lehmans' and help with the chores—and ask Mary Kate if she'll ride along with me. Unless you think the sleigh might need some repairs."

"No, no—the sleigh'll have some dust on it, but it's plenty sturdy. Nothing like the roof that gave way under me." Amos pulled his pants over his legs, allowed Roman to help him stand, and then got his pants fastened. "Seems to me Gloria's the girl who's trying to look after you, Roman. What'll she say when you take her sister sleigh-riding instead?"

Roman shrugged, although he'd been thinking about this very situation. "I'm going to have to say it straight out, and tell Gloria I'm not interested in dating her. Never have been."

"*Jah*, that's what you have to do with women sometimes—tell them how it's going to be, if they can't see reality for themselves." Amos sat back down in his wheelchair with a sigh. "That's why I broke up with your mother. I really didn't want to, Roman, but I couldn't shackle her to a man who'll need so much care, maybe forever. It was in Mattie's best interest. For her own *gut*."

Roman didn't reply. Did Amos truly believe he'd done himself or Mamm any favors by calling off the wedding? From what Roman had observed, his mother was moving beyond her broken engagement a lot faster than Amos was—but he suspected a part of her would always be disappointed.

And Gloria's going to be mighty disappointed when you tell her you're not interested in her, Roman thought as he strode up the road to the Lehman place after breakfast. *How will you handle her reaction? It won't be pretty . . .*

Mary Kate lolled in the recliner, tilted all the way back, feeling very bulky and uncomfortable. Her legs were swollen, she was exhausted from not sleeping well for the past few weeks—and she was ready to deliver the baby and be done with this discomfort. Minerva had checked her over a couple of days ago and was predicting an early December birth, but Mary Kate wasn't sure how she could possibly endure this pregnancy for another week or more.

It didn't help that her *dat* had hobbled into the front room to stare at her. He pointed to her belly and tried to say something—spoke very slowly and with great deliberation—but Mary Kate couldn't understand a word he said. It bothered her to look at him, because one side of his face hung slack and motionless while the other side displayed his agitation at not being able to speak clearly.

"I'm all right, Dat," she assured him. "Just feeling as big as a house. Wishing this baby could be born *right now.*"

The eyebrow above Dat's good eye rose as he waved her off. When they heard loud knocks on the door, he went to answer it, rocking unsteadily from side to side as his cane tapped the hardwood floor. Mary Kate prayed he wouldn't stumble and fall again, as he had last night. She hoped Mamm would steer their visitor into the kitchen rather than into the front room, where she was sprawled in the recliner, looking as though she'd swallowed a beach ball.

When Mary Kate heard Roman's voice, she groaned. Even though she enjoyed his company a lot, she really didn't want him to see her this way.

"I've finished your barn chores," Roman was saying, "and I found a shovel and cleared your walk and your porch steps. What else can I do for you while I'm here?"

"*Denki* so much, Roman," Mamm said. "We appreciate it, especially because you're helping out over at Amos's place, too."

"Oh, Roman, that's so *sweet* of you to do those chores for us again," Gloria gushed.

Mary Kate closed her eyes, trying not to imagine the cloying expression on her sister's face. Sensing he might come into the front room, she pulled the afghan on her lap up higher, to camouflage the bulge of her belly—but now her midsection resembled a beach ball with a ripple-striped sweater stretched over it. She struggled to raise the chair back into a sitting position, but either her arm muscles had degenerated into wet noodles or the chair's mechanism was broken.

"It's *gut* to see you, Mary Kate," Roman murmured as he approached her chair. "Let me help you. You're at an awkward angle to be—"

"Everything about me feels a lot more than *awkward*," she muttered. "And I don't think I have a single angle left. I'm all bulges and curves and—"

"This, too, shall pass, sweetie." Roman smiled at her as he righted the recliner and then stood beside her.

"They tell me you forget all about this discomfort once you're holding your baby. But truth be told, I think you're beautiful."

Mary Kate was ready to protest, but she saw Gloria coming into the front room—probably to horn in on her conversation with Roman. "You're very kind," she whispered. "Minerva says it'll be another week or so. She thinks I'm doing very well."

"That's what we like to hear." Roman's face lit up and he leaned closer. "What would you think of joining me for a sleigh ride, Mary Kate? Amos has a wonderful old sleigh in the shed, and he says I can hitch it to his mare—"

"A sleigh ride! Oh, Roman, I'd love to go!" Gloria said. She hurried around to the other side of the recliner, where she could look directly at Roman. "Mary Kate's been lying around feeling fat and cranky all day, so I doubt she'll be up to going, but I—"

"Gloria, with all due respect," Roman said in a low, firm tone, "I invited Mary Kate to go with me. She can answer for herself."

Mary Kate's heart thudded in her chest. Her sister looked stunned—and then incredulous.

"You can't really want to spend your time with Mary Kate," Gloria protested. "Why, in another week or so she'll have a baby to tend and—and she won't have time to—"

"I'm fully aware of that, Gloria," Roman continued in that same purposeful voice. He straightened to his full height, looking directly at Gloria as she began to clasp and unclasp her hands. "I appreciate your interest in me," he murmured gently, "but I don't want to date you, Gloria."

Mary Kate braced herself. Her older sister's expression was undergoing one change after another, displaying surprise, then outrage, disbelief, and mortification. Gloria suddenly reached across the recliner to give Roman's cheek a resounding slap.

"Gloria Margaret Lehman!" Mamm called from the kitchen. "That was uncalled for. You're to apologize to Roman—and your sister—this instant!"

But Gloria was already hurrying upstairs. The sound of her crying echoed in the stairway, followed by the heavy tattoo of her footsteps in the upstairs hallway and the *bang!* of her bedroom door.

"Sorry," Roman murmured.

Mary Kate fought a smile. It was wrong to enjoy her sister's hissy fit, but she was feeling a whole lot better than she had a few moments ago. "Did she draw blood?" she murmured. "A few times when we were kids, Gloria put some fingernail into it when she slapped me."

Roman chuckled. "Well, I probably deserved that slap," he said as he rubbed his stinging cheek, "but I said what I had to say. I'm not interested in your sister, and I've never liked the way she puts you down, Mary Kate."

Mamm was hurrying up to them, wringing her dish towel between her hands as Dat hobbled awkwardly behind her. "Roman, I'm so sorry Gloria struck you," she said as she studied his cheek. "Envy's not a pretty emotion, and my daughter doesn't handle it well."

Dat appeared very agitated, as well. He glanced from Roman to Mary Kate and back to Roman, expressing his dismay with a one-sided shrug and a stiff shake of his head. Dat pointed toward the stairway, as though to say that either he or Mamm ought to go upstairs and give Gloria a talking-to.

"Let's leave Gloria be for now, Floyd," Mamm said. "And let's you and I sit in the kitchen so the kids can have some time without us gawking at them. I'll make us some cocoa. Come on, now."

Mary Kate's heart swelled with gratitude to her mother. Did Roman really believe she was beautiful? Or was he just saying that to be nice?

Is that a problem, him being nice? For once, somebody stood up to Gloria and told her what's what—a very fine young fellow who wants to spend time with you.

"A sleigh ride sounds like fun. And it's so pretty outside, with all the fresh snow," Mary Kate murmured. When she dared to reach toward Roman, he gently held her hand between his two much larger, stronger ones. "Soon enough, I probably won't be able to go—"

"I'll take you anytime you want, Mary Kate. We can wrap the baby in blankets and take off across the hills."

What a picture he painted. Mary Kate badly wanted to believe his interest in her would continue while she was confined to the house with her newborn baby, but for now she didn't concern herself with the future. She smiled up at Roman. "If you can give me a few minutes to dress more warmly—"

"I have to clean the sleigh and polish it up a bit," Roman said. "Name a time that suits you, and I'll be here."

Mary Kate suddenly felt as giddy as a little girl at Christmas. "How about two? I'd ask you to have dinner with us, but Gloria will still be in a snit."

Roman squeezed her hand and released it. "See you at two, then. I'm so glad you want to go, Mary Kate."

She watched Roman stride toward the kitchen to say good-bye to her parents. Was this turn of events real, or was she caught up in a dream? All those times Gloria had had a date and she'd been stuck at home, Mary Kate had imagined herself going out with someone even cuter and more wonderful than her sister was seeing—and today her fantasy had come true.

She slid out of the recliner and waddled toward the stairs, feeling better than she had for days. Roman deserved a girl wearing a fresh dress and a smile, a young lady-in-waiting who could rise above her weariness to have some fun.

So that's who Mary Kate decided to be.

Chapter Eighteen

"What a beautiful afternoon," Rosetta murmured. "Is it just me, or does the snow have a special sparkle to it today?"

Walking beside her, Truman chuckled. "Far as I can see, all the sparkle starts with you and spreads over everything else, Rosetta. You're right. It's a fabulous afternoon."

Rosetta tightened the arm she'd slung around his waist. "I suppose part of this sensation is enjoying our first winter at Promise Lodge," she said softly. "The lodge and the new houses look so pretty with snow on their rooftops and smoke rising from their chimneys. The hillsides are so clean and crisp—so perfect, without so much as a footprint."

"Unlike the yard around the lodge and Noah's place, where he's been throwing Queenie's Frisbee. From our place up on the hill, Mom and I love to watch out our front window when they play in the snow." Truman reached the end of the road, just past where Marlin Kurtz's family lived, and turned around to survey the expanse of property around them. "Do you—or any of these other folks—ice-skate, Rosetta? By Christmas the ice on Rainbow Lake will support us, most likely."

Rosetta shook her head. "My sisters and I have never lived close enough to a pond to learn how," she replied. "We had roller skates when we were kids, but I suspect it's an entirely different skill, balancing on a single blade rather than having four wheels underneath each foot."

"That can be my winter mission, then—teaching you to skate. The church camp was always closed during the winter, so my older brothers and I had the frozen lake to ourselves," Truman reminisced. "We played pretty rough hockey games, but it was all in *gut* fun. Now Stan and Dave are married and raising their families out in Indiana. We lost our younger brothers, Pete and John, when a car crashed into the back end of the buggy they were in, back when we were all still in school."

"Oh, I'm sorry to hear that," Rosetta murmured. "I'm blessed that all of my sisters are still alive—and living in the lodge with me."

Truman's smile brightened and he tightened the arm he'd slung around her shoulders. "*Jah*, you sisters are a tight-knit bunch. An inspiration to us all about moving past your losses and making the most of your lives. My mother goes on and on about how she enjoys spending time amongst you."

"Your *mamm*'s a special lady."

"She is," Truman agreed as a pensive expression stole over his face. "And how's Mattie doing? When Amos told me he called off the wedding—and why—

I gave him quite an earful about how he'd probably take longer to recover now, on account of how depressed he's getting. Not that I changed his mind."

"Mattie's sad, but like you say, she's moving forward and finding other purposes for her life." Rosetta sighed. "We're all concerned about Amos, though. Roman tells us his legs seem to be getting weaker from not getting any exercise. Eli and Marlin are figuring to construct a ramp up to his porch and install some grab bars in his house—and Noah has suggested a workshop added on to the back of Amos's place, where he'd be able to build small furniture and do some woodworking, even if he's confined to his wheelchair."

"He needs something to occupy himself, for sure," Truman agreed. "I've told him I'll drive him to his doctor's appointment this week and then we'll get his physical therapy set up. Maybe those therapists can get Amos motivated to work with his hands and focus on doing things he enjoys."

"If he finds a new way to generate some income, I think he'll feel better about himself—and about life in general," Rosetta added with a nod. She shielded her eyes from the sun to gaze toward the entry to the Promise Lodge property. "Is the snow glare affecting me, or is that a sleigh turning off the road?"

"It is." Truman rested his head against hers, pulling her closer as they watched the horse-drawn vehicle glide across the snow. "Oh, but it would be fun to take you for a sleigh ride, sweetheart," he murmured. He quickly kissed her cheek. "Who's the sleigh belong to? The two folks riding in it are so bundled up I can't tell who they are."

"Let's find out." Waving her arm high above her head, Rosetta grasped Truman's hand and they jogged down the hill toward the lodge. She grinned when the passengers returned her wave, and the sleigh headed up toward them. "Why, I think that's Roman and Mary Kate under those blankets! I didn't know he had a sleigh."

"But he does have a girlfriend, obviously—and I'm pleased to see Gloria didn't play the third wheel," Truman remarked. "Don't get me wrong. Gloria's a nice enough girl—"

"But she's been trying so hard to make Roman notice her, we're all embarrassed for him." Rosetta's smile widened as the sleigh came closer. The horse's harness had bells on it, and the merry sound of their jingling made the perfect accompaniment to the snowy, happy scene. "Isn't that Amos's mare, Mabel?"

"I believe you're right. Hullo, you two!" Truman called out. "What a fine sight you make, dashing through the snow."

Mabel whickered, shaking her head—and the bells—as she halted a few feet away. Even though Mary Kate was swaddled in blankets up to her chin, with her black bonnet tied tightly over her head, she appeared as light-hearted as Rosetta had ever seen her. Roman seemed delighted to be keeping her company.

"What a beautiful sleigh," Rosetta said as she approached it. She ran her gloved hand over the seat's curved wooden back, which was upholstered in deep green velvet. "How long have you had this sleigh and not told me about it, Roman?"

Her nephew's laughter rang out over the snowy

hillside. "Amos had it stashed under a tarp in the shed, so I asked if I could borrow it. Cleaned it up a bit—"

"And it's padded in all the right places," Mary Kate chimed in. "I was feeling pretty achy at home in the recliner—until Roman talked me into coming along for a ride."

Rosetta smiled. That was young love talking, if ever she'd heard it.

"Could we possibly take it for a spin after you two are finished?" Truman asked eagerly. "I'll tend to the mare—"

"Or we could give Mabel a rest and hitch the sleigh to my gelding," Rosetta suggested. "Chuckie could use a *gut* run, and he's sure-footed in the snow."

Roman looked at Mary Kate. "What do you say? Have you had enough for now, or do you want to loop around the campground one more time?"

Mary Kate's brown eyes sparkled. "What if we went inside to visit with your *mamm* and the others while Truman switches the horses? Then he and Rosetta could give us a ride back up to the house and be on their way."

"Sounds like a plan," Roman replied as he took up the lines again. "I'll pull up closer to the lodge so you don't have to walk through so much snow."

As the mare took off toward the tall, timbered lodge with another shake of the sleigh bells, Rosetta felt happy all over. "Unless I miss my guess, my nephew's going to be getting hitched in the near future. Did you see how both of them were glowing?"

Truman tucked her hand under his elbow as they walked the rest of the way down the hill. "If anybody can handle starting out married life with a wee one, I think Roman's the right fellow for the job. Got a steady head on his shoulders and a *gut* heart—not to mention a house all set up for a family."

Rosetta nodded, thinking those qualities applied to Truman, as well. And someday, God willing, she hoped to be the woman he took as his wife. To have and to hold . . .

After Truman harnessed Chuckie, he ran his hand along the bay's back, checking the leather, the lines, and the tarnished bells. "This tack could use some saddle soap to soften it up," he remarked to Rosetta, "but the sleigh looks to be in fine condition. Makes me wonder how long Amos has had it, because you don't often see such carving details in the wood these days."

He watched Rosetta running her gloved hand along the rounded back of the seat. Truman had found her lovely in the bright sparkle of the afternoon, yet here in the unlit barn she appeared even more enticing. When she met his gaze, his pulse thundered. "Oh my," he said in a breathy voice. "We'd better move along or I'm likely to find a warm spot in the hay for some serious kissing."

Rosetta's low chuckle lingered like the wisps of vapor framing her face. "I'm not supposed to encourage that sort of talk," she whispered, "but I'd be lying if I said I wasn't thinking the same thing. Roman and Mary Kate will be watching for us, wondering what we're—"

"They can wait."

Truman started around the back of the sleigh,

pleased when Rosetta met him halfway and reached for him as he slipped his arms around her. Their heavy coats formed a bulky barrier between their bodies, but not so much that he couldn't savor her soft curves as his mouth explored hers. He reminded himself that they were adults in total control of their hormones and emotions, yet with every sweet taste of Rosetta's willing lips Truman yearned for more.

He broke away with a final, lingering kiss and a sigh. "I'm not supposed to let my mind wander in this direction, I suppose," he murmured, "but if Floyd doesn't recover from his stroke—can't carry out his duties—maybe there's hope that a new bishop will allow us to marry."

"Or maybe I'll tire of following that Amish rule about marrying outside the faith and become your wife anyway," Rosetta whispered. She gazed into his eyes, her expression intense. "Every day lately, I've asked Jesus if He would cast me into the fire for loving a man who's not of the Old Order."

Truman swallowed so hard his Adam's apple hurt. The last thing he intended was to tempt Rosetta beyond her religion, causing the potential separation between her, her sisters, and her close Amish friends. Yet her question sent a tingle up his limbs. "What's His answer?"

"I'm still waiting, to be sure it's God I'm hearing rather than my own selfish, wayward heart," she replied.

Truman rested his forehead against hers, praying that he, too, wasn't allowing his thoughts to stray. "Much as I dislike the punishment of shunning—as many ways as I would have to reorganize my land-scaping and snow plowing business—I've wondered if I shouldn't convert to your faith," he admitted in a tremulous voice. "I'm not sure how much longer I can . . . wait."

Rosetta hugged him hard and then stepped away. "I—I wish this love were simpler."

"We'll figure it out," he vowed as he, too, put some distance between them. "Meanwhile, Chuckie is wondering why we hitched him up, if we're just going to stay in the barn."

With a nervous laugh, Rosetta got up into the sleigh while Truman slid the barn door open. The bright snow glare made him squint as he sucked in a few deep breaths of the frosty air to settle himself. When he realized Rosetta was clucking to the gelding, he stepped aside to let them out—and then hollered when she urged the horse into a fast trot.

"Hey! Aren't you forgetting somebody?"

Rosetta's laughter drifted back to him, as merry as the jingle of the sleigh bells. As Truman closed the door, he watched the horse-drawn sleigh race across the garden plots, now covered with snow, and then loop around the row of brown cottages behind the lodge. Roman and Mary Kate stepped out onto the porch with Mattie and Christine, who clutched their shawls around their shoulders as they waved at their sister. Truman figured he might as well start walking toward them. Would Rosetta take off without him again after the kids settled into the sleigh's backseat?

Moments later, she steered the sleigh toward Truman and stopped the horse a few feet away from him. "Going my way?" she teased. "I'm not one for picking up strange men, but for a cute fellow like you I'll make an exception."

Truman had to chuckle. Roman and Mary Kate were laughing in the backseat, assuming he would take the lines and insist on being the driver—but why not let Rosetta have her fun? She was prettiest this way, when an expectant smile lit her face and her brown eyes sparkled. Truman slid onto the seat and adjusted the blankets around them.

"Forward ho!" he exclaimed, waving as they left Christine and Mattie behind.

When they'd let Roman and Mary Kate off at the Lehman place, Rosetta offered him the lines. "You're a *gut* sport, Truman. The look on your face when I shot out of the barn was priceless."

"*You* are priceless," he insisted. "How about if you drive, Rosetta? I've not allowed that before, but for a sweet girl like you, I'll make an exception. My fate's in your hands."

Rosetta laughed as she lightly clapped the lines on Chuckie's back. "You're in big trouble now, Wickey," she teased. "We might not make it back anytime soon."

As Truman scooted closer and slipped his arm around Rosetta's shoulders, he felt alight with sheer happiness. "It's not how far you travel, but who's beside you that counts," he murmured. "Let's roll."

Chapter Nineteen

"What's your plan for happiness today?" Rosetta asked. She stood beside Mattie at the kitchen counter mixing apple chunks, grapes, and walnut pieces into their favorite salad for Thanksgiving dinner. "In a few minutes, Roman and Noah will be bringing Amos over. I know you'll be polite, of course, but I suspect it'll be a little tricky to have him here for most of the day."

Mattie shrugged. "Everyone who lives in Promise Lodge will be here," she pointed out. "It's a fine idea for all of us to celebrate Thanksgiving together rather than in our separate homes. I don't dislike Amos, you know," she said softly. "I've simply chosen to honor his wishes by staying out of his home. Out of his life."

Rosetta smiled knowingly. "From what Ruby tells me, he's not been keeping himself up—and he's been really moody when they've gone over to clean. Maybe he'll see how well you're doing and realize what a mistake he's made."

"And maybe, what with the curtains all closed, it'll be so dim he won't see me at all," Mattie teased. Perhaps a change of subject was in order. She didn't think there was anything left to say about the relationship that had ended a week ago today. "I'm pleased the Kuhns went back to their brother's place for a few days, but it'll be different, not having them here for dinner with us."

"I'm glad Lester went back home to his family in Ohio, too," Rosetta said. "His wife surely must've missed him while he was helping Floyd establish their siding business here."

"She and the kids have a nice new home to move into, though," Christine chimed in as she slipped her hands into oven mitts. "And they've got time between now and next spring to sell their place in Sugarcreek."

"I suspect Frances and the girls will really miss having Lester around," Mattie added. "Lester's *gut* at keeping Floyd busy at things—focused, instead of wandering aimlessly from one activity to the next. Every time I see the bishop, I think he's slipping further away from us."

"Beulah thinks Amos has also slipped a notch or two, as far as being the fellow whose company we all enjoyed so much," Christine said. She opened one of the ovens to check the three big hens she was roasting. "When I was cleaning his place, I told him he needs to get out amongst folks—needs to get busy at something—but Amos said his headaches are so bothersome he can't focus long enough to finish anything, or even to read."

Mattie nodded. "Dr. Townsend said he might have a short attention span until his concussion has healed."

"Truman was none too pleased when Amos refused to go for his appointment yesterday," Rosetta said with a shake of her head.

Mattie sighed. She'd never figured Amos Troyer for

a man who'd give up so quickly, or who would allow his health to deteriorate . . . the way Marvin had when he'd ignored his diabetes. Maybe Amos had done her a favor, after all, when he'd called off the wedding. "Did anything ever come of the idea for building Amos a ramp and a woodworking shop?" she asked. "He needs something to do. Needs a way to be more independent if he's going to be stuck in that wheelchair for any length of time."

"You're exactly right," Christine said. "He's never been one for sitting around."

Rosetta shrugged, appearing rueful. "Truman's told me Amos turned down the ramp and shop offer flatter than a pancake," she murmured. "Amos seems to be sinking deeper into depression, even though the doctor gave him some pills to help. I never figured Amos for a quitter."

"I'll check the venison roasts," Mattie said. She was more concerned about Amos's well-being than she cared to admit to her sisters, but she'd done as he'd asked. She hadn't become his caretaker. As the aroma of the carrots, onions, and meat wafted around her, Mattie couldn't help recalling how Amos enjoyed the way she prepared venison with vegetables.

"Is it time to cut the pies? We've got the tables all set," Phoebe said eagerly. "The Kurtzes are coming down the hill—"

"And the Peterscheims are on the way, too—and of course the boys are running ahead and throwing snowballs at each other and Queenie," Laura put in as she glanced out the window.

"Hah! We'd better stick these fried pies in the pantry if we're to have any left for later this afternoon," Rosetta teased as she grabbed the container they were in. "Lavern, Johnny, and Menno eat more than any six men. Makes me wonder how Alma keeps any food in the house."

Mattie glanced out the other kitchen window, wondering who'd gone to help Roman with Amos and how they were going to get him here with his wheelchair. When a big pickup rumbled up the road, she had her answer. "I'm certainly thankful for Truman," she murmured. "Think of all the times he and his truck have come to our rescue lately."

Rosetta stepped up beside Mattie at the window, watching as Roman rolled Amos out onto his porch. The two younger men joined hands and made a chair for Amos, with arms behind his back and under his backside. "*Jah*, he has," she murmured. "And yet Truman's considered joining the Amish Church, selling his truck and his motorized equipment to the fellows on his landscaping crew—"

"No! Really?" Mattie gazed into Rosetta's deep brown eyes. "I thought he had serious objections to some of our ways."

Her younger sister shrugged. "We're trying to find an honorable solution. Bishop Floyd's bluster doesn't change the way we feel about each other."

"Glad to hear that! Don't give up on such a *gut* man," Mattie said, hugging Rosetta's shoulders. When the front door opened and voices filled the lobby, they went to welcome the Kurtzes. Minerva was carrying a large lidded pan, and Harley followed her into the kitchen with jugs of cider.

"I think we've got enough mashed potatoes to feed the five thousand," Minerva teased. "Which oven shall I put them in to keep them warm?"

"And we've got candied yams, too!" Deborah said

as Noah followed her into the kitchen carrying a large glass casserole dish. "Someone we know says it wouldn't be Thanksgiving dinner without them."

"That would be my younger son," Mattie teased as she hugged the newlyweds. "Roman won't give you two cents for sweet potatoes with syrup and marshmallows all over them."

Coming in behind them, Irene Wickey smiled and greeted everyone. "I figured some pumpkin crunch would be a *gut* choice," she said as she handed the pan to Rosetta. "All the flavor of a pumpkin pie—"

"But you don't have to make a crust!" Rosetta teased. "We'll let one of the girls cut this—and I'll take your coat for you. We're so glad you and Truman have joined us today."

As the women brought their food into the kitchen and the men congregated in the dining room to chat, Mattie became immersed in the details of getting their big meal ready to serve. It was such a blessing that Mary Kate looked perkier today, and that she and Gloria worked as a contented team, filling water glasses and pouring milk for the kids. As the venison and roasted hens were carved and bowls were filled with potatoes, gravy, stuffing, and other favorite dishes, Lily, Fannie, Laura, and Phoebe carried the hot food to the tables—and kept the younger boys from roughhousing in the dining room as they awaited the meal.

At last everyone sat down at the two long tables that had been placed end to end. Mattie noticed that Floyd was seated at one end, with Frances and Mary Kate on either side of him to help him eat. It bothered Mattie to look at their bishop for very long, because the left side of his face was still sagging and he appeared very withdrawn. He was a far cry from the man who'd come here to set the folks of Promise Lodge on the proper path to salvation. As she gazed along the other side of the table, taking in her sisters and the friends who were bowing their heads, she saw that Amos sat at the other end in his wheelchair, between Roman and Truman.

Mattie gasped. Amos needed a haircut, and he sat bent over—*and he looks about a hundred years old*, she thought as she quickly closed her eyes to join in the silent prayer. How had he gone so far downhill in only a week? Was Amos becoming physically incapacitated, or had he given up?

Looks like Amos needs the kind of help only You can give him, Lord, Mattie prayed fervently. She blinked repeatedly, determined not to cry. While it wasn't her fault that she and Amos had separated, she wondered if she should've defied his wishes and kept on helping with his housework—

"Mattie? Would you like some of this fabulous chicken?"

Mattie opened her eyes to see Preacher Marlin patiently holding the platter for her. Had she been so immersed in praying for Amos that she hadn't realized when everyone else had begun to pass the food?

"*Denki*, Marlin," she murmured, choosing a golden, crispy thigh. "Rosetta picked out the largest of her hens, and they've roasted up nicely, haven't they?"

Marlin smiled. "One of the things I'm most thankful for today is that my family came here to join you three sisters," he said as he held her gaze. "You all contribute so much to this new colony. It was a wonderful idea to have everyone gather together today for our first Thanksgiving at Promise Lodge."

"Like the Pilgrims we've been studying, right, Teacher Minerva?" Johnny piped up.

"Except without the funny hats," Lowell added.

As folks around her chuckled, Mattie passed the platter of chicken to Alma. Was it her imagination, or had Marlin just paid her a special compliment? She'd always found him to be a pleasant fellow, but he'd rarely singled her out for conversation . . . and she'd just realized that he'd chosen to sit beside her at the center of the table rather than in the midst of the men. The food was all being passed in the same direction, so each time a bowl or platter came to him, Marlin held it for her so she could help herself before he took his portion.

"I suppose this acorn squash came out of your garden? And the sweet potatoes and lima beans?" he asked as he glanced at the bowls of vegetables making their way around the table.

Mattie focused on the creamy white mashed potatoes she was spooning onto her plate. "If you count the fact that my Noah shot the deer, nearly everything we're serving today was grown here at Promise Lodge, *jah*," she replied. "We didn't make the flour in the bread, but all the milk and cheese and honey was also produced here."

"Pretty amazing, considering you and your sisters didn't move here until this past spring," Marlin remarked. "Many of our Plain neighbors in Iowa weren't nearly so self-sufficient."

Mattie was wondering why that would be so, because the Amish families she knew had always raised most of their food. She blinked, realizing she'd been holding the other side of the mashed potato bowl while Marlin had been talking with her—and observing her with a soulful brown-eyed gaze that lingered longer than usual.

Is Preacher Marlin flirting with you? He's being so polite and attentive—

"How about some cranberries, Marlin?" Noah asked from the preacher's other side.

Mattie quickly passed the mashed potatoes, wondering if anyone else had noticed their private pause. She made a point of helping herself more quickly, to keep the food moving—so much food they had!

"Maybe you should've set two plates at each place," Marlin remarked as he shook his head. "I've run out of room, and not nearly all the bowls have been around yet."

"Truly a cornucopia of flavors and textures," Irene said from across the table. "I can't recall the last time I sat at a table so loaded with deliciousness!"

"And we've not even put out the desserts yet," Mattie said, happy for a diversionary topic of conversation. "I'm looking forward to some of your pumpkin crunch."

"That's always been one of Truman's favorites," Irene replied, smiling at her son. "And my favorite is whatever somebody else has cooked!"

The women sitting nearby laughed and agreed. When all the food had been passed at last, Mattie was grateful for a chance to eat so many special dishes in the company of so many dear friends. She hoped that Ruby and Beulah were enjoying their visit with their brother's family, and she sent them a silent thank-you for suggesting that Promise Lodge residents should celebrate their first Thanksgiving together. It gave them all a chance to catch up with Amos and Bishop Floyd—and it seemed Marlin Kurtz was taking the opportunity to catch up with *her*.

When Mattie noticed that Marlin was smiling at her again—and that other folks seemed to be noticing— she quickly chose a topic of conversation that everyone might join in. Was it her imagination, or did the room's dimness encourage Marlin to cozy up to her? With so many folks seated close together around the table, Mattie could feel the brush of his knee against hers every now and then.

"Is your barrel shop up and running full-tilt now?" Mattie asked. "What sorts of things do you make there, Marlin?"

"I'm off to a *gut* start, in a shop that's bigger than I had before," he replied as he split a roll and smeared cranberry sauce on it. "Right now it seems rain barrels are all the rage, and I'm getting more orders than I can fill—to the point I may need to hire somebody besides Harley to help me. My newest model has a hand pump in the lid so you can fill buckets for watering your flowers—"

"And we make cool barrels with checkerboards on the top," his son Lowell piped up. "The mercantile at Forest Grove just ordered a whole bunch of those!"

"I really like your tables made from a half barrel with a nice round wooden top," Minerva said from across the table. "Not only are they pretty, but when you lift the top, you can store stuff inside the barrel base."

"Rain barrels would be just the thing for the downspouts around the lodge!" Rosetta said excitedly. "Think of how much easier it would be to water the nearby plants and bushes—or to carry water to your produce plots for planting the tomatoes, Mattie. Especially if there's a pump in the lid."

Mattie nodded. "Makes a lot of sense to use rainwater rather than just drawing water from the lake. Sounds easier than dragging hoses around."

"Maybe you should take a look at what-all's in my shop," Marlin said as his gaze lingered on Mattie. "I've got a catalog, but you'll get a better idea of the various barrels and sizes we produce if you look at them first-hand. Come on up and I'll show you around."

Mattie felt her face tingling. She wasn't sure how she felt about Marlin's attention, but what could it hurt to look at his rain barrels—especially because supporting his shop would be an investment in her produce business? "I'll do that," she murmured. "We've been so blessed to attract new residents with such diverse skills."

Chapter Twenty

Amos concentrated on his plateful of food so he wouldn't have to watch Bishop Floyd missing his mouth with his fork at the opposite end of the table—and so he wouldn't see Marlin making eyes at Mattie. Was there no end to Kurtz's nerve, flirting with her in front of everyone who lived at Promise Lodge? Each time Mattie looked at the new preacher and encouraged him with her bright-eyed questions—or held a bowl of food between them for far too long—Amos felt steam coming up out of his collar. He was becoming so upset, he didn't even want to stay for pie.

"Get me out of here," he murmured when Truman had cleared the last of the gravy from his plate with a roll. "I want to go home—*now*—but don't make a big fuss about it. Just roll me out."

Truman frowned. "You're not well?" he asked, leaning closer. "By the way you were tucking away your food, I thought you were doing a lot better."

Roman, too, lowered his voice so the other conversations covered theirs. "You've not even been here an hour," he said as he studied Amos's face. "Is it not dark enough in here? Would some sunglasses help, or your pain pills or—"

"I've had enough. I—I need to go home and rest," Amos hedged. His sudden exit would bring on a lot of concerned questions—more pity that he didn't need—but the sooner he got out of this difficult situation, the sooner he'd feel civil again. If he let slip a remark about Marlin's behavior—and the way Mattie was eating it up—he'd get himself into hot water for sure.

"I'll head for the bathroom," Amos murmured, "and when you two come to assist me, we'll just keep on going."

Truman's raised eyebrow expressed his doubts about this scheme, but Amos didn't let it stop him. Nodding at Preacher Eli as though nothing was wrong, Amos backed away from the table and wheeled himself out of the noisy dining room, presumably toward the bathroom tucked beneath the big double staircase in the lobby. A few moments later, Truman and Roman joined him, grabbing their coats. Before anyone came out to ask what they were doing, the two younger men rolled Amos out to the porch and then hefted him, wheelchair and all, down the steps.

Amos could tell his companions weren't keen on leaving the dinner. Once they were situated in the truck, with him in the backseat and the two of them up front, the interrogation began.

"So what's really going on here, Amos?" Truman asked as he started the engine. "You know *gut* and well that Roman and I will have to answer everyone's questions when we return without you."

Amos shrugged. What went on in his absence didn't

really concern him. "Say what you want. Tell them my headache was making me cranky—"

"Last you told me, your headache was nearly gone," Roman interrupted. "I was glad you felt like joining everyone for dinner today—getting out of your house—but you didn't even wait around for pie."

"*Jah*, something's fishy about that," Truman put in, watching Amos in the rearview mirror as he drove. "You were feeling fine when we picked you up. Next thing we know, you'll become as antisocial—and maybe as incapacitated—as Floyd. Why do I suspect you're not taking the antidepressants Dr. Townsend prescribed?"

Amos recognized a jab when he heard one—and he avoided answering about the meds, as well. "I was shocked to see how far the bishop's slipped, considering that Roman's told me Floyd's getting in-home therapy," he said earnestly. "It bothered me to watch the poor guy fumbling with his fork. From where I sat, I couldn't ignore it."

"Even with medication and therapy, Floyd's recovery will be slow," Roman pointed out. "We have to wonder if he'd be doing better had he accepted treatment right after you two fellows fell. I suspect he'll be a burden to his family for quite some time," he added ominously. "If that's God's will for our bishop, I have to wonder what He's got in mind for you, Amos, if you choose the same stubborn path Floyd first took."

Amos scowled. Up until now, Roman and Truman had been very patient with him, so he couldn't miss their criticism. The truck halted in front of his house. Without ado, his two assistants helped him down from the truck, positioned him in his wheelchair, and pushed him into his curtained front room.

Before Amos could thank them for humoring his whim, Truman stood in front of his wheelchair with his hands jammed into his coat pockets. His expression was none too tolerant. "What's this really about, Amos?" Truman demanded again. "I have a sneaking suspicion you got all bent out of shape watching Mattie chat with Marlin. The whole time you were staring at them, you looked ready to spit nails."

Amos glared. He had *not* been that obvious about watching them. "I was appalled at their shameless display of—have they been seeing each other, and you've not told me?"

"You turned her loose, remember?" Truman challenged.

"Seems to me that Mamm asked Marlin about his shop, and he was just making conversation," Roman remarked with a shrug.

"She's your mother. You don't think about her trying to attract a man's attention," Amos countered. "I found it discourteous—disconcerting—that Mattie would flirt so openly in front of—"

"As I recall, Amos, you told Mattie to leave you be—and not to grow old alone," Truman reminded him bluntly. "Now that she's doing as you told her, you don't like it much, do you?"

"I still think Marlin was just being polite," Roman insisted, "because Mamm's never shown any inclination toward him before today. But if you want to stew about it, that's your choice. I'm going back to have my pie and some of Irene's pumpkin crunch. Then I plan to spend the rest of the day with Mary Kate. Don't wait up."

"You have another choice, as well," Truman said as he grabbed the doorknob. "You can let your jealousy darken your heart—and strain a lot of relationships— or you can end this problem instead of becoming a part of it. Your call, Amos. God helps those who help themselves."

After the door closed firmly behind them, the house echoed with silence. Amos remained in the middle of his shadowy front room, reeling with emotions he didn't know how to handle—not to mention the criticism from Truman and Roman.

You told Mattie to leave you be—and not to grow old alone. Now that she's doing as you told her, you don't like it much, do you?

Amos slumped in his chair. In truth, Mattie might as well have thrust a butcher knife into his heart and given it a vicious twist. What could she possibly see in Marlin Kurtz? Amos had broken his engagement to Mattie for her benefit . . . but he'd never imagined she would seek out another man's company. Mattie's wide-eyed attention to Marlin and the roses in her cheeks told Amos that she was interested in the other preacher. And when she visited Marlin's new shop, Amos could imagine all sorts of scenarios where the two of them would be alone. Rain barrels would be the furthest things from their minds . . .

Amos wheeled himself into his bedroom, sinking into the lonely gloom that was such a contrast to the lively chatter and wonderful food he'd left behind in the lodge dining room. After asking a few questions, everyone there would continue enjoying their holiday with no further thought of him. The pies would be passed around, along with whatever other goodies the women had baked—and Irene's pumpkin crunch . . .

You should've at least stayed for dessert, he chided himself. *You can blame Kurtz for getting your dander up by making sure he got to sit by Mattie, but it's you who left that door wide open.*

Meanwhile Truman would be enjoying Rosetta's company, and Roman would spend the day with Mary Kate—maybe taking her for another sleigh ride. Amos thought back to the rides he'd taken with his wife, over frosty hillsides that sparkled with snow. He sighed loudly, regretting that he'd never had the chance to take Mattie in his sleigh. He'd originally built it with Mattie in mind, for courting her that winter so long ago when he'd intended to marry her . . .

This is your own stupid fault, you know. You should've known better than to put your weight on the corner of the shed roof, his conscience mocked him. *You could've followed the doctor's advice, too—could be taking those pills and physical therapy instead of sitting here in the dark alone, letting another man make Mattie smile. Twice you've lost her now, because you lacked the gumption to hang on to her.*

Amos glanced around his dim room. The rant inside his head had sounded so much like his father, he wondered if Dat's spirit had come to give him a talking-to. His *dat* had lectured him again and again after Mattie's father had insisted she must marry Marvin Schwartz—telling Amos he would be eternally sorry if he didn't reclaim the young woman he loved.

"And you were right, Dat," he murmured.

Bothered by these unpleasant thoughts, Amos stripped down to his long johns and crawled into bed. It wasn't even two in the afternoon, but if he went to sleep, he could forget about how everyone else was having a fine Thanksgiving . . . and the way Mattie was probably smiling at Kurtz even more, now that Amos wasn't there to witness their flirtation.

As soon as Amos closed his eyes, however, his father started in on him again.

So you're going to take this lying down? Going to sleep your life away? Dat's voice hammered at him. *What happened to all those grand plans you made when you came to Promise Lodge? Will you sit idly by—in that blasted wheelchair—while other folks carry on in your place—while other men take up where you left off? I raised you better than that, Amos.*

Amos turned to face the wall, hoping that if he ignored his father's spirit, it would go away. In all the years since his *dat* had passed, Amos had never sensed his presence, so why was the voice of Tobias Troyer haunting him now? After turning their small farm over to Amos's older brother, his father had died peacefully in his sleep at the ripe old age of ninety-five. Why had Dat stopped playing his harp up in Heaven to pester the son who'd never quite measured up—and never would, by the sound of it?

It was downright annoying, the way Amos couldn't seem to fall asleep—and he was too spooked to turn over and see if Dat's ghost was visible in his dark room. Amos concentrated on breathing in and out, suspecting there was a message or a lesson in this situation, if he would sit up and figure it out. But he didn't.

Next thing Amos knew, he was back home in Coldstream, in the house he'd built for Anna the third year they were married. His wife was very large with their first child, terribly fearful about being pregnant, worrying at every turn whether eating this or doing that would hurt the baby. She complained about how badly her back ached and how her ankles and feet had swollen in the unbearable summer heat. Amos grew so impatient with her fretting that he took a construction job in the next county, knowing he'd be away from home for at least a couple of weeks . . .

Amos sensed he was dreaming, recalling the difficult days of a marriage that had felt second-best, yet he couldn't seem to wake up. When he entered the house again after he'd finished the construction job, the neighbor lady, Ruth, informed him he had twin daughters—scornfully adding that Anna might have died birthing them had Ruth not heard her desperate cries through the open windows. When Amos saw his wife sitting up in bed with a red, puckered infant in each arm, his first thought was that he now had two more mouths to feed so he'd need to work even harder. Although having children was the natural order of things for married couples, he was terrified by the idea of being a father.

"You weren't much of a husband, Amos," Anna lamented as she looked at him from their bed. Her voice sounded far away, coming at him from the past, yet her gaze remained piercing. "Always had other things on your mind. You were married to me, but you were in love with someone else."

Amos gaped. Hadn't he given Anna and their kids the best he had? Hadn't he made a point of living on the far side of Coldstream from Mattie and Marvin Schwartz? Even after he'd become a preacher, he'd resisted the temptation to spend much time in the Schwartz home—except to advise Marvin that he needed to get treatment for his diabetes, and needed to curb his temper. When Schwartz had broken Mattie's nose, Amos had still kept his distance, even though he'd been tempted to give Marvin a dose of his own abusive medicine.

But Amos had never guessed that Anna had any inkling of his deep feelings for Mattie. Maybe—because he realized he was caught up in a dream—some of the things Anna was saying were skewed. As Amos walked closer to the bed, intending to ask his wife more about her thoughts, the twins disappeared from her arms. Anna sensed his questions, yet turned her head and refused to answer, pouting. In a matter of seconds, her face underwent several rapid changes, from being young and fresh to appearing sallow and lifeless. She slumped sideways, tumbling out of bed and beyond his reach—

"No—wait!" Amos awoke with a gasp. His long johns were soaked with sweat and his heart was hammering. The memory of how he'd found Anna dead one wintry morning felt excruciatingly vivid, as though it had happened only moments ago. She'd been feeling puny from a bad case of the flu for more than a week, and there hadn't been much he or the doctor could do for her. After Amos had fed Anna some soup, she'd nodded off and he'd spent the rest of that night in the barn with a mare that was having a difficult time foaling.

"I always thought you were more attached to that horse—to all of your fine horses—than you were to me, Amos," Anna said.

Amos stiffened with apprehension. He was fully awake, yet Anna's plaintive voice rang with near-tears misery—so strident and accusatory that she might be standing behind him, staring at him in the darkness.

He knew he'd been dreaming—realized that some of the images in his dream had not actually happened—yet the sensations felt so vivid and real. Remorse made Amos's throat so thick he couldn't swallow. For a moment he wondered if he might die, because it seemed he couldn't breathe—

But when a sob escaped him, Amos knew he'd survive—if only because dead people seemed compelled to remind him of his shortcomings. After enduring the spectral presence of his father and his wife, Amos wasn't so sure he wanted to doze off again.

He fumbled for his flashlight and focused its beam at the clock on his dresser. Four thirty. Still Thanksgiving afternoon, judging from the faint light around the edges of his curtains.

Amos sighed. The hours of this day seemed to be crawling like a fly through molasses. After his big dinner, he wasn't hungry, so he had no reason to wheel himself into the kitchen. He wasn't interested in the latest issue of *The Budget*, because he still had trouble concentrating . . . figured Roman was out in the sleigh by now, and that no one else would be likely to visit him, after the ungracious way he'd ducked out of the dinner gathering at the lodge. For lack of anything better to do, Amos burrowed beneath the covers. *It'll soon be dark, anyway, so I might as well sleep.*

Once again Amos became aware that he was dreaming. This time it was Christmas, yet the house showed no signs of the fresh evergreen boughs or candles with which Anna had always decorated. The Nativity scene their three kids had loved was nowhere in sight, either. Amos's heart shriveled and a heavy sadness settled over him when he realized that his wife had passed on. He somehow had to get through the holiday even though he'd lost all interest in stars and carols and even the Christ child.

"I'm headed out. No more of this nonsense from you and Bishop Chupp about either joining the church or suffering eternal damnation," Allen announced sullenly.

Amos turned to see his twenty-year-old son at the door with a duffle in each hand and a scowl on his handsome young face. "I wish you'd reconsider," Amos pleaded, mostly because he couldn't bear the thought of being totally alone. "If your *mamm* knew you were jumping the fence, it would break her heart."

"You're a fine one to speak of *that*," Allen retorted as he crammed his black hat on his head. "You broke her heart first—and then the girls hitched up with a couple of spineless redheaded guys, just to get out of this place. No point in me staying around, either. I've had it with your thou-shalts and thou-shalt-nots."

When the door closed behind his son, Amos felt as though his coffin had shut with him inside it. "You'll be sorry, Allen!" he hollered. "Someday you'll realize I'm right—"

Amos sat bolt upright in bed, fully awake as the anger of a few Christmases ago made his head throb. Once again his pulse was pounding and he was dripping with sweat, yet he had a sudden flash of realization.

He'd driven away—or demoralized—everyone he loved. As a husband and father, Amos had believed his way was the right way, so Anna had borne the brunt of his harsh, autocratic attitude and his three children now had nothing more to say to him. Had he become so demanding, so domineering, because his father had constantly criticized him? Had he known the pain of feeling unworthy when he was growing up, only to perpetuate his *dat*'s critical attitude as an adult because it gave him a sense of control and self-worth?

Amos blinked. In recent years he'd made a sincere effort to emulate Jesus and his teachings of love and patience rather than modeling himself after Old Testament prophets of doom, yet now that the chips were down he seemed to have reverted to his former bad attitude. He'd wallowed in self-pity because he couldn't walk—and then he'd driven Mattie away and treated Truman and Roman poorly, as well.

"At this rate, you're digging your own grave, man," Amos muttered as he struggled to free himself from the sheets and blankets. "Folks here will be happy to see you gone, too—just as Allen, Barbara, and Bernice want nothing more to do with you."

And now you're talking to yourself. Pull yourself together, Troyer.

Amos landed in his wheelchair with a *whump*. As he caught his breath, still thrumming from the impact of the voices of his past, he knew one thing was startlingly clear: he had to change. At fifty, he might have many years of life ahead of him. He could not go on this way, thinking that he was right and his friends and Dr. Townsend were wrong. He'd seen what such an attitude had done for Bishop Floyd, after all.

And he'd seen what it had done to Mattie, too. He'd broken her heart when she was trying her best to help him. He was no better than Marvin Schwartz, allowing his illness to get the best of him without heeding any medical advice that might make him better.

Amos wheeled himself into the bathroom and took the bottle of antidepressants from the cabinet. After

he'd washed one down with water, he thought about
what he needed to do to make amends. He would ask
Truman to set up his physical therapy sessions. He
would find a way to apologize to Mattie—soon. But
another, more urgent task pressed heavily upon his
heart.

He dressed as quickly as he could—he didn't dare
fall while he stood to pull up his pants, so he left them
unfastened around his hips. Amos pulled his coat
down from its peg beside the back door, mentally assessing his odds of making it to the phone shanty by
the road. It was dark and cold out. If he overturned
his wheelchair, he might be stuck in a snowbank for
hours before anyone found him.

So you can't let that happen, Amos told himself as he
opened the back door. *You have to prove to yourself you
can get around on your own—and then you have to face
the harder task of contacting your kids. No way around it.
You have to make the first move. You must attempt a reconcil-
iation and convince your family and friends you love them.*

Amos was relieved that the moon brightened the
twilight and that he could clearly see the paths Roman
had shoveled to the barn and down to the road. If he
was lucky, the bare surface was wide enough so that
his wheels wouldn't sink into any snow—and if he was
even luckier, he wouldn't slide out of control on any
ice. *It's in Your hands, Lord—so please, please be in my
hands, as well,* Amos prayed as he rocked himself over
the threshold and out the mudroom door. He hadn't
realized that having the back doorway on ground
level would come in so handy.

Amos sucked in the frosty air, grateful for the darkness that didn't hurt his eyes—and thankful, as well,
that his headache had gone away. He put on his gloves

and began to turn the wheels of his chair, intent on negotiating the uneven snow where the shoveled paths to the barn and the road didn't quite meet. Across the road, the windows of the lodge glowed with lamplight, but he saw no one outside—and that's how he wanted it.

Focused on the white phone shanty that gleamed in the moonlight, Amos held tightly to his wheels to keep the chair from racing out of control as he started down the hill—and then he went into a skid that whirled him in a circle and landed him at the road a lot faster than he'd intended.

When his wheelchair came to a stop, Amos caught his breath, planning his moves. He maneuvered the wheelchair as close to the shanty's door as he could, thrust his body forward, and grabbed the doorframe to remain upright. Moments later, when he landed on the wooden chair beside the table where the phone sat, he felt as though he'd done hours of physical labor. As he pulled his pants up over his long johns, he realized that he could've tripped over them and reinjured himself. But there was no time to dwell upon how many ways he'd been a fool.

Amos pulled the cord of the wall-mounted battery lamp, checked the list of phone numbers he'd taped beneath it, and made the easiest call first.

"Truman, it's Amos," he said when the Wickeys' answering machine beeped. "I've behaved badly and I'm ready to begin those physical therapy sessions Dr. Townsend authorized. If you'd be so kind as to set those up for me, I'll be eternally grateful, friend. *Denki* for all you've done for me—and let's not tell Mattie about this, okay? It'll be our secret for a while."

Was he being silly and vain, wanting to see if the

therapy sessions helped before he told Mattie about them? Amos sighed, rubbing his bare hands together as he sat in the cold shanty. He badly wanted to talk to Mattie, to apologize for the way he'd hurt her feelings, but he was starting to shiver. Before he lost his nerve, he had other calls to make.

Amos opened the drawer of the table and pulled out the small catalog he'd been saving ever since Barbara and Bernice had married Sam and Simon Helmuth, whom they'd met at a cousin's wedding the summer before Anna had passed. His breath escaped him as he realized that the girls would be twenty-five now . . . and that three years had gone by since they'd joined their husbands' families in Ohio. The Helmuths operated nurseries and garden supply stores in three towns—very successful businesses, judging from their catalog. Sam and Simon were slim and they sported unruly mops of auburn hair, which had prompted Allen to consider them less than masculine. But then, Allen had always been judgmental.

And where did he get that? The sins of the father visited upon the son, perhaps?

Amos sighed, closing his eyes. *Help me do this, Lord. If the girls really did leave because of me, I have to give them a reason to end this separation that goes against Your ways.*

He quickly dialed the phone number printed on the catalog, recalling how Anna had read in one of Barbara's letters that she and Bernice lived next door to each other and shared a phone shanty. Amos held his breath, listening to the message. "Hello from Helmuth Nurseries near Zanesville, Ohio! To leave a message or place an order at the store, please press one. To leave a message for Sam and Barbara, press two—"

Amos jabbed the keypad, praying the right words

would come to him. "Barbara, this is your *dat*," he said breathlessly. "First I wanted you and Bernice to know that I've moved to a colony called Promise Lodge, and my new phone number is—"

He looked at his handwritten list to be sure he got it right before he said it, because it was different from the number they'd had for all those years in Cold-stream. "But mostly I—I wanted you girls to know that I'm sorry for the things I said and did that made you leave home, and that made you stop writing to me after your *mamm* passed . . ."

Amos swallowed the lump in his throat. Apologies didn't come easy. "I hope you can forgive me," he said in a breathy voice, "and I'm wondering if you could let me know Allen's address and phone number. I—I miss you all. Give my best to your family."

As he hung up, Amos worried that he'd sounded hopelessly old or muddled, but he'd followed through—he'd taken the first step by asking for his daughters' forgiveness. The ball was in their court now, and if they didn't respond . . . well, that part was beyond his control. Amos turned out the light with a sigh. He'd had no idea it would take so much emotional energy to contact his daughters, or to think about reconnecting with them. Amos hadn't given his headstrong son much thought since Allen had walked out, yet now he felt keenly aware that he had no idea where his boy might be or what trade he'd taken up.

Amos sighed. Why had being Anna's husband and fathering her children seemed like such an effort? Not long ago he'd told Mattie he would welcome any children they might have together—

Not that you'll get a chance at that unless you make up with her.

Amos shook his head. He would figure out how to win Mattie back when he was warm and rested. It occurred to him, as he prepared to step out of the shanty and into his wheelchair, that his chances of getting back up the lane to the house were slim to none. His arms were probably strong enough, but the same iciness that had made him spin in a circle on the way down would send him sliding backwards, helpless, when he tried to go back up the lane. There was just enough of an incline to cause him a problem.

"Phooey," Amos muttered. He was cold and tired now, and it might be hours before anyone came by. For all he knew, folks were still at the lodge enjoying a light supper, or maybe playing board games and visiting. *No fool like an old fool, right, Troyer?*

When he stuck his head out the door, however, a compact black body with a wagging tail gave him hope. Sometimes angels came in unexpected forms. "Queenie!" he hollered. "Hey, Queenie—go fetch Noah. Or Roman! Go get 'em, girl!"

The Border collie stopped in the road, turning toward his voice.

"Go on, Queenie!" Amos urged. "Fetch Noah! Fetch Roman for me!"

The dog barked loudly, circling a few times before she took off across the snow-covered field. Amos slumped in the wooden chair, wondering why Queenie hadn't headed for the lodge or toward Noah's house. He braced his hands on the table to stand up, leaning heavily against the shanty's wall while he fastened his pants. He'd have enough explaining to do without his drawers dropping around his ankles once somebody found him.

Then he waited.

As his feet and face got colder, Amos reflected on what an odd, uncomfortable day it had been. But hadn't he set himself upon the path of major change? Hadn't he listened to those voices from his thoughts and dreams and, for once, taken their lessons to heart? As Amos replayed the heart-rending scenes in his mind—when Anna and his *dat* and his son had spoken directly, harshly, to him—he swore he heard distant sleigh bells.

He really was losing his mind. As the minutes dragged, he closed his eyes. His fingers and toes went numb . . .

"What've we got here?" a familiar voice called out. "That's a wheelchair by the phone shanty."

"Amos? Are you in there?"

A dog barked urgently. Amos roused himself, grinning when Queenie jumped up to look through the glass in the shanty's door. "Queenie, you're a *gut* girl!" he cried.

After Noah and Roman helped him into the sleigh, where Deborah and Mary Kate sat in the front- and backseat beneath the blankets, Amos didn't lie, but he didn't elaborate either. He simply told them he'd called his daughter, and by that time Mattie's boys were helping him into the house. Noah went back to get the wheelchair while Roman and the girls sat down at the kitchen table with Amos.

"How about if I fix you some cocoa? You look half frozen, Amos," Deborah said as she found a pan for the water.

"That sounds mighty nice," he replied. Amos gazed at their rosy young faces, briefly recalling when he and Mattie were their age. "If you want, you kids could stay and have cocoa with me—but I'll understand if you've got more sleigh riding to do. Never miss a chance to have fun with folks you love."

The boys gazed knowingly at the girls, who were peeling off their coats and bonnets. By the time they'd all sipped cocoa and the kids had caught him up on the chit-chat from the afternoon at the lodge, Amos felt better than he had since he'd fallen from the roof. Mattie's boys were truly a blessing, and he was pleased that both of them had found young women who suited them so well.

Someday soon, Amos would figure out how to restore Mattie's faith in him. He knew better now than to let his vanity and stubbornness prevent him from living with the love of his life ever again.

Chapter Twenty-One

"Roman! Roman, come quick!"

As Roman left the barn Tuesday morning after he'd finished milking the cows, the alarm in Gloria's voice made him break into a jog. He peered through the early morning snowfall, and saw her rushing down the road toward him, her scarf fluttering behind her. He'd been on the way to tend the Lehmans' animals anyway, and he hoped Gloria's father hadn't taken a turn for the worse.

"The baby's coming!" she cried as she approached him. "We need to find Minerva."

Roman's heartbeat accelerated. As he imagined Mary Kate struggling with labor pains, he sent up a prayer for her strength and comfort. "Minerva's probably setting up for school," he reminded Gloria as he pointed toward the lodge. "How about if I bring her to the house, so you can go back and help your *mamm* and Mary Kate with—"

"I've heard all the moaning and crying I can take," Gloria muttered. "Her pains started in the middle of the night, so—why don't *you* go to the house, Roman? Mary Kate will feel a lot better knowing you're there."

Roman's eyes widened. From what little he knew about birthing, men weren't welcome because the women either found their presence inappropriate— or because guys got in the way.

"Go on," Gloria urged him. "Maybe by the time I get there with Minerva, you'll have Mary Kate calmed down and ready to have that baby."

As Roman rushed up the snow-covered road toward the Lehman home, his mind spun like snowflakes caught in a whirlwind. What if he got nervous and only made Mary Kate more uncomfortable? What if Frances shooed him away, incensed that Gloria had sent him to their house?

If nothing else, I can sit with Bishop Floyd so the women don't have to keep track of him while the baby's coming. Maybe he'll come to the barn with me to feed and water the horses.

When Frances opened the door, however, she welcomed him in. "Roman, I'm glad you're here," she murmured. "Mary Kate's out of her head, I think, and if you could just hold her hand—"

A sudden cry of pain rang out in the bedroom above him. Roman swallowed hard.

"Let's go upstairs," Frances murmured, grasping his hand as they left the kitchen. "Floyd's beside himself, thinking something horrible must be happening to Mary Kate. If you can calm her down, you'll be doing us all a big favor."

Roman sensed this request was highly unusual— and that Frances was so concerned about her daughter, she was willing to overlook the usual propriety. As they passed through the front room, Roman saw that Floyd was on the sofa fidgeting with a magazine. Roman spoke to him, but the bishop's only response was a fast, wide-eyed glance.

At least he's sitting upright, trying to read, Roman thought. *That seems like an improvement.*

Upstairs, Roman stopped in the doorway to Mary Kate's room and inhaled deeply to settle his nerves. The poor girl in the bed looked pale and exhausted, and her next wail set him on edge. She was covered by blankets, so it wasn't as though he'd be seeing body parts he wasn't supposed to look at.

"Hey," Roman murmured as he approached her. "Looks like the baby's making a grand entrance, eh?"

When Mary Kate's brown-eyed gaze held his, Roman's heart went out to her. She looked so young and frail—not much different from the way he pictured the Virgin Mary, bearing her first child as an unmarried young woman caught up in circumstances other folks considered extremely dubious. At Frances's nod, he went to the bedside and took Mary Kate's hand.

"Sit with me," she pleaded. "Stay with me, Roman. It hurts so bad I think I might die—"

"No, no," Roman hastened to reassure her as he gingerly eased onto the mattress beside her pillow. "Minerva's on her way. She'll know exactly what to do."

"Hold me. Give me your strength."

How could he refuse? Frances nodded her consent, so when Mary Kate shot bolt upright with the next labor pain, Roman slipped behind her and sat against the headboard. She felt as weak as a kitten when she settled back against him, yet her sigh suggested she already felt calmer, cradled in his arms. Somehow he found quiet words to comfort her, not expecting her to respond. He heard Minerva speaking loudly to Floyd downstairs, and when Frances left the room to greet the midwife, Roman nuzzled Mary Kate's temple. He took the liberty of stroking her wavy brown hair away from her flushed face, aware that only husbands were allowed to see a woman with her hair down. The thought made his heart flip-flop.

"I won't leave you, Mary Kate," Roman murmured, his heart in his throat. "Stay strong for the baby, and we'll get you through this. It's a big day—and you'll feel a lot better about all of this when you see your little one's face."

Why was he telling her these things? What if they weren't true? Or, God forbid, what if the baby was breech, or Mary Kate developed other complications? Roman knew from assisting cows and mares that the birthing process was messy in the best of circumstances and downright terrifying when things went wrong. But he dismissed these negative thoughts. Mary Kate seemed calmer now, and he didn't want her to pick up on his concerns.

When Minerva entered the room, she nodded at him. "Roman, you're a *gut* man," she said. "Keep her still while I see how she's progressing."

He wrapped his arms more snugly around Mary Kate as the midwife went to the end of the bed and folded the blankets up onto Mary Kate's bent knees.

"We're moving right along." Minerva opened her black bag and slipped on latex gloves. "Mary Kate, I want you to push back into Roman and at the same time push the baby toward me. Take a deep breath first. You're doing fine."

"Give it your best shot," Roman murmured as he

felt Mary Kate gathering her strength. "It'll be over soon—"

"Oh, *oh!*" Mary Kate hollered as another pain wracked her body. But she pressed her slender shoulders against his chest, clenching her jaw as she pushed the baby. Mary Kate put her whole body into the effort for as long as she could, and then she collapsed.

Roman admired Mary Kate beyond belief. Birthing seemed to be so much easier for animals. When he considered how large she had grown, he had a hard time imagining what she was going through as the baby came out. *Lord, please help us. Don't let her rupture anything—and please let the baby be strong and healthy.*

"Here's the head!" Minerva announced as she leaned in closer. "Give me another big push—that's the way—"

Hovering beside Minerva, Frances was watching anxiously. "Oh, here it comes! Don't stop, Mary Kate—you're almost there!"

Rivulets of sweat had dampened Mary Kate's flushed face and her breathing sounded shallow and desperate. She screwed up her face, and with great determination she pushed again.

"It's a boy!" Frances crowed.

"He looks fine and dandy, and now we're going to open up his lungs," Minerva said from the other side of the tented blankets.

Roman heard a wet smacking sound. When a shrill wail filled the room, his heart thudded in his chest. "You did it, Mary Kate," he whispered against her temple. "You have a son!"

"We'll tend to the finishing details and clean him up for you, sweetheart," Minerva said as she worked efficiently behind the other side of the blankets. "*Gut* work! Rest for a minute and think about what to name this fine fellow."

Mary Kate managed a smile as she sank into Roman's embrace. "*Denki* so much," she murmured as she gazed up at him. "Dat was frantic and Gloria ran off, but you stuck by me."

"It—it was an honor," Roman replied in a breathy voice. After Frances helped Minerva give the howling baby a quick bath, Mary Kate's *mamm* approached the bed with the blanketed newborn cradled in her arms.

Roman saw a puckery red face and tiny hands flailing above the blanket as the baby continued to fill the room with his cries. When Frances stopped beside him and he got a look at the little boy's fuzzy dark hair and bow-shaped lips, Roman fell head-over-heels for the helpless little fellow who'd just undergone the tremendous effort of being born. "Ohhhh," he murmured, daring to stroke the boy's pudgy cheek. "Wow. Aren't you something? Just plain amazing."

Mary Kate sat up straighter, gazing at the baby as her mother handed him over. "So here you are," she whispered in awe. "Maybe you were worth all this trouble after all."

When Mary Kate smiled at her newborn son, Roman suddenly knew he was meant to be the man of this little family. Was it his imagination, or had a glow settled over the three of them? Roman could hardly breathe, knowing full well that under normal circumstances he wouldn't have been present for this miracle—let alone encouraged to sit behind Mary Kate while she was giving birth. He felt immensely grateful that Frances and Minerva had ignored the traditional boundaries their faith placed between unmarried men and women . . .

"We're so blessed that everything went well, and that the baby's perfect," Frances murmured as she gazed at Mary Kate and her son. "And we're blessed that you were willing to lend us your strength and compassion, Roman. I—I don't know how I'd have gotten through these past few weeks without you helping us in so many ways."

Roman blinked. "Whatever you folks need, let me know," he murmured. "It's no trouble at all."

Minerva joined them at the bedside, her bag in hand. "I'll be back later today to check on you all," she said. She smiled at Roman. "Maybe you could walk me out, Roman? I suspect our boy's hungry."

The thought of Mary Kate nursing her newborn made Roman's face flush, but he nodded. "See you later," he whispered to Mary Kate. He longed to kiss her cheek, but thought better of it with the two women looking on. "Can't wait to hear what you name him."

When they reached the bottom of the stairs, Roman saw Mary Kate's *dat* standing at a window, gazing out. "Congratulations, Floyd!" he said as he approached the bishop. "You have a fine new grandson, and your daughter's doing well."

When Floyd turned around, his words came out in an unintelligible rush. Because half of the bishop's face was sagging, Roman couldn't tell if he was pleased about the baby or not. Floyd's expressions gave little clue about what was going through his mind.

"I'm going outside now to do your horse chores," Roman said slowly and distinctly. "Would you like to come with me?"

The bishop waved him off with his good arm and turned to stare out the window again. Roman and Minerva were silent as they put on their heavy coats, until they stepped outside.

"I don't know what to think," the midwife murmured with a shake of her head. "Floyd seems steadier on his feet now, but I can't tell that his speech is progressing any. If he's not able to talk clearly soon, I suspect he'll dismiss his speech therapist."

"It's very sad," Roman murmured. "Frances has a load on her shoulders."

Minerva's face glowed within the confines of her black bonnet as she gazed upward into the snowfall. "I wish this snow could brighten the Lehmans' household the way it refreshes the landscape," she said wistfully. Then she gazed speculatively at Roman. "Are you thinking of marrying Mary Kate? Not that it's any of my business."

Roman smiled with more confidence than he felt. "When I saw the baby for the first time—and the way Mary Kate held him in her arms—I was totally sucked in," he whispered. "Had you and Frances not been there, I might have proposed right then and there."

Minerva's happy laughter rang out as the snow began falling more heavily. They stopped at the spot where she would head for the lodge and Roman would turn toward the Lehmans' barn. "I think you'll make a wonderful husband for her, Roman—and you'll be a blessing to that entire family. But it's not a decision to be made lightly, considering Floyd's condition and Gloria's, um, crush on you."

Roman nodded. "I think Gloria and I have reached an understanding now," he said, glancing toward the

Lehmans' big home. Was it his imagination, or had a curtain fluttered when Gloria stopped looking out the window at him? "But, *jah*, the whole family can use our prayers and our help."

Minerva nodded. "I'd best get back to my scholars. I'm sure Rosetta and Christine have them reciting their addition and subtraction tables and working on their spelling lessons for the week, but the Peterscheim boys and Lowell can get distracted in the blink of an eye."

"Especially with Christmas coming," Roman said with a chuckle.

"So true! We're going out this afternoon to cut evergreen branches," Minerva said. "Your *mamm* has volunteered to show the kids how to make fresh wreaths, and Rosetta has offered us a lesson in making sugar cookies. We'll bake and decorate them for the meal after church on Sunday."

"If any cookies are still around by then," Roman teased. "Have a *gut* rest of your day, Minerva."

"You too, Roman. God be with you as you make your important decision about hitching up with Mary Kate and her baby."

As Roman strode toward the Lehmans' barn, he hummed a Christmas carol. He was guessing at least three inches of snow had fallen since Gloria had summoned him to help with Mary Kate, and the dull gray sky suggested that the snow wouldn't stop anytime soon.

He slid the barn door open, smiling as the horses all turned to look at him. "'What child is this, who laid to rest, on Mary Kate's lap is sleeping,'" he sang softly. It seemed his heart was filled with Christmas cheer earlier than usual, and every fiber of his being was telling him he belonged with Mary Kate and her newborn son, to care for them and provide them a home as Joseph did so long ago for the Virgin Mary. It was indeed an important decision, yet Roman sensed he'd already made it.

Chapter Twenty-Two

Rosetta sighed happily on Thursday afternoon as she and the children stood looking at the long counter-top covered with decorated sugar cookies. "What a pretty picture! And what a gift these cookies will be to everyone after church," she added.

"We're grateful to Rosetta for our lessons in fractions and kitchen math as we measured and baked," Minerva remarked as she stood with them. "As our treat, we'll each choose one cookie to eat now—and then we'll clean up the kitchen. Let's start with the youngest, and we'll take our cookies to the dining room. Mattie's made us all some cocoa and she'll pour you a cup when you take your seat."

Johnny Peterscheim chose a snowman with candy eyes and buttons, and his brother Menno snatched up a star that was thick with yellow frosting and multi-colored jimmies. Twelve-year-old Lowell could easily have devoured five or six cookies, but he limited himself to a large holly leaf frosted in green with cinnamon imperials for berries. Lily, Lavern, and

Fannie chose a wreath, a chocolate-frosted camel, and an angel that sparkled with big white sugar crystals.

"This was a *gut* lesson and fun for all of us," Rosetta remarked as she chose a yellow bell. "Lily and Fannie kept their brothers focused on figuring the fractions for the flour and sugar, too."

"They'll make fine teachers someday," Minerva agreed, lifting a frosted poinsettia from the countertop. "It helped that they reminded the boys we'd all be eating their mistakes if the cookies didn't turn out right."

Rosetta chuckled as she joined the kids at a table in the dining room. By all appearances, the cookies had turned out delicious: the younger boys had frosting smeared on their mouths, and all the scholars were smiling. Mattie poured three mugs of cocoa for the adults and went to the kitchen to choose her cookie. "I see an angel with my name on it," she teased.

"Teacher Minerva, I think we should take some cookies to Preacher Amos—especially if he's not able to sit through church," Fannie suggested.

"Let's take some to Bishop Floyd and Mary Kate, too!" Lily said exuberantly. "We have baby booties and blankets to take over anyway, so cookies would be something everyone in their family could enjoy."

"That's a very thoughtful idea," Minerva remarked. "And maybe we could sing them a few Christmas carols when we deliver them."

"And we could do it during schooltime, *jah?*" Menno asked hopefully.

"Our teacher in Coldstream would've *never* let us make cookies and called it a lesson," Lavern put in. "We were too busy memorizing looong Christmas poems and Bible stories for the pageant to have any fun like this."

"*Jah*, but we didn't have a kitchen in the school-house, either," Lily pointed out.

Minerva chuckled. "Now that you mention it, Lavern, it's time to begin working on our Christmas Eve program. I'm thinking we could do a simple version of the Christmas story, with shepherds and Wise Men—"

"What if Mary Kate played Mary, with her little David as baby Jesus?" Fannie asked, her eyes wide with excitement. "The Christ child was born in the city of David, after all."

Mattie chuckled along with Rosetta and Minerva. "I don't think we should plan for that until you ask Mary Kate if she's willing to participate," she said. "David will only be a few weeks old—"

"But if Roman plays Joseph, he'll be with them!" Menno insisted. "And we'll be indoors where it's warm—"

"And we promise not to sneeze in the baby's face or feed him too many cookies!" Johnny put in.

Rosetta was amazed at how quickly the notion of including Mary Kate, Roman, and the baby had captured the children's imaginations. "If the three older boys play the Wise Men, that leaves you as the only shepherd, Johnny," she speculated aloud. "And what parts will you play, Lily and Fannie?"

"I'm an angel, of course," Lily replied demurely.

"Hmm . . . I could be the star," Fannie murmured, "or I could dress up like a shepherd with Johnny."

"*Jah!* Those guys all wore dresses back then, anyway!" Menno blurted.

"And we could have Queenie help us," Johnny said,

so excited that he stood up to bounce on his toes. "She's a sheepdog, ain't so? And if the girls sewed up some stuffed sheep and a donkey—"

"Fannie can be the donkey! She's a natural," Lowell said with a hoot.

Fannie swatted at her younger brother while the boys began to bray like donkeys, filling the dining room with their ruckus.

Minerva held up her hand for silence. "I understand why you'd like to see David in your Christmas Eve program, but I'm going to insist that you not even ask Mary Kate about participating. She and the baby need time to get strong—and David's way too young to be exposed to such a crowd yet. Do you understand?"

When the boys appeared ready to protest, Mattie spoke up. "I believe we should go along with what Teacher Minerva says, because she's a midwife—and because we want little David and Mary Kate to stay healthy, ain't so?"

Fannie nodded. "It would be easier to use a doll for baby Jesus anyway," she said. "A doll wouldn't start crying or fussing during the program—"

"And a doll wouldn't poop its pants, either!" Menno put in.

"Excellent points," Minerva said as the boys all started laughing and holding their noses. "We've eaten our treats, so it's time to clean up the kitchen. We'll start by gathering our mugs and napkins. Lowell, you and Lavern can wash the cookie cutters, bowls, and utensils," she instructed, pointing toward the sink, "and the girls can put the leftover frosting in containers. Johnny and Menno, you're just the right height to wipe down the tables. Many hands make light work!"

Rosetta stood back to watch the children carry out their assigned tasks. She smiled at Mattie. "I'm glad the girls suggested visiting our shut-ins," she murmured. "Now that Fannie and Lily have joined our crochet club, we've got several booties and little blankets finished for the baby. If we join the granny squares we've crocheted, we could take an afghan to Amos, ain't so? It'll be a *gut* chance to look in on him, all of us together."

Mattie considered this idea. "I suppose so," she murmured. "And we could make a big wreath for the Lehmans. I suspect Frances and Gloria will be too busy tending Floyd and the baby and Mary Kate to do much decorating for Christmas."

Rosetta slipped her arm around Mattie's shoulders as they headed toward the kitchen with the empty cocoa pot and ladle. She suspected her sister was more curious about Amos's well-being than she was letting on—and an outing with the kids would give them all a chance to be neighborly without Amos thinking they were being nosy, too. Truman had taken Amos into Forest Grove for an appointment a couple days ago, but he was being very tight-lipped about the preacher's progress. It would be a blessing, indeed, if Amos could resume his preaching duties—he could certainly deliver a sermon from his wheelchair, after all—now that Eli Peterscheim and Marlin Kurtz were the only able-bodied church leaders they had.

It's in Your hands, Lord, Rosetta prayed as she watched the children cleaning the kitchen. *You've given us these fine kids and a new baby and interesting ideas for the scholars' first Christmas Eve program at Promise Lodge. I know it'll be the most wonderful Christmas ever!*

Amos raised his eyebrows as Roman began removing their supper dishes from the kitchen table. "What's going on that you think I should change my shirt?" he asked. "It's Friday night and we've made no plans—"

"Just saying," Roman replied in a suspiciously cheerful tone. "Ruby hinted at a surprise this morning when she brought over those wonderful-*gut* sweet rolls for our breakfast, remember? Christmas is the season of mystery, after all."

"Oh, *jah?*" Amos asked, secretly enticed by whatever might be about to happen. "Now tell me true. Has your *mamm* been cooking something up?"

Roman widened his eyes and looked directly at Amos. "That's not the way I heard it. But that's not to say she won't be involved," he said. "The Peterscheim boys mentioned cookies and caroling to me, they were all excited about the event. You don't want to be wearing that baggy old soup-splattered sweatshirt if company's coming."

"Ah. In that case I suppose I'd better be more presentable."

Amos turned his wheelchair and headed back to his bedroom, almost giddy with the prospect of having kids stopping by . . . and maybe Mattie. Thank God he was feeling much better these days: his headache had disappeared, and the antidepressant had improved his mood, as well. He hadn't told anyone except Truman, but a couple days ago Dr. Townsend had pronounced his concussion nearly healed. The physical therapist had referred him to a massage therapist after a closer look at his X-rays . . . something about his leg nerves getting pinched when he'd fallen from the roof.

Amos didn't know why therapists would have better ideas about treating his condition than a full-fledged doctor would, but he wasn't asking any questions. His first massage had made some of his muscles ache, but wasn't that an improvement over total numbness in his legs? He was doing his exercises—a few more repetitions than the physical therapist had suggested— and he was feeling a lot more motivated, more hopeful about making a recovery. And didn't hope and belief account for a lot of healing? Hadn't the people Jesus had healed regained their strength because they had believed He could make them well again?

Amos took a clean flannel shirt from the drawer and changed out of his old sweatshirt. *Good thing Roman trimmed your hair and beard yesterday, so you don't look like a caveman,* Amos thought as he also put on a clean pair of TriBlend trousers. He was tickled that he could pull them up and fasten them by himself now— he could stand for nearly a minute without any support and without falling back into his wheelchair.

But Roman didn't know these things, and Amos didn't figure on sharing a lot of details just yet. He hadn't told a soul about those nighttime visits from his *dat* and Anna and Allen, either.

In the light of day and rational thought, Amos wasn't entirely sure he'd heard their voices, but their presence had felt very real to him. If Mary and Joseph had received messages from God in dreams and from angels, Amos believed the Lord might have sent those three members of his family to deliver the most important warning of his life. Only a fool ignored God's messages. And Amos was finished with being a fool.

When he'd wheeled himself out to the front room, Amos lit the two battery lamps on his tables. It was December fourth—still three weeks from Christmas, yet Amos yearned for the season's peace and joy. He felt ready to receive whatever gifts the Holy Spirit delivered. A sense of expectation filled his soul. Centuries ago the world had awaited a Savior's birth, and this year Amos prayed for his own delivery from the bondage of illness and physical limitations.

A few minutes later someone knocked very loudly on the door. Roman came out of the kitchen, but Amos had already wheeled himself across the front room to answer it. When he saw the young Peterscheims and Kurtzes, with Rosetta, her sisters, and Minerva standing behind them, he opened the door. "Come on in, folks! What a nice surprise on a snowy evening!"

Johnny flashed a smile with a couple of teeth missing as he thrust a plate of frosted cookies toward Amos. "We brung you some goodies!"

"And we *brought* you a wreath for your front door," his big sister Lily added as she held it up for Amos to see.

"We made the cookies ourselves, and Mattie showed us how to make the wreath!" Menno exclaimed. "Teacher Minerva lets us do really fun stuff in school."

Amos's heart was beating happily as he grasped the hands of the kids who stood around his chair. "It's so *gut* to see you all again," he said, aware that his voice sounded tight with emotion. "And *denki* so much for these wonderful gifts, and for thinking of me, too."

"We're glad to see you looking so much better, Amos," Rosetta spoke up from behind the children. She held up a large, bulky item wrapped in a white trash bag. "The crochet club also made you a little present. I'll put it on your sofa so you can open it whenever you'd like. No need to wait until Christmas."

"It's from the PPCC," Lavern said with a roll of his eyes. "Only *girls* would belong to a Pajama Party Crochet Club, ain't so, Preacher Amos?"

Amos laughed, imagining a roomful of the women and girls he knew, all of them crocheting in their nightgowns. "Well, at least they get something done besides gossiping and eating," he remarked with a smile for Rosetta and her sisters. "I've known fellows who don't have anything but dirty dishes to show for the time they spend together."

Amos was pleased that his remark brought a smile to Mattie's face, even if she wasn't meeting his gaze. He'd been in such pain the last time he'd seen her, he couldn't recall some of the things he'd said and done—except, of course, he remembered that he'd called off the wedding and ignored her birthday. Was it any wonder Mattie didn't want to look at him? Amos was keenly aware that he needed to ask her forgiveness, to repair the damage he'd done to their relationship. And he would find a way.

"Now we're gonna sing some carols," Lowell said brightly, "and then we're taking cookies and baby things over to Bishop Floyd's house."

"I'm sure Mary Kate and the bishop—and the whole family—will be blessed by your presence," Amos said with a nod. "Start up a song and I'll join in with you. I love Christmas carols!"

The kids looked at each other for a moment, and

then Lavern began singing in a clear voice. "'God rest ye merry, gentlemen—'"

"'Let nothing you dismay,'" everyone else joined in. Amos sang along, thinking the words of this old carol were good advice: it was best to listen for tidings of comfort and joy, to appreciate the blessings of God rather than allowing earthly toils and tribulations to take their toll. By the time he and Roman and their guests had also sung a verse of "Hark! The Herald Angels Sing," Amos felt happier than he had in weeks.

As he said goodnight to his visitors, Amos wore a big smile even though Mattie didn't linger behind the others to speak with him. He vowed to find a way to make her smile again, to make her believe in him the way she had for so many years of their lives.

"I'm going to join those folks at the Lehman place," Roman said as he came from the mudroom with his coat. "It'll be fun to sing some carols and see how the baby's doing."

"Not to mention Mary Kate," Amos added with a chuckle. "Give the bishop and his family my best. And kiss baby David for me. One of these days I intend to meet the little fellow in person, but for now you can be my messenger, Roman."

When Roman nodded and closed the door behind him, Amos let out a contented sigh. He lifted the edge of the plastic wrap and took an angel cookie from the plate on his lap. She was frosted in white and liberally sprinkled with crunchy white sugar crystals, and she had blue eyes, a pink O for a mouth, and a yellow halo. As Amos bit into the moist, chewy cookie, he gave thanks for the small pleasures of the season and for the joy the children of Promise Lodge wore on their pink-cheeked faces.

Amos wheeled over to the sofa and unfastened the ties of the white plastic bag. When he emptied it, his mouth fell open. An afghan of multicolored squares rolled out, big enough to cover the sofa.

Big enough to cuddle under, he thought as Mattie's face came to mind.

What other incentive did he need? Amos rolled his wheelchair to the back of the sofa, placed his hands on it for support, and stood up. He would walk again—he *would.* He would once again become the active, purposeful man Mattie Schwartz deserved, and—Lord willing—his love and devotion would become the most wonderful gifts she had ever received for Christmas.

Chapter Twenty-Three

Mary Kate stood in the front room with her son on her shoulder, swaying gently in time to the music as the carolers sang "Away in a Manger." Except for Minerva and Roman, these folks were the first visitors she'd had since David was born three days ago, and their smiles and songs lifted her spirits. The young boys who were usually running around and teasing each other looked almost angelic as they sang with their sisters, Laura, Phoebe, and Roman's *mamm* and aunts.

Roman seems to be enjoying this outing a lot, Mary Kate thought as she heard his steady baritone blending with the other voices. She wanted to believe that his eyes held a special shine tonight because he was here with her—although Gloria, who sat on the opposite end of the couch from Dat, was also gazing steadily at Roman as he sang.

Mary Kate closed her eyes, focusing on the tiny beat of David's heart against her chest. He was flapping his little arms as though the music excited him, and she gave thanks that her son was healthy and whole. His presence was such a blessing now that Dat seemed to be fading before their eyes.

The carol ended and Mary Kate smiled at their guests. "It's so *gut* to see you all," she said, "and what a pretty plate of cookies you made for us!"

As Lowell and the Peterscheim boys pointed to the various cookies they had decorated, Mary Kate noticed Lily, Fannie, and the Hershberger sisters exchanging secretive glances.

Laura slipped out the front door and came in again with a large white basket tied in pale blue ribbons. "For you and David," she said as she handed the basket to Mary Kate. "We've started a crochet club, and we wanted you to have a few things."

"And we could hold the baby while you look at what's in the basket," Phoebe hinted.

Mary Kate's mouth fell open. She handed her son to Phoebe, tickled when all the girls and women gathered around to coo at him—but she was even more delighted as she picked up pairs of tiny pastel booties, little caps, and silky-soft crocheted blankets. "Ohhh," she murmured as she held up each item to admire it. "And look at these toys! How adorable!"

Mamm came to stand beside her, her face alight. "What wonderful gifts," she said as she picked up a white crocheted lamb and a bright yellow duck. "You ladies have been busy with your hooks! It's been a long while since I crocheted, but seeing these baby things makes me want to start again."

"You could join our crochet club," Christine said as she took her turn holding David. "We started it as a pajama party for these cold winter nights, but you wouldn't have to wear your nightie if you came over.

We'd love to have you, Frances—and Gloria and Mary Kate, too, if you want to come."

"We have a great time," Laura said. She glanced at the bishop, who seemed to be dozing with his head lolled back against the sofa. "We're nearly finished with an afghan for Bishop Floyd, too," she whispered. "We'll bring it over as soon as the squares are joined together."

"What a lovely gesture," Mary Kate's *mamm* said wistfully. "Floyd will probably appreciate a warm afghan more than anything else we can give him."

The front room got quiet for a moment, until David let out a squawk of apparent delight. When Mary Kate looked up, she saw that Roman was holding the baby, making funny faces at him as he tickled David's nose with the crocheted duck. She suspected little David was too young to realize Roman was having fun with him, yet the sight of her son seeming to return Roman's gaze, gurgling and wiggling, touched Mary Kate deep inside. In her heart of hearts, she hoped that this would be the first of many times she could watch Roman and her son playing together . . .

After the carolers sang a rollicking rendition of "Angels We Have Heard on High," Mattie went out to the porch and came back with a fresh greenery wreath. "We want you folks to have this, and we wish you the peace of the season," she said. "Let us know what else we can do to help."

Mary Kate thought her mother might cry. "We'll put this above the fireplace, where we'll all enjoy it," Mamm said in a tight voice. "What a lovely gift—and it smells so fresh and pretty. Roman, if you could hang it for us—tall as you are—"

"I'd be happy to," Roman said. He showed no inclination to let go of David as the women and girls said their good-byes with another round of smiles for the baby. When the visitors had gone back out into the cold, Roman smiled at Mary Kate. "Any idea where I can find a hammer and a nail—or whatever sort of hanger you want me to use?"

"I know where they are!" Gloria said. As she hurried out of the front room, the baby began to fuss.

"Let me take him upstairs," Mary Kate suggested as she reached for her son. "It won't take all that long to feed him, if—if you'd like to stay for a while," she added shyly.

"I will," Roman replied. He smiled at her and nodded toward the basket. "I might have to play with his new toys—unless you're taking them upstairs, too."

Mary Kate felt a giggle bubbling up from deep inside her. "I want to look everything over, too. We can play with them together and check out those little caps and booties. I'll just take a blanket for now."

As she headed upstairs with David, Mary Kate gently stroked her son's cheek with the pale yellow blanket she'd grabbed. She was still in awe of the basketful of handmade gifts—and amazed at how comfortable Roman seemed to be with her baby. She settled into the rocking chair in her room, wrapped David in the soft blanket, and held him to her breast. As he suckled, Mary Kate relaxed, anticipating a quiet visit with Roman. Downstairs, she heard pounding on the wall and envisioned how cheerful the wreath would look above the fireplace.

When David had finished nursing and was beginning to doze off, she quickly changed his diaper, slipped him into pajamas, and gently laid him in the bassinet beside her bed. Mary Kate sighed. She and Mamm had found some basic, inexpensive baby clothes and the bassinet at the thrift store in Forest Grove, and they'd sewn a stack of cloth diapers a few weeks ago, but she didn't feel she could press her parents for a lot more. With Dat no longer working—and his medical bills mounting up—Mary Kate suspected money would get tight very soon.

Putting on a cheerful smile, she smoothed her dress and apron and went back downstairs—only to find Gloria seated next to Roman on the couch. Mary Kate reminded herself to give Roman the benefit of the doubt, knowing how her sister took every opportunity to impress their handsome blond neighbor.

"It would be a fine night for a sleigh ride, Roman," Gloria was saying in a sticky-sweet voice. "The moon is out, and—"

"And here's Mary Kate," Roman said in a purposeful tone. He rose from the couch, smiling as he reached for Mary Kate's hands. "If you're interested, we could go for a stroll," he suggested. "It's not really very cold—"

"I'll get my coat and ask Mamm to look in on David," Mary Kate said eagerly. "The fresh air will do me *gut.*"

When she returned to the front room wearing her coat and snow boots, Mary Kate was pleased to see that Gloria had gone to the kitchen with Mamm. She tied on her black bonnet and buttoned her coat before arranging a long green scarf around her neck. "Ready?"

Roman's eyes widened as he took her hand. "More than you know," he murmured.

They stepped outside and went down the porch stairs. Mary Kate sighed happily as she gazed up into the night sky. The stars looked like sparkling snowflakes embedded in deep blue velvet, and the hillsides around the lodge and the houses were blanketed with fresh, flawless snow. The evergreens across the road whispered as the wind shifted their branches, and Mary Kate could almost hear them saying her name in the deep silence of the evening.

"Oh, Roman, it's so beautiful here—so different from Ohio," she murmured. "We didn't have these hills and woods where we lived before."

"I like it here, too," he said. He led her behind the windbreak of pine trees, and then he turned so he was standing in front of her, close enough that their coats were touching.

When Roman slipped his arms around her, Mary Kate stepped into his embrace, encircling his neck with her arms. In a twinkling she knew he was going to kiss her, and before she could worry about doing it all wrong, Roman's lips lingered gently on hers. Mary Kate closed her eyes, giddy with the way he was holding her, sighing as he deepened her first kiss—or the first kiss that counted, anyway. The stranger who'd knocked her into the ditch hadn't cared a thing about affection, after all—and Mary Kate realized now that he hadn't even seen her as a person. That man had forgotten about her as soon has he'd gotten back into his car—so Mary Kate decided to put him out of her mind, as well. He wasn't worth remembering.

Roman eased away to look into her eyes. "Is this all right? I—I probably should've asked you if I could—"

Mary Kate rose onto her tiptoes and kissed him again, wishing this blissful moment could last forever. Roman held her as though he never wanted to let her go, his lips telling her what he'd been hinting at with words.

"Mary Kate, I—I didn't want to push you too fast, considering how—" Roman searched her face, his brown-eyed gaze intensified by the night. "Well, I thought you might be afraid of—might not want to be this close to a man, after the way . . ."

She smiled ruefully. "There was a time when I thought I'd never want another man to touch me," she admitted, "but you've been very patient and considerate, Roman. After the way you helped me when I was birthing David—the way you marvel over him and play with him—I know you'll never be mean to us. I feel so safe and protected when I'm with you."

Roman let out a relieved sigh. "It surprises me, how your little boy has already grabbed me by the heartstrings," he admitted. "I've not been around many babies, but when I first saw David, moments after he was born, something inside me just . . . changed."

"*Jah*, he's very real now," Mary Kate murmured. "There's no putting off his needs or thinking my time is my own anymore, even though he sleeps a lot. It's kind of scary."

When Mary Kate shivered, Roman held her close again. "Maybe we should get you back into the house," he said as he took her gloved hand in his. "I don't want you catching a chill."

"The wind is finding its way through the thin spots in my coat," she admitted as she walked quickly alongside him. "I should sew myself a new one—but I've been busy making baby clothes."

As they carefully climbed the snowy porch steps, Mary Kate chided herself for sounding as though she was desperate or begging for Roman's sympathy. *Why would he want to hear about your worn-out coat? Moments ago he was kissing you—*

They stepped into the front room, and when Roman saw no one but her sleeping father—still on the sofa where they'd left him—he kissed her again and then held her close. "Mary Kate, I—for a long time I've wanted to take care of you and make you smile and share my home with you and—will you marry me?" he murmured earnestly. "I love you so much."

Mary Kate felt as though she might explode with joy. "Oh, Roman, *yes!*" she blurted. She wrapped her arms tightly around his waist, thrumming with a whirlwind of emotions. Just a few days ago she'd delivered a healthy son, and now the young man of her dreams had asked her to marry him. What a remarkable week this had been!

A noise behind them made Mary Kate and Roman turn. Dat was getting up off the couch, and as he approached them his cane thumped loudly against the floor. He was talking forcefully, but his words were mushy despite his agitated tone of voice. Roman released Mary Kate and focused on her father.

"If I'd known you were awake, Bishop Floyd," he

began cautiously, "I would have asked you first if I could marry Mary Kate. I love her, and I want to—"

Once again Dat railed at them, gesturing toward the door with his cane.

Mary Kate swallowed hard. She couldn't understand what her *dat* was saying, but he was clearly very unhappy. "Are you sending Roman away? Shall I get you paper and pencil?" She'd gotten used to asking very simple questions he could answer with a nod or a shake of his head, because he only wrote things down when he felt like it.

Dat glared at her and then at Roman, once again pointing toward the door.

Mamm rushed out of the kitchen, clutching a dish towel. "Floyd, what's wrong?" she demanded. She glanced at Mary Kate and then at Roman with a bewildered expression.

Mary Kate was trying not to cry. "Roman asked me to marry him," she murmured. "We—we thought Dat was sleeping, but now he's all upset, and—"

"I'll leave," Roman said in a low voice. "We'll sort this out another time, Mary Kate, but right now I'm concerned about your *dat* being so riled up. *Gut* night, all."

Blinking rapidly, Mary Kate nodded. "No matter what happens, you have my answer, Roman," she whispered.

"My offer will always stand." Roman slipped out the front door, taking a piece of Mary Kate's heart with him. Why had her father gotten so upset? Dat had been very appreciative of Roman's help with the horses and other outdoor chores, yet when he'd seen her in Roman's arms, his attitude had changed dramatically.

When the door was firmly shut, Dat stood staring at it, breathing rapidly. Mamm tried to take his hand, but he muttered at her and swatted her away.

"Floyd, please, settle yourself," Mamm pleaded. "We don't want you waking the baby—or having another stroke, God forbid."

Dat waved them off and hobbled back to the couch. Mary Kate wondered if he was losing his mind along with his ability to speak—but she was more concerned about what Roman must be thinking. What if he had second thoughts about marrying her now? What if Roman could see how difficult life with her family would be if her father kept objecting to his presence?

Greatly saddened, Mary Kate said goodnight to her parents and went upstairs. As she gazed at her sleeping son by the glow of her bedroom lamp, she wondered what the future held. She believed with all her heart that Roman wanted to marry her, but she sensed he might delay the wedding until her father could no longer object to it . . . and thinking about that alternative made tears run down her cheeks.

It was too soon to go to bed, so Mary Kate slipped into the rocking chair to watch David sleep. She heard Mamm fussing at Dat again downstairs, and his garbled response sounded even more vehement than before.

Sit with me, Jesus, Mary Kate prayed with her head in her hands. *It's going to be a long night.*

Chapter Twenty-Four

A week later, on Friday afternoon, Amos thrummed with the progress he'd made during his physical therapy session. He felt so good, partly because the massage therapist had given him a thorough rubdown, that he couldn't contain his excitement. He grinned at Truman from across the cab of the pickup.

"What do you think of getting everybody at Promise Lodge a pair of ice skates—or at least everybody who'd like them?" Amos asked. "I want it to be my Christmas gift to my friends here, because where would I be without them?"

Truman's eyebrows rose. "That's a lot of skates, Amos," he remarked. "I've been skating on Rainbow Lake since I was a kid, so I think it's a fine, fun idea—"

"Would you mind taking everybody to the mercantile in Forest Grove tomorrow?" Amos asked excitedly. "You might have to make a couple of trips—and with so many folks wanting skates all at once, the store might have to order some of them in the right sizes, but—"

"I'll be happy to!" Truman declared. "A while back

I offered to help Rosetta learn to skate, so this would be the perfect opportunity to get her fitted for a pair. If lots of other folks are learning at the same time, maybe she won't feel so bad about landing on her backside until she gets the hang of it."

"Let's do it!" Amos blurted. "Who knows? Maybe I can even coax Mattie onto the ice."

After Truman drove the truck beneath the curved iron Promise Lodge sign, he stopped in the lane. "Are you planning to teach her to skate, Amos?"

Amos knew a fishing question when he heard one. He held Truman's purposeful gaze. "When I was young, I spent all year looking forward to the joy of gliding across a frozen pond, feeling the snowflakes on my face in the hush of a winter's day," he murmured, reliving the scene again in his mind. "Let's consider this skating scenario my incentive for working really hard at my physical therapy. If I set the goal of being able to skate sometime around Christmas— or whenever the lake's frozen solid enough—my mind will talk my body into regaining its strength faster, don't you think?"

"Always *gut* to have a goal," Truman said. He glanced at his wristwatch as they drove closer to the lodge. "The kids are nearly done with school for the day. Do you want to tell them about going to pick out skates, or shall I?"

"How about if you do it—but don't tell them who the skates are from. I want it to be a mystery gift," Amos explained in a lower voice. "It's the season of mystery and giving, celebrating the *gut* and perfect gift God gave us all—and it's a way for everyone to enjoy this first winter in our new home."

"Let me ask the fellows on my landscaping crew to

help with the driving," Truman mused aloud. "We could make it in one trip that way—and the clerk could ring all the skates up at one time. I'll see what I can do about getting Mattie interested, too."

"The trick is to convince Rosetta and Christine they want to skate. Mattie wouldn't dream of letting her younger sisters get ahead of her at learning something new."

Truman laughed as he pulled the truck up to the back of Amos's house. "You've got that right! If one sister goes for this idea, they all three will—and they'll encourage each other out on the ice, too," he said as he opened the door of the truck. "You and I won't have to do nearly as much teaching that way. We can be demonstrators. Encouragers."

Amos opened the door on his side and very carefully slid out of the seat until his feet touched the ground. He waited for Truman to get his wheelchair out of the back—but instead of sitting in it, Amos took hold of its two handles on the back.

"This is what they're having me do during my sessions," he said as he slowly walked toward the back door. "But don't let on to anybody, all right? I want to be walking free and clear—no walker, no cane— before other folks are watching me, making me lose my concentration. I had no idea how I took it for granted, being able to walk and talk and do a bunch of other things all at once, without falling."

"You'll get there, Amos," Truman said as he jogged ahead to open the door. "Oh, but it makes me feel better to see your legs supporting you again. It's like getting a gift weeks before Christmas."

"You're the best friend a man ever had, Wickey,"

Amos said in a voice that was tight with emotion. "I'll call the mercantile to tell them you'll be arriving with a bunch of folks tomorrow, and that the skates are on my tab. Quick and easy—and a secret we'll enjoy keeping."

"*Jah*, it'll be our little secret," Truman teased as he stepped inside to hold the door. "I'll go tell the kids right now, and have them spread the word about what time we'll leave in the morning. It'll be our Christmas adventure!"

"And you can tell me all about it when you bring everyone back." Amos stopped in his kitchen to catch his breath, but he couldn't wipe the smile from his face. "You're the best, Truman. I owe you for another favor."

After he watched Wickey's truck back down his lane and head toward the lodge, Amos sat down at his kitchen table. He ate the last frosted cookie the kids had given him—a green wreath with red sprinkles—hearing their merry carols in his mind as he chewed.

It was going to be a wonderful-*gut* Christmas after all. He could *feel* it.

That same Friday evening, Rosetta sat among her sisters, nieces, and friends, all of them crocheting happily. The wind was from the north, so the old lodge windows were making her apartment drafty, but everyone stayed cozy by wearing sweaters over their nightgowns or by wrapping quilts around their shoulders. Beulah sat in an armchair adding the final round of border to the granny square afghan they'd made for Bishop Floyd, while the younger girls worked on toys for baby David. Rosetta and her sisters had decided to crochet a few lambs for the kids to use in the Christmas Eve program. The hum of happy chatter filled her main room, and for that Rosetta was grateful.

"I can't wait to go to the mercantile for ice skates tomorrow!" Laura said excitedly. "And Truman says if it stays below freezing this whole next week, he'll come test the ice for us."

"*Jah*, and as we've been roller-skating since we were kids," Phoebe chimed in, "I can't think it'll be too hard to adjust to balancing on a blade. We can wear extra clothes for padding until we get the hang of it."

Beulah shifted her afghan so she could continue crocheting the border. "I've got some padding I'd like to loan you," she teased.

"Ice-skating's all well and *gut* for you young folks," Ruby remarked, "but I'll be content to keep the hot chocolate and cider warm for everyone instead of falling all over myself on the ice."

Rosetta chuckled as she gazed at Christine and Mattie. "We three sisters aren't so young anymore, but we've decided to give it a go," she said. "I see it as something Truman and I can enjoy together—after he coaches us all."

"The Lehman girls and the Kurtzes already have skates, so they'll be able to help us, too," Laura said. She playfully raised her eyebrows. "Maybe Preacher Marlin will give you private lessons, Aunt Mattie."

"And maybe he won't!" Mattie shot back, laughing along with the others. "What I want to know is who's footing this bill. What with more than a dozen folks wanting to get skates tomorrow, that'll come to a whopper of a total."

It's a mystery. A plan for happiness, Rosetta thought as she focused on the lamb she was crocheting. She had a pretty good idea who was paying for the skates, and she admired him for his generosity—and considered it another sign of his recovery. For the next few minutes Rosetta listened to the conversation around her, lost in thoughts of gliding effortlessly across Rainbow Lake on her skates . . . smiling at Truman as he held her hand . . .

"I can still smell that fabulous meat loaf you made for supper, Ruby," Christine remarked as she worked another row on the fluffy white lamb she was making.

"It's Rosetta's pumpkin pie I smell," Phoebe said with a smile. "It's the cinnamon and ground cloves that make it taste extra-special *gut*."

"Speaking of food," Rosetta teased, "who's in the mood for one of those lemony cherry candy cane cookies Mattie made today? I had to hide them away in the pantry to keep from eating them all before anyone else got to try one."

"Well, if confession is *gut* for the soul, I'll confess that I've sampled one of those new cookies—or two," Beulah added with a chuckle. "I want to make a batch and send them to Delbert's kids with their presents, in case the weather keeps us from getting there on Christmas."

"I'll bring those cookies upstairs. We might as well be eating them as anyone else!" Rosetta stood up and laid her yarn and the lamb she'd been crocheting in her chair. "I'll tell myself that going up and down the stairs is enough exercise to work off some of those calories."

"Work off my calories while you're at it!" Ruby called after Rosetta.

As she started down the steps, Rosetta smiled at the lively chatter that continued in her apartment. What could be better than the friendships that had developed since all of them had moved to Promise Lodge? She anticipated many more winter evenings filled with this love, and with the joy she and the other ladies shared as they crocheted together. Truman had mentioned that his church encouraged donations of blankets, stocking caps, and scarves for homeless folks in Kansas City, and Rosetta sensed that once their crochet club members had made Christmas gifts for their family members and friends, they would be eager to donate time and yarn to this worthwhile cause.

As Rosetta entered the kitchen, which was still fragrant from the simple but delicious supper they'd enjoyed, she couldn't imagine being homeless. *Denki, Lord, for finding our families and friends homes in Promise— and in Your world to come,* she prayed as she opened the pantry door. When the phone rang, she quickly set the covered pan of cookies on the counter.

"Hello? Promise Lodge Apartments—and this is Rosetta," she added. "How can I help you?"

"Rosetta, it's Lester Lehman. And it's *gut* to hear your voice!"

"Lester! How are you—and your family?" she asked excitedly. "I suppose you have snow on the ground, like we do here? We've had at least seven or eight inches. Truman's thinking it won't be long before Rainbow Lake is frozen hard enough to skate on."

"We've had our share of cold and snow, *jah*," Lester

replied. He cleared his throat. "Thought I'd talk to you first, before I phoned Floyd's place. It's been a couple weeks since I last spoke with Frances. So . . . how's my brother doing by now?"

Rosetta sighed. "I wish I could say he's recovering," she murmured, "but when we took some cookies there last week, and sang carols in the front room, Floyd didn't even raise his head. I wasn't sure if he was asleep on the sofa, or if he didn't have the energy to respond to our visit."

"Oh my. Frances must have a lot on her mind," Lester said ruefully. "I wish Floyd had stayed in the hospital after Amos fell on him, but that's water under a bridge we won't be crossing again."

"*Jah*, I'm afraid so," Rosetta said. "It's very hard to tell what's going through Floyd's mind because we can't understand anything he says. On a brighter note, though, you have a bright, bouncy new nephew named David, born on December first. Mary Kate's doing fine, and we love that little boy to pieces."

"Glad to hear it. That family needs some happiness." Lester paused for a moment. "With Floyd unable to work any longer, I'll need to reorganize our siding and window business . . . will need to hire some more fellows to help me keep it going," he said in a faraway voice. "And meanwhile, Frances has no income."

"You know we won't let Floyd's family do without," Rosetta insisted quickly. "We look in on them every day now. We're all one big family here at Promise Lodge."

"*Jah*, you *gut* folks are the main reason I'm moving to Missouri," he said. "I'll send Frances a check to tide them over—but don't tell her that, or she'll fuss at me."

"You can count on us," Rosetta stated. "We're all looking forward to you and your family moving here, so you can live in your new home and get your business up and running again."

"And how's Amos doing? Last I heard from Frances, he'd told Mattie the wedding was off."

Rosetta smiled, gripping the receiver. "I suspect he and Truman are keeping a few secrets about his condition," she replied quietly. "When we stopped at Amos's place with cookies and carols last week, I thought he seemed much better—in attitude, anyway. Still in his wheelchair, though."

"They say attitude's ninety percent of everything we do," Lester remarked. "Amos impresses me as the sort who'll find a way to stay useful, even if he can't walk. I'm looking forward to hearing his sermons again, and spending time with him. He's a fine fellow."

"We were hoping he'd feel up to being in church last Sunday, but I still suspect he's improving more than he's telling us about." Rosetta glanced up the narrow stairway to be sure Mattie wasn't coming downstairs for the cookies. "The way Amos was looking at Mattie while we were singing, I could tell he hasn't put her out of his mind entirely."

Lester laughed. "A man's got a right to his plans and dreams—and so does Mattie. Say, it's been real *gut* talking with you, Rosetta. I'd best give Frances a call now."

"We'll keep you in our prayers, Lester. Give our best to your family."

"*Denki* for your honest appraisal of Floyd's condition," he said sadly. "Sometimes I suspect Frances isn't telling me the whole story—or maybe she doesn't have the heart to admit how seriously ill he is."

As Rosetta finished the conversation and hung up the phone, she sighed. *The Lehmans could use a big helping of Your comfort and peace, Lord,* she prayed as she picked up the pan of candy cane–shaped cookies. *And meanwhile we here in the lodge thank You for blessing us with an evening of comfort and joy.*

Chapter Twenty-Five

By Wednesday of the following week, the temperatures had dropped dramatically and more snow was falling. As Mattie washed the dishes after the noon meal, she overheard occasional remarks from the big room where Minerva was trying to keep the scholars' attention—but the boys were focused on the snow.

"After school we gotta go drill a hole in the lake to see how deep the ice is!" one boy said.

"Nuh-uh! Truman says we're not to go anywhere near Rainbow Lake until he checks the ice," came another boy's reply. "But we can sled down the big hill in back of the Kurtz place!"

"Menno and Lowell, you'll be staying after class to make up for the time you've wasted chit-chatting," Teacher Minerva said firmly. "Your parents won't be happy if I have to report your disruptive behavior to them."

Mattie smiled at Rosetta and Ruby, who had also overheard the schoolroom conversation. "Sounds like the kids are getting restless. Ready to be out of school for a couple weeks' vacation."

"*Jah*, I recall feeling that same way at their age," Rosetta murmured. "Truman has no idea how he's captured the boys' imaginations by taking them to buy their skates and then telling them how cold it had to stay before he'd allow them on the ice."

"Let's hope they all follow his precautions," Ruby remarked as she dried a big blue enamel roaster. "A boy down the road from Delbert's place wasn't careful about where his sled went."

"He fell through the ice on their farm pond and drowned," Beulah added ruefully.

"We'll need to watch out the lodge windows every now and again, to be sure nobody gets too excited and sneaks out to the lake," Mattie said as she peered outside. From the kitchen sink, they could see past Roman's house over to where Rainbow Lake appeared frozen and snowy. "After Amos and Floyd had such drastic accidents, I sure don't want to see anyone else get . . . hmm. There goes Queenie, barking like crazy. Who could that be coming down the lane?"

The other women crowded around Mattie to look out the window. Nobody recognized the large, green van approaching the lodge, so Rosetta set aside her tea towel. "Could be somebody wanting to buy soap or honey," she said as she started toward the lobby. "I'd better restock my display."

"Let me know if we need to open the cheese factory shop," Beulah called after her. She smiled at Mattie and Christine. "After the big order the mercantile fellow picked up yesterday, we'll need to make a few more batches tomorrow. Seems folks are loading up on our cheeses for the holidays."

Mattie resumed her dish washing, unable to recognize the folks getting out of the van—the three fellows in broad-brimmed hats and the two women bundled in their black coats and bonnets resembled most of the folks they knew. One man who seemed vaguely familiar leaned down to ruffle the fur behind Queenie's ears, and the dog jumped up to lick his cheek—something she only did to folks she knew. When the visitors entered the lodge lobby, Rosetta's exclamation made Mattie and Christine dry their hands excitedly.

"Barbara and Bernice, is it really you?" Rosetta cried. "And your husbands are here—and Allen! Oh, but it's *gut* to see you all!"

Mattie's heart sped up as she and her sister hurried to the lobby. That had been Allen Troyer patting the dog! What had brought Amos's kids all the way to Promise? She hadn't seen the Troyer twins since they married the Helmuth brothers and moved east. Allen left Coldstream right after his mother died. But now that all five of the guests in the lobby had removed their hats, there was no denying they were Amos's kids. "What a fine surprise," Mattie said as she rushed in to greet them.

"We had no idea you folks were coming," Christine put in as she, too, began hugging Barbara, Bernice, and a somewhat reluctant Allen. "Your *dat* will be so happy to see you."

The three siblings glanced at each other as though they were uncertain about how to respond to this. Then Barbara gestured toward the two tall redheaded fellows behind them. "You remember Sam and Simon—"

Mattie smiled and nodded at the girls' husbands. It tickled her, the way the Helmuth men's names were always said together—*Sam 'n' Simon*—so they sounded like one word. "And it's *gut* to see you fellows, too," she remarked. "I hope your nursery business is doing well?"

The redheads nodded. "Looking to expand," one of them remarked, while the other brother curled the brim of his hat in his hands.

"*Jah*, we were saying as we came in that this area looks to be *gut* for growing trees and shrubs and such," he said. "Do you know of any land that's for sale?"

Allen grunted. "Kind of putting the cart before the horse, aren't you?"

Barbara and Bernice seemed surprised about their husbands' remarks. Mattie had always been hard-pressed to tell Amos's daughters apart, so she wasn't certain which one was speaking. "We got a call from Dat a while back," one of them said.

"And we thought we'd better come for a visit," her sister continued. "Dat's doing all right, isn't he?"

Mattie exchanged glances with Rosetta and Christine. "I suspect Amos will be much better when he sees you've come to visit," Mattie hedged. "Your *dat* lives in the second house up the road."

"The smaller one," Rosetta clarified. "And up the hill we've got a nice place where you can all stay during your visit, as Lester—the owner—won't be back until next spring."

"Or Roman's got spare rooms in his place, a couple doors down from your *dat*," Mattie said. Then she got a better idea, knowing the Kuhn sisters wouldn't mind and Bishop Floyd was in no shape to object. "You're also welcome to stay in rooms upstairs here in the lodge. Either way, we'll be glad to catch up with all of you—"

"And don't worry about meals," Christine insisted.

"We'll set you places at our table right here—and we've got a place for your driver to stay, as well."

Sam and Simon glanced at each other and then one of them said, "If it's all the same to you, we'll stay here in the lodge where the food is."

"*Jah*, whatever you had for dinner still smells mighty fine," his brother put in. Then he smiled at Barbara and Bernice. "That way the girls won't have to hike through the snow before they have their breakfast."

"Or their coffee," the other Helmuth twin added wryly.

Mattie and her sisters laughed. "That settles it, then! We'll get three rooms ready—and one for your driver, as well," Mattie said.

"Her name's Vicki Winstead, and she'll appreciate that," Allen remarked. "She's been putting up with the five of us for a lot of miles, and she's ready to be off the road."

"We started out yesterday afternoon and then stayed over when we picked Allen up in Indiana," one of Amos's daughters explained.

"And we've been on the road all this morning," her sister finished. "It's so *gut* to be here and to see you all again! We'll go on over and surprise Dat now."

The five visitors put on their hats and went back outside to board their van.

"There's a story there," Mattie murmured as she watched the vehicle head slowly up the road. "Amos never mentioned it, but I had the idea there'd been some misunderstandings or hurt feelings after Anna died."

"Allen was always the rebel, hinting that he'd move away and jump the fence," Rosetta recalled as they all headed back into the kitchen. "Mostly to spite his preacher *dat*, I always thought."

"We'll hope for the best from this visit," said Christine. "What a blessing, that Amos's kids have shown up at Christmastime."

"And we'll plan for some happiness while they're here," Rosetta chimed in. "Wouldn't it be wonderful if they stayed through the New Year?"

Amos's eyes widened as he finished shaving above his silver-shot beard. He'd come into the bathroom to clean up after lunch, and he'd heard Roman open the front door.

"Allen! Barbara and Bernice—and Sam and Simon!" Roman called out in surprise. "Wow, it's been a long time. Come in! Come in!"

His kids were here? Amos hadn't heard a word from them since he'd left his message on Barbara's answering machine. He quickly rinsed his face and blotted it with a towel, wondering what on earth to say to them now that they'd shown up without any warning. How would he explain his wheelchair? The accident? And what would he say to soften their hearts . . . to convince them to forgive him for being such a stern, hard-hearted father?

You're a preacher—a man who delivers the Word of God, Amos reminded himself. In his private moments, he'd often envisioned the conversation he so desperately needed to have with his children, yet now that the moment was at hand, he was at a loss for words that might end their separation. But the longer he took getting out to the front room, the more his children might assume he was stalling. When the kids had lived at home, he'd been up before dawn and had done most of a day's work by this hour—

Life has changed directions for all of us. You can't go back and repair the past, but your future with your kids starts right this minute.

Amos slid into his wheelchair and propelled himself out to where Roman was taking his visitors' wraps. "What wonderful music to my ears, hearing your voices again!" Amos called out. "Did you have any trouble finding us here in Promise? It must have been a long trip for you."

Allen appeared impatient—as usual. "English drivers have computerized gadgets that show you the way," he pointed out. "But you did find a place out in the middle of nowhere, compared to Coldstream. So what's with the wheelchair?"

Amos felt his temper prickling—as it always had when Allen spoke in such a sardonic tone. But it was his place, his sincerest desire, to put an end to the animosity that had come between them, so Amos smiled. "We moved here because we could no longer tolerate Bishop Chupp's way of chastising everyone except Isaac," he replied cheerfully, holding his son's gaze. "Mattie, her sisters, and I felt Obadiah had lost his sense of perspective. His loyalty to God and his congregation were no longer his highest priorities. You were right about him all along, Allen."

Allen's eyes widened. "Well, that's a first, you giving me credit for—"

"Allen, be kind," Bernice warned her brother.

"*Jah*, we came here to make our peace," Barbara

reminded him sternly. "Don't put us at odds before we even have a chance to talk things through."

Amos was pleased that his girls were still putting their younger brother in his place after all these years—and he took heart because Barbara and Bernice were taking their father's side, wanting to reconcile. "How about if we all sit down," he suggested, gesturing toward the sofa and chairs. "I've not quite gotten my new place put together, but—"

"It's a sweet little house," Bernice said as she gazed around. "I see lots of furniture from our home in Coldstream."

"And Promise Lodge looks like a wonderful-*gut* new colony, from what we've seen," Barbara said as she headed for the sofa. "We sent our driver back to the lodge, figuring she'd feel right at home there with Mattie, Christine, and Rosetta."

"We're looking forward to taking them up on their invitation for meals, too," Sam remarked as he angled his lanky body into the armchair nearest Barbara.

"*Jah*, some mighty fine smells were coming from that kitchen," Simon said with a chuckle. "I remember meeting those three gals at our wedding, and they kept things pretty lively."

Amos rolled his wheelchair so he was sitting between the end of the sofa and the two chairs that faced it. Despite the kids' easy chatter, it felt a little awkward, seeing his son and two daughters—now adults—and the girls' husbands gathered here in his front room. He would probably have had more—and newer—furniture if he'd married Mattie, but he set that thought from his mind.

"I've put the percolator on the stove," Roman called from the kitchen. "If one of you girls would keep track of it, I'll leave you to visit with your *dat*."

"*Denki*, Roman. You're a lifesaver—not that I'm comparing you to the candy," Amos teased as he swiveled in his chair. "If you're going to the Lehmans', give them my best."

When Roman waved and slipped out the kitchen door, Amos turned back to his kids. "You probably wonder why Roman's looking after me," he said, patting the arms of his wheelchair for emphasis. "I'll give you the abbreviated story of how your old *dat* should've known better than to put his weight on a rotted roof."

As Amos explained the fall that had caused his concussion and the weakening of his legs, he relaxed. It felt good to see his children's matured faces, to watch their expressions become more intense, more concerned, while he was telling them about his trip to the hospital and the physical therapy he was receiving. He didn't mention the part about canceling his wedding, because he hadn't ever told them he and Mattie were engaged.

Yet another mistake you made, not keeping the kids informed about your plans to remarry, Amos mused as Barbara excused herself to fetch them some coffee. He'd thought his children would believe he'd swept their mother out of his life if he took another wife—and Amos realized now that he'd done Mattie yet another disservice by not telling his kids that she'd resumed an important place in his life. So many mistakes he'd made . . .

"So the bishop here is laid up, as well? And he's in

worse shape than you are?" Simon asked as he raked his red hair back from his face.

Amos nodded, grateful for a topic that didn't require any remorse on his part—or did it? "I couldn't believe it when Floyd rushed over with his arms out," Amos murmured. "In fact, I thought he was talking crazy, demanding that God send angels to catch me. I—I owe Floyd more favors than I can count for the way he risked his own safety on my behalf. He had a stroke shortly after our accident, and he might never recover the use of his left side, or his ability to speak."

And I'd better find a way to make amends and make myself useful to his family, Amos thought.

"You don't suppose Obadiah Chupp will want to move here and take Floyd's place, do you?" Bernice teased with a sparkle in her dark eyes.

Amos laughed out loud. "We had a run-in with Bishop Obadiah, concerning Isaac and Deborah Peterscheim—who's now married to Noah Schwartz," he added to update them. "I don't see the Chupps coming here, but Preacher Eli's family has joined us, and we've welcomed Preacher Marlin Kurtz and his family from Iowa, along with Bishop Floyd's brother, Lester, who's bringing his family back with him next spring."

"Sounds like Promise Lodge has more than its share of preachers," Allen remarked under his breath.

"And it won't hurt you one little bit to associate with fellows who're serving God, living responsible lives, little brother," Barbara said as she carefully set a tray of filled coffee mugs on the end table. She handed Amos the first mug, letting her hands linger on his.

"Dat, when you called and said you hoped we kids could forgive you, I didn't know what to think," she said softly. "Bernice and I listened to your message again and again, and honestly, it's we girls who need to apologize."

"We should've kept writing to you after Mamm passed," Bernice continued earnestly, "but we got caught up in our married lives and—and we didn't know what to say, what with her being gone."

"It's a poor excuse," Barbara insisted as she cupped her hands around Amos's, "and we told Sam and Simon that the only true way to apologize was to come and see you. So they closed the nursery for the rest of the year, and here we are."

Amos's heart was thumping so hard he couldn't speak for a moment. "You girls were always closer to your *mamm*, but I really should've been better at keeping in touch. I was pretty harsh at times while you were growing up, and not always very kind to your mother, either—"

"Oh, Dat, how can you say that?" Bernice asked. She rose from the sofa to join her sister, slipping her arm around Amos's shoulders. "Mamm seemed perfectly happy to me, always humming while she worked around the house and looked after us. We lacked for nothing while we were growing up, and—well, we weren't exactly angels. We needed a firm word now and again."

"*Didn't* we, Allen?" Barbara challenged as she gazed at her brother. "After all the talking we did on this subject during the ride to Missouri, don't you dare leave Dat hanging, thinking it was his fault that you left home."

Amos didn't know what to say. Scenes from his vivid dreams of Anna replayed in his mind. He clearly recalled his wife telling him he cared more for the horses than he did for her—and that he'd been a lousy husband for abandoning her when the twins were born. And in the next dream, Allen had said a few choice words before he'd walked out, too. Yet his girls didn't seem to believe their childhood had been particularly difficult or onerous.

Allen sighed loudly and began handing mugs of coffee to Sam and Simon—as a diversion, Amos sensed. His son had never been one to express his feelings or to apologize.

The apple hasn't fallen too far from the tree, ain't so?

Amos smiled ruefully. Allen had matured into a ruggedly handsome young man with dark hair and penetrating brown eyes. He would probably remain rough around the edges until some young woman took pity on him and agreed to be his wife—which meant Allen would either join the Old Order or marry someone of a different faith, a thought that twisted an imaginary knife in Amos's gut.

When Allen had resumed his seat and taken a noisy slurp of his coffee, he gazed directly at Amos. To Amos, it was like looking in a mirror from when he'd been in his early twenties. And in some ways it was a painful reminder of what an *attitude* he'd had back then, too.

"It was mostly Chupp I couldn't stomach," Allen said in a low voice. "And *jah*, after Mamm died I wasn't much on being in that house without her, so I took off to become my own man. Not that I've been hugely successful at it."

Amos's eyebrows rose. It had taken considerable courage for Allen to admit that he'd not done as well as he'd hoped. "What're you doing these days, son?" he asked softly. "You had the aptitude to take up any trade you set your sights on."

Allen's face registered surprise. "Could've fooled me," he murmured. "I took some course work in plumbing and electricity, figuring I'd be able to hire on with English contractors. But come time to take the licensing exams, I . . . I chickened out."

Amos bit back a remark about how Allen would have no use for knowledge of electricity if he joined the Amish Church—which was exactly what Preacher Amos would've said a few years ago. Something in his son's tone made Amos listen more carefully, hearing the fear and insecurity Allen wouldn't have owned up to when he'd lived at home. "So you've learned a lot of useful skills, but you're not officially a plumber or an electrician?" he asked gently. "What's stopping you, son? I always figured you'd take on a trade I never had the smarts to master."

With a short laugh, Allen shook his head. "Remember how I learned math and reading well enough when I was a scholar, but come time to take big tests, everything I knew flew out the window?" he asked sheepishly. "Well, I didn't want to pay the fees and show up for the licensing tests only to flunk out. So I didn't go. I've been getting a few jobs with fellows I took those classes with, but they can't let me work on the commercial jobs because I'm not licensed."

Amos felt terribly sorry for his son, just as he'd agonized over the way Allen's poor grades in the Coldstream school had never reflected his true intelligence. What could he say to fix this dilemma? Amos recalled chiding and chastising Allen when he was younger, but that approach hadn't worked, had it? His boy still lacked confidence when it came to written tests. Allen still feared failure.

"If you were to stay in Promise a while, maybe our Teacher Minerva could give you some practice at taking tests like the ones you need to get your licenses," Amos mused aloud. He held his son's gaze, pleased that Allen had admitted his need. "I'm not telling you what to do, understand. You probably want to head back to Indiana already, after seeing how small our new colony is."

Allen's lips twitched. "Truth be told, I sort of miss Missouri. But maybe you've hit on an idea," he murmured. "Some of my trade school buddies got copies of sample tests on their computers and practiced with them before the exam."

"And if you asked them, those fellows would probably give you printed copies to work with," Simon said.

"Any one of us would help you practice with those tests," Bernice continued eagerly. "Remember how Barbara and I used to make you play school with us?"

"You were our best scholar, Allen—even if you were our only scholar," Barbara said. "What's family for, if not to help you along?"

"If you called those friends tonight, and they put sample tests in the mail right away," Sam speculated, "we could drill you while we're all here for the holidays. Once we head home and drop you off in Indiana, we can't be much help."

"I'll think about it." Allen appeared to be closing off this topic of conversation, yet Amos sensed his son might have gotten enough encouragement to carry through on what his sisters and brothers-in-law had suggested.

For a moment they all sipped their coffee. Amos's thoughts were spinning as he considered what his children had said—how they had refuted the painful messages he'd received in those dreams. Even so, Amos felt compelled to wipe the slate clean. Who knew how long it might be before he had his kids together again?

"You'll never know how grateful I am that you've all come here to see me," he began softly. "And if I said or did things that seemed hurtful or hard-hearted— to you or to your mother—I hope you can forgive me. I regret the separation I might've caused—"

"Enough said, Dat," Bernice insisted, holding up her slender hand to stop him. "Barbara and I moved to Ohio with these redheaded Helmuth fellows because they so badly needed our guidance—"

"And it had nothing to do with our life at home with you and Mamm," Barbara finished. "Amish parents believe in discipline and obedience. Nothing wrong with that. Matter of fact," she added, blushing as she looked at her husband, "Sam and I plan to raise our kids the same way."

"So do Simon and I," Bernice put in, reaching for her husband's hand. "We're expecting our first ones in June, you see."

Amos's mouth dropped open. "You—you're starting your family?"

"Both of us are, *jah.*" Barbara nodded happily, wrapping her arm around her midsection.

Bernice laughed. "It was the craziest thing, when we both realized we were carrying—and that we'll both give birth around the same time, too. It's a twin thing, I guess."

Allen gazed first at Sam and then at Simon, shaking his head in disbelief. "Are you kidding me? Did you guys plan this out?"

Simon shrugged at the same time his brother did. "Bernice said it exactly right. It's a twin thing."

"We were just doing what we were told," Sam teased as he looked at the two girls. "It was their idea to come here and make the announcement to you in person, Amos, and it seemed like the perfect reason to shut down the nursery shop for a while. Nothing's worth more than being with your family."

Grandchildren! Two of them—next summer! Amos wanted to laugh and cry and sing all at the same time as he gazed at his daughters. "I—well, it seems I've just received the best Christmas gift a father could ask for," he blurted.

Simon smiled secretively. "Maybe we'll have another surprise after we've been here long enough to see your new colony," he said. "We've got a younger brother looking to get hitched soon, and he'll be needing a business that'll support him—"

"And you know how all the best land out east is either passed down through generations of a family, or it's too expensive for a fellow just starting out," Sam added with a smile that matched his brother's.

Amos blinked. Did he dare believe his daughters and their husbands would relocate to Promise Lodge? He decided not to press them for an answer—or to entice them by offering plots of land. Some gifts were meant to be anticipated and savored, opened in their own good time.

Amos felt extremely grateful because he would have another couple of weeks to spend with his children, who apparently loved him despite all of his perceived faults. Those painful dreams he'd experienced had served their purpose, but Amos was even more grateful because they hadn't come true.

Chapter Twenty-Six

On Saturday morning—with only six more days until Christmas—Mattie sang along with the other ladies in the kitchen. The old carols rang sweetly as some of them baked and decorated cookies while others prepared a special noon meal for everyone at Promise Lodge, as a way for folks to get better acquainted—or to catch up—with Amos's three kids and the girls' husbands. Barbara, Bernice, and their driver Vicki already seemed right at home with the Kuhn sisters. They were asking a lot of questions about the cheese factory as they helped Beulah make a large pan of macaroni and goat cheese.

"Oh, that's a real treat," Phoebe remarked as she walked by the counter where Amos's twins were pouring the macaroni mixture into a big glass casserole. "And when Ruby tops it with slices of her fresh mozzarella cheese, you'll want to take seconds—"

"And thirds!" Laura teased as she rolled out dough on the counter. "But I'll be saving room for lots of these sugar cookies. Seems the ones the kids made last week all disappeared before I got any."

"Did someone say sugar cookies?" a male voice called out from the lobby. "Make lots of stars with frosting and jimmies on them!"

When Roman entered the kitchen, followed by Allen Troyer, Mattie had to chuckle. Her sons had always loved frosted sugar cookies, and when Roman, Noah, and Allen were growing up, the three of them had devoured dozens of cookies in her kitchen before heading outside to play. It did Mattie's heart good to see the young men renewing their friendship—just as she enjoyed seeing the big stack of mail her son placed on the worktable.

"Lots of Christmas cards," Roman remarked as he snatched a warm bell from the wire rack where the cookies were cooling. "We'll be back when you've got these frosted, Laura. Better mix up another batch of dough, don't you think?"

As the young people teased each other, Mattie stepped over to the pile of mail at the same time Rosetta did. "Several cards from our friends in Coldstream," Rosetta said as she leafed through the colorful envelopes. "This small one's addressed to you, Mattie. Who could it be from?"

When Mattie noted that the return address was U NO HOO, her heart thudded faster. She snatched the envelope from Rosetta's fingers. "None of your beeswax, little sister," she murmured.

Rosetta's dark eyebrows rose. "Hmm, could Marlin be writing you a special invitation to visit his barrel shop?" she teased. "He asked you quite some time ago, but I don't think you've gone—"

"Nor do I intend to," Mattie put in crisply. "I told Marlin I was glad he moved here, but that I wasn't interested in a private tour of his shop—or a serious relationship." She glanced around, pleased that the other women were singing again and paying attention to their own tasks rather than following this whispered conversation. "Carry on, Rosetta. I'll be back shortly."

Feeling as giddy as a schoolgirl whose sweetheart had passed her a note at recess, Mattie headed into the lobby and up the double stairway to the privacy of her apartment. She had recognized the small, uneven handwriting—and U NO HOO—immediately, and before she'd entered her doorway she'd ripped the envelope open.

Mattie,

I've been such a blind, hard-headed fool. Please, please, will you forgive me? Can we be lovebirds again, singing and winging our way through the rest of our lives together?

"Oh, Amos," Mattie murmured as tears sprang to her eyes. When they'd been head over heels for each other years ago, he'd written her the sweetest letters—and that's when he'd made up his whimsical return address. That was also when she'd known Amos Troyer was unlike any other man she would ever meet.

How about a sleigh ride Saturday afternoon? I'm guessing my kids and yours—and lots of the others—will be ice-skating then, so if you'll slip away with me, maybe we can get our act together again. At least I hope so. I never, ever meant to break your heart, dear Mattie. I love you more now than I ever knew how, back when we were kids.

Your man always,
Amos.

Mattie sucked in her breath. She'd longed for such a letter since the moment Amos had sent her away on that awful afternoon when his depression had gotten the best of him. She'd insisted that it didn't matter to her if he'd be in a wheelchair—but Amos hadn't been ready to believe her that day. This brief, compelling letter said far more between the lines than Amos's affectionate words spelled out.

Amos had stopped wandering in the wilderness of his affliction. He'd come back to himself—and he wanted her again.

"Oh, Amos!" Mattie repeated as she went to her closet. She pulled out a dress the color of cranberry sauce and slipped into it, then put on a fresh *kapp*, as well. In a few hours she would be accepting Amos's invitation for a sleigh ride—and whatever else he suggested.

When Mattie returned downstairs and began setting the big tables for their festive meal, Rosetta came out to help her. "Why do I suspect somebody's got a date?" she teased.

"*Jah*, the way I understand it, you're taking another skating lesson from Truman this afternoon," Mattie replied without missing a beat.

"Puh! You think you're keeping a secret, but it's written all over your face, Mattie," Rosetta said as she finished putting the plates at each chair. She slipped her arm around Mattie's shoulders and pulled her close. "And nobody's happier than I am that Amos has come to his senses."

Mattie felt her cheeks tingling. "Well, don't go shouting it from the rooftops just yet. But I think you're right."

As everyone began arriving just before noon, the

women came into the kitchen while the men chatted in the dining room. Mattie was busy slicing the turkey and the ham, chatting with Frances and Minerva as they filled serving bowls with stewed tomatoes, creamed corn, and steamed broccoli. When Mattie set the platter of ham at the end of the table, she couldn't miss the way Amos was gazing at her, his dark eyes wide with a pressing question. He sat taller in his wheelchair. He was wearing a shirt of deep green, and his hair was neatly combed.

He's better looking now than he was at twenty, Mattie thought as she held his gaze. When she smiled and gave him a thumbs-up, Amos grabbed her hand.

"See you later," he whispered.

Mattie nodded eagerly. "*Jah,* you will."

After everyone was seated and had joined in the silent prayer of thanks, the bowls and platters made their way around the extended table, which comprised three tables placed end to end. Mattie smiled as she looked at every resident and guest who graced their home . . . the two Kuhns, the six Peterscheims, the five Kurtzes, three of the Lehmans—because Mary Kate had remained at home with little David— her sisters and nieces, her two sons and Deborah— not to mention Amos and his three kids, two sons-in-law, and Vicki. Truman and his mother had joined them, as well. What a sight, what a blessing, that all of them were here together!

"Floyd, it's *gut* to see you," Amos called to the bishop, who sat at the other end of the long table. "I want you to know how grateful I am that you tried to catch me when I fell, and how sorry I am that you came out of that accident in much worse shape than

I did. If there's any way I can help you and your family, I want to know about it, all right?"

The dining room got quiet. Bishop Floyd straightened in his chair. He didn't say anything, but he gestured to Frances, who pulled a notepad and pen from her apron pocket.

Mattie watched as the bishop laboriously wrote a few words on the paper with his good hand. When she caught Frances's eye, Frances smiled.

"The occupational therapist told Floyd he should be communicating in whatever way he can, and we're grateful for this advice—and thankful to God that Floyd can still use his right hand." Frances paused to glance at the note her husband shoved toward her. "It says, 'Amos, seeing that you feel better makes me feel better, too. Just be my friend.'"

Everyone around the table smiled and murmured their agreement. Mattie felt hugely relieved by this statement, considering the difficulties the Lehman family had experienced since Floyd's stroke.

"What a wonderful thing to say," Amos replied to the bishop. "I'm proud to be your friend, Floyd. Keep up the *gut* work with your therapists."

For the next several minutes, everyone concentrated on eating, talking among themselves. Every time Mattie glanced at Amos, he was already looking at her . . . a man with a plan, apparently. He turned toward the redheaded son-in-law who sat beside him and murmured something.

Sam—or was it Simon?—smiled brightly. "This seems like a fine time to share our news," he began as he gazed across the table at Barbara and Bernice. "My brother and I have spent these past few days looking over the land here, and talking with Amos, and we've decided to move to Promise Lodge! The girls want to be near their *dat* when our kids are born—and Sam and I believe a garden center and nursery like we have in Ohio will do very well here."

"Oh, I'm so glad to hear that!" Christine said, clapping her hands. Rosetta grinned and added her congratulations, as did other folks.

"That's *gut* news for me, too," Truman put in happily. "I'd like nothing better than to buy my trees and shrubs from my neighbors instead of having to drive so far to find reliable stock. Welcome to Promise Lodge, you Helmuths!"

"We'll move early in the spring," Barbara said, smiling at everyone around the table. "Dat has offered to build us houses by then, and it'll be the best time for Sam and Simon to transport nursery stock to start this branch of the business."

"And what about you, Allen? Are you coming, too?" Gloria asked sweetly.

Mattie bit back a laugh. Gloria's question, accompanied by the batting of her eyes, left no doubt about her interest in Amos's handsome son.

Allen shrugged, but he was smiling. "Might be. Once I take my exams—and *pass* them," he insisted as he looked at his *dat*, "I think I could find plenty of work around here as a plumber or an electrician. Of course, Dat has been reminding me that I also need to join the Old Order, and that maybe I shouldn't be as interested in electrical matters—"

"But at least we're talking about it," Amos finished. "We all know plenty of young men who have equipped themselves with education and skills and then put them to *gut* use after they joined the church. I'm tickled that Allen's even considering coming home."

Mattie could tell that Amos felt immensely gratified by his children's presence, and by their decision to relocate from the Helmuth family's thriving nursery business in Ohio. "Seems to me that God's been very busy amongst us lately," she said as she rose to fetch the cookie tray and the pies from the sideboard. "We've seen such improvement in Amos and Floyd, and now the two Helmuth couples are joining us—not to mention their babies and maybe Allen! That's a lot of blessings to celebrate."

"*And* we get to go ice-skating today!" Johnny piped up. "That surely is a blessing—thanks to whoever gave us our new skates."

As everyone murmured their assent and their thanks, Mattie held her breath. The expression on Amos's face told her he wasn't nearly finished bestowing blessings—and she hoped everyone would be excited enough about skating that they wouldn't linger too long over their dessert. About half an hour later, when most of the pies had disappeared and the tray had only a few cookies left on it, folks began to push back from the table. Amos winked at Mattie and then murmured something to Allen, who wheeled his *dat* toward the lobby, where the coats were.

Ruby, Beulah, and Christine all gathered around Mattie and Rosetta. "You girls have afternoon plans that are much more exciting than cleaning up the kitchen," Beulah said.

"So get ready for your fun!" Ruby insisted. "We've got plenty of help today."

"If anyone deserves time out to enjoy life, it's you two," Christine added with an emphatic nod.

Mattie raised an eyebrow at Rosetta. "You told everyone I was going to—"

"Hah!" Beulah blurted. "The way Amos was gawking at you during dinner, I thought the tablecloth might catch fire. Maybe his kids talked some sense into him."

"Or maybe," Rosetta said playfully, "Amos decided it was his turn to show a special gal a *gut* time in his beautiful sleigh. After I take a few tumbles on the ice, I'll probably wish I could trade places with you."

Mattie couldn't help grinning—and she didn't argue about leaving the kitchen cleanup to the other women, either. By the time she freshened up and came back to the lobby in her deep red cloak and black bonnet, she saw that Amos was waiting in the sleigh, out by the lodge's front porch. It was such a treat to see him settled on the plush velvet seat without his wheelchair, she didn't even mind that the other women would be gawking out the windows, watching them leave.

"I suppose Allen helped you by hitching Mabel to the sleigh and tucking the blankets around you," Mattie said as she took her place at Amos's left.

Amos shrugged, smiling mysteriously.

"And what do your kids think about us being together?" she asked as she arranged part of the quilt around her lap.

Amos grabbed her hand under the blanket and squeezed it. "They said it was about time I got on with my life," he replied in a tight voice. "I'd been so concerned, thinking they'd resent my leaving their mother's memory behind—which is why I didn't tell them when you and I originally got engaged. Turns out I've been mistaken about several things. But enough about the kids."

Mattie didn't dare drop her gaze, even as Amos clapped the lines lightly across Mabel's back. Amos seemed to be keeping secrets, wondering how to say what was on his mind as the sleigh lurched and then slid over the snow-covered ground. The bells on the mare's harness kept time with Mabel's leisurely trot, and a few snowflakes kissed Mattie's cheek. As they passed near Rainbow Lake, several skating kids waved to them, as did Truman and Rosetta. Once the sleigh started up the hill and away from watchful eyes, Amos slipped his arm around her.

"Mattie."

She scooted against him, deliriously happy that he wanted to hold her again. "*Jah?*" she whispered. "I'm listening."

"Of course you are. And had I followed your lead—had I listened with my heart instead of my hard head—we wouldn't have spent the past month apart," Amos murmured. "Can you forgive me for shutting you out, sweetheart? I've been such a stupid fool."

Mattie rested her head against Amos's shoulder. "We all take our turns at playing the fool, Amos. I'm so tickled that you're feeling better now—and you know, it doesn't matter one bit to me about your being in a wheelchair."

"Well, it matters to *me*," he retorted. He kissed her cheek, returning to his amiable mood. "But what matters more is that you've agreed to be with me again, to let me start over at trying to win your heart."

"Oh, Amos," Mattie said with a dreamlike sigh. "You've had my heart since we were kids. I—I might've set aside my feelings while we were married to Marvin and Anna, but I've always loved you, Amos. I don't know how to stop."

"It's been the same for me," he insisted. "But I've got to settle something today. I just hope I won't fall flat on my face. Or my backside."

Mattie blinked. Amos had steered the sleigh past the orchard and Ruby's beehives, up the gently rising hill behind the two Lehman homes. Despite the carefree jingle of the sleigh bells, Amos now seemed so serious, so set on doing something exactly right for her. *Surely he knows he doesn't have to impress me anymore. We're beyond those adolescent expectations . . .*

When Mabel slowed down on the snow-covered path that led into the woods, Amos pulled the mare to a halt. With a nervous sigh, he looked at Mattie. "Why don't you walk ahead of us, into the shelter of those old evergreens? Wait for me there, okay?"

Mattie's eyes widened. She hadn't seen Amos's wheelchair folded in the backseat—not that he'd be able to propel it across the uneven ground, or through the snow that had piled up over the past few weeks. What on earth was he thinking to do?

The earnest expression on Amos's dear, weathered face told Mattie not to ask any questions. She slipped out from under the quilt and onto the ground, glad she'd put on her boots before she'd left the lodge. Mattie walked toward the impressive evergreens, which were dressed in their lacy-white winter finery, praying that whatever Amos had in mind, it would go smoothly.

When she reached the edge of the woods where the evergreens formed a windbreak, she turned—and gasped. Amos was following her! His progress was slow, but with the aid of a cane he was carefully lifting one foot and putting it in front of the other. Mattie wanted to rush to him, shouting for joy, except she didn't want to distract Amos from a task that was requiring his utmost concentration.

Lord, denki *so much for whatever it's taken to get him walking again!* Mattie prayed as she watched each step he took. Her heart was thumping so hard Amos could probably hear it, because she felt such joy—such pride in his accomplishment. Now she understood why Amos had been secretive. He'd probably stashed his cane beneath the seat of the sleigh so she wouldn't quiz him about it. No doubt he'd been working very hard with his physical therapists, but the real proof of his recovery—at least to Amos—depended upon his ability to walk without anyone else's help.

A couple of yards away, Amos stopped. He placed his cane in front of him to lean on it for a moment as wisps of his breath encircled his head. "How's that?" he murmured, fighting a grin.

"Amos, look at you! It's our Christmas miracle!" Mattie cried, rushing toward him with her arms open wide. "I'm so—I'm so proud! And excited!"

"Watch out, now. Pride goes before a fall," he murmured as she wrapped her arms around him. "And now that I'm this far from the sleigh, I *don't* want to fall!"

Mattie laughed, exhilarated when Amos slipped an arm around her waist and claimed her lips in a long, thorough kiss. "Oh, Amos," she whispered when she'd caught her breath. "This is the best Christmas gift ever, seeing you up and walking again. You've been working very hard."

"You've got that right," he said with a chuckle. "But when the therapist looked at my X-rays and found a few nerves that appeared pinched, he suggested some massage and some exercises that would get the blood pumping where it needed to be again. And I have to admit that taking the antidepressant Dr. Townsend prescribed was what got me on the road to recovery."

"You could've ignored the doctor's advice, like other men have done."

When Amos smiled, the lines around his brown eyes deepened. "I was on a mission to walk—to be a whole man again—for *you*, Mattie. By the New Year, I hope to get you out on the lake, skating alongside me. Sometimes I'm too vain for my own *gut*, but this time that vanity spurred me on to get well. I never wanted to see pity in your eyes again, sweetheart."

Mattie blinked back tears, speechless. She'd assumed Amos had cast her completely out of his life and thoughts these past lonely weeks, so it was a sweet relief to realize she'd served as an incentive for his recovery.

"I want to marry you as soon as we find a bishop who can tie the knot," Amos murmured. "Is that still all right with you?"

"All right?" she challenged breathlessly. "It's all I've ever wanted, Amos."

"Shall we seal that intention with a kiss?"

Mattie's cheeks went hot as Amos straightened to his full height. When he took her in his arms, she lifted her face to receive the blessing of his affection. At long last they were ready to marry, to become life partners in the truest sense. Amos lingered over the kiss, and when he eased away, Mattie stood on tiptoe to press her lips to his again.

Amos chuckled low in his throat. "What a happy day this is, and what a wonderful woman you are," he murmured as he gazed into her eyes. "I'm a blessed man, Mattie. Now let's turn around and survey our domain."

When Mattie pivoted, her breath caught. From this vantage point, they could watch a few skaters gliding across Rainbow Lake, while other folks practiced walking on their skate blades by holding on to partners or to the dock that extended out over the ice. Wisps of smoke curled up from the lodge chimney. Snow covered the hillsides in a flawless blanket and decorated the rooftops of all the new houses and barns, while Rosetta's goats, Christine's cows, and Harley's sheep munched contentedly at the hay in their outdoor feeders.

"It looks like one of those miniature villages you see in the stores around Christmas—except prettier," Mattie murmured. "All we need is a train—"

"No, all we need is each other," Amos corrected gently. "And with all of our kids settling down here at Promise Lodge, the world feels cozy and complete now, *jah?*"

"It does," Mattie agreed. "You've said it all, Amos."

Chapter Twenty-Seven

As Roman watched the scholars' Christmas Eve program from his seat in the large lodge meeting room, he had to smile. Who would've thought Lavern Peterscheim would play such a concerned, compassionate Joseph beside his twin sister, Lily—who, at thirteen, wasn't much younger than Mary had been when she'd given birth to Jesus? Lily tenderly cradled a doll while Fannie Kurtz told the familiar Christmas story from the book of Luke.

"'And she brought forth her firstborn son and wrapped him in swaddling clothes, and laid him in a manger,'" Fannie recited with a peaceful smile on her face, "'because there was no room for them in the inn. And there were in the same country shepherds abiding in the field—'"

Roman chuckled. On cue, Menno and Johnny came in from the other room, wearing old bathrobes with towels tied over their heads. Queenie walked obediently beside Johnny, panting slightly, as though the two crocheted lambs Menno carried were real sheep that needed her attention. As a kid, Roman had played the part of a shepherd with Noah many times, until he'd been promoted to being a Wise Man. His final year in school, he'd had to memorize this same passage from Luke so he could recite it with meaning, allowing time for the younger kids to find their places and act out their parts in this perennial Christmas tradition.

Roman smiled at Teacher Minerva, who stood off to the side watching her scholars. She'd worked hard to get the Peterscheim boys and Lowell Kurtz to wear costumes and listen for their cues when their young minds were more excited about ice-skating than a story that had happened so long ago and far away.

But the coming of the Christ child became pertinent again with the birth of each new baby, didn't it? Wasn't a newborn a sign that God wanted the world to move forward with the new opportunities for grace and meaning He would provide?

Roman shifted in his chair, eager to visit Mary Kate and David after the scholars' program ended. The Peterscheim boys had told him of their plan to invite her and the baby—and him—to play the holy family, but Roman was pleased that Teacher Minerva's wisdom had prevailed. Mary Kate was adamant about keeping the baby at home, away from crowds, for several more weeks.

She's such a loving, levelheaded young mother. Roman was sorry Mary Kate wasn't able to watch the program this evening, but her sense of responsibility was one of many reasons he'd set his heart on marrying her . . . even if they had yet to convince her father that their union was a good idea.

Roman glanced across the room at the bishop, who sat slumped to one side in his chair. A lot of folks had felt Floyd Lehman was too conservative—and too outspoken—to serve as their new colony's leader, yet now that a stroke had robbed the bishop of his ability to speak clearly, everyone felt compassion for him and his family. Floyd's condition put the Amish residents of Promise Lodge in a difficult position: Old Order bishops were chosen to serve for the remainder of their lives. What if Floyd never recovered his ability to speak? How would he be able to tell them of God's will?

As a stirring in the crowd brought Roman out of his deep thoughts, he realized it was time for refreshments— food he would skip in favor of enjoying whatever Mary Kate might have baked. She had convinced Roman to visit with her and David whenever he could, hoping that her father would someday accept his presence again.

When the folks around him stood up, Roman did, too. He spoke with Preacher Marlin and Harley, moving toward the lobby to get his coat—until something made Roman turn around. Bishop Floyd was thumping toward him with an awkward, purposeful gait, leaning heavily on his cane. The bishop's facial expression seemed harsher than usual, but because his stroke had frozen half of his face, it was hard to determine his mood. Maybe Floyd sensed Roman was headed over to the house to spend time with Mary Kate, and he intended to prevent the visit.

Roman braced himself for the possibility of another loud, unintelligible lecture as Mary Kate's father stopped in front of him. "*Gut* evening, Floyd," he said cordially. "I thought our scholars did a fine job portraying the folks who were present for Christ's birth. If it's all right with you, I'd like to go and tell Mary Kate about the program—"

An expression that resembled a grimace crossed Floyd's face as he fumbled in the pocket of his baggy brown sweater. He pulled out a small piece of paper and waved it toward Roman.

"For me?" Roman asked. He certainly hadn't expected

a note from Mary Kate's *dat*, but when Floyd grunted and gave him a lopsided nod, Roman accepted it.

Be gut to MK. She needs you, Roman. You have my blessings.

The words were written in an uneven scrawl, but there was no mistaking their meaning.

Roman looked up and thought—for a fleeting moment—that he saw a sparkle in Bishop Floyd's eyes. "*Denki* so much!" he whispered. "I'll take very *gut* care of her and David—and I'll watch over you and the rest of your family, too."

With his good arm, the bishop waved him off.

Roman rushed through the lobby, grabbing his coat as he went. When he opened the door, Queenie raced past him, and when they got outside they were pelted with huge, white snowflakes. This new winter storm had piled another few inches of snow on top of what was already on the ground, and it showed no sign of stopping.

Roman looked again at the scrap of paper in his hand. He let out a whoop—which inspired Queenie to bark and jump around him, snapping gleefully at the snowflakes. Roman began running down the snow-covered road toward the Lehman place, eager to share his news with Mary Kate. He had asked Mamm to crochet a simple shawl for Mary Kate and another stuffed toy for David, as his Christmas presents to them, but who could've guessed her *dat*'s acceptance of him would be the greatest gift of all?

Chapter Twenty-Eight

"My word, would you look at that snow coming down!" Rosetta murmured as she peered out the kitchen window. "I was so engrossed in the kids' program, I haven't looked outside in a while. I'm glad Truman won't have far to go when he takes his *mamm* home."

Beside her, Mattie chuckled and placed more cookies on a tray. "Why do I suspect Truman won't be staying home once he gets Irene inside?"

"And why do *I* figure Amos's kids will be heading upstairs to their rooms long before their *dat* is ready to go home?" Rosetta fired back.

When Mattie giggled, Rosetta slung her arm around her sister's shoulders. "And aren't we glad it's worked out that way for us?" she murmured. "Now, if we could only find a worthwhile fellow for Christine."

"Keep the faith, Sister. He'll show up when God decides it's time." Mattie picked up the big tray she'd loaded with cookies. "Let's enjoy this first Christmas Eve with all our friends, shall we? Everyone's in a *gut* mood after the kids put on their program, and we've got so much to celebrate and be grateful for."

"We do," Rosetta agreed. She followed Mattie into the dining room, where their friends and neighbors had gathered for refreshments. Rosetta smiled over the top of the coffee urn she carried when she spotted Truman at the end of a table. "And I, for one, am grateful that a solemn Christmas Day gives my poor backside a chance to recover from falling on the ice so many times. I'm sure Truman will want to resume my lessons on Second Christmas."

Mattie laughed. "Maybe I can learn from your mistakes. Amos seems determined to get me on skates when his legs are stronger—and after the recovery he's made, I wouldn't dream of disappointing him."

Christine came over to help Rosetta and Mattie set out the second round of coffee and cookies. "Can you believe how many of these treats we're going through tonight? You'd think nobody ate supper before the program."

"Oh, let's be honest," Rosetta teased. "The three of us Bender sisters, teamed up with the two Kuhns, have baked the best goodies any of these folks have ever— What on earth can Queenie be barking at? Sounds like we've got company."

"Who would be out on such a snowy night?" Christine asked as she, Rosetta, and Mattie hurried into the lobby. "Surely can't be anyone local, so maybe they're lost."

When Rosetta swung open the front door, snowflakes swirled inside with a cold blast of wind. "Hullo out there!" she called loudly when she saw an enclosed buggy had pulled up beside the porch. "Queenie, come here! Stop your barking."

"She's got every right to bark," a melodious male voice replied. A very tall, burly fellow was getting out of the buggy, shielding his face from the snow with a gloved hand. "Dogs only bark at strangers—and there's nobody stranger than me! But I guess I should let you folks form your own opinion. I hope I've reached Promise Lodge?"

"*Jah*, you have," Rosetta replied, holding the door open for him. "We weren't expecting anybody on such a night—"

"And I wasn't expecting to get waylaid by nasty weather and snow-clogged roads. I'd hoped to arrive in time to see your scholars present their traditional Christmas Eve program," their guest replied. "But I couldn't ask the kids to do it over, just for the likes of me."

Rosetta stared as the fellow removed his broad-brimmed black hat. He sported thick brown hair and his curly beard framed a friendly, masculine smile. She was guessing he was in his forties—and he was the best-looking man she'd ever seen. He was gazing at her with eyes as green and serene as a pine forest.

"Would you happen to be the Rosetta Bender who writes the *Budget* posts for Promise Lodge?" he asked.

"I am!" Rosetta replied. "And these are my sisters, Christine Hershberger and Mattie Schwartz. The three of us—and Mattie's fiancé, Preacher Amos—sold our farms and pooled our funds to start this place up last spring."

"You have no idea how happy I am to be here." The man removed his heavy coat and leaned cordially toward them. "I'm Monroe Burkholder. I was the bishop of my settlement in Illinois, but the district's growing so large we're reorganizing—not that

I need to burden you with all the details," he added apologetically. "Just from reading your weekly column in *The Budget,* I've felt compelled to come to Promise Lodge. See? I told you I'm strange! But I've followed God's lead and here I am."

Rosetta exchanged glances with her sisters, smiling widely. "You have no idea how happy we are that you've come, Bishop Monroe," she murmured.

"And your timing is perfect," Mattie insisted as she gestured toward the meeting room. "Nearly everyone's still here, and we've just set out more cookies and coffee."

"May I take your coat, Bishop Monroe?" Christine asked. In the subdued light of the lobby chandelier, her face took on a hopeful glow as she gazed up at their attractive guest.

Rosetta exchanged a quick glance with Mattie, unable to suppress a grin. "We'll go tell everyone you've arrived, Bishop, and whenever you're ready, Christine will be happy to introduce you around," Rosetta said. "Before the evening's over, we'll find you a place to stay and you'll have lots of new friends!"

"I'll get a couple of our boys to tend your horse," Mattie put in. "We've got plenty of room in the barn across the road."

"*Denki* so much," Monroe murmured. "I feel at home already—and Clyde's ready for a *gut* rubdown and some feed after our day's journey."

Rosetta grabbed Mattie's hand and hurried into the meeting room, feeling ready to burst with excitement. "Did you *see* that man? He could be our new bishop!" she exclaimed in a whisper. "He could perform weddings!"

"I heard no mention of a wife, so he could be the man of Christine's dreams, too!" Mattie murmured. "But we can't let our wishful thinking color our impression of him. And we can't assume he'll be taking Floyd's place. The preachers and Floyd—and God—have the final say on that."

"*Jah*, but Monroe Burkholder certainly gives us something fun to think about," Rosetta said as she slipped behind the serving table to pour coffee. She spotted Truman chatting with Preacher Amos across the room, and she gave him a little wave. "If you ask me, it's time to start planning for a whole new kind of happiness."

Amos felt his entire body thrumming when he saw Mattie approaching him and Truman with a freshly loaded cookie tray. While his fiancée had always been a hostess who saw to everyone's needs, Amos sensed she had more than dessert on her mind as she made her way through the crowd. Mattie stopped and whispered something to Lavern Peterscheim and Lowell Kurtz, who set out toward the lobby as though a great adventure awaited them.

"Here comes a woman with a story to tell," Amos remarked to Truman. "She and Rosetta both look ready to let some big cats out of the bag."

Truman laughed. "Who knows, with those two? Wherever they are, excitement seems to follow. We'll never lack for entertainment in our lives, you and I."

Amos stood taller when he caught sight of a stranger entering the large, crowded room. "And who might that be with Christine? Is he a local fellow—someone you know?"

Before Truman could reply, Mattie reached them. "You won't believe this!" she said in an ecstatic whisper. "The fellow Christine's introducing around is Bishop Monroe Burkholder, and he's coming to live at Promise Lodge! He got waylaid by the weather—"

"You'll never lose him in a crowd," Truman murmured. "My word, he must stand seven feet tall."

"—but he saw Rosetta's columns in *The Budget* and felt God was leading him here," Mattie continued in a rush. "He's the answer to our prayers!"

Amos's eyebrows rose as he chose a dark chocolate fruitcake bar from Mattie's tray. "Be careful what you pray for, dear," he murmured. "We've already got a bishop who came here for the same reason, and Floyd's been a challenge at times—at least before he had his stroke, he was."

"Floyd's a challenge for a different reason now," Truman remarked as he took a sugar cookie shaped like a sleigh. "Have you folks decided whether he can continue as your bishop, seeing's how he can't talk anymore?"

Amos looked around the room until he spotted Eli Peterscheim and Marlin Kurtz. "No, we haven't, but that will be a hot topic in a matter of minutes, as folks here find out about this new fellow. Excuse me while I call an informal preachers' meeting, will you?"

Amos held Mattie's gaze for a moment. Her pretty face was an open book: she saw this Burkholder fellow as the bishop who could perform their marriage ceremony—and who might be open to Rosetta's marrying Truman, as well. A lot rode on what Amos might learn about their guest this evening. He wanted to ask the right questions and listen very carefully to the answers.

As Amos made his way through the crowd toward Marlin, he caught Eli's eye and waved him over. *Give us Your guidance, Lord,* Amos prayed as he carefully crossed the floor with his cane. *Help us to see with eyes fully open and minds attuned to Your will for us.*

Marlin smiled as Amos approached, pulling a chair from a nearby table. "Take a load off, Preacher," he said. "It's mighty *gut* to see you walking again, and we don't want you overworking those legs."

"I've got a better idea," Amos murmured, gesturing toward a quiet corner of the room. "Let's you and Eli and I have a quick conference before that new fellow makes his way over here to meet us. He's a bishop. Told Rosetta and Mattie that God has led him to Promise Lodge, to live here."

"You don't say," Marlin murmured as he looked toward the man Christine was showing around. "You hear that, Eli?"

"Another bishop, eh?" Peterscheim asked as he followed Amos and Marlin to the corner. "And what do you suppose Floyd's going to say about that?"

"Frances took Floyd home a few minutes ago because she thought he was getting too tired." Amos looked earnestly at Marlin and Eli, both of them good, solid leaders of the faith and of this colony. "What we find out about this Burkholder fellow tonight may well decide the future of Promise Lodge. It's in our best interest to ask him some pertinent questions, because we've all invested a lot of ourselves and our money to make this place home."

"*Jah*, and after dealing with Bishop Obadiah in Coldstream—and putting up with some of Floyd's quirks," Eli murmured, "I'm not of a mind to let just any bishop take the reins here. God has the final word, certainly, but we preachers have a responsibility to our congregation—and to our families."

"I say we mosey on over and introduce ourselves," Marlin proposed quietly. "If we take the initiative and stand together, we'll be able to sound him out—and he'll get a feel for how we do things here. He might decide, after he visits for a few days, that we're not the sort of flock he's looking to shepherd."

"Let's do it." Amos stood tall, leaning his cane against the wall. He felt stronger, more in control of this situation, walking without assistance as he made his way over to the knot of friends who surrounded the newcomer. Amos could tell by the rapt expressions on their faces that Minerva, Harley, and Alma Peterscheim were already impressed by the man who stood among them—and Christine seemed even more taken by Burkholder than her two sisters.

When Minerva noticed the three of them approaching, she waited for their guest to finish his sentence. "Bishop Monroe Burkholder, I'd like to introduce our colony's leaders," she said, gesturing to each man as she named him. "This is Preacher Amos Troyer, a founder of Promise Lodge," she began. "On either side of him are Preacher Eli Peterscheim and my father-in-law, Preacher Marlin Kurtz, who's serving as our deacon. I believe Bishop Floyd has gone home—"

"*Jah*, Frances took him just a few minutes before you arrived, Bishop Monroe," Amos said as his hand got swallowed in their visitor's firm grip. "He's recently suffered a stroke, so we're watching over him and his family pretty closely these days."

"Christine has mentioned your bishop's infirmities, and I'm sorry to hear about them," Monroe said as he shook hands with Eli and Marlin. "Please don't think I intend to take over Floyd's position—unless God and your congregation decide I will. When folks break away to start a new colony, they often want things to be different from what they could no longer tolerate in their previous place," he continued in a flowing baritone. "I have no way of knowing your preferences, so I can't presume to become your leader."

The folks around Burkholder were nodding in agreement. The Kurtzes and Lehmans had found their own reasons for pulling up roots and relocating, but everyone who'd left Coldstream had a very specific reason for coming here: a bishop they could no longer tolerate. "So where'd you come from, and why did you break away, Monroe?" Amos asked in a purposeful tone. "And what made you choose Promise Lodge— besides reading Rosetta's columns in *The Budget*?"

Burkholder clasped his hands in front of him, gazing down at Amos with penetrating green eyes. "Why do I suspect you three preachers are checking me out?" he teased. "Would it be best if we went somewhere quiet to talk amongst ourselves?"

Marlin glanced at Amos and Eli. "I've got nothing to ask that anybody else in this room shouldn't hear the answer to," he remarked with a shrug.

"Me neither," Eli said. "Folks are naturally curious about anybody who wants to come here, and when he's a bishop, well—we've got our reasons for asking some important questions."

"*Jah*—so will you be bringing your family with you?" Christine put in quickly.

Amos had to smile even though he suspected his line of questioning had already been derailed. He couldn't miss the way Mattie's sister was gazing up at Burkholder with hopeful awe on her face. Monroe's smile made his dimples deepen as he responded to her.

"My dear wife, Linda, God rest her soul, passed on last year about this time," the bishop replied in a subdued voice.

"Oh, I'm so sorry," Mattie murmured. "Always harder to lose folks you love during the holidays."

"*Denki* for understanding," Monroe said, his gaze never leaving Christine. "Linda and I weren't blessed with any children, and I lost my parents when I was very young. House fire."

"Oh my," Minerva whispered. "Who raised you?"

"My *dat*'s brother and his wife took me in," Burkholder replied. "And I was very blessed that Uncle Herman taught me all he knew about horses—and that Aunt Lena convinced me to join the Old Order when I was seventeen. They gave me a *gut*, solid foundation for leading a responsible life."

"What sort of trade are you in?" Eli asked. "Or do you run a shop?"

Burkholder smiled. "I breed and train draft horses—Clydesdales," he replied. "Would I be interfering with anyone else's business if I set up a stable here for that?"

"Oh, we've got nobody else in the horse business," Harley replied enthusiastically. "And any Plain community needs *gut* horses."

"Clydesdales, eh?" Marlin put in. "Most folks I know farm with Belgians—"

"Perhaps I should clarify," Burkholder cut in with a debonair smile. "Most of the horses I raise are destined for the show ring, for owners who enter them in competitions or drive them in parades. My Clydesdales are magnificent, spirited animals that are more likely to perform in a crowded arena than out in a hayfield."

Amos was listening carefully, noting how the crowd around them was growing larger as folks caught bits and pieces of the conversation. Kids and adults alike seemed drawn to Monroe Burkholder's resonant voice and cordial demeanor, yet the more Amos heard, the more questions he wanted to ask this newcomer. A man's chosen occupation revealed a lot about his character.

"What got you into raising show horses rather than farm stock?" Amos asked. "I'm wondering how successful such an enterprise might be here in rural Missouri. Promise and the nearby towns are very small, you see."

"That's one of the things I'll need to ask you about—location, that is," Burkholder replied. "I'm following in Uncle Herman's footsteps, as far as dealing with Clydesdales, because his reputation—and mine—rest upon the fact that Amish breeders and trainers are known for their meticulous methods and the dependability of the animals they produce."

Amos noticed that Lowell and Lavern were making their way through the crowd, their cheeks rosy with the cold as they shrugged out of their coats. "*Jah,* that's some horse you've got, Bishop," the Kurtz boy said with a grin.

"We got him all rubbed down—had to stand on a tall stool to do it!" Lavern added as he and Lowell came up beside Burkholder. "We put him in a stall with fresh rations, hay, and water . . . and I hope you don't mind that we took him for a short spin up and down the road before we tended him. He sure does love the snow."

Burkholder's laughter filled the large room as he grasped the boys' shoulders. "Clyde never passes up a chance to strut his stuff, and I appreciate you fellows taking *gut* care of him. If you'd be interested, I'll be needing some hands—dependable guys like you— when I get my stables built and transport my breeding stock here."

Lavern and Lowell gawked at each other, wide-eyed, and then back at the bishop.

"Wow, really?" Lavern asked. "Come time for school to be out next spring, I'd be mighty happy to have a job—"

"*Jah*, you betcha!" Lowell blurted. Then he looked longingly at his father. "Will it be okay if I work for Bishop Monroe sometimes, Dat? I—I know you need me in the barrel factory, too."

Marlin smiled. "I'm a firm believer in young men trying out several trades rather than being told they have to carry on their father's business."

"Same here," Eli said with a nod to his son. "What with Noah and me both being welders, I don't expect—or encourage—you and your two younger brothers to follow my trade. Not enough work in this area for all of us."

"We won't have to be too concerned about that just yet," Alma pointed out as she smiled at the boys. "At twelve and thirteen, you'll both be living at home a few more years before you have to earn your livings."

"Twelve and thirteen—and preachers' boys," Monroe said with a glimmer in his eyes. "Perfect qualifications—full of energy and raised to be responsible. You'll learn very quickly that if you don't focus on those huge horses every minute, they'll get the best of you. It'll be a challenge I hope you'll grow to love."

Once again Amos noted how folks in the crowd were nodding, and how Burkholder seemed to know exactly what to say to win them over effortlessly. Mattie was offering Monroe the cookie tray and Rosetta, on the bishop's other side, was handing him a cup of cocoa—while Christine appeared years younger and totally enthralled with him.

"Maybe we should call Lester—ask if Bishop Monroe could stay at his place until you men can get a house built," Christine suggested. "I'd think it would be better if that Lehman place weren't sitting empty all winter, anyway. Less chance for the pipes to freeze."

"*Jah*, that's true," Marlin said. "More than likely, you'll want to choose land up that direction anyway, Bishop, because a lot of the property close to the road has already been claimed."

"If it wouldn't be any trouble for me to stay in that house, it sounds like a fine arrangement. I really appreciate the welcome you folks are giving me," Burkholder added as he happily raised his cookie and his cup. "This is much more than any fellow could expect, showing up unannounced."

"I'll give Lester a call right now!" Rosetta said as she started toward the kitchen.

"And I'd like you to meet my daughters, Phoebe and Laura—as well as the two Kuhn sisters," Christine said, gesturing toward the refreshment table where those four ladies stood. "It's fortunate that you came while most of us are still in the same room, after the scholars' Christmas Eve program."

Once again Amos sensed he couldn't press Burkholder for the information he wanted this evening, so he relaxed and observed the way their guest paid special attention to Laura, Phoebe, Ruby, and Beulah—and the rest of the folks who eagerly introduced themselves, as well. Minerva, Harley, and the others around Amos were making their way to the table for more cookies and cocoa, leaving him with the two other preachers.

"I suppose our questions will have to wait until Second Christmas—unless Burkholder volunteers the information," Amos murmured to Eli and Marlin. "Wouldn't be proper to quiz him tomorrow, on our Lord's birthday. And I suspect Rosetta and her sisters are already planning for his meals—and they'll get him settled into Lester's place for however long he stays."

"Best to let the women extend their hospitality first and ask our church questions later," Marlin agreed. "We'll probably learn what we need to know while we visit with him these next few days, anyway. Seems like a mighty nice fellow, if you ask me. We'd be lucky to have him here."

Amos nodded, bidding Marlin and Eli goodnight.

He fetched his cane from the corner, smiling when Mattie came up and tucked her arm through his.

"What if you and I slip out for a walk? Are you up to that?" she asked quietly. "The snow's stopped and the moon's shining and—"

"A short walk sounds like the perfect end to this Christmas Eve," Amos said, squeezing her hand. "It'll help me settle my mind before I go to bed."

When he and Mattie had slipped into their wraps, Amos was glad he'd agreed to go outside. The night sky was such a clear indigo, scattered with shining stars, it took his breath away. Moonlight glowed on the freshly fallen snow, and as he and Mattie carefully descended the stairs from the porch, the soft flakes fluttered like shimmering diamond dust around their feet.

Mattie gazed upward, smiling serenely. "What a wondrous night," she murmured. "Perfect for welcoming the Christ child into our hearts—and for meeting Bishop Monroe, as well. Why do I sense you're not nearly as taken by him as the rest of us are, Amos?"

Amos slipped his arm around Mattie's waist as they strolled slowly toward the road. There was no dodging her question, because she was extremely perceptive. He'd always loved that about Mattie.

"Can't put my finger on it," he murmured. "As I watched Burkholder beaming at everyone and responding to them—not to mention winning their sympathy by mentioning the loss of his wife and parents—I kept wondering why he ducked my questions about where he's coming from and why he's leaving."

"There's no denying that Christine's glad he's here,"

Mattie murmured. "And *jah*, I saw how the women all flocked around him, even the married ones. Monroe has a way about him. Charisma, I guess you'd call it."

"That's part of what's nagging at me. Why does a successful fellow like Burkholder—almost too handsome for his own *gut*—leave his home and established business to come to Promise, Missouri, to start over amongst total strangers? And why on earth does he do this during the Christmas holiday?" Amos asked. He took a few more steps, heading toward his house because his legs were getting tired. "Do I sound too suspicious? Have I lost my faith, wondering if Burkholder's motives are as open and honorable as he makes them out to be?"

When Mattie gazed into his eyes, Amos felt the same thrill he always did—yet there was something exceptionally beautiful about her face as they stood together in the hush of the evening.

"Do you suppose the folks at the manger had serious doubts, too?" Mattie mused aloud. She took his hands in hers, continuing in a solemn, stirring voice. "What must poor Mary have endured, bearing a child out of wedlock? Did she ever wonder if her boy was really the Son of God, or if she'd been led astray by her youthful imagination?

"And Joseph—now there was a man who had every reason to doubt whether his beloved's condition was an act of God," Mattie continued, shaking her head. "*Jah*, an angel told him he should go ahead and take Mary for his wife—and there were angels bringing *gut* tidings of great joy to the shepherds, as well, but they were scared to death by that heavenly proclamation. Even the Wise Men went home by another way after

God told them in a dream to steer clear of Herod's evil intentions," she added. "If I'd been any of those folks, I'm not sure I would've had the faith to believe that all those sensational goings-on were part of God's plan."

Amos nodded, soaking up the words that flowed so freely from her. He might have questioned Monroe Burkholder's motives, but he would never doubt that Mattie Schwartz was utterly sincere and devoid of deception. It still amazed him that she wanted to be his wife.

"And even though we have the Bible as God's Word that He came to earth for us in Jesus, to save us from ourselves, Christmas is still a mystery," Mattie continued in an awe-filled voice. "Some things we have to take on faith until we can fully understand them—but don't stop asking your questions, Amos. We depend upon your wisdom to steer us straight, about Monroe Burkholder and everything else we encounter."

Amos wrapped his arms around her, swaying gently with the rhythm of the carols that had begun playing in his head. "Ah, but you're the wise one, Mattie, always seeing through the extraneous details to the heart of the matter," he murmured. "And for me, you're the gift of joy—a part of God's grace I don't deserve, but for which I'll be forever grateful. Maybe that's what I should focus on, instead of wondering if Burkholder's too *gut* to be true."

Mattie eased away so she could gaze into Amos's face. She tenderly stroked his cheek. "You are *gut*, and you are true, Amos," she said with a sparkle in her dark eyes. "That's all I need to know. We'll soon learn what we need to about Monroe—and meanwhile, I feel a great sense of hope and anticipation because a healthy, successful bishop wants to join us."

"He might be God's answer for us, considering how Floyd isn't fully functional anymore," Amos admitted. He chuckled, rubbing Mattie's nose with his. "But right now all I can think of is how badly I want to kiss you—"

Mattie stood on tiptoe and pressed her lips sweetly to his. "Sometimes you talk too much," she teased softly. "Merry Christmas, dear Amos. I love you."

He pulled her close, savoring the sweetness of another kiss and the dream that had finally come true for him after so many years. Bishops would come and go, but Amos believed with all his heart that Mattie would stand by him forever. What greater gift could he possibly receive than her precious, abiding love?

"Merry Christmas, sweet Mattie." Amos closed his eyes as a wondrous sense of completeness filled his soul. When he looked up again, one of the stars beamed brighter and bolder than the rest, beckoning him with its peaceful, powerful rays—just as the star over Bethlehem had led the Wise Men to worship the Christ child.

Or is this a figment of your wishful Christmas imagination?

Amos sighed wistfully. Some things were best left unquestioned.

"You're right, Mattie," he murmured. "Christmas is still a mystery—and a miracle. And I'm blessed to be sharing it with you."

From the Promise Lodge Kitchen

Rosetta Bender and the Kuhn sisters love to cook, and as they settle into their lives at Promise Lodge, they'll be sharing favorite recipes the way you and I do! In this recipe section, you'll find down-home foods Amish women feed their families, along with some dishes that I've concocted in my own kitchen— because you know what? Amish cooking isn't elaborate. Plain cooks make an astounding number of suppers from whatever's in their pantry and their freezers. They also use convenience foods like Velveeta, cake mixes, and canned soups to feed their large families for less money and investment of their time.

These recipes are also posted on my website, www.CharlotteHubbard.com. If you don't find a recipe you want, please email me via my website to request it—and to let me know how you liked it!

~Charlotte

Beulah's "Marriage Meat Loaf"

Amish cooks tend to use fewer spices than I prefer, so I tweaked this recipe by adding the soup and salad dressing mixes. This feeds 10–12 guests, and they repeatedly ask for the recipe.

- 1 lb. each lean hamburger, pork sausage, turkey breakfast sausage
- 1 cup rolled oats, uncooked
- 3 eggs
- ¾ cup tomato juice
- 1 envelope dry onion soup mix
- 1 envelope dry Good Seasons Italian salad dressing mix

Sauce

- 3 T. ketchup
- 3 T. mustard
- 3 T. brown sugar

In a large bowl, combine all meat loaf ingredients thoroughly. Pack firmly into 2 loaf pans sprayed with non-stick spray OR shape into 2 loaves and place in a large slow cooker, adding ¼ cup water in the bottom of the cooker.

Mix the sauce ingredients and spread over the meat loaves. Bake the pans at 350° F. for an hour. Bake slow cooker loaves for about 6 hours on low. Remove from pan/cooker and allow to sit on platter for about 5 minutes before slicing.

Pumpkin Bread

This is a fall favorite at our house, and it was my mom's recipe! Moist and flavorful, and it freezes well. You can also make this as muffins or mini loaves by adjusting the time: allow about 15 to 20 minutes for muffins and about 25 to 30 minutes (or until the tops are firm and a toothpick comes out clean) for mini-loaves.

> 1 15-oz. can pumpkin puree
> 2 cups sugar
> 1 cup milk
> 4 eggs
> ½ cup softened butter
> 4 cups all-purpose flour
> 4 tsp. baking powder
> 1 tsp. baking soda
> 1 tsp. salt
> 1 T. cinnamon, or more to taste
> 2 cups chopped walnuts or pecans

Preheat the oven to 350° F. and coat two 9"x 5" loaf pans with non-stick spray. In a large bowl, combine the pumpkin puree, sugar, milk, eggs, and butter with a mixer until well blended. In a smaller bowl, combine the flour, baking powder, baking soda, and spices, then gradually blend these dry ingredients into the pumpkin mixture. Stir in the nuts. Divide the dough between the prepared pans and bake for 55 to 65 minutes, until the centers are set. Cool in the pan about 10 minutes, then remove to a wire rack to cool completely. Freezes well.

Butterscotch Cashew Bars

These thick, chewy bars are rich and satisfying. They have a place on my Christmas cookie trays every year!

Crust

> 1½ cups flour
> ¾ cup packed brown sugar
> ½ cup butter, softened
> ¼ tsp. salt

Filling

> ½ cup light corn syrup
> 1 11-oz. pkg. butterscotch chips (2 cups)
> 4 T. butter
> 2 T. water
> ½ tsp. salt
> 3 cups cashew pieces

Preheat oven to 350° F. Coat a 9" x 13" pan with non-stick spray. Combine crust ingredients with a mixer until you have coarse crumbs. Press firmly into the prepared pan. Bake for 10 minutes.

Meanwhile combine all filling ingredients except cashews in a microwavable bowl. Microwave on high for 1 to 2 minutes, stir; repeat until smooth and blended (OR melt over low heat in a pan on the stovetop, stirring often). Stir in cashews. Spread filling on the partially baked crust and bake another 10 to 12 minutes or until bubbly and just starting to brown. Cool completely. Cut into 20 squares, and cut each square into 2 triangles.

Orange Date Bars

These moist, dense bars are fabulous. When I can't find orange cake mix in the store, I substitute lemon cake mix. I've also substituted dried cranberries or chopped dried cherries for the dates.

> 2 boxes orange cake mix
> 2 3.4-oz. boxes instant orange or lemon
>   pudding mix
> 1 cup vegetable oil
> 4 eggs
> 1 8-oz. box chopped dates
> 1½ cups coarsely chopped pecans

Glaze

> 1½ cups powdered sugar
> 1 T. orange juice
> Milk

Preheat oven to 350° F. and coat a 11" x 17" x 1" pan (or two 9" x 13" pans) with non-stick spray. Blend the cake mixes, pudding mixes, oil, and eggs. Add in the dates until distributed evenly. Spread the batter in the prepared pan(s) and sprinkle with the pecans, pressing them lightly into the dough surface. Bake for 20 to 25 minutes, until center is firm. Cool on a wire rack. Stir the powdered sugar and orange juice together, adding just enough milk (a tablespoon or so) to make a thin glaze. Drizzle the glaze over the bars and allow glaze to set before cutting. Freezes well.

Bread Pudding

Here's a basic bread pudding recipe using any bread you have around (even if it's stale). As Rosetta did, you can also use leftover rolls or muffins, as long as you measure out 4 cups. You can also substitute other dried fruits, and add nuts to taste.

  2 cups milk
  4 cups bread scraps, in pieces
  ¼ cup butter, melted
  ½ cup sugar
  2 eggs
  Dash of salt
  ½ cup raisins
  2 tsp. or more of cinnamon or nutmeg

Preheat oven to 350° F. Coat a 1½ quart casserole with non-stick spray. Place bread scraps in a large bowl. Scald the milk (heat just until bubbles form) and pour it over the bread, stirring to blend. Stir in the remaining ingredients and pour mixture into the prepared casserole. Bake 40 to 45 minutes, or until a knife inserted in the center comes out clean. Serve warm. Refrigerate leftovers. Serves 6.

Cheesy Rice Casserole

Here's another dish Amish cooks stir up from ingredients in their pantries. This basic comfort food goes well with just about anything and feeds a crowd! You can use any sort of white/brown/wild rice you prefer.

½ cup butter or margarine, divided
½ cup chopped onion
8 cups cooked rice
1 cup sour cream (or plain Greek yogurt)
1 can cream of mushroom soup
2 cups shredded cheddar cheese or Velveeta
2 cups crushed corn flakes

Preheat oven to 350° F. Sauté the onion in ¼ cup of the butter. Stir this into the rice with the sour cream, soup, and cheese, then spread the mixture in a 9" x 13" baking dish that's been coated with non-stick spray. Melt the remaining ¼ cup of butter and stir in the corn flakes, then spread this mixture on top of the rice. Bake for about 45 minutes, until bubbly and hot. Serves 15.

Pumpkin Cornbread Muffins

I enjoy just about any sort of cornbread—and to save you from having half a can of pumpkin puree hanging around, I've doubled the original recipe. If you only want a dozen muffins, use 1 cup of pumpkin and halve the remaining ingredients!

1 15-oz. can pumpkin puree (NOT pie mix)
2 cups milk

¾ cup honey
½ cup sugar
4 large eggs
2½ cups yellow cornmeal
1½ cups flour
2 T. baking powder
1 tsp. baking soda
1 tsp. salt
1 T. cinnamon
½ tsp. nutmeg
½ tsp. ground cloves
1 stick butter, melted

Preheat oven to 375° F. and coat two regular-sized 12-cup muffin tins with non-stick spray. In a medium bowl, whisk together the pumpkin puree, milk, honey, sugar, and eggs. In a large bowl, whisk the dry ingredients and spices, and then stir in the pumpkin mixture and the melted butter. Mix until just combined. Spoon batter into the muffin tins and bake about 20 minutes, or until tops are lightly browned and firmly set. Cool in pans for 10 minutes and then remove to a wire rack—or to a basket for your table!

Kitchen Hint: These are best served warm. To reheat, place desired number of muffins on a microwavable plate, tuck a wet paper towel around them, and microwave for about 30 seconds.

Chocolate Gravy

Perfect for parties or any other time you're in the mood for a decadent treat!

1½ cups sugar
4 T. flour
2½ T. cocoa
½ cup water
1½ cups milk
A few drops of vanilla (optional)

Mix sugar, flour, and cocoa in a medium skillet, then stir in the water to blend. Add the milk and cook on medium heat, stirring, until gravy is thick. Stir in the vanilla as you remove the skillet from the heat. Serve over hot buttered biscuits, muffins, etc. Refrigerate leftovers.

Lemon-Cherry Candy Cane Cookies

I baked this shaped shortbread cookie for the first time this year, and it will be on my Christmas trays for a long time to come! The lemony dough and chewy dried cherries are an unexpectedly yummy combination, and a squiggle of pink frosting makes them stand out on a cookie platter. Makes about 2½ dozen.

Dough

1 cup butter, softened
1 cup powdered sugar
1 large egg
1 T. fresh lemon zest
1 tsp. vanilla extract
2½ cups flour
¾ cup dried cherries, chopped

Frosting

  1½ cups powdered sugar
  3 T. cherry or pomegranate juice
  Few drops of liquid red food coloring

To make the dough, cream butter and powdered sugar until light and fluffy. Add egg, lemon zest, and vanilla, beating until blended. Gradually beat in flour, and then stir in the cherries. Wrap dough in wax paper or plastic wrap and chill at least 2 hours.

Preheat oven to 350° F. Line cookie sheets with parchment paper. Divide dough into 30 equal sections and roll each section between your hands, into a rope about 5 inches long. Bend the tops to form candy canes and place the canes 2 inches apart on baking sheets. Bake cookies for 10 to 12 minutes, rotating cookie sheets halfway through, or until just starting to brown. Cool on sheets for a couple minutes before transferring cookies to wire racks to cool completely.

For the frosting, whisk the powdered sugar, juice, and food coloring in a small bowl until smooth. Fill a pastry tube with frosting, and use a plain tip to form frosting stripes or make a zig-zag design. Allow to dry/set completely before storing between sheets of waxed paper. Freezes well.

Kitchen Hint: _You can also spoon the frosting into a sandwich bag and nip off a tiny corner to substitute for the pastry tube._

Please read on for a sneak preview of a special new
Amish romance from Charlotte Hubbard,

A Mother's Love,

coming in hardcover from Kensington Books
just in time for Mother's Day!

Rose Raber looked away so Mamma wouldn't see the tears filling her eyes. As she sat beside her mother's bed, Rose prayed as she had every night for the past week. *Please, Lord, don't take her away from me . . . I believe You can heal my mother's cancer—work a miracle for us—if You will.*

Tonight felt different, though. Mamma had taken to dozing off more, and her mind was wandering. Rose had a feeling that Mamma might drift off at any moment and not come back.

"Was church today?" Mamma murmured. "I don't . . . recall that you and Gracie . . . went—"

"We stayed here with you, Mamma," Rose reminded her gently. "I didn't want to leave you by yourself."

Her mother let out a long sigh. As she reached for Rose's hand, Rose grasped it as though it could be a way to hold on to her mother, to keep her here—keep her alive. They didn't speak for so long, it seemed Mamma had drifted off to sleep again, but then she opened her eyes wide.

"Is Gracie . . . all tucked in?" Although Mamma's voice sounded as fragile as dry, rustling leaves, a purpose lurked behind the question.

"*Jah*, she is, but I'll go check on her," Rose replied, eager for the chance to leave the room and pull herself together. "Planted some of the garden with me today—all that fresh air—should make her sleep soundly."

"Gracie was mighty . . . excited about doing that, too. She asked me again and again . . . how long it would be before the lettuce . . . peas, and radishes shot up." Mamma chuckled fondly as she recalled the conversation with her granddaughter. Then she gazed at Rose, her eyes fiercely bright in a face framed by the gray kerchief that covered her hairless head. "When you come back, dear, there's something I . . . need to tell you about."

Nodding, Rose carefully squeezed Mamma's bony hand and strode from the bedroom. Out in the hallway she leaned against the wall, blotting her face with her apron. Her five-year-old daughter was extremely perceptive. Gracie already sensed her *mammi* was very, very ill, and if she saw how upset Rose had become, there would be no end of painful questions—and Gracie wouldn't get back to sleep anytime soon.

The three of them had endured a heart-wrenching autumn and winter after a fire had ravaged Dat's sawmill, claiming Rose's father, Myron Fry, and her husband, Nathan Raber, as well. The stress of losing Dat had apparently left Mamma susceptible, because that's when the cancer had returned with a vengeance, after almost thirty years of remission. The first time around, when Mamma was young, she'd survived breast cancer, but this time the disease had stricken her lungs—even though she'd never smoked.

With the family business gone, Rose and Gracie had moved into Mamma's house last September. Rose had sold her and Nathan's little farm so they would have some money to live on—and to pay Mamma's mounting bills for the chemo and radiation that had kept her cancer manageable. Until now, in early April.

Little Gracie has lost so many who loved her, Rose thought, sending the words up as another prayer. She composed herself, took a deep breath, and then climbed the stairs barefoot. She peeked into the small bedroom at the end of the hall.

The sound of steady breathing drew Rose to her daughter's bedside. In the moonlight, Gracie appeared carefree—breathtakingly sweet as she slept. Such a gift from God this daughter was, a balm to Rose's soul and to her mother's, as well. For whatever reason, God had granted Rose and Nathan only this single rosebud of a child, so they had cherished her deeply. Rose resisted the temptation to stroke her wee girl's cheek, feasting her eyes on Gracie's perfection instead. She'd seen some religious paintings of plump-cheeked cherubim, but her daughter's innocent beauty outshone the radiance of those curly-haired angels.

After a few more moments, Rose quietly left Gracie's room. Standing in her daughter's presence had strengthened her, and she felt more ready to face whatever issue Mamma wanted to discuss. Rose knew of many folks whose parents had passed before they'd had a chance to speak their peace, so she told herself to listen carefully, gratefully, to whatever wisdom Mamma might want to share with her. Instinct was telling her Mamma only had another day or so.

Pausing at the door of the downstairs bedroom, where Mamma was staying now because she could no longer climb the stairs, Rose nipped her lip. Mamma's face and arms were so withered and pale. It was a blessing that her pain relievers kept her fairly comfortable. When Mamma realized Rose had returned, she beckoned with her hand. "Let's talk about this before I lose my nerve," she murmured. "There's a stationery box . . . in my bottom dresser drawer. The letters inside it . . . will explain everything."

Rose's pulse lurched. In all her life, she'd never known Mamma to keep secrets—but the shadows beneath Mamma's eyes and the fading of her voice warned Rose that this was no time to demand an explanation. Rose sat down in the chair beside the bed again, leaning closer to catch Mamma's every faint word.

"I hope you'll understand . . . what I've done," Mamma murmured. "I probably should have told you long ago, but . . . there just never seemed to be a right time—and I made promises—and . . . your *dat* believed we should let sleeping dogs lie."

Rose's heart was beating so hard she wondered if Mamma could hear it. "Mamma, what do you mean? What are you trying to—"

Mamma suddenly gripped Rose's hands and struggled, as though she wanted to sit up but couldn't. "Do *not* look for her, Rose. I—I promised her . . ."

Rose swallowed hard. Her mother appeared to

be sinking in on herself now, drifting in and out of rational thought. "Who, Mamma?" Rose whispered urgently. "Who are you talking about?"

Mamma focused on Rose for one last, lingering moment and then her body went limp. "I'm so tired," she rasped. "We'll talk tomorrow."

Rose bowed her head, praying that they would indeed have another day together. She tucked the sheet and light quilt around Mamma's frail shoulders. It was all she could do. "*Gut* night, Mamma," she murmured. "I love you."

She listened for a reply, but Mamma was already asleep.

Rose was tempted to go to Mamma's dresser and find the mysterious box she'd mentioned, but desperation overrode her curiosity. She couldn't leave her mother's bedside. For several endless minutes Rose kept track of her mother's breathing, which was growing slower and shallower now, as the doctor had said it would. He had recommended that Mamma stay in the hospital because her lungs were filling with fluid, but Mamma had wanted no part of that. She'd insisted on passing peacefully in her own home.

But please don't go yet, Mamma, Rose pleaded as she gently eased her hands from her mother's. *Stay with me tonight. Just one more night.*

Exhausted from sitting with Mamma for most of the past few days and nights, Rose folded her arms on the edge of the bed and rested her head on them. If Mamma stirred at all, Rose would know—could see to whatever she needed . . .

In the wee hours, Rose awakened with a jolt from a

disturbing dream about two women—one of them
was Mamma as she'd looked years ago, and the other
one was a younger woman Rose didn't recognize.
They were walking away from her, arm in arm, as
though they had no idea she could see them—and
didn't care. Rose called and called, but neither woman
turned around—

"Oh, Mamma," Rose whispered when she realized
she'd been dreaming. Her heart was thumping wildly
and she felt exhausted after sleeping in the armchair
beside her mother's bed. She lit the oil lamp on the
nightstand. "Mamma? Are you awake?"

Her mother's eyes were open, staring straight
ahead, but unblinking when Rose gripped her bony
shoulder. Mamma's breathing was so much slower
than it had been yesterday, and in the stillness of the
dim room the rasping sound of each breath was mag-
nified by Rose's desperation.

Rose stared at her mother for a few more of those
labored breaths, trying again to rouse her. Mamma's
expression was void of emotion or pain. She was
unresponsive—as the doctor had warned might
happen—and Rose curled in on herself to cry for a
few minutes. Then she rose and slipped out the front
door to the phone shanty.

"Bishop Vernon, it's Rose Raber," she murmured
after his answering machine had prompted her. "If
you could come—well, Mamma's about gone and I . . .
I don't know what to do. *Denki* so much."

Rose returned to the house with a million worries
running through her mind. Soon Gracie would be
awake and wanting her breakfast and—how would
Rose explain that her *mammi* couldn't talk to her

anymore, didn't see her anymore? How could she manage a frantic, frightened five-year-old who would need her constant reassurances for a while, and at the same time deal with her own feelings of grief and confusion? After days of watching and waiting, suspended in time, Rose suddenly had a funeral to plan and white burial garments to sew and a house to clean so the visitation and funeral could be held here. All the frightened moments Rose had known this past week, when she'd thought Mamma was already gone, were merely rehearsals, it seemed.

"Oh, Nathan, if only you were here," Rose murmured as she walked through the unlit front room. "You always knew what to do. Always had a clear head and a keen sense of what came next."

Rose paused in the doorway of the room where Mamma lay. Her breathing was still loud and slow, and the breaths seemed to be coming farther apart. Rose hoped it was a comfort to Mamma to die as she'd wanted to—even though it was nerve-racking to Rose.

There had been no waiting, no doubts, the day she and Mamma had returned from shopping in Morning Star to discover that the sawmill had caught fire from a saw's sparks. The mill, quite a distance from any neighbors, had burned to the ground with her father and husband trapped beneath a beam that had fallen on them. Their men's deaths had been sudden and harsh, but quick. No lingering, no wondering if she could be doing some little thing to bring final comfort.

Once again Rose sat in the chair beside Mamma's bed, and then rested against the mattress as she'd done before. The clock on Mamma's dresser chimed three times. It would be hours before the bishop checked his phone messages. Rose didn't want to rustle around in the kitchen for fear she'd waken Gracie, so she placed a hand over her mother's and allowed herself to drift . . .